LORNE RYBURN

THE MENOCHT LOOP

THE MENOCHT LOOP
BOOK 1

Edited by Silas Sontag and Paul Martin
Cover by Jeff Brown

Timeless Wind Publishing LLC

First edition

Editing by Silas Sontag
Editing by Paul Martin
Cover art by Jeff Brown

THE MENOCHT LOOP

CONTENTS

CONTENTS

CONTENTS

MAP OF THE WORLD

THE WEST

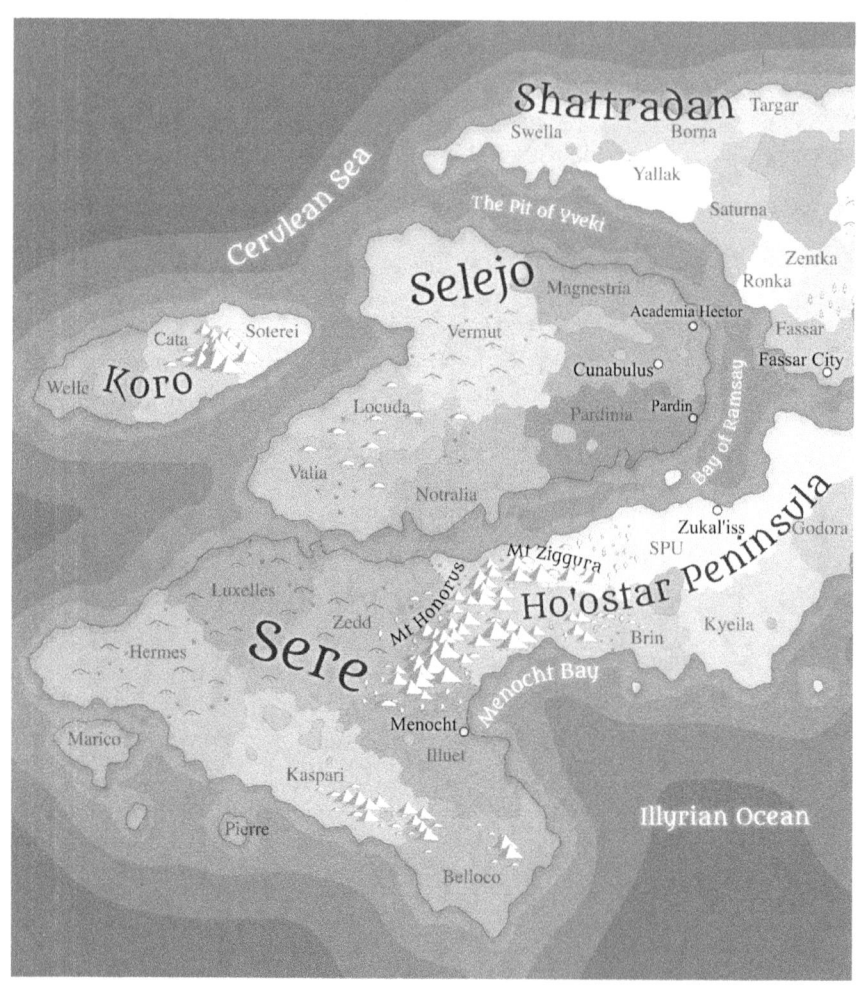

MAP OF THE WORLD

THE EAST

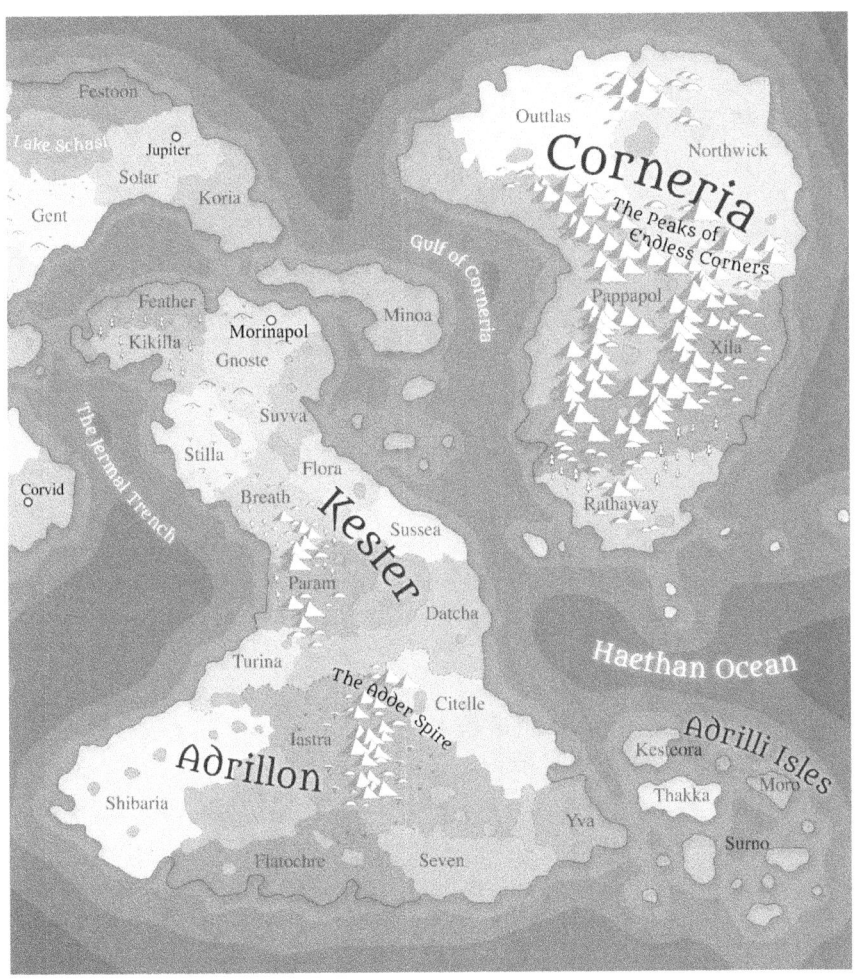

For my patrons, who made this possible. For my family and friends, who believed in my vision.

And finally, for Emil, who makes every day better.

YET AGAIN

I open my eyes, dilated pupils protesting the intense glare of sun reflecting off waves.

My first instinct is to punch the dinghy's weathered side out of spite, but I'm too exhausted to bother. Instead, I sit there, thinking, *Oh, come on, not again.* Useless thoughts, but still there.

I squint my eyelids shut and cover my face with my hands, feeling mucus grits in the corners of my eyes.

I've already done this so many times before. *Not. Again.*

I'm curled up into a ball, my forehead on my knees and my bare feet braced against the raw wood of the floorboards. The boat's as small as it's always been—a small dinghy that anyone might mistake for a freshwater fishing boat.

I let out a low moan, then open my eyes once more. *Be cool*, I think. Anyone could be watching. Well, not *anyone.* I've narrowed it down to either scientists, corporate goons, or a god.

Why else would I be going through this hell if not for someone else to watch?

So I throw up a deadpan mask, crossing my arms and legs to stop them from jittering in the sea breeze's chill. To be honest, it takes all my strength to not hyperventilate, to not just dive over the boat's edge and sink into oblivion.

Why can't I? I ask myself, suppressing a smile that would probably scare even my mother. Scare anyone, really. I've seen that smile in the mirror and it scares me. It's the smile of someone with nothing to lose.

But I do have things to lose, I know I do. Just...I can't focus on them. They seem so far away. Mother...I picture her face in my mind. I can see her clearly, but it feels like I haven't seen her in years. "Mother," I murmur aloud, my lips forming the word with care. Mother: the unfortunate center of my life's brief orbit.

Suddenly, I hear a seagull overhead—the first sign of life since I've woken up. I swallow my growing nausea and lean forward, pressing my stomach into delicate knuckles.

After the seagull, I know what's next.

I almost giggle when I hear it: the moaning, clanking girth of a ship, the toot of its low horn. The cruise ship approaches, evil hiding behind its sleek white exterior. It comes closer, rocking over the waves, inevitable and ponderous. I feel the burn of the sun on my face and ignore it.

I glance into the water. I tell myself that the cold will soothe my hot skin and slide in. Swimming in this heat is better than flying. I kick and paddle over to the ship, locating the nearest ladder with practiced ease, its silvery sheen stark against the ship's black side stripe.

Then I'm on board and I see the first of the barely mobile skeletons, the joints between bones poorly formed. I wave my hand and the five nearest to me stand erect, their bodies reinforced, their loyalties turned.

Effortless.

I don't smile; it'll just give the watchers pleasure. This is what they want, I know by now. They want this. Why else would they go through all the trouble of sending me here?

The skeletons grin all around me, violet lights in their eyes replacing the pale green of before. At the same time, sunset-red flows from their eyes to their bones, cushioning them and keeping them in place as surely as skin, ligaments, and tendons. It makes the skeletons look pink or slightly pink-orange on the skeletons that are yellowed by age.

I walk over the deck, turning the loyalties of the skeletons that cross my path. There are always twenty.

Then I head to the rear of the boat. Tens of people lay submerged in a large on-deck swimming pool with water up to their necks, their shackled arms splayed over their heads while their fingers gnash at the sky.

"Help, please!"

"Ah, ah, It's so cold..."

"I'm blind!"

I ignore them. I used to say, "I'm sorry," but that only ever made things worse. Silence is the best tool in my possession if I'm playing to win.

Or maybe it's indifference? But I have the suspicion that indifference might be like a callus grown over bone. Let me explain: If you break a joint, like your elbow, the bone will grow back new, hard, and strong. Left unchecked, the new bone will grow *differently* than what once was, ruining the joint by preventing proper motion. I didn't *use* to be indifferent; rather, I cared too much. And now, I wonder at what I've lost: Indifference is like that newborn bone, patching a warped wound but ultimately holding me back.

I walk past the clamoring captives to the back of the ship and the engine. I know from experience that the steering mechanism on the ship is broken and that the only way to change course is by manually steering the rudder. I hold out my hand and wave it to the side. At my command, one of the fourteen people who died in the pool breaks free of her shackles. Her bony wrists are too small for them to contain after I instruct her to rub them free of flesh.

She stands up and exits the pool of moaning captives, her skin glowing softly with red. I used to flinch when she walked past me and into the rudder, when her flesh spattered before the bones broke into pieces that I could easily manipulate from afar.

But it's been a long time since my range was that short. I stand far enough back that I'm safe from her splatter. I could throw her into the propeller from a hundred meters away at this point. Probably even farther than that. I manipulate her bones into place, forcing the largest fragments into the base of the rudder and nudging the ship's course to the right.

I depart from the back of the deck, glancing furtively around me. I *still* don't know how they watch me. I've checked for gloss-cams and thralled bugs...nothing.

I walk to the front of the ship where the prow juts off a few feet into the distance. I rest my arms on the railing and feel the ocean spray against my forehead.

The ship started out as a near-insurmountable puzzle. Defeat the skeletons, reconstruct a map, find the grimoire, master decemancy. I used to think that rescuing the people was part of the task. I have a sour taste in my mouth as I think of the moment when I really and truly realized my idealistic folly. My job was to *ferry* them, not rescue them—there's nowhere to rescue them *to*, not out on the ocean. And bringing them into Menocht Bay delivers them into the hands of a city gripped by outbreak.

By the time I get on the ship, they're all already half-dead and unable to stand from weakness. I once tried bringing them out of their fetid pool and onto the deck, and they all collapsed and died. Suspended in the cool water—their narrow profiles and sardine-packing limiting exposure to the sun—is the best way.

Once I carried all of them below deck, enlisting the skeletons for help. Even then, out of the sun, they died. *Every possible action* aside from keeping them in their aquatic holding container has led to their untimely deaths.

I realize, as I think of this, that I've never once tried rescuing *one* of them and talking to them about why they're on the boat in the first place.

It seems like a most logical thing to do. I almost feel like crying from frustration, aimed entirely at myself. I look over my shoulder at a seagull overhead. Have I dehumanized them so much, after all this time? Thinking of them as some kind of test or obstacle?

I know I have. And I know why I didn't talk to them in the beginning.

First, I was dealing with *a lot*. Like the fact that I kept continuously *dying* and reliving the same nightmare scenario.

Second, I was more interested in beating back skeletons than chatting with a bunch of emaciated, horrifyingly sunburned people.

And third...those people scared me. They looked like standing corpses: Just one look at them was enough to know that they'd never recover from this ordeal. And whenever they called out to me, it was with such desperation and anguish that...well, it disturbed me. And to someone who generally avoids human interaction, it was too much.

And so I kept my distance, tuning out their cries as I did pretty much anything else to keep busy.

I sigh and return to the moment. I almost consider heading to the back of the boat but think better of it. Instead, I instruct two skeletons lazing about to fetch someone from the pools. I direct them towards the human with the smallest aura of death in the hopes that they will be...less fragile.

The skeletons come back a minute later. I feel the feeble struggles of their chosen human as he's brought to kneel behind me.

"Why...why..."

I turn around. All the skeletons need is a glance to know that they've been dismissed. I look at the pathetic person in front of me, at his bony form and blood-shot eyes. Are they...? Ah, so the blind one. And considering the meat remaining on his bones, I reckon that when he first came into the care of...whoever captured him and the others, he wasn't exactly thin.

It's served to keep him alive, at the very least. And maybe the blindness from looking at the sun has saved his brain from the horror of looking at the people around him.

I can tell from the pauses between his words that he's thirsty and out of breath from the small walk. From what I understand, the only thing the people on the boat have to drink is their pool water—also their wastewater—and rain that falls every other day or so from the sky. It's probably been at least a day since he's had anything to drink.

One of my skeletons comes forth with a bowl of water, my desire calling him forth just as surely as a gesture of my hands or a glare from my eyes. I grab it from his warm, bony clutches and step forward. The person tenses at the motion, even though my feet are quiet on the plank floor.

It must be so silent here, I notice, compared to in the back. Any sound would go noticed. He's latching onto anything he can to understand what's happening.

I clear my throat, and he stills. "Hello," I say, surprised at how smoothly the word rolls off my tongue. "I have taken over this ship and have changed its course for the closest shore."

"Oh, oh Y'jeni, please..."

I almost smile to reassure him before I remember that he's blind and it won't matter either way. I'll have to encourage him with words, then.

"I'm—" I pause internally, shaking my head. I hold my mother's image firmly in my mind, her aquiline features and cold expression anchoring me to my past.

"I'm Ignatius," I finish. Named after her husband's father, and the father before him...and so on. "But you can call me Iggy."

"Iggy?" Incredulity saturates the man's voice. The name sounds innocuous—what kind of villain is named Iggy?

I chuckle. "Yes, I know, it *is* a bit silly. Now, if I'm to do anything to help you and the others on this ship—" I begin. But I pause. "My apologies, I didn't realize you were so thirsty." I say this as the man licks his bleeding, cracked lips. I wonder if he notices my disingenuity. "Here, let me give you some water." I step forward, the bowl of water secure in my hands. "Open your mouth: I'll pour water down your throat."

"Thank...you..."

I place the bowl by the man's lips, then use one hand to hold the bowl and the other to direct the man's hands onto the bowl's sides. I leave him, stepping back to watch.

I've never seen a person drink the way this man did.

After he finishes with the bowl, he begins to lower it down but drops it a few inches from the floor. From the spasms in his hands, I can tell that the action wasn't intentional. Either way, the bowl is fine: I leave it where it is.

"So," I say, "tell me. What happened to the lot of you?"

He begins to sniffle, tears running down his face. *Don't be impatient, don't be impatient...* "I know it's been difficult," I say consolingly, "but I need to know who did this to you."

"I'm blind," he moans, covering his face with his hands. He collapses to a sitting position, no longer kneeling before me. It...irritates me. Maybe because it seems so sloppy and unpoised. Maybe because I am used to fear, and this man has none.

"Who—"

The man interrupts me. "I don't know the name of the person who did this," he murmurs, his face looking up as though trying to pinpoint the location of my eyes. "But I can tell you what I know."

MENOCHT BAY

A skeleton comes by with a chair—the kind that's intended for reclining. This one even has an overhead umbrella attached.

"What's your name?" I ask. I hoped that when I introduced myself earlier, he'd tell me of his own accord.

"J-Jeremy."

I hum soothingly. "Now, Jeremy, I've brought over a chair for you to sit in." I walk over and grab onto his hands, lifting him up. He can't be more than a hundred and twenty pounds. Based on his height, a healthy weight would lie somewhere around one-sixty. He's as unsteady on his feet as a newborn foal. I remember how the skeletons had labored bringing him to me. I was wrong in assuming it was because Jeremy was struggling. No: They'd practically dragged him because he'd been unable to move.

He shouldn't be that weak, especially since I'd given him water. He should be able to stand. Maybe he's just that pathetic. But I don't say anything—doing so would be counter-productive. If I do this right, it seems like I might actually have new, valuable information on the situation.

I ease Jeremy into the chair, helping him to adjust his head onto the neck cushion while positioning the umbrella to fully cover his body.

As I step back, I notice that he looks incredibly embarrassed. "Is something wrong?" I ask.

"I—I'm not wearing clothes," he says, his voice practically a whisper.

No shit.

"Nothing to be self-conscious about," I say. The malnourishment has rendered his sensitive parts...shriveled. "But let me fetch you a towel." A skeleton comes forth and drapes one over the man.

"Who—who's with you?"

"Oh, just my subordinates," I reply. "They're all mute." Perhaps it's useful that the man is blind. Most people would refuse to talk to me on principle after seeing me control the skeletons. Given how desperate the people in the pools are, though, I don't think his ignorance matters too much.

"Oh."

"...You were saying?"

"Right..."

I wait for a solid ten seconds, but the man's mouth remains closed. I cough, and he jerks as though startled.

"This used to be an actual cruise ship," he explains, his voice soft, almost reverent. "We were on vacation."

I 'mhm' to show him I'm paying attention. "Go on."

"And...well, I woke up in the morning to a legion of skeletons. I opened the door to my room, went upstairs, and then—"

"Then what?"

"They knocked me unconscious. "Next thing I knew, I was in the pools."

"Did the pools always used to be there?"

The man shook his head limply, barely moving it over the surface of the cushion. "No."

"Did you ever hear anyone speak?" I asked. "Anyone with a semblance of authority?"

"Only Miles Walker," Jeremy admits. "The captain of the ship...though I think...he..."

"He what?"

"I think he's already dead."

I tsk. "Shame."

"Right."

"Anything else you have for me?" I ask. *Be patient, be patient.*

"I only went blind a few days ago," Jeremy says. "Before then, I saw...some things."

"Really?" I say, feigning interest. I doubt Jeremy has anything worthwhile to give me—yet another wild goose chase. Besides, what was I expecting? Rescuing the captives is hopeless.

"There used to be a man on a bone wyrm," he begins, "but he left a week ago, taking at least fifty skeletons with him."

Must have been a massive wyrm to take on so much extra mass, I reckon. My gaze sharpens. I'm oddly...surprised. Jeremy actually did have useful information after all.

A skeleton comes forth with refrigerated food. It looks a little...dated, but it should be fine.

I leave the skeleton with Jeremy and walk away. "Enjoy the food," I call out. "I'll be back later."

I head into the captain's quarters and sit down at the man's desk. I pull a book out from the shelf—the third volume of Hercates' Grimoire. A bone construct... Perhaps a way to leave the ship before it reaches the shore?

Maybe a way to break the vicious cycle of this game.

I page through the grimoire, scanning for the illustration of bony wings... Ah, yes, flying constructs.

Difficulty: expert, requirements...I skip over them, they don't matter...description doesn't matter...reagents: a bare minimum of twenty full, intact human skeletons or suitable equivalent. Two soul gems. A flight focus.

I gaze coolly at the requirements. I return to the surface, then look up at the seagull that's been circling overhead for the past thirty minutes. As I pinch my index and middle fingers to my thumb, the bird seizes and falls, crashing onto the deck with a splat.

"Who's there?" Jeremy's startled voice rings out, muffled by half-chewed food.

"It's nothing," I call back. I walk over to the bird and rake my fingers over its chest plumage. As they come up, I see the bird's energy swirling around them like inky, violet water. I distill the dark energy into a soul gem. Afterward, I suspend the bird over the ship's aft and swipe one hand right, effectively skinning the bird and cleaning it of flesh. I swipe again; this time, 70% of the bird's skeleton falls away into the water, joining the superfluous meat. What's left is my flight focus—a double-triangle formed by the bird's spine and wings. It's too big to place in my pocket, so I deposit it onto the deck.

I still need one more soul gem. I glance over at Jeremy...and mentally shake my head. He could be useful, I think, justifying mercy to myself.

Instead, I direct a pair of skeletons to head over to the pools and kill someone at the very edge of death. Then, I direct them to bring me the corpse. I place my fingers upon the emaciated human's chest, pulling them back to form a violet soul gem. I have twenty skeletons on board, not even counting the dead captives. Enough to make a large skeletal mount and have servants left over.

I direct the closest skeletons to my side while holding onto the flight focus with both hands. On either side of the focus float the violet soul gems.

I collapse the skeletons en masse, watching as their bones fall away like broken teeth. They begin to take shape, flowing like water over the focus, soul gems, and myself. I step away to let the process continue to completion, watching the wyrm's construction with interest.

It's said the exact form of a wyrm depends on the psyche of its creator. The thought almost makes me giggle but for the watchers...and Jeremy. If I had to describe wyrms in simple terms, they're supposed to look like snakes with crested lizard heads. Given the simplicity of the design, I'm curious to see what variations in form might arise.

The wyrm finishes self-assembling in five minutes. It's long and definitely wyrm-like, though I don't see anything unusual about it. Maybe all decemancers are as fucked up in the head as me.

The wyrm roars, though it doesn't sound like the cry of any living creature. It's hoarse, like the grinding of metal, the sizzle of a pan. Jeremy panics, screaming, "Oh no, he's back! I shouldn't have said—"

"Relax!" I bellow. All is silent. "This wyrm is taking me—us—to safety." Why "us?" Am I too soft? Was it Jeremy's noticeable drop in vitality when I said "me?"

I suppose deserting the man would push him closer to suicidal depression and loss of will to live.

"Really?" Jeremy doesn't ask the question I know he must be thinking—how I summoned a wyrm if I, myself, am not a decemancer. He's undoubtedly figured it out if he has two brain cells to rub together.

"Really."

"Thank you so much," he says, his voice catching in his throat. He begins to shake, then sob, then wail, until the only sound in the whole world is the peeling joy of Jeremy's restored hope.

I swallow. "It's nothing." It isn't nothing, but I'm not sure what it is yet. "Can you stand?"

"Yes"—Jeremy gasps—"I can stand." And he does, though he grabs onto the chair for support. I direct one of the remaining servants to lead Jeremy over to the wyrm's ribcage—an area generally designated as the guest seating area. At least according to Hercates, though given the man's notion of safety...

Not that there are any alternatives.

"Your servants," Jeremy begins, licking his chapped, sun-blistered lips. "They're quite warm."

"The same temperature as you or me," I reply.

"...Right."

"Hold tight," I warn. His hands currently grip two arcing ribs with all the strength of a starved, traumatized man—not enough force. I sigh, then collapse the skeleton that led Jeremy into the rib cage. I wrap its bones around Jeremy's torso and secure them to the wyrm. "I'm strapping you in with a harness."

Good thing that Jeremy's blind.

"A-alright." Jeremy licks his lips again. "Very...warm... Are you bringing anyone else?"

"No." One passenger is already enough for this time. I'll see where this change in events takes me before I escalate things further.

I climb onto the back of the wyrm, eventually positioning myself firmly onto the crest of its head. There, my hands once more take control of the flight focus, wrapping around its spongy, delicate bones. With a thought, the other nine skeletons on deck collapse into their components and fly onto the tail of the wyrm, extending its length by another seven feet for a final length of twenty-five feet from head to tail tip.

Though Hercates draws the image of a bony winged dragon on the cover of the flying construct chapter, he never discusses the creation of such a mount. Wyrms are superior in that they're aerodynamic, can be made with bones from a plethora of sources (even though Hercates only uses human bones in his reagent list), and are easily extended out to account for additions—and subtractions—of bone.

"Ah," Jeremy exclaims as the wyrm rises off the ground. I ignore him, lifting the construct farther into the air. Once we're around a hundred feet above the water, I direct the wyrm forward, towards the mainland. In minutes, the ship is a speck on the horizon behind us.

"Where are we going?"

"The mainland," I reply.

"But whe—"

"Menocht Bay."

I hear Jeremy audibly gape. "Menocht Bay? We're saved!"

If only that were true.

"Don't get your hopes up yet." Maybe a day or two's head start in the city will give me a better chance at preventing the worst of the outbreak.

The city is within sight after four hours of flying, its skyscrapers towering over the horizon. The glass reflects the sunlight and magnifies the glare coming off the water, so much so that it's difficult to look at the city directly.

I touch the wyrm down onto the waves, disengaging myself from its head and lowering myself down to Jeremy. Since he's already in his 'harness', I simply detach him from the wyrm's ribcage and float him next to me.

"What's happening?" he asks, flustered.

"We need to travel inconspicuously. I'll lead you along next to me; you won't have to do anything."

Jeremy breaks the silence after a minute. "How—"

My head snaps around. "Hmm?"

"Do you have a harness too?"

Funny. "No."

He's quiet for a moment. "Before this nightmare, I worked at an Arts academy. To cover all our bases, we ensured that we had personnel proficient in all practitioner domains."

I see where he's going with this. "So you have a basic familiarity with decemancy."

"Something like that."

"Then you should understand why we should travel inconspicuously." It's best to avoid headaches, even in a world with no consequences.

The man grimaces. "I know how you're moving me"—he spits the last word, shivering with disgust—"but how are you moving?"

I yawn. "We're all made of bones, after all." Sure it's considered dangerous to manipulate your own bones, but I've done it enough times now that it's old hat. I can't blame him for being surprised—most would never dare experiment with their own bodies. "But you're not far off the mark: I'm not using a harness like yourself, but I have a few bones stashed in my clothes." A blatant lie but easier to digest than the truth.

Jeremy settles down with that revelation. "Of course."

"When we arrive," I begin, "I'm going to remove your harness. You're going to have to walk with me... Can you do that?"

"I'll do my best. It'd be easier if I had eyes."

He's obviously hinting that I should bring him to a healer. But, seeing as neither of us has money or identification, I can't see it working out. I could try to fix his eyes myself, but my practice is more suited for destruction than restoration.

"I can whip something up for you. It'll make people look at you funny, but it should serve as a stop-gap until you can see a proper Life practitioner."

His lip curls up. "A stop-gap?"

"Well?"

"Fine."

I pull the soul gems I used to animate the wyrm from my pockets. I crunch them, turning them into a liquid, and direct them into Jeremy's eyes.

He jumps. "Everything's in shades of gray!"

I smile and tap my head. "You're seeing the world in shades of vitality." In other words, with the sight of Death.

"You're white," he murmurs.

"I'm alive," I point out. "Look at your own arm. You're a pale gray because you're still teetering on the cusp of death."

He pales. "I am?"

I need to find him a pair of sunglasses—his eyes are glowing violet. "Yes, you are." I really need to work on my patience as I keep snapping at the man. "But you've already lightened up quite a bit," I say encouragingly.

"I didn't realize how quickly we were moving," Jeremy comments, probably referring to the speed of the wyrm over water. He looks at me, his eyes narrowing. "Who are you?"

"Ignatius."

He snorts. "I should've heard of a decemancer of your caliber."

"It doesn't matter," I murmur, directing us around the docks and toward the cliff by the left edge of the city. There's a small overgrown area that I use as cover to sneak us in. I lower our feet onto the ground and strip Jeremy of his skeletal overcoat.

I sigh. I'm not here to rescue them, I tell myself. Every time I've gone down that route in the past... And yet, what else is there to do? Screw it.

"Let's go to the consulate and try to get in touch with an official."

CHAPTER

3

THE FLOWER DISTRICT

"Are they really that conspicuous?"

"Yes." I give him a look while he readjusts his sunglasses.

"Thanks for the clothes, by the way," he mutters.

"I couldn't have you walking around in a towel." Before we left, I scrounged up a set of clothing from one of the guest cabins—a simple black patterned shirt, a loose pair of gray trousers, and cheap sandals.

It doesn't take long before the consulate building is just up ahead, its golden tresses sparkling in the sunlight.

"What business?" an attendant asks as she scrolls through a collection of names and appointments.

Jeremy gives me a look.

"A ship containing civilian captives is going to arrive at Menocht Bay in a little more than one day," I explain. "I have a cohort that has taken over the ship and steered it on course for this city."

The attendant's finger pops off her glosspad. "Excuse me?"

"Who should we speak to about this incident?"

"You'll get in big trouble if you aren't serious," she warns us.

I nod. "We're serious."

She shakes her head, then stares at her glosspad. "Since this is...urgent, follow me." She gives us a reluctant look before motioning for another guard to stand at the white-and-gold-filigreed entrance.

Soon, we're standing before a large mahogany door. "One moment." The attendant knocks, then enters. She emerges a moment later and beckons us in.

Jeremy and I enter the professional office of whom I immediately recognize as the captain of the guards.

"Esmerelda Conningway," she says, introducing herself. She's standing by the window, looking out. It's not a particularly nice view, framing city instead of bay.

"Ignatius Black," I lie.

"But you can call him Iggy," Jeremy interjects. My eye twitches. "I'm Jeremy Sanderson."

"...Mr. Black," Captain Conningway calls out, "I see Death energy around you. Speak your business."

It's by no means illegal to practice the Dark Art, though I've found that decemancers typically enjoy lukewarm welcomes at best. When engaging with Menocht authorities, I've learned that it's strategically useful to deny any decemantic association. Conningway, I suspect, will be no exception.

"It's unsurprising that the taint I fight has seeped into my vestments," I rebut, sighing. "A day ago, my assistant, Claude, and I traced the path of a peak decemancer back through the Illyrian Ocean. We thought it suspicious that a decemancer would use a flying construct to follow a circuitous path over water."

The captain hums her assent. "Quite suspect. It's faster and safer to travel over ground, especially for the decemantic type. But why were you chasing a decemancer?"

I smirk. "There was a bounty on him—wanted for human sacrifice."

Conningway frowns, then makes a gesture for me to continue.

"To our surprise and dismay, we soon found a ship that had been boarded by undead. Moreover, not only was it filled to the brim with skeletons, but it also held over two hundred shackled people in a pool on deck."

Captain Conningway's eyebrows rise, her expression turning grim. "Heavens."

"Jeremy was one of the better off that I managed to rescue," I say, gesturing to the bony man. Even dressed in clean clothes and sunglasses, he looks half-dead. It's not exactly difficult to believe that he'd just been liberated.

Conningway's eyes widen. "So, what happened to the ship and its captives?"

I clear my throat. Y'jeni, I've talked more today than I have in ages. Not that I didn't *use* to talk in this looping nightmare: There just hasn't really been a need in the past however-many months.

"As I said, we only found the ship a few hours ago. Since then, we've defeated the skeletons and taken over the ship's steering mechanism. With my partner at the helm, it should arrive at Menocht Bay soon—in about thirty-six hours." While there was no human steering the ship, I did leave a skeleton in charge of keeping it on course.

The captain fingers her jaw. "Okay. Excellent." She exhales while clenching her fist. "I swear, I can only handle so much evil in this world..."

I cock my head. "Has there been anything else going on in the city?" I take a step forward. "You probably haven't heard of my name because I usually operate across the ocean in Turina, but I'm quite accomplished in the Arts."

Jeremy gives me a look, and I wink at him.

The captain groans. "Nothing worth troubling a guest over."

"I insist." The problem at hand most certainly *is* my business after all the trouble it's put me through.

She waves a hand dismissively but paces back over to the window. "We've been having problems with a drug called ginger," she explains. "It afflicts people with a mild bout of insanity that only grows worse with further usage. Moreover, it's contagious," she spits. "I know, it sounds preposterous. However, when someone exchanges fluids with another on the drug...the insanity spreads." I know from experience that even a sneeze is enough to spread the contagion, with fluid droplets lingering in the air for hours.

"How long has this been going on?" I ask.

"Two days"—she sighs—"and it's already grown into a terrible headache."

It'll be far more than that if it isn't stopped now, I think scathingly. Her information is correct, though: given that I've arrived a day and a half earlier than usual, it's only been around two days since ginger began to be produced in the city.

"Do you have any leads?" I know the drug's source, but I might as well see if the captain knows anything I don't.

"We only know that the drug's maker is skilled in the Arts," she replies helplessly.

The consulate guards really don't know anything, then. Disappointing.

"Is there a way that I can contact you?" she asks suddenly.

I blink. "No."

"You can contact me through quantum channeling," Jeremy interjects. "You do have a channeler in your office, correct?"

She nods. "I do."

I'm mildly taken aback by this. Quantum channelers have been largely rendered obsolete by the emergence of glossYs, so it's surprising Conningway has one on hand. They do have their uses, though, allowing for communication without a physical device serving as a medium.

In exchange for convenience, they're much more invasive. Just thinking of Mother screaming at a marketing agent over quantum channeler is enough to give me goosebumps. Granted, the agent deserved it: you can't ignore someone contacting you via channel as their voice tunnels *straight* into your mind. Unsurprisingly, the marketer contacting Mother over quantum channel was illegal—a fact she repeated with feverish gusto.

"Excellent," Jeremy says as he heads for the rectangular black receiver in the office's corner. "I'll input my signature into the system... There." He turns back and smiles. "Remember: Jeremy Sanderson."

She smiles back. "I'll contact you if I have any further updates or questions, and I'll keep men stationed at the docks to await the arrival of the ship. I presume that we'll have much more business together sorting out everything when your partner arrives."

I bow my head. "Excellent. You've been a pleasure to work with, Captain Conningway."

"Likewise."

* * *

"We're going to the Flower District," I call out as we exit the consulate building. Jeremy follows behind, his steps sure enough that he no longer slows me down.

"Why?"

I give him a grim smile. "That's where the root of the trouble is."

He doesn't ask any more questions, for which I'm thankful. I don't have any good answers. None that are simple, anyway.

The Flower District is, on the surface, beautiful and decadent. That's because it has two levels. Flowers line pathways and shopfronts on the surface, gardens of rose bushes and shrubs interrupting the monotony of the trimmed lawn. Throughout the Flower District are strategically placed lifts leading down to the lower level. Sections of the upper level peel away from below, allowing the sun to cast slits of light into the underground.

Instead of the park-like upper level, the lower level is a veri-table warren of buildings. Thin streets crisscross shopfronts and lead off into seedier areas with less-than-legal businesses—such as drug dens where the ginger manufacturers worked. From my understanding, the lower level is largely left to its own business, so long as the debauchery and crime stay below.

I take Jeremy down one such lift to the lower, sunless level, not that he'd be able to tell. "What happened down here?" He breathes through his mouth, holding his nose. "Smells like some-thing died."

"Lots of things have died down here," I murmur as I sidestep past a group of stringy-haired loiterers. "It's only going to get worse until this drug is out of the picture."

I almost can't believe I'm in Menocht before the drug has reached the Central District. Things haven't gotten out of hand yet. While I don't want to get my hopes up, I feel like I might have a chance to nip this entire humanitarian crisis in the bud.

I shake my head to clear my thoughts. "Pay attention to peo-ple's vitality as we walk," I murmur. Jeremy looks my way, his face rapt. "People who are taking ginger will look gray."

Jeremy blanches. "They're dying?"

"Something like that. We need to find the spot with the great-est density of people with low vitals."

It doesn't take us more than fifteen minutes to do so. We stand before the door of an abandoned factory.

"They're making it inside," I whisper. "But don't worry." I wave my hand.

"Holy shit," Jeremy hisses. "You just killed all of them! They're all black!"

Look behind you, Jer. I killed everyone else on the way over. "The drug's new, so the captain doesn't know...but the insanity is permanent."

"So? I'm sure some healers could—"

"Do you trust me, Jeremy?"

He stops and looks at me, his eyes narrowing. "I shouldn't, but I do."

"Then trust that this is the only way."

I place my palms together, then split them apart. I can't use these bodies; the only thing they're good for is a fire. I strip them of moisture, expelling it from their flesh, though even for someone like me, the process is inefficient. It would be much easier if I were a water elementalist.

"You're a practitioner, right? What do you specialize in?"

He sighs. "I'm a fire and water elementalist."

I give him an appraising look. Opposite elemental affinities of Sun and Moon? That's a rare combo. He's almost certainly been able to feel me moving water out of the bodies. Then he should have already guessed...

"You want me to light these bodies up, don't you?"

"As if they're all infected with plague."

He runs a hand through his hair. "They're already dead..." he mutters, as though trying to convince himself to light the dehydrated corpses up. "I need to see what I'm setting on fire to do it correctly," he says, stepping toward the factory door.

"Fine. But if you need to get close, hold your breath." I move the dead over to the far side of the factory and follow him inside. Tables of syringes and vials of yellow litter the inside, taking up a third of the factory's floor space. Mummified people lay strewn over the ground.

He stays within a foot of the doorway, keeping his distance, hands shaking. "Before the ship, I would've vomited at this sight." He immolates the corpses, his orange flames quickly turning shriveled skin black.

When we go back outside, Jeremy sets the rest of the people I killed aflame. The entire process takes around half an hour.

"Is that it? Crisis averted?" he asks.

I chuckle. "If only it were so simple. We need to kill all the infected, Jeremy. That's the only way to prevent the city from going under." I glance back at him. "But it's easy to tell who's infected, at the very least."

"Can we stop for dinner?" Jeremy asks, his tone defeated.

"Why?"

"It's been seven hours since I last ate," he retorts, anger creeping into his voice. "I'm hungry."

"Fine. If you can pay for it." I mean this as a joke, but he takes my words seriously.

"Don't you have money?"

"No," I reply, cracking a smile.

He licks his lips. By now, we've returned to the upper level of the city, and the consulate is within view. "Why don't we see if we can get money from the captain?"

I scoff. "For doing what?"

"F-for taking care of the ginger problem..."

I narrow my eyes and glare at him. "People don't take kindly to solving problems with killing, even if it's the only way." I sigh. "We'll be busy ridding the city of infected for the foreseeable future; we're bound to get money or food off the culled infected."

"Oh..."

"We can take food then. Fair?"

He doesn't reply.

WORLD SHIFT

J eremy held an auri in his palm, rubbing his fingers over its smooth, blue, jade-like surface.

"What are you thinking about?" I ask.

Jeremy looks up, his eyes widening. "...How did you know where to go?"

I tilt my head in consideration. Using stolen auris, I brought Jeremy on over twenty hovergloss trips around Menocht Bay. Wherever we disembarked, I led him to budding groups of infected, striding through back alleys and commercial districts alike. In just under five hours...I did it: I eradicated ginger.

"You know the city like the back of your hand, but I'm willing to bet you're not from Menocht Bay—you're too powerful. Are you from Kaspari?"

"No."

"Did you grow up in Menocht, perhaps?"

I scoff. "Definitely not. Don't you hear my accent?"

Jeremy's brow furrowed. "...Shattradan?"

I grin. "You guessed it."

"But..."

I sigh and fold my arms across my chest. "Look, Jer, it's complicated, but have I steered you wrong thus far?"

"You consider culling over two percent of the city's population a success and somehow convinced me to be your accomplice. You can't blame me for still trying to figure out what's going on. What kind of person are you to kill so many without blinking an eye?"

I snort and avert my gaze. "The kind of person with nothing to lose."

* * *

Inevitably some of the infected had access to store registers. I easily puppeted their corpses into giving us enough money to pay for two rooms at a hotel.

We're in the hotel room now, a luxurious suite with two king-size mattresses. Jeremy falls asleep almost the second his head hits the pillow, not that I can blame him. I lie down on my own mattress, though I keep my eyes open to stare at the ceiling.

"Was this what I was supposed to do all along?" I murmur. "In hindsight, it seems so close-minded that I stayed with the ship until it docked. I can't believe I never thought to go on ahead and stop the crisis from escalating."

I chuckle bitterly. Sometimes when you linger on a problem for too long, you grow blind to the way forward. Even a single external comment can help you to see things differently and illuminate a flawed pattern of thinking.

Unfortunately for me, I've been alone. Maybe that was the first mistake I made, here, in the loop: failing to treat people like *people*. Just because they won't remember anything in a few days doesn't mean they don't have anything to offer besides raw information.

Thinking of the potentially uncertain future, a part of me is terrified. The loop always restarted when I lost, which was inevitable after the city completely went off the rails. I normally could hold the ginger-infected people off for a few days, taking out strategic points and disabling lines of communication, but the end result was always my failure.

Was this the one time...that I would succeed?

* * *

I'm awake after Jeremy—surprising considering that the man hasn't had a proper bed in weeks. Based on the position of the sun, I'd say we've been sleeping for seven hours.

"What now?" he asks.

"We wait for the boat to arrive."

"...That's it?"

I raise an eyebrow. "Am I missing something?"

He recoils. "You seemed to be in a hurry yesterday," he observes. "I find it hard to believe that there's nothing for us to do but wait."

"I was in a hurry to stop ginger's spread," I explain. "Now that that's done with, we can relax."

"The captain hasn't called us."

"Should she have?"

"Well...the guard must have realized that someone went and killed over five thousand people."

"Why would they blame us?"

Jeremy's jaw drops. "Forget it." He turns away for a moment. "Speak of the devil," he exclaims. "Look who's making contact."

I can't but feel that Jeremy jinxed us. "What is it?"

"Conningway's freaking out."

"Well—"

"She wants us to come in now."

I pause for a moment, then shrug. "Fine."

* * *

When we step foot onto the steps of the consulate, a different attendant from yesterday comes up to us and leads us inside. Before I know it, we're once more within the office of Captain Conningway.

"Black, Sanderson," she says, her voice strained. "Welcome back."

"Is there a problem?"

"No, no, nothing at all. Just the deaths of 4,243 people." She takes a drag from a cigarette and clenches her fist. "And that's just what's been called in so far. I can't help but suspect the dark art is involved."

"On what grounds?"

She snorts. "Only Death practitioners have anything to gain from the wanton destruction of human life."

Conningway...I might be more willing to actually work with you if you weren't so intolerant of all decemancy.

"What kind of city is this?" I murmur, feigning surprise. Jeremy clears his throat and looks the other way as I continue. "First, a cruise ship full of captives, now mass murder. Were the deaths concentrated in any one area?"

"At least five hundred came from the lower level of the Flower District alone, but they're also scattered all over."

"Anything linking the bodies together?"

She gives me a worried look. "That's just the thing: all the bodies have been burned to ash."

"We'll look into it while we continue our investigation into ginger," I say encouragingly. "It couldn't have just been one person. More likely it was a group of people working in tandem, or"—I stare at her—"Ginger's so new that you know very little about it, right?"

"...That is correct."

I grab my jaw. "It might, in fact, be the case..." I look over at Jeremy. "While we were conducting our own investigation, we ran into evidence that pointed towards the lower level of the Flower District being a manufacturing center for ginger." I begin to pace. "Perhaps...the creator of ginger put some kind of deadly substance in it that can be activated remotely? Something that sets someone on fire from within?" I freeze in place, giving the captain a hollow stare. "But why? Why kill off the users of a successful drug?"

The captain rubs her arm, appearing more confused than ever. "I don't know if that's possible..."

"Regardless...the ship should be here in an hour. You do have guards stationed at the docks, right?"

"Of course."

"We'll go down to the docks to wait, then."

* * *

It only takes forty-five minutes for the former cruise ship to arrive within sight of the docks. The guards hail it down, and upon realizing that its course is set, they deploy anti-velocity nets to slow the vessel down. Then, they send out a team of tugboats to haul it to one of the piers.

I rush past them onto the boat. "Claude!" I call out. "Claude!"

By now, the captain has made her way to the dock to see the ship herself.

"Claude?" Jeremy whispers.

"He's my assistant, remember?"

Jeremy gives me a dubious look. "Right..."

"Where could he have gone?" I murmur, looking dejectedly off into the distance. The captain boards with the other guards and stops by my side.

"Can't find your associate?" she asks, concern visible in her eyes.

"I'm worried that the decemancer came back. If so, Claude probably left the ship to chase him off." I groan. "But now I have no idea where he is..."

"Chasing off a peak decemancer by himself? Your friend must be incredibly strong."

I shake my head. "He'll be fine...but this entire situation of us being separated is an inconvenience."

"Captain!" a guardsman calls out. "We found the captives."

"Excellent!" she shouts back. "I'll come and see for myself."

"You sure that's a good idea?" I say, grabbing her arm before she can leave.

She jerks her arm away. "Who do you take me for?" she growls.

I hold out my hands in defeat. I did warn her.

She comes back a minute later with a hand resting on her stomach. "Only the most depraved of men," she hisses, "could ever do something like that."

"I can't disagree."

She looks to Jeremy. "And you, Mr. Sanderson...you were there, in those pools?"

"I was."

Her face turns ashen. "You seem much better off than most. No doubt thanks to Mr. Black's assistance." She shakes her head and exhales. "We're taking them all off the ship in the next few minutes. Unless you're going to help...it'd be best if you leave."

I blink.

And suddenly, the world shifts.

* * *

I'm back in my room.

My room?

My eyes are wide open, unbelieving. Some human is in the bed across the room, sleeping, his chest moving up and down beneath his pale sheet. Xander? My eyes open even wider. It's really him. I feel his vitality from across the room, feel the vitality of others housed within the building.

I jump out of bed and rub my eyes. This isn't real. It can't be.

I don't believe it. It must still be this damned nightmare loop. It *has* to be.

The dorm room is as I remember it, like some kind of bad dream, socks strewn about near the hamper, the walls covered in frayed posters, and the window's cheap metal screen still torn.

The worn wood of the floor calls me like an old friend, my slippers the most beautifully familiar object in the world. I haven't seen a pair of slippers in years! Menocht denizens all wear *sandals* instead of proper, warm, fuzzy...

I step from the bed, my legs practically shaking from shock. I trip and fall over my shoes on the way to my fluffy sheepskin beauties. My eyes flash in annoyance.

Xander stirs. "Ian," he murmurs, yawning. "You alright?"

Y'jeni, after everything I've been through, I'm *actually* hyperventilating. "Mmm," I grunt in response.

Me, hyperventilating after being *spoken to* by my roommate. I shake my head.

"Okay, well...I'm going back to sleep. Quiet please." He rolls over to face the wall, the bed so thin width-wise that his nose practically touches the plaster.

I gingerly place a foot into a slipper, then the other. My hands are unsteady as I undress and grab a towel hanging from my dresser. I wrap it around my hips, doing everything I can to keep my teeth from chattering.

I need a damn shower.

I walk out of the room in a daze. It has to be a dream... There's absolutely no way I'm out of the loop.

Of course, when I get to the shower, I remember that I really *should* be wearing my shower shoes (sandals...) and not my slippers. I double back, regretfully extract my feet from the slippers, don my sandals, and return to the bathroom.

I slam the door of the shower behind me and toss the towel on a hook outside. The water streams over me in a hot torrent, helping to ease my muscles and calm my thoughts.

I think through the possibilities in my head for what's happening.

1. I'm dreaming, likely trapped in some kind of illusion because the captain suspected that I killed the people in Menocht. If this is true, then I've severely underestimated her.
2. I'm awake, and I've managed to break out of the time loop. I've beaten the puzzle. I'm in the loop...but the loop has *changed*.

With each passing minute, I'm leaning towards option number two...but I can't bring myself to accept it. After all those times waging a one-man war on Menocht Bay and its drug-zombified inhabitants, I refuse to believe that the answer I was always searching for—the way to win—was just going ahead of the boat and stopping ginger before it took over the city. It seems too simple. Not at all like the kind of resolution that would satisfy whoever made the loop in the first place.

After fifteen minutes of letting the water run, I realize I forgot to grab my shampoo. I sense the vitality in the area and note that nobody's even close to the bathroom. Nude, I step out of the shower, grab the bottle of hair product, and return to the warmth.

Ten minutes later, I'm brushing my teeth and marveling at how long it's been since I did so.

"You've been in here for a while," Xander says as he enters the bathroom, unwashed brown hair sweeping around his forehead. He grabs his toothbrush and a tube of toothpaste. He glances at me. "You okay?"

I give him a toothpaste-filled smile. "Fine."

Just seeing him makes me want to panic, and I don't know why. I shake my head. Hordes of insane humans and armies of skeletons don't make me panic. Facing off against the entire armed Menocht Bay armada doesn't make me panic. So why am I so jittery and anxious?

"Not shaving today?" Xander asks, raising an eyebrow.

I pause as though struck. Right. "Thanks for the reminder." I chuckle, feigning normalcy. "I didn't get much sleep last night. Nightmare."

He nods. "Must've been some dream."

I add another selection to my list of possibilities: The time loop was a nightmare.

Though that seems even more unlikely than the other options. What kind of nightmare turns you into a decemancer?

"It was pretty terrible."

"Wanna talk about it?"

My breath catches in my throat. "It started on a boat," I explain dryly. "No matter what I did, after a few days, I always ended back up on that boat."

"Sounds awful."

"It really was."

I head back to our room, donning the university uniform and a pair of dress shoes. I shuffle downstairs and head off to the dining facilities to get breakfast.

I barely get five feet out the main door before I turn around. *It's a weekend,* I berate myself, scowling. *You wear casual clothes on the weekend. This is the real world, and in the real world, you need to pay attention to how you dress.* I shake my head as I angrily throw off my clothes, stripping the robe-like uniform off to don a T-shirt, zip-up jacket, and jeans. Not exactly the eerie black robe and greasy-haired look I always spawned onto the boat with.

I check myself in the mirror before I go out.

"Whoops," I murmur as I grab my brush. *Nearly went out with wet shower hair.* The drybrush sucks the moisture from my hair as it passes over the follicles.

"So, I've escaped." I sigh, glowering at the mirror's reflection: brown eyes, pale skin, and dark hair. Utterly average. "Now what?"

Giving myself one last look, I reason that I look sallow and on edge but presentable. I head back out the door and make my way once more to the dining hall.

GETTING AWAY

"Hello, Ian," the card swipe lady says as I walk through an archway into the dining atrium of Campus Central—the main hub of Academia Hector's regular campus. I'm surprised I remember her name. The regular facilities supposedly aren't as nice as those on the practitioner campus, but I've never complained about the dining room's wide, sunlit windows and a view of the far-off Bay of Ramsay on a clear day.

"Octavia," I reply, stretching my mouth into the approximation of a smile. "How are you?"

"Fine." Her expression grows pensive. "You okay?"

What? "I'm fine, why?"

"Oh, nothing. Have a good one, dear."

I'm not acting any differently than usual...am I? I've gotten my act together, and I'm no longer outwardly jittering. I suppose it's more than possible that my mannerisms have changed; it's been a few years, to say the least. I almost feel like I'm going to overdose on normalcy.

Regardless, I head over to get some food. At 8:30 in the morning on a weekend, the line is only two people long. I help myself to eggs, hash browns, and sausages and grab a glass of soda.

As I sit down, I think about what I'm doing.

I'm back at school, in the cafe. I'm about to eat a plateful of food. Warm, hot food—nothing like the cold stuff I poached yesterday. Y'jeni, I'm hungry.

I grab a fork and hold it out in front of me. Out in Illuet, where Menocht Bay is situated, people use their hands to eat everything. How long has it been since I used a fork?

"Ian!" someone calls out from behind. "Eating with anyone?"

My eye twitches before I turn around. It takes me a moment to remember the girl with curly black hair and green eyes. "Oh, hey, Veronica." I gesture to the seat across from me. "Be my guest."

"Great! Be right back."

Veronica lives in the dorm underneath mine. We're in the same year, so I've known her for a while. We're on generally good terms but by no means close friends. Thinking back, I didn't really *have* close friends: I surrounded myself with a network of friendly acquaintances.

By the time she returns, I'm almost done with my plate. I consider getting seconds as she asks, "So, what's up?"

"Nothing really. Why?"

She tilts her head. "Just asking."

"He had a nightmare," Xander says from behind. He pulls out the chair to my right. "Right, Ian?"

Thanks for telling Veronica. But hey, what do I care? "Yep. Horrible nightmare. I'm super tired because of it."

"Oh no! Have you considered going to the nurse's office at Campus Central? She can probably give you a boost to get you through the day."

I snort, replying, "I don't need to go to the nurse because I'm tired."

"I've done it before!" Veronica exclaims. "Seriously. One night I was so worried about an exam that I couldn't get any sleep at all. I was so worried about going into the test unrested that I called up my dean and asked her for help. She told me to go to the nurse and, as you can guess, problem solved."

"Maybe." Going to the nurse because of fatigue, worrying about tests? Heavens, I'd trade tests written in classical Thakkish in exchange for dealing with ginger any day of the week.

Xander returns with a plate of food and settles down to eat. "What're you guys planning to do for winter formal?" he asks.

Literally the furthest thing from my mind. "Um..."

"I'm going with Rod," Veronica says after swallowing a bite of food. "Already have my dress and everything."

"When is winter formal?"

The two of them raise their eyebrows. "Seriously?" Xander says. "You're pretty dense, but they've been advertising it all over."

"Even in the bathrooms," Veronica chimed in. "Every single stall has a flyer in it."

"Guys, I'm tired as all hell. When is winter formal? Just tell me."

"In five days," Xander says. "Friday."

I breathe in deeply. "Okay. Well, I'll let you know once I have any updates."

"Aw, man, you mean you didn't ask Laura?"

Who? "...No."

Veronica looks between the two of us, then laughs. "Better get your act together, Dunai," she says, her expression playful. "The clock is ticking."

"Y'know what, Veronica, I think I will check out the nurse. I'll see you guys around." I gather up my plate, silverware, and cup and push in my chair. Before I leave, though, I give them both a forced smile.

I'm really not up for conversation right now. What I really want is to get off-campus and away from a life that feels like it belongs to someone else.

I head out from Campus Central, winding down the stairs from the dining hall and into a broad hallway. I pass through the main doors and brace myself against the wind, though the chill is somewhat refreshing after spending the last epoch in Menocht's warmer climes.

I walk through a cramped courtyard and turn left, arriving at the foot of a hovergloss terminal. I climb a short series of steps and sit down on a bench, the exposed terminal providing no shelter from the wind. As I wait for the next hovergloss, I can't help but think that things were much easier in a world with no consequences. I could whisk myself into the air and raise an army of dead without worry. Now? I'm waiting outside in the cold.

I end up at a cafe with barely any recollection of how I got there. I took the hovergloss for twenty minutes, hopped off, and walked around, trudging through fresh snow until I ended up here. The cafe is warm, unfamiliar, and open—the perfect combination.

All I want is a space to be alone without someone interrupting.

The plan works...at least, for twenty minutes. Then, a random person taps on my shoulder. If I hadn't sensed them coming, I would've been startled.

"Um, excuse me, is that seat open?" The man is referring to the seat in front of me, of course.

I roll my eyes before turning around. "It's open."

He nods. "Excellent." Then he sits and just stares at me.

"Who are you?" he finally asks.

I run a hand through my hair. "Excuse me?"

"You can't be more than twenty-five," he remarks. "How is the energy of death so strong around you?"

I blink. "You can see that?" I cycle the energy that I picked up on the way over. Honestly, it's not very much energy at all, just some leftover remnants from roadkill and animals dead of natural causes. The hovergloss hadn't even passed a hospital.

"I see it clear as day," the man replies, folding his arms over the table. "What are you planning on using that energy for if you don't mind me asking?

I speak the truth, for once. "Not planning anything." The restrictions on decemancy are numerous enough that I might just end up with an outstanding warrant for arrest if I'm careless.

"What's your family name?"

I sigh. "I think I'm just gonna go." He doesn't stop me, but by the time I'm back at the hovergloss terminal, I realize the man slipped a business card into my pocket.

Maybe he did it when he tapped on my shoulder, back when he asked for the seat. I can't think of another time that he had access to my pocket.

I flip the card between my fingers as the bus drives off. Walter E. Cristien. Wind Elementalist. Investigator of Preternatural Affairs at the Bureau of Issues and Answers.

I cough dryly. An investigator, huh? Does he think that just because I'm a decemancer, I'm involved in the occult? I'm surprised that he had the affinity to even notice my aura. Maybe he has some kind of device that lets him sense it or a minor Life or Death affinity.

I ponder what to do next. Not just school but *everything* in my damned life from before seems trivial. I never gave serious thought to what would happen once I escaped the time loop.

Maybe I should have.

I *definitely* should have.

* * *

Temple Beach is cold and overcast so I'm the only one here—which is the point. The feel of the wind buffeting my hair is familiar, along with the sounds of the ocean and the countless blips of vitality around me. As I stare off into the distance, I half expect to see that familiar ship...

I shake my head and flex my hands, circulating warmth back into them. I wave my hand, bringing a cluster of shells up from the sand to cover my face like a mask.

Good. Anonymity, in case anyone sees.

Then I drag myself forward over the water, putting on speed until I'm gliding over the gray waves. I'm going faster than anything in the water below me, though slower than if I were riding a wyrm.

I'm glad that at least this much is real. Whatever happened—or didn't happen—in the time loop, learning how to move around like this is undoubtedly a boon.

After I proceed about five miles out, I start to gather up bones beneath me. Soon, a giant, pink-red bone-whale crests out of the top of a wave and falls back down on its back. I smile at the spectacle and make more bone constructs, adding an entourage of dancing dolphins and a school of flying fish.

I did something like this several cycles back, when I was passing time on the cruise ship before it docked into the bay. They aren't truly animated bone constructs like the wyrm since they lack soul gems and foci, but they're outwardly similar if I'm actively controlling them.

Flying myself over the ocean while wet is agonizing, especially when my hair is starting to freeze and my shoes are soaking wet. My teeth begin to chatter, and I realize that I might actually want to go to the nurse after all: Not for exhaustion, but for hypothermia.

Why did I decide to do this? Because I wanted to make sure I still could?

Shit. I see my vitality graying before my eyes. *Definitely need to go to the nurse.* I'd forgotten just how cold northern weather could be. *Am I really so obtuse?* I wonder in incredulity. I know that my sense of pain has dulled after everything, but to not realize that I'm freezing to death is something else entirely. Maybe

I've also lost survival instincts after carelessly dying so many times.

I really don't have time to wait for the bus. Maybe going into a warm building will be enough. I just need to warm up a little…

Upon reaching the end of the beach, I choose to glide rather than walk on the sidewalk. Snowbanks frosting the sides of the road offer decent cover—I simply glide behind them, obscuring my feet.

By the time I return to the more populated part of town, the cold has thoroughly seeped into my bones. *If only I could dry my clothes or walk as fast as I could fly.* Having someone like Jeremy who could conjure up a fire and banish moisture would be invaluable.

This part of town seems kind of run-down, with a few store windows barred up. I walk into the first one I see with an "open" sign and lights on. The sign outside reads, *Pan's Precious Stones and Other Goods.*

"Welcome," an elderly woman says from across the room, her hands resting on the counter. "Welcome to Pan's."

I give her a small wave and thank my lucky stars that the room has a space heater. I give her a smile. "Going to be honest with you, I'm just looking for a place out of the cold." When I hold my hands out over the heater, I notice how much they're shaking.

"Oh, goodness!" she exclaims. "You poor thing! You look half-frozen." She sets something down on the counter and runs back to a closet. She emerges with a yellow towel and hands it to me. "Take this off," she scolds, helping me out of my sweatshirt. She wraps the towel over my shoulders and places my unzipped sweatshirt over one of her chairs. "Went outside without a jacket…all wet…" I hear her grumble.

"Thanks for the towel," I say once my teeth stop chattering. By now, the vitality has crept back into my extremities.

No need to go to the nurse after all. Maybe.

"So tell me about this place," I say. It's a local shop, probably owned by the woman herself.

"Well," she begins, "this place—Pan's—has been in my family for three generations now."

"Long time," I observe.

"It is."

"So what exactly do you sell here?"

She laughs. "Well, in terms of what we actually manage to sell, mostly these books over here." I turn around to see her point at a bookshelf full of Spirit Art guidebooks on the beyond. I scoff.

"I know, I know"—she sighs—"but people want what they want."

"What's the rest of this stuff taking up ninety percent of your floor space?"

She smiles. "Everything else is precious stones. Not the kind you'd use for jewelry—though many people come in and make that mistake. Specifically, they're tools and reagents for practitioners of the Arts."

I nod along.

"Not many people skilled in the Arts trust privately owned shops like this for their reagents," she says and sighs. "Too many things could go wrong if they use the wrong kind of focus or stone."

Makes sense, unfortunately. What she said is right: using the wrong kind of reagent could backfire, especially at the lower affinity levels when stone foci are most commonly consumed.

"Shame," I murmur. I'm feeling well enough to leave the immediate proximity of the heater and begin to walk around the shop. I appreciate how cozy the place is with its rustic wood paneling and carpet-covered floors.

"Did someone die here?" I murmur out loud, not intending to be overheard.

"Hmm?"

I shake my head. "Nothing."

She sighs. "My husband died a few months back. We lived in the loft above."

So *that* explains the residual energy of death dripping down from the ceiling like an unpatched leak. I draw the energy out, leaving the space above clean.

She pauses for a moment, then asks, "Are you a student at the university?"

I nod absently.

"Well, if you're the sort who can see vitality...we have a few foci that might be of interest and some soul gems in the back."

I smile gently, though my stomach is in knots. "Thanks. I'll keep that in mind." *If I keep being so careless, everyone is going to know I'm a decemancer.* Which isn't necessarily a bad thing...but I need to be careful how I reveal that information.

I make my way around the shop, looking at the various reagents and inspecting those that give off subtle auras. After a few minutes of warming up, I'm feeling ready to make the journey back.

"I'm feeling better," I state as I come to the front counter. I grab my still-damp jacket off the chair and grudgingly stick my arms into it, then run the towel through my hair one more time before draping it over the chair in my jacket's place.

The woman looks at me carefully. "If you ever need a place to be at peace, you're always welcome in this shop."

I give her a nod before sliding my shoes back on and heading out into the snow and sleet, reaching the nearest bus stop just in time to catch the next shuttle heading back to Academia Hector.

When I step into my room, Xander's working at his desk. "Hey," he says in greeting. "See the nurse?"

"Nah," I reply while hanging up my jacket. "I got some coffee, though."

Xander grunts. "Well, at least that's something."

"Yeah, I'm feeling much better now."

"Why are you all wet?" he asks, frowning.

"It's snowing," I point out, cocking my eyebrow.

"Not that hard."

I shrug. "Hard enough to make my sweatshirt wet." I take off my shoes and place my socks in the hamper. While I'm at it, I also pick up the socks piled around the hamper on the ground.

Seeing Xander working on homework reminds me...I probably have things to do, though who knows what: I sure don't remember.

"I really think you should see the nurse," Xander insists. "You're still acting out of it. Maybe you're coming down with something."

I look over in his direction. "Maybe."

"It'd make me feel better if you went and got checked out," he replied. "If you get sick, there's a ninety-nine percent chance that I'm gonna get sick, too."

I give him an exasperated sigh. "Fine." Besides, maybe the nurse can restore more heat into my body. I still feel cold, even after the hospitality at Pan's.

POTENTIOREADER

Thankfully, our residential building is connected by an underground tunnel to Campus Central, and I can get there without needing to return outside. I change out of my wet garments and walk down a stairwell leading to the underground, following the half-circle passage to Campus Central's primary atrium.

As I've never been to the nurse's office before, I don't know what to expect. It thankfully wasn't hard finding the office due to clear signage, but when I arrive, all I see is a lady sitting behind a window. The office is otherwise completely empty.

I walk over and clear my throat. "Hello?"

"Are you here to see the nurse?" the woman asks, her white lab coat affording her a subtle air of authority.

"Yeah."

"Okay, just fill out this sheet of paper and bring it up to me when you're done." She hands me a clipboard with a questionnaire attached to it.

I fill out my full name—Ignatius Julian Dunai—and peruse the questions. Most of them have the option to check N/A, which is convenient. I check the boxes indicating that I feel "tired", "fatigued", and "cold" and hand the questionnaire back. The lady nods, then tells me to wait until my name is called.

I shrug my shoulders and sit down in the waiting area. Two minutes later, a man comes out with a glosspad. "Mr. Dunai?"

I look up. "Here."

"Come with me, please."

I stand and follow him down a hallway into a small room with a table and a counter.

"So, just to confirm, you have symptoms of fatigue and chill."

I nod slowly and steeple my fingers in my lap. "Right."

"Has anything happened to you lately? Have you had any arguments with your peers?"

I hold up a hand. Does he think I've been cursed? "Wait, wait, slow down," I say. "I never said the chills and the fatigue are connected."

He taps his pencil on the clipboard. "They aren't?"

I sigh. "I wasn't able to sleep at all last night," I explain. "And then I was outside too long this afternoon, and my jacket got drenched by the snow. By the time I returned to my dorm, I was cold to the bone."

"Oh, alright. I'll let the nurse know."

"Thanks," I reply.

The official nurse comes in a minute later with a good-natured smile on her face. "Hello, Mr. Dunai. Tell me how you're feeling."

I notice immediately that she's trying to charm me, making me feel trusting and at ease. I frown. *A dual Life and Remorse practitioner?*

"I had a nightmare last night and couldn't sleep, so on one hand, I'm exhausted." I yawn right on cue. "On the other hand, I spent too long outside in the cold, and my jacket and shoes were soaked through by the snow. My roommate told me to come and get treatment, so...here I am."

The nurse nods. "Okay, hold tight—" She walks over and places a hand on my shoulder. I feel the energy in her touch as it flows into me, feeding warmth and alertness into my body.

I stretch my back. "Thanks, I feel a lot better now."

The nurse gives me an odd look. "You're not a practitioner, are you?"

Why is she asking? I made sure to dispel any Death energy before I entered the nurse's office.

I give her a pleasant smile. "No, I'm not."

She jots something down on her glosspad. "Feel better, Ignatius."

"Thanks."

"You know...if you're having nightmares..."

I freeze in place.

"I recommend the counseling services. They're provided free of charge by the school, and everything you say to a counselor is confidential."

...Except if they think you're a danger to yourself or others. No thanks.

Her expression quirks. "They even have a few counselors that have true confidentiality," she continues. "I know many practitioners of the Arts tend to seek them out, for whatever reason. They are bound by a life-death oath to never disclose anything that you discuss."

Life-death oath? If true, then anything I spoke of to a counselor really would be confidential.

As I leave the office, I linger for a bit in the hallway. *Wouldn't it be nice to finally tell someone about everything?* I reason. *Someone who can help me think this all through, plan for the future.*

I chew my lip, then look at the time on my glossY. It's still only 2 pm.

Before I know it, I'm standing in line at the counselor reception desk. Unlike the nurse's office, I have to wait a solid twenty minutes in line before I talk to the receptionist.

"Hello," he says, voice cheerful. "I haven't seen you here before. Looking to make a first appointment?"

I blink, a bit taken aback by his jubilant personality. "Yeah."

"What's your full name?"

"Ignatius Julian Dunai."

The receptionist scrolls through some things on his glosspad before punching in some numbers. "Great. So, why don't I give you our selection of counselors?"

He turns the glosspad around to me so that I can see names and faces.

"How do I know if they have total confidentiality?" I ask.

His warmth flickers. "That's a different list. Apologies. I usually only provide those counselors to practitioners."

"It's fine." Soon, he turns the glosspad back my way.

I give him a look. "You could've just told me there was only one available."

"So would you like to meet her?"

I shrug. "Sure. What's the waiting time?"

"She's available now. That's why she was on the glosspad."

"Oh. Great."

He points to the hallway. "Second to last door on the right. Room nineteen."

I make my way down the hall until I stand outside of room nineteen, its number displayed in clean white letters on the door. I knock, then open the door. Inside is a woman sitting at a desk, her face illuminated in the warm light of a floor lamp.

"Sit down," the woman says, her short blonde bob accentuating the movement of her jaw. I sit down on the provided couch. The woman sits down in a chair across from me and gives me a wry grin.

"Before we begin," she says, "I'm going to recite the life-death oath." She holds a slip of cardstock in front of her. "I, Jasmina Hermina Fernandez, do swear on my life and death to never divulge the contents of this meeting and all meetings henceforth between"—she looks over at her glosscomp screen—"Ignatius Julian Dunai, the Fourth of his name, and I. Even should I be under the effects of charm or compulsion, may all memories of these meetings be effaced from my mind and wiped from my lips. I do give this vow thus." The slip of cardstock spontaneously bursts into yellow flames and burns up into nothing.

I give a sigh of relief. "Thanks."

"Now, it indicates in your file," she says, "that you aren't a practitioner. But, Mr. Dunai, I suspect that this *might* not be the case."

I raise an eyebrow. "What gives you that impression?"

"The way you move, the way you look around you. There's a certain...arrogance to it." She gives me a look as though daring me to disprove the observation.

"You're right; I am a practitioner," I admit. "And you can call me Ian, by the way."

She smiles, though the gesture doesn't reach her eyes. "Call me Jasmine."

I look around. "What happens next?"

"Don't worry, I'll get us started," she says. "First, I'm profoundly curious: how did you forge the documents regarding your affinities and status as a practitioner?"

"I didn't."

"You can be honest with me; remember, I can't tell anyone about what we discuss."

"Before this morning, I wasn't a practitioner."

Her eyes flash with curiosity. "Care to explain?"

"Well, this is going to sound"—I cock my head as though doing a mental calculation—"improbable, at best, but...it's the best explanation I have." I take in a deep breath. "I've spent the past...well, it's definitely been more than just a few years, though I can't say how long it's been exactly...let's just say...I've spent an epoch of time in a dilation loop." I give her a look. "Do you follow me?"

"Dilation loops...are rare, but they do exist," she murmurs, eyes narrowing. "Continue."

"The loop always starts the same way."

Jasmine jots something down on the glosspad. "How does the loop start?"

I chuckle humorlessly. "On a boat...a little dinghy, in the middle of the Illyrian Ocean."

Jasmine snorts. "Y'jeni, what a horrendous start."

"Every time, a cruise ship comes from afar. I found out that I'm supposed to board the ship, defeat the minions of undead on its surface, piece together a map of the cruise ship's current location and target trajectory, and master decemancy from a grimoire in the captain's cabin." I pause. "Oh, and stop an outbreak from destroying Menocht Bay."

Jasmine's face doesn't change. "Menocht Bay?"

"It's in Illuet Province, near Mt. Honorus."

Jasmine raises an eyebrow. "Interesting location."

"So, in the past however-many hundred loop iterations, save the last one, I always rode the cruise ship into Menocht Bay. Oh, and I forgot to mention something: On the cruise ship are captives that used to be passengers. At the time I find them, they've been stewing in a cesspool for weeks. Most of them are on the brink of death."

Jasmine's eyebrows furrow, her lips separating.

"Anyway. So, I usually ride the ship into Menocht. However, when I arrive, the entire city is always embroiled in a war against a contagious drug-borne pathogen that causes incurable insanity." I sigh. "The entire time I'd been convinced that the way to escape the loop is to become strong enough to single-handedly win against a city of insane, hyper-aggressive, trigger-happy humans with access to defensive artillery."

Jasmine coughs lightly. "...Seems like that wasn't the case?"

"No." I sigh, resting my head on the couch. "The way I was supposed to win, evidently, was by leaving the ship on a bone wyrm, getting to Menocht Bay before the city succumbed to insanity, and killing the five thousand or so infected before they passed the pathogen on.

"When I did all of that, the cruise ship had no issues docking into the bay and everyone was rescued. Just as they were being lowered out of the pools and onto the deck...I blinked." I start to laugh. "And then I woke up and was here, with all of my memories."

I know it must sound absurd, but I don't have any reason to lie. "Do you believe me?"

She pushes up her glasses. "I believe that you've told me the truth."

She doesn't appear fully convinced, however, and believing that I've been truthful isn't the same as believing that what I've said is true. To offer up concrete evidence, I begin to levitate myself above the couch. It takes Jasmine a few seconds to notice, but when she does, she swallows, and her heart rate increases. Seeing that I've made my point, I let myself drop back down, bouncing against the cushion.

"So...you woke up this morning in your room a decemancer?"

"Yes. One second, I was on the docks of Menocht, the next, I'm lying in my bed."

"You say that you were in the time loop for a few years. Correct?"

I nod.

"...And after only a few years, you were able to fight off against the entire armed city of Menocht?"

"Look," I say. "Technically, yes. But it was never enough to stop the plague, and in the end, everyone always died. That's beside the point. In a world without consequences, decemancy is the most powerful kind of practice there is."

Her lips press into a line. "How many creatures do you think you've killed over the course of your time in the loop to further your practice?"

I stare at her. There were entire cycles of time where I razed the city of Menocht almost to the ground. Then there were the cycles when I killed all the neighboring cities in an attempt to bring the situation under control with an army of undead...then there was the time when I flew all the way to the capital of Illuet Province to request an audience with the high counselor. The loop controllers hadn't liked that plan one bit, the loop promptly restarting as soon as I entered the high counselor's chambers.

"Not sure," I say. "The number's probably too high to count, honestly."

"You must have *some* kind of estimate."

I give her a hard look. "I've killed in excess of ten million people, conservatively."

She gives me a blank stare. "People?"

"Yes, people. They always came back in the next loop, so I saw nothing wrong in killing them."

She inclines her head, looking as though she's trying to decide what to say next. "I understand you. Have you ever had someone measure your affinity in the loop?"

"No."

"Want me to measure it now in the office?"

I frown. "You can do that?"

"I have a potentioreader in the closet I can bring out."

"The result would be considered as part of the life-death oath, right?"

"It counts, don't worry," she assures me.

I look at the ceiling. To be honest, I'm curious. I never worried too much about my power while in the loop. After awakening, I simply tried to do my best and didn't dwell on what kind of status and opportunities my raw affinity percentage would give me. But now that I'm back in the real world, and I need to start planning for the future, figuring out where my affinity stands is important.

"Sure, why not."

She brings the potentioreader out and places it on the desk. It's a black sphere the size of a skull, resting on a small three-legged metal stand.

"What do I do with it?" I ask. The last time I was read by a potentioreader, I was too young to remember.

She grabs the ball in her hands. "Just hold it like this. It'll change color." Even as she speaks, the ball turns a muted blue color.

"Fine, hand it over." Soon, it's warming the space between my fingers. I expected it to be cold, to suck something out of me, but instead, it feels like the sphere is churning the energy up within my chest like a blender.

I give Jasmine an uneasy glance. "How do we know when it's done?"

"When it stops changing color."

Okay then. Its surface is red and swirly, almost like a red-tinted ocean swell.

"I use the colors to measure potential by inputting them into an algorithm on my glosscomp," Jasmine says, breaking the silence.

"Interesting."

"Aren't you at least a little excited to see what the results are?" she teases.

I shrug. "Excited or not..."

"...It's the Dark Art," she finishes. "Decemancy."

"...Right."

"It still has its uses, even if it's restricted."

"In wars, maybe," I murmur. Now that my actions have consequences again, I can't see myself using decemancy for any notable purpose besides flying around or creating soul gems. What use would I have for animating corpses or killing people?

Even if I want to get to the bottom of the dilation loop and who trapped me inside it, I've decided not to go about finding the truth in a violent matter. At the end of the day, I left the time loop without having aged a day and obtaining a powerful affinity. If anything, I should technically be...well, *thankful* is the wrong word, but I don't have a better one.

"I can see that you're skeptical of your own affinity's use," she observes.

"It's not that I'm unaware of my practice's utility, but I'm resigned to the reality that decemancy's expression is strictly regulated. Most of what I can do probably isn't permitted."

"This school has a track of study in pursuit of the Dark Art. It's small, but it exists; I think you'll find it better than nothing."

I think back to Jeremy and our conversation. The school where he worked employed a single decemancer.

"How many students are enrolled in the decemancy track?" I ask.

"I can check while we wait for the potentioreader to calm down," Jasmine offers.

"Sure."

"Four students are studying decemancy. All of them are also pursuing studies in another, primary affinity."

She sits back down on the couch. "It's still going?" she murmurs, giving me an appraising look. "Did you really make a bone construct?"

"Wasn't that difficult," I say. "The reagents are really flexible. Anyone with an affinity for the Dark Art could make one given two soul gems, enough time, and sufficient animal bones."

"Oh, really?"

"You can use human bones, whale bones, dog bones, even fish bones." You just need a lot of fish bones, but they're not exactly in short supply. "Aside from that, you need two soul gems and a flight focus. The latter you can get from any bird bigger than a sparrow."

"It does seem suspiciously easy when put that way," Jasmine admits. "For some reason, I bet there's a catch."

"Well, I can't think of any."

She folds her arms and leans back into the chair. "How did you get the bones to align properly?"

"That's the job of the flight focus," I reply. "The skull falls into place around it, then you keep adding links to the back of the skull to form the backbone. The ribs are simple, and the backbone just repeats itself." The wyrm only has those three components. If anyone has any experience in decemancy at all, they'd be able to form a composite skull and rib cage with their eyes closed.

"Why don't more decemancers exist, then? If it's that easy, we'd see more bone constructs flying the skies, I guarantee it."

I stare at her blankly, unable to muster a response.

"I'm just pointing out...your affinity test is taking way too long. I'd say that you aren't being fair to others pursuing the Dark Art."

"Are you saying that I'm not being fair to people who had actual teachers and reagents laid out for them on wood tables?"

"How *did* you learn the Dark Art, Ian?"

I give her a level look. "On the ship. It's a long story. Honestly, I've already been here for a while... It's probably easier to talk about it next time we meet."

She nods. "Fine with me." There is silence for a moment as though she's considering her next words with care. "Ian, did you ever spend long periods of time alone in the loop?"

"Sometimes. Why?"

"Why were you alone?"

My brow furrows. "There wasn't anybody to talk to."

"Didn't you have people on the ship or in Menocht?"

I avert my gaze to the ceiling. "The people on the ship died whenever I tried to help them, so I stopped interacting with them early on."

"What about in Menocht?"

"Whenever I arrived there, everyone was insane."

"What about nearby towns and villages?"

"I didn't see the point in reaching out to them: I didn't like talking to people who weren't real. Besides, I'm used to being alone. I *like* being alone."

Jasmine jots something down, then looks back up and readjusts her glasses. "Did the time loop feel like a game to you?"

I close my eyes and sigh. "Sometimes it felt *exactly* like a game. Other times..."

Just then, the potentioreader stops changing color. Jasmine walks over with her sensor bar to read the results and convert them into a hexadecimal code.

"It's red," I observe.

Jasmine frowns. "We've known that since the beginning. The sphere wasn't going to randomly change to *blue* halfway through."

Does she really not see what I mean when I say that the sphere is *red?* It isn't red like a flame or roses. It's so red that the color burns my retinas. It's pure, unadulterated, *red.*

"It's hideous," I explain, shuddering. "It's unnatural. *Nothing* is this red."

"Hideous?" she replies. "I'm not seeing it."

I take in a deep breath, then exhale. "You see this?" I ask, holding out my palm. Usually, Death energy manifests as oily black, but with intention, I can draw out the violet-pink energy that animates constructs. It dances across my palm like the cross between lightning and fire. "This red is the color of the setting sun"—I point to her desk—"and it's natural." I now point to the sphere, which I've since placed back on the pedestal. "This red is *fake*."

She's still looking at my hand when I point to the sphere. She doesn't seem to know quite what to say, her chest constricting as she silently exhales a breath.

"Sorry, I'm still waiting for your results to load." Considering the distributed network speed on campus, I'm surprised the results are still loading: She typed in the hexadecimal output code from the sensor bar thirty seconds ago.

"Ah, they just finished," she adds, her voice rising in pitch at the end. *She's trying to hide it, but she's nervous.* She disconnects her glosspad from the glosscomp hub and hands it over, her hands trembling.

I breathe in and out. This doesn't mean anything. It's not like I'm a kid, getting the potentioreader test to decide which path my life is going to follow. I already know what the results will be. Or at least I can guess.

RESULTS:

Color: Red II

Type	Affinity (± 0.10%)
Light	0.50%
Dark	1.01%
Life	3.01%
Death	99.91%
Mountain	1.20%
Cloud	1.20%
Sun	0.01%
Moon	0.00%

Beginning	7.79%
End	8.00%
Regret	12.23%
Remorse	12.67%

Any affinity less than 20% is considered too low to even consider pursuing. Before, none of my affinities exceeded that threshold.

As the gravity of the situation sets in, my hands join hers in shaking. I look up at Jasmine and shrug. "My Death affinity *is* quite high. Who knew?"

Her face is aghast. "Ian, you cannot tell *anyone* your affinity for Death is over 99%. Once Cunabulus gets wind of your power, you're not going to be allowed to do anything without your every move being under watch." Cunabulus is the capital of Selejo—where Academia Hector is located—and the Eldemari's seat of power. I don't know the specifics on how the Eldemari's powers work, but word is that she keeps tabs on people all over the country from the comfort of her palace.

I meet her worried gaze. "Perhaps I *should* be under watch."

"Ian...that would only be the beginning." She sighs, her expression conflicted, her leg tapping rhythmically on her chair leg. "For now, what I'm going to do is write up a report. With your help, of course."

"About what?"

"About how you've recently undergone a traumatic incident and unlocked the Death affinity."

I frown. "That could happen?"

"It could; different things trigger different affinities, but awakening a Death affinity is within the reasonable realm of possibility. Usually, when it happens to someone, their affinity might increase by a few percentage points, putting them over the edge and turning them into a practitioner. According to my records..." She makes a swiping gesture on her glosspad. "Your affinity for Death was 17.38% before you woke this morning. It's within the realm of possibility that it might have been bumped up to 25 or 30% affinity."

The corners of my mouth curve downward. "You're going to forge a potentioreader result for me?"

"Yes."

I doubt Jasmine has ever looked more severe than she does now. Honestly, I'm not sure why she's taking it upon herself to help me. I stepped into her office for the first time less than an hour ago. While she's bound to keep silent on what we discuss, she most certainly isn't required to forge official school documents.

"You're welcome," she says as she hands me a freshly printed potentioreading.

Everything is the same as the results I received, except for the fact that instead of reading 99.91%, Death reads as a mediocre 29.91%. More than a ten percent increase from the former affinity level is probably pushing things, but I agree with her choice. Placing me as anything less than around 30% affinity would be...possibly risky. Below 30% affinity, people struggle to do even the most basic things. It would be far easier to slip up pretending to be a 23% affinity practitioner than one with 30% affinity.

"Thank you."

"Come back and give me an update as soon as possible."

I smile. "Trust me, I'll be back here as soon as I know anything." I would have already been dead in the water without her help, struggling to conceal any manifestation of power. "Who am I supposed to go to about this, anyway?" I ask, holding up the potentioreading.

"Talk to your dean right away," she instructs. "He's the one you should be giving that report to. He'll put it on file and send out copies."

Hand on the doorknob, I turn around one more time. "Thanks for everything."

"Of course," she says after taking in a deep breath. "See you soon, Ian, and please...be careful."

* * *

"Ian," Dean Harley says as I enter the room, pushing aside his glosscomp projection display. He smiles and gestures to the chair before his desk. "Take a seat. Now, why did you request a meeting?"

I cough lightly. "I've recently gone through a harrowing experience"—I shake my head—"and I went to see a counselor to talk about it."

Dean Harley nods politely, though his eyes flicker over to the glosscomp. "I'm glad you're taking advantage of our counseling services."

"She decided to do a potentioreader test on me because of some odd things that had been going on."

The dean's eyes light up, the glosscomp forgotten. "Don't tell me...you've awakened as a practitioner?"

I hand him the potentioreading results sheet. "Nothing to be proud of."

He places his finger over the lettering and hums to himself as he looks it over. "Seems like your affinities have all improved a little across the board. But, of course, the most notable jump is in your affinity for Death."

I sigh. "The Dark Art." Now that I think about it, the title is a bit vague. Why isn't a Dark affinity called the Dark Art?

He gives me a sympathetic look. "So, I assume you'll want to continue studies in your current track, in addition to an elective in the arts."

"Is it too late to join an extra class?" I ask. It's almost the end of the semester if the winter formal is in a few days.

"Not in this case. The arts electives are more like guided independent studies."

My eyes light up. "Really?"

He nods. "Yep."

I had been concerned that I would need to sit through lectures about the basics of decemancy and safety—lessons I've learned through painstaking trial and error. It seemed like this wasn't at all the case.

"That'd be great if you could add it to my schedule, then, Dean Harley."

"Remember, Ian," the dean says. "Even if it's a Death affinity, it's better than none. Go make us regs proud, eh?"

"I'll do my best."

I get a notification on my glossY practically before I leave the room.

Subject: [Dean's Office Notice] Placement into Death Affinity I

Recipient: Durning, Kelsey J.

CC'd: Dunai, Ignatius J.

This is a notice indicating that Ignatius J. Dunai has been placed into the class Death Affinity I at the discretion of Dean Harley of the Regular College, to be effective immediately.
If any parties affected by this change have any questions, they should reply to this message.
Best,
Dani Lee,
Office of the Regular Dean

The message doesn't state when the class—or independent study in disguise—meets. I pull up the list of academics and search for Death Affinity.

In the results, I see five classes. The first four are labeled Death Affinity I through IV, while the final class is just Advanced Death Affinity.

I tap Death Affinity I and wait for the page to load. It meets on Mondays and Wednesdays from 8:00 pm to 10:00 pm.

Why so late? That's a horrible time to meet for class! Do these people think that the cover of darkness lends itself to decemancy? Maybe it's at such an unfortunate time to discourage people from attending.

I add the class to my online schedule, then return to the full schedule view. I see all my classes laid out and let out a groan.

Tomorrow is Monday...and I still haven't done any work. Given that it's been years since I've looked at any of this subject material, I'm probably screwed.

I take a deep breath and remind myself to think positively. *At the very least, this place is free of ginger.*

DEATH AFFINITY

I wake up almost calmly, my eyes shut, shoulders stretching to either side. But something's wrong: I notice the scent of salt, the touch of a breeze, and wetness soaking my feet. My eyes snap open and stare out uncomprehendingly.

Why am I on a tiny wooden boat in the middle of the open ocean? Where is this, and how did I get here? Wasn't I at school?

I wrack my mind for answers, but I can't remember. The past is clouded in a haze.

I feel a cold chill settle in my stomach to war with the heat of the sun. I lick my lips and gaze out over the sparkling waves, my body starting to shake. I hold myself tightly as though it'll provide some protection from reality, but that doesn't stop the onset of an anxiety attack. I grit my teeth and cower into the wood, my heart racing.

Afraid as always, I think in self-deprecation. *Didn't realize I was afraid of being alone in the middle of the ocean, but that seems like an unsurprising addition to the list.*

Mother would probably tear off a piece of wood from the seat and start paddling, but I can't bring myself to move, let alone disassemble the dinghy.

Why am I so useless?

* * *

I snarl as I hurl a glass table at an animated skeleton. It shrugs off the blow, the shattered glass inflecting at best minor scratches.

Y'jeni, this is impossible. I shudder in place, eyes locking onto the approaching skeletons. *They're not even rushing over here. They don't need to: I'm nothing to them.*

I narrow my eyes in indignance, unwilling to submit to the never-ending nightmare. But more fundamentally...the thought of dying again sends a fear-fueled spike of adrenaline through my body. *Not again.*

I remember the very first time I died. The skeletons caught me off guard, two slamming me into the deck before another finished me off with a swipe to the face. Its bony hand flared with green light as it tore through my left eye and ripped into my mouth, shattering my jaw. It was over pretty quickly after that, the skeleton forcing its reinforced hand through the roof of my mouth.

I'd never felt more pain in my life.

The second time I curled up on the dinghy paralyzed in fear, waiting to be rescued. I lasted two days before succumbing to heatstroke and dehydration, not to mention blistering sunburn.

* * *

I swore I wouldn't lose track of how many times I died, but the reality is that after the twentieth death I became somewhat delirious. I couldn't get up, couldn't do anything. Time was a blur, and it wasn't easy to measure. Whenever I died, the day reset to mid-morning.

I'm at least certain that the death count is over thirty.

I no longer shake like a leaf as I climb the ladder to the ship deck. Wedged in my shirt is a plank of wood I tore off the dinghy. It was surprisingly loose; perhaps it'd been left there on purpose by whoever put me in this nightmare.

I take in a deep breath and peek up over the railing at the deck, eyes passing over two skeleton guards. My one advantage is speed: If I move quickly, I'll catch the unwitting guards by surprise. If I get lucky, I might even take one out by smashing in its skull.

I tighten my grip on the plank. *One...two...three!*

I leap over the side of the ship and draw the plank out from under my shirt. The nearest skeleton seems surprised when I land a solid whack to its head, dislodging its skull.

Of course, it's not enough. The skeleton holds its head with one hand while swiping out with a green-tinged claw.

"Just *die!*" I snarl, slamming the wood plank into its head again. I overstep and find myself too close to its claws, losing the reach advantage of my weapon, but I honestly can't bring myself to care.

Even if it kills me, I'm taking this fucker down. Only when I land another blow do I realize that the skeleton failed to take advantage of my mistake, never staging a counterattack. Its eyes flicker and fade in color until the green embers wink out.

Stunned, I barely sidestep the other skeleton's swipe, its bony talons knocking the plank from my hands and clawing me across the chest. The four lacerations are like liquid fire. I let out a shuddering groan as the skin around them begins to turn yellow. *Necrosis.*

Panic races through me as I watch the plank clatter to the ground...out of reach.

I throw myself to the side to avoid another swipe and nearly fall to the deck, tripping on the fallen skeleton. Whatever energy had kept the skeleton together had dissipated, and since any connective tissues had long since rotted away, I feel no resistance tearing the femur off the ground. The bone is still slightly tinged green with residual energy, but that doesn't seem to matter. It's a nice, solid femur bone: the perfect club.

I come swinging at the other skeleton, ramming the femur into its skull. It does significantly more damage than the plank; perhaps whatever energy empowered the skeletons is still at work. But after being on the wrong side of the equation for so long, it feels *so good* to finally have the upper hand.

In four strikes the second skeleton falls, scattering into a heap of bones.

Tears of relief pool at the corners of my eyes, arms slacking like deflated balloons. I begin to laugh, barely even recognizing the feral, desperate sound coming from my own lips. Nobody is coming to help me, but here is proof that I'm not useless, that I can, in fact...save myself.

As I stand panting, my eyes rove over the fallen skeletons, their eye sockets devoid of emerald embers. Blood pumping with adrenaline, I begin to go over the first exchange with the skeleton. It occurs to me that I have no clue why it didn't originally claw me when I got too close. I walk over to the first skeleton and push part of its rib cage with my foot. I kneel down and frown as I notice something I've never seen before: part of the skeleton's claws are tinged not green but a light violet-red.

I freeze, my heart pumping audibly in my chest. For some inexplicable reason, I just *know* that the discoloration is my fault. I drop the femur and flinch back. It's also tinged violet, glowing subtly from the inside. I crouch down and hesitantly nudge the skeleton's small, violet-tinged hand bones. Pinching a segment between two fingers, I can feel something—some kind of foreign connection.

"Whatever is happening to me...it's going to mean the difference in getting out of here."

I carefully inspect the violet bones, trying to understand what I did so I can do it again. I have the suspicion that whatever power I'm using is the same kind that empowered the skeletons in the first place, but...power is power: I'll take what I can get.

* * *

No matter how much I want to be calm, my body shakes with sobs and my breathing comes in messy gasps of air and tears. Everything feels hopeless.

I can't do anything for the people in the pools. I've tried over ten separate times to help them, but no matter what, they always died. Whoever captured them and imprisoned them on the deck without food, clean water, or shade, chaining them in place...monster is an inadequate descriptor. Just the stench coming from the pool at the back of the ship is enough to make me gag, but the vision of people packed like sardines in filthy water, sun-blistered faces crying out helplessly when I approach...it's enough to drive me insane.

"Fuck this nightmare," I curse, teeth gnashing together. "You win!" I holler, holding my arms to the sky. "Whoever you are, whoever invented this sick place, you win."

Tears continue to stream down my face. "What...am I...supposed to do?"

I try to imagine what Mother would say. It helped before when I used the plank from the dinghy as a weapon.

"Stop being so pathetic," I murmur, raising my voice to imitate hers. It's bland but a phrase of choice.

"It's not like this nightmare came with a set of instructions," I retort, hissing through the tears flowing over my lips.

I imagine Mother's cruel, gentle smile: "Whatever you do, do it with the dignity of a gentleman. Stop crying and toughen up. People are always watching for a sign of weakness, Ignatius. Don't forget what happened to your father and this family."

Her words are such crap, but thinking them through seems to help, my tears beginning to subside.

The next sentence I didn't speak out loud, but instead, I envisioned Mother delivering the words directly while sitting straight-backed at the dining table.

"There's a reason for your troubles—you just have to find and dissect it. Enter the mind of your opponent; think like your enemy."

* * *

I wake up breathing heavily. I'm surprised to find a veritable blanket of Death energy draped over my torso and immediately dispel it. *This is the kind of thing that I need to be wary of,* I remind myself. *Nobody with a middling 30% Death affinity would be able to condense energy like this.*

As soon as the energy mantle is gone, a slight gnawing sensation returns to my stomach. It's been like this ever since I stopped constantly using decemancy. Back in Menocht, I used it freely, not worrying if others noticed. Now I don't have that luxury if I want to keep myself hidden.

If I had to describe the sensation, I'd say it's like withdrawal, as though I've grown dependent on having Death energy around me. Still, it's nothing I can't handle. I'd rather face a bit of discomfort than return to Menocht.

After a period of slowly breathing in and out, I lean over and check the time: 9:34 am. I rub my eyes and turn in on my side, curling into the fetal position.

I'm not on a boat, I tell myself. *Not on a boat, not in the middle of the ocean, and not in a dilation loop.*

"What the hell happened to you?" Xander asks. I sit up and look over my shoulder.

"What?"

He looks at me with concern. "You kept talking in your sleep," he says. "You've never done that before," he adds quietly.

I laugh dismissively. "I have a lot on my mind with exams and everything."

He narrows his eyes. "Ian"—he pinches the bridge of his nose—"I couldn't sleep for hours because you were saying the word 'why'. Repeatedly." Then he starts to show me what it sounded like. "Why, why, why...why, why!?"

"Stop, please, Xander, that's enough. I'm sorry you couldn't sleep."

"What happened to you? You're suddenly so...*different*."

I suppose it was going to come out sooner or later. "I had a...death-defying experience, the details of which I'm not going to share."

"...Oh. Wait, what? When?"

I shake my head. "I was never in any real danger, but I was terrified." I give him a small smile. "Hence the nightmares..."

"...Right."

I better tell him about the affinity bump, though. That's the kind of thing I don't want him to find out later from someone else.

"Also...the experience raised my Death affinity."

He recoils. "To what?"

99%, Xander. Worried? "29.91%."

"Well...congratulations, right? Any affinity is better than no affinity." He hops off his bed and walks over to me, pulling me into a side-hug. As I'm half-under the bedsheets, the gesture is awkward at best. "You're going to start taking classes in the Arts?"

"Yeah...the dean actually just placed me into Death Affinity I if you can believe it."

"This late in the semester?"

"Right? That's what I said. Apparently, the Arts classes function more like independent studies than anything else, so he said it shouldn't be a problem."

Xander steps away and we stare at each other for an uncomfortable moment. I can tell he wants to ask something...

"What's it like?" he asks.

"What's *what* like?"

He rolls his eyes. "Does anything feel different now that you have an affinity above 20%?" I can tell that he's genuinely curious.

"I don't know... It's hard to explain. Not really." I grin. "Though I'll try to find a way to let you see the way I see now, just you wait."

Xander freezes. "Wait! You just said there's no real change, so what d'you mean you're gonna find a way to make me see differently?"

"I can kind of see the vitality of people and objects," I explain. "You and I, we're both alive, so we're white. It looks like we're glowing a little bit. Everything else in this room is dead and appears in various shades of gray. Except for the stuff glowing black."

He looks spooked. "What glows black?"

I laugh at his expression. "Aside from the orange peels, the succulent in the trash."

He laughs along with me. "I was hoping you wouldn't notice that."

"I made a bet with you that you'd forget to water it, right?" I'm surprised that detail surfaces from the morass of faded memories.

He grins sheepishly but stays silent, his eyes fixing on the trash. After a moment, he clears his throat and faces me again. "Well, let me know if it's possible to let me, um, see too."

"Hey, Xander," I begin, "when I was dreaming...did I say anything else besides 'why'?"

Xander frowns. "You said 'Mother' once."

Of course, I did.

"Thanks for checking in on me."

He beams. "Of course. You'd do the same for me."

I pause as I let his words sink in. *No*, I think, *I really wouldn't.* Not before the loop, and not now.

* * *

I go to my reg classes and desperately try to pay attention. Because they're all higher-level classes, though, the subject matter is technical and difficult to follow without adequate background.

How long was I stuck in the time loop? I ask myself. I can still generally remember people's names, and how to navigate the school...but remembering how to make a distributed glossY algorithm feels akin to waging a one-man war on Menocht Bay with a ninety-percent infection level. Even looking at my past notes and going through old code doesn't help.

Mondays, I have two glossprog classes, but only the first deals with algorithms. The second deals with networks, but it goes about as well as the first.

As I sit down to lunch in the Regular College dining hall and think about how I'm going to keep myself from failing out of my classes, a few familiar faces sit down around me.

"Ugh, I need to do so well on the next algo exam."

"Baxter's a terrible lecturer, but the TAs are decent."

My eyes snap up. *Right, there are TAs.* "When are the TAs meeting this week?"

My five classmates give me amused looks. "The same time as every week," one of them says. Jaime, I think.

Laura laughs. "It's every Tuesday and Thursday from seven to nine," she says. "Why, you need help?"

"I should probably make sure I understand everything with the exams coming up," I retort.

A few people make hoots of surprise.

I give them dirty looks. "Why, do none of you use the TAs?"

Laura rolls her eyes. "We're messing with you 'cause you're the only one who doesn't use them."

Oh, right. I vaguely remember this being true, though I'm pretty sure the only reason I originally avoided the TAs was because of social anxiety.

"What do you need on this final, anyway? I thought you were doing fine."

While I wasn't very productive last night, I did do some final grade calculations. To get an 80% flat in the class, I need to get a 40% on the final. The problem is that I actually don't think I can do that. Of course, nobody's going to take me seriously if I say that I'm aiming for a 40% on the exam. To get a 90% in the class, however, I need to get a 73%. That's a more believable target.

"I need a 73% to get an A," I reply. Groans erupt around me. "But I haven't reviewed the material in weeks, and I don't remember a lot of it from the beginning of the year."

We all finish our meals and get up. Before I leave the dining hall, however, Laura comes up to me.

"You feeling okay?" she asks.

This again? "Why?"

She bites her lip. "You just seem kind of out of it...and you haven't been answering your texts."

How does she...? *Oh.* I vaguely remember her sending me a message to meet up, but I didn't respond. I'm no longer used to having a glossY around after going without one for so long.

"Thanks for asking," I say. "I'm actually fine. Just got a lot on my mind."

"Well...I'd still like to meet up sometime. Maybe see a movie?"

The way she's looking at me... Is she asking me out? I think of the winter formal. *It's just in four days, right?*

"Laura," I begin, "are you going with anyone to the winter formal?"

Her expression lights up. "No; are you?"

My heart thumps as I smile back. "Want to go together?"

"Sure."

What do I do now? After a short pause, I say, "Well, it was nice talking with you." *Y'jeni, I'm so awkward.*

"See you around. And don't ignore my texts!"

"Right."

She's gone, and I'm left standing by the card swipe.

"Smooth," Octavia says, chuckling softly from behind her glosscomp.

I turn around. "How are you?"

She cackles. "I'm fine, hon. That the first time you've ever asked a girl to a dance?"

"I asked a girl once back in high school, but we were friends." And if I recall correctly, I'd only done it after Germaine—my older sister—took my glossY and asked her out for me.

"Well, good on you," she says.

"Have a nice day, Octavia."

* * *

The rest of the day passes quickly. I spend most of my time going over old notes, lecture slides, and problem sets. Things are starting to come back when I go from the beginning and work my way toward newer material, which is a relief.

Eventually, the time comes for Death Affinity I. The meeting space for the class is, unfortunately and unsurprisingly, located on the Arts campus around fifteen minutes away. I don snow boots, a jacket (a real, waterproof one), a hat, and gloves before setting off.

Except for the moon and the occasional street light, it's pitch-black outside. It's a change from Menocht and the ocean. I'm used to seeing the white flits that signal the movements of insects and small mammals, but here, in the heart of winter, I see very little vitality at all.

I arrive at the classroom building five minutes early, only to find it locked. The building is tall and looks like it's almost made of cobbled gray stones. It looks old and grim in the cold evening, the wrought iron fence surrounding the area contributing to the graveyard aesthetic.

I knock on the door. "Hello?"

"One moment," a female voice responds. I step back just as the door swings inward. "Come inside, Ignatius. I'm Professor Durning."

The woman is dressed in a robe identical to my own with the exception of its color: pure black. It reminds me of the black clothes I wore in the time loop. Is she trying to live up to a stereotype?

I go inside and take off my jacket. She looks somewhat disapprovingly at my shoes—not dress shoes as expected of the dress code—but doesn't say anything.

"So," she says after clearing her throat, "I've been informed that you recently had a near-death experience that increased your Death affinity."

"Yeah. And I prefer to go by Ian, by the way."

"Well, Ian, the nature of the experience often affects the way your affinity will manifest itself. For instance, a person who is almost crushed to death—"

I hold out a hand. "My experience is private," I say, "but I'm sure it won't matter that much. My affinity is only 29.91%."

She shakes her head. "That's just your base affinity. You know the saying, you have to have money to make money? It's the same with affinity. The more you have to start with, the better, but in the end, affinity is like a muscle."

I smile knowingly. "The more I practice, the greater my affinity will become?"

She smiles at me. "Exactly. And the more powerful your Art as a result."

Just then, another knock comes at the door. As Durning turns to get the door, I take a moment to inspect my surroundings. The room is small, with oddly high ceilings and gray stone walls. I peer into the room beyond an open archway, noting that the large Shibarian carpet is hiding all sorts of odd stains in its whirling patterns.

When Professor Durning comes back, she's followed by four other students. Did they all come together? Their dress loafers are covered in a dusting of snow, suggesting that they walked maybe fifty feet out in the open to get here. That's a fairly long distance considering that most people never need to go outside to enter their classes on the Arts campus.

They all seem surprised to see me and give Durning questioning looks.

"Class, this is our newest addition, Ian Dunai."

They continue to give me blank stares.

What? I want to ask them, feeling conspicuous. They shouldn't see anything suspicious.

"Hello," I say. "Nice to meet all of you."

"Do you really have Death affinity?" a guy with red hair asks.

I smile pleasantly, suppressing the urge to roll my eyes. "Why else would I be here?"

Professor Durning chooses this time to step in. "Ian only recently had an experience that caused his affinity to increase," she explains. "He hasn't had any formal training yet."

Hercates' grimoire described a basic circulating exercise that had only taken me a few hours to master in the loop. I reckon it's believable that I looked up a decemancy manual on the distributed network and started practicing.

I consider carefully the kind of first impression I want to make. I don't want them to assume I know absolutely nothing—if only because it'll be difficult to completely feign inexperience—but I don't want to draw attention to myself.

"I've been experimenting a bit on my own," I interject. I circulate the tiniest bit of ambient energy in the room I can manage, distilling it onto my palm in a rough, barely coherent blob. Accompanying the energy is a sensation of profound release, as though I've received a glass of water after trekking through a bone-dry desert. I hadn't realized the gnawing sensation in my stomach had grown so severe.

The redhead snorts, clearly unimpressed. Good. "So you *are* a practitioner, then."

Why else would I be here?

"Oh, you do have an understanding of the basics," Durning says. "That'll make things easier. Does anyone want to work with Ian today?"

"On what?" the brunette asks, her demeanor relaxed.

"Whatever you think he should learn for a first lesson in the Art."

She shrugs. "Fine." She looks at me and smiles.

"Everyone else should know what they're working on," the professor says. "I'll be walking around to check on your progress."

CHAPTER

8

WYRM

"I'm Sarah," the brunette says as she walks me over to the far-right side of the room.

"Ian," I say, even though I've already been introduced by Professor Durning.

"What year are you?" she asks.

"Fourth year," I say.

"I'm a third-year." She looks at me appraisingly. "You don't look like a fourth year."

I chuckle. "I get that a lot."

"You look at least twenty-five."

"I took a gap year before school."

"Oh," she murmurs. "How old are you?"

"Twenty-four."

She scowls. "Shouldn't you be twenty-three?"

"I got held back in kindergarten."

She coughs to conceal a laugh.

"Anyway," I say, clasping my fingers together, "what am I going to learn for my first real lesson?"

She puts a hand on her hips. "How squeamish are you?"

I deadpan. "Do your worst."

"Fine. We can start with carnimancy, then."

I grimace internally. Personally, I hate carnimancy. Under the harsh Menocht Bay sun, flesh rots and putrefies in hours. Flesh as a whole is messy and spreads disease, particularly dead flesh. On the other hand, bone remains relatively constant over time. Bone is clean, doesn't smell...

I hear a thud and realize that Sarah's placed a chest onto the table in front of us. "Here." She's breathing a little heavier from the exertion. I realize that I can't sense the vitality of whatever is in the chest; my guess is that it has been warded.

She opens the chest, and I have to take a step back. Seriously, why carnimancy? My eyes dart to her face. Is she trying to scare me off?

"See this? It's rotten flesh. That means it's great for manipulation."

Well, it *is* oozing Death energy, but I'd prefer to get energy from *un*-rotted corpses. I can't even tell what animal the meat is from.

"What is this good for?" I ask. "I can't see this being useful for anything." It's literally just a rotten slab of meat. Maybe you could make a poison out of it?

"It's good for *practice*," she says, smiling. "Getting squeamish?"

Not squeamish...just...*annoyed.*

I crack my knuckles. "Tell me what to do."

"I want you to try to gather as much of the Death energy up as you can," she says while pulling out a flask from a nearby cabinet. "Then I want you to put it in here. It's specially made to hold energy."

"Just like when I pulled ambient energy from the room?"

"Just like that. But be careful, the energy from this kind of meat is a little...strong."

I'll say. "Ok, here goes nothing." I hold my right hand out over the meat and begin to circulate energy. Soon, I have a small orb of black energy writhing like a flame in my hand.

"Put it in the flask, then do it again."

I bring my hand toward the flask...and the energy is vacuumed right out from my palm. I hold the flask out and note that its interior has taken on a black-gray color.

I repeat the energy-siphoning a few more times until the meat's aura has been significantly reduced. Sarah grabs the flask from my hand and inspects it.

"Great, you got that quicker than I expected. Now that we've extracted all the energy that we can, it's time to practice on the meat itself." She holds out her index finger and hovers it about two inches over the meat's mushy surface. "You want to make the meat move. That's it. It's easier the first few times if you inject a bit of Death energy into a certain area and try to move that."

I step forward and hold out my index finger next to hers. "Good," she says. "Now draw a bit of energy out of this flask." She holds it out to me, and I drain a little bit of the energy out.

"Now," she continues, "point and shoot."

I point my finger at the chest, expel a sliver of energy, and wait for it to sink into the meat. Then, I curl my fingers up and watch as the death-darkened patch writhes as though infested by maggots.

"Wow, great job!" Sarah cheers. "I think you must be a natural at carnimancy. Maybe it's even your specialty."

I give her a questioning look. "Specialty?"

"Let me explain. Most people who have any affinity will have a specialty. That's why not everyone who has Sun affinity can manipulate both plants and fire."

I nod slowly. The grimoire didn't mention any 'specialties' or divisions. The distributed network held little information either. Most articles on the Dark Art spiraled into occultism.

"It's much more expedient for a person to pursue their specialty than the affinity as a whole. With a subject like decemancy, where there are so many different paths to choose, it's particularly important."

I look off to the side. "What about bone manipulation?"

"You mean osteomancy?"

"Sure."

"Why do you ask?"

I raise an eyebrow. "Wouldn't it be cool to make a bone construct and use it to fly around?"

She laughs. "Those are banned unless you have a license."

License?

"How hard is it to get a license?"

She stops laughing. "I was just joking. Nobody here practices osteomancy. Most of the existing research was done hundreds of years ago on human captives and doesn't scale well with animal bones."

What research is she talking about?

"Besides, making a bone construct is supposed to be prohibitively difficult. You'd never be able to make one, even if you raise your affinity to 50%."

"Still, is there anything else I can try? I don't really like carnimancy."

"Hah; I knew you were squeamish."

I give her a look. "Not *squeamish*. I just don't like working with pieces of rotting meat."

"Fine, let me ask the professor if she can help us out. I don't really know anything about osteomancy."

* * *

"Osteomancy?" Professor Durning exclaims. "There's no money to be made in it."

Isn't this a school of higher learning? Since when do professors care if there's money to be made?

"I'm not going to pursue the Dark Art as my career. My affinity is low, and I'm almost done with my glossY programmatics major. After I graduate, I'm going to focus on that." Everything out of my mouth is a blatant lie, but in truth, I have no idea what I'm going to do after leaving Academia Hector.

"While it isn't as lucrative as elementalism," the professor argues, "the Dark Art has many specializations that will easily net you more money than a glossprog degree."

She's right: there's a reason why so many people are desperate to receive some kind of affinity.

"I really like programming," I retort. "I'd rather do that than mess around with rotting meat all day."

The professor sighs and looks at me sadly. "That's not what carnimancers do, you know."

"What kinds of specializations are there, anyway? I only know about carnimancy and osteomancy."

"Sarah, care to explain?"

She nods. "Right, um, aside from those two, there's animancy, thralling—though that's just as unpopular as osteomancy—and one more..." She looks at the professor for help.

"You missed diagnosty," Professor Durning admonishes. "To give you a quick rundown, carnimancy, animancy, and diagnosty are the most popular specializations. Carnimancers usually work in the agricultural industry. A single carnimancer can replace an entire factory's worth of labor and machines."

So, not rotting meat then.

"They also can work in the medical industry performing autopsies and even helping to conduct certain delicate surgeries."

I suppose I can see why carnimancy might be popular.

"Animancers generally work in the exterminator industry," she adds. "They snuff out the lives of small, invasive insects. Moreover, they can collect Death energy and create soul gems. These can be used for a plethora of purposes and are as valuable as they are hard to make.

"Finally, diagnosticians are usually employed as spies and guards. Diagnosticians focus on developing their ability to scope out environments on the basis of perceived vitality."

She smiles at me. "Do any of those sound appealing?"

None of them sound particularly attractive; the way I learned didn't make any distinctions between the categories. While I consulted the grimoire to learn my practice, it was only a guide: I ultimately taught myself everything I know about decemancy, and based on my potentioreading, I trust my intuition.

The professor continues: "For the others, I'll be brief: Thralling generally involves controlling small creatures like bugs and rodents for tasks like espionage and security; while osteomancy, as the flip side to carnimancy, focuses on shaping not flesh, but bone. I would personally advise choosing one of the other three specializations."

While osteomancy is an obvious choice, it's probably best to pick animancy for utility's sake: It would be useful to 'learn' how to make soul gems. I sold them a few times in Menocht Bay, though only after decomposing larger gems into the small, low-grade variety.

"How much do soul gems sell for?"

Sarah rolls her eyes and shoots me a lazy grin. "*If* you can make one, they normally sell for upwards of 5k."

5k? "As in, five thousand auris?"

She nods. "Right."

"I want to do animancy, then."

Professor Durning looks at Sarah. "Why don't you bring Justin over here?"

"Sure."

The professor turns toward me to speak. "Justin's specializing in animancy, so I'll let him take over showing you the basics."

Justin is a well-built guy with sandy hair and a babyface. He comes over with a grin. "So, you wanna learn animancy?"

Professor Durning walks away, leaving me alone with Justin. I note that Sarah has gone back to the right side of the room and is currently unlocking a different, heavier chest than she showed me.

"Animancy sounds pretty useful," I observe.

"Come over to my workstation," he says. I see that his desk is filled with jars of insects and a few white, quartz-like rocks. "See these rocks? They're foci to help concentrate Death energy into a soulstone. Even then," he adds, seeing my conflicted expression, "forming a soulstone is really difficult. I've only ever formed *one*—and that was a fluke." He then gestures to the jars of insects. There must be at least seven jars covering the desk. "I usually spend my time working on drawing the energy out of these guys. By the time I graduate, I should be able to drop them all dead with a wave of my hand." He sounds smug about it.

"What year are you now?"

"I'm a second year."

I nod. So this guy has been working on sucking the life out of bugs for the past year? I don't envy him.

"What's your primary affinity?" I ask, curious. Honestly, I'm not surprised that he—and the rest of the people here—haven't progressed too far. This is only an elective for them.

He grins. "Sun."

"Huh. Fire elementalist?"

"Correct!"

"Why even bother with this, then?" I ask.

He laughs. "I hate bugs," he admits. "If I can keep my future house bug-free, this is all effort very well spent."

Way to aim high. "Makes sense. So, what's the first step of animancy?"

He spends the next twenty minutes lecturing me about the regulations regarding the internationally accepted intelligence and size quotient for what decemancers can and can't kill. I was already familiar with said regulations, but it's helpful to hear them stated clearly.

All insects are fair game, along with anything the size of a rat or smaller. Anything larger, like raccoons, is off-limits. Smaller things with higher intelligence, such as a few kinds of rare birds, are also banned, though Justin assures me that I'll never run into one unless I go to the Ho'ostar peninsula or Kester.

I personally believe that the laws are far too limiting, given the fact that any elementalist can go off and kill whatever animals they'd like with a fist of earth or a tongue of fire. Not to mention, any regular can kill using conventional methods.

"Of course, there are always exceptions," Justin adds. "Most carnimancers in the meat industry obtain special permits that allow them to slaughter livestock."

I nod slowly. I actually had no idea that decemancers could get permits to kill larger animals. Maybe the laws are more reasonable than I thought. "Any others?"

He pauses, taking in a deep breath as he mulls the question over. "Well, the other major exception is in war. But I don't think you need to worry about that."

My chest constricts, a sense of foreboding coming over me. *I hope you're right, Justin. I've had enough conflict for a lifetime.*

* * *

After class ends, I find myself by the ocean again, though this time I didn't bother taking the bus, electing to fly the whole way there under the cover of darkness. It's freezing, but at least this time I'm in my waterproof jacket and boots.

Germaine would like the tension in this place, I think, suddenly missing my sister's presence. I haven't seen her in years, so why haven't I yet reached out? The ocean is a dark void into which the moonlight endlessly sinks after breaking lightly on the waves.

I gaze out over the empty water, wondering if Germaine sees her clean canvases as I see the Death-dappled dunes of sand beneath the water's surface: latent potential, like a slab of marble whose true form has yet to be revealed by the sculptor. With a sigh of exultation, I let loose. Death energy surges around me like a tide, easing away the ache of abstinence, its oily tendrils mine to manipulate and mold.

I send myself out over the waves and flex my fingers, once more reanimating the bones I left the day before. Instead of forming a whale and an entourage of other sea life, I now form them all into a wyrm. There are plenty of bird skeletons underwater, so finding an undamaged flight focus doesn't take me more than a few minutes. Of course, killing a seagull for a fresh focus would be easier, but now that I'm outside the loop, I'd prefer to use the bones of the already dead.

There's also the fact that using decemancy to kill a seagull is probably illegal.

For the soulstones, I swipe out with my right hand, prompting two fish to come flying out of the water and hover before me. I extract their Death energy and distill it down into two diminutive, violet soul gems. While I doubt soul gems made from these fish are very powerful, they should function fine for a construct.

It takes me longer to make the bone construct this time—probably because the majority of the bones I'm using come from smaller animals than humans. Binding them together takes more effort on my part, but the end result is better than I could have hoped for. The smaller bones have resulted in a more sinuous, life-like wyrm. I step up onto the skull crest and insert the soul gems into the eye sockets. Then, before I know it, I'm off and flying over the ocean.

INVITATION

I get back to my room two hours later feeling refreshed. On the way back, I fixed a series of bones over my exposed face and under my clothes, insulating me against the dropping temperature and the whipping wind.

I left the wyrm a few hundred feet out from the shore, sunken beneath the waves; I'll be able to reanimate it without issue if I return. The soul gems are in my pockets, though, since I have a plan for them.

"Hey, you're back late," Xander says, waving to me as I enter the room. "You had your first decemancy class." He leans back in his office chair. "How'd that go?"

I shrug. "It was underwhelming. Nobody there seems to be able to do much. I'm not surprised, given that they all have other primary affinities."

"Ouch," Xander says, grimacing. "Well, I'm sure you'll learn at least something when you're there."

I smile. "I've already learned one thing, at least. Here: I have these." I hold up the violet soul gems. "If I crush them, they'll turn into a liquid. And if I pour them on your eyes, you'll be able to see vitality." I grin devilishly. "Want to try it?"

He blinks twice. "Seriously? I thought you said that nobody there knew how to do anything!" He jumps out of his chair and stands at my side. "What are they?"

"Rocks," I say. Given how valuable soul gems are, I should keep what they are secret.

He gives me a dubious look. "This isn't going to make me blind, is it?"

"No. It will make your eyes glow violet, though."

"You can take the, um, rocks out of my eyes, right?"

I chuckle. "Why else would I offer to put them in your eyes in the first place?"

"Fine, I'll trust you, master decemancer."

I roll my eyes and crush the stones between my palms. I direct the energy out and spool it into Xander's eyes. "There," I say when the energy has been depleted. "What do you see?"

He blinks a few times. "You look paler, kind of like...you're glowing. And there are swirls of black around you."

Whoops. I dispel the energy I gathered over the course of the evening. "How about now?"

"They're...gone."

I nod. "Just a residual effect of channeling the energy into your eyes."

Xander turns around and looks at the trash can. "Holy crap," he murmurs.

He must be looking at the dead flowers. He turns around again and looks at me. "Is this how you see all the time, now?"

"Yup. It's a bit disconcerting, but I'm getting the hang of it."

Xander stares at the floor. "I can see glows coming from below...is that from people?"

"I think so," I answer noncommittally. "I'm almost as new to this as you are."

"This is so cool..." His gaze lands on the mirror, and he stops moving, staring at his own reflection. "You weren't kidding," he says. "My eyes are glowing purple."

"Definitely don't go out in public without sunglasses," I joke. "Okay, you done for now?"

He looks back at me reluctantly. "...I suppose."

I gesture for him to come close, then hold my hand in front of his eyes and direct the energy out. I subsequently distill it back into the form of two soul gems, placing them on my desk.

"Don't try to use them without me here," I caution. "The rocks can be explosive if cracked open the wrong way." A blatant lie. Unless he's a disguised practitioner, Xander won't possess the power to break a soul gem. The warning is meant to discourage him from investigating them too closely.

He leans back and runs a hand through his hair. "Thanks for the warning."

I nod, then sit down at my desk and resume my coursework. I have a feeling that it's going to be a long night.

* * *

I see Jasmine the next day. I tell her about asking Laura to the dance, about my glossprog classes, and, in particular, about the new addition to my schedule.

"Sounds like a waste of time," she says.

"Nobody there had a clue what they were doing." I sigh. "The professor seemed content to let people mess around with what-ever they wanted, so long as they were being safe about it."

"And they dissuaded you from osteomancy?"

I give Jasmine a severe look. "They said that *nobody* practices osteomancy."

"Does that make you angry?"

I sigh and look off at the ceiling. "Kind of."

"Be honest."

I look at her. "Yes, it pissed me off."

"Why?"

"Because...osteomancy's such a versatile tool. Moreover, I hated how they subdivided decemancy and tried to get me to specialize down one path." I look down at my hands. "For instance," I begin. "To make a bone construct, you need to first use carnimancy to strip the flesh off any fresh bones. Then, you bind all the bones together using osteomancy. Finally, you use animancy to bind two soul gems to serve as the construct's core."

She pushes up her glasses. "So just pursuing one specialization isn't enough."

"No. This isn't elementalism," I say, narrowing my eyes.

"How do elementalism and decemancy differ?"

I look off to the side, my eyes lingering on Jasmine's steel lamp. "How does controlling water make it easier to use fire?"

"Dehydration leads to better ignition."

"How does controlling flesh make it easier to control bone?"

Jasmine pauses for a moment. I stop her before she continues, saying, "It doesn't. Each element specialization provides a different skill set to complete the same kinds of tasks. Granted, some are better suited than others for certain situations, but an adept hydromancer will be able to complete any task just as well—and usually better—than a novice pyromancer."

"If you ask a hydromancer to light a match, could they ever do so better than a pyromancer?" Jasmine asks.

"Depends on how quickly the hydromancer could draw out water. Anything dry enough will ignite in the open air."

"I suppose, though I believe you're simplifying things." Jasmine scratches her wrist. "With respect to decemancy, no specialization can accomplish the job of another—is that right?"

"Exactly." She still doesn't look convinced.

"Say you need to raise an army of dead," Jasmine proposes. "Couldn't you animate them with thralling, carnimancy, *or* osteomancy?"

"I suppose you could."

"Or," she continues, "can't you kill someone with a flick of a hand with either carnimancy, osteomancy, or animancy?"

"While I see your point...it feels different to me."

"Tell me your thoughts about elementalists, then."

"They're abundant and inflexible," I remark. "They're obnoxious to fight at range but have limited utility on the whole in a siege."

"Outside of a conflict, what is your opinion of them?"

Outside of a conflict? I haven't ever had extended contact with elementalists outside of the time loop, obviously. When not attacking me, manning defenses, or assisting me in burning corpses (in the case of Jeremy), I have little personal familiarity with what they can do.

"What *do* elementalists normally do?" I ask.

She seems surprised by my question. "What do they work as?" she clarifies.

"Yes."

"They normally join a company," she says. "Many of them take up professional dueling due to its resurging popularity. Others go into politics. A minority attend to other professions, such as those involving agriculture, water purification, and so on."

Taking up dueling...it's not entirely unsurprising. Going into politics doesn't surprise me either—bloodline affinity inheritance was proven over five decades ago. Dynasties of practitioners in politics should be no surprise to anyone—not that having an affinity makes you any better at politicking, of course.

"Why don't we move on to other updates," she says, redirecting the conversation. "Tell me about the person you're bringing to the Winter Formal. Is she a friend?"

"Yes, I'd call her that."

"How long have you two known each other?"

"Well, we've been acquaintances since freshman year. We have a class together this semester, so I've gotten to know her better there."

"How do you feel about going to the dance?" she asks.

I groan. "Not particularly enthusiastic. I'm only going because Xander would worry about me if I didn't go."

Jasmine laughs. "It's good that you're going," she says. "Even if you don't want to do the things you used to do, you should still get back into the habit of doing them."

While this sounds reasonable, I still have to ask: "Why?"

She crosses her arms. "You've been in isolation for a long time, Ian."

"Just one night," I joke.

"You might be inclined to cut people off, and that isn't healthy," she adds. "It might seem like work, but you need to put effort into maintaining your relationships with people around you."

"I'll do my best," I murmur, "but I think you're overestimating how social I was before the loop."

"Tell me more about the loop."

I frown. "I've been trying to forget."

"Why?"

"If I don't think about it, I can almost imagine the time I spent in it was just one long dream."

She tilts her head to the side. "Is it possible to really forget what happened?"

I chuckle bitterly. "No." I sigh in exasperation. "Maybe."

"Distance helps," Jasmine adds, her eyes sympathetic. "Time most of all. I think that one day, you'll be able to think about your time in the loop without regret. Until then, trying to push the experience away is a valid response."

"Glad to hear it isn't just...running away from my problems."

"The issue isn't running away but running away forever."

I mull over her words. "That's an oddly encouraging way to think about it."

Jasmine smiles, then looks down at her wrist and frowns. "I'm sorry to cut us off," she says, voice contrite, "but I have another appointment in a minute."

"It's fine," I say. "You've already given me enough to think about. Thanks for meeting with me."

"Of course!" she replies. "Are we down for Tuesday of next week?" A week from today.

I smile. "Yes. Looking forward to it."

* * *

By the time Wednesday rolls around, after attending a few office hour sessions, I'm feeling much more confident in my ability to not fail spectacularly out of school. Now that I'm starting to get my feet back under me, I've been questioning what it is I want to do.

I narrow my eyes at the glosscomp screen before me. When my fingers slide over the glosscomp keypad, my thoughts wander to the boat, where this all started. The loop gave me power, but it also made it difficult to work a normal job as I once planned.

Every day, every minute I'm not practicing decemancy, a hunger gnaws at me from within, a terrible desire to use my gift. It distracts me from doing classwork and sometimes keeps me up at night, though if I'm really overtired, I can get away with using my practice to swiftly knock myself out.

Jasmine is probably right that with time, I'll be able to live a more normal life, but...even if I'm no longer scarred by my memories, the reality of the situation is that a 99% peak practitioner can't hide forever. If—when—others discover my potential...I don't think they'll see anything but a weapon.

* * *

When I get back to my room later in the evening, a note is waiting for me on my desk. Xander isn't in, so I doubt he saw how it got there. I check the window but it's locked.

I open the wax seal on the exterior and shake out the contents.

Mr. Dunai,

practitioner of the Dark Art,

is invited to congregate this Sunday at the residence of Dr. Sylvestri, practitioner foremost of the Dark Art with a specialization in carnimancy, as well as practitioner of the Lightless Art with a specialization in cryptomancy.

Food and drinks will be served along with pleasant and stimulating conversation.

Please mark the box indicating attendance.

At the end of the letter are two boxes: one reads "I will attend," the other, "I will not attend."

Even though I know that message has been mass generated by a fabY, the entire thing makes me feel uncomfortable. Meet at a stranger's house? The letter doesn't even mention an address.

Still...not going would be *rude*, wouldn't it? At least that's how I justify satisfying my curiosity regarding a *real* decemancer gathering. I sigh and apply pressure to the box on the left, waiting until it turns a faint green. Whoever Dr. Sylvestri is, he should have received my response.

I open up my glossY and search up the man's name. Before I do so, I realize I have a few unread messages.

From Laura: *Hey, do you want to get a movie sometime this week before the dance? I'm free in the evenings.*

From Mother: *Call me.*

From Germaine: *Mother says you're a practitioner. What the hell? Care to explain?*

I sit back in my office chair and hold the glossY out in front of me. What should I tell my family?

I probably should meet them in person to explain things directly. Even so, I can't just ignore their messages. I decide to call Mother first.

The line connects almost instantly. "Julian," she says, her voice clear over the connection despite the distance. "Are you alright?"

"I'm fine," I reply. My hands begin to shake. "I see that the school has informed you that I'm a practitioner now." I'm surprised: They usually don't contact parents about anything.

Her bell-like laugh comes over the line.

"Did they tell you my affinity?"

"They sent over your potentioreader results."

So she really does know. "What do you think?"

I can feel her unsatisfied gaze over the line. "I suppose you're less of a wasted effort than before."

My mouth curves into a smile. "Thanks." Her manner of speaking is just as I remember it. Of course, she's still unsatisfied, even when I finally unlock an affinity. In her defense, it *is* officially recorded as a fairly low Death affinity, which is *almost* less useful than a glossprog degree.

I feel a bead of wetness fall down my temple and quickly wipe it away.

"Though it's a little late...You're just a semester away from graduating with a glossy programmatics degree." She sighs. "I'd hate to think you've put in all this effort for nothing." *And wasted all your money*, I add mentally. She pauses for a moment. "What are your plans?"

"Why don't we wait until I get home to talk about everything. There are only two more weeks until winter recess, after all."

"Sure, if that's easier." She coughs. "I heard that this all...happened because you got into an accident." Is that a modicum of concern I detect?

"I'll tell you about it when I get home, okay?"

"Fine. Do keep in touch if anything happens though."

"Will do."

The line cuts off.

I exhale and hold my head in my hands. I don't feel like starting up another conversation, not with bubbly Germaine. Hopefully, Mother will talk to her and clear things up, but I should still give her a message.

To Germaine: *I'll tell you everything when I get home in two weeks. I presume you'll be returning for the holiday?*

I finally return to the message from Laura—the one I've been avoiding. She wants to see a movie? Based on the way she was looking at me...she intends for this to be a date.

I think I liked Laura before the time loop: she's cute, kind, and hardworking. But now, I'm not up for any serious human relationships: I need time to remember how to be a normal person again. Even so, I think back to Jasmine's admonishment regarding my anti-social inclinations. I should probably do *something*: becoming a hermit won't help me readjust.

To Laura: *I'm free tomorrow if you want to meet up.*

I frown, remembering that I have my Death Affinity I class in the evening.

To Laura: *I'm free Thursday if you wanna meet up. I know it's the night before the dance, but*

I pause, deleting the message again. I suppose we could meet tonight if she's able to make it on such late notice.

To Laura: *You free tonight?*

I finally send the message off.

What was I doing before looking at the messages? I turn back to the table and see the opened invitation. Right: I was looking up this Dr. Sylvestri figure. I plug the glossY into my desk glosscomp dock. Now that I have a larger screen and a full-sized keyboard, I look up his name on the distributed network.

> Sylvestri practitioner Dark Art Death affinity decemancer

I submit the request, then look through the results. To my surprise, the first entry seems to be a Dr. Sylvestri living in Portwood—a town only twenty minutes away by public hovergloss. I follow the link to his official government profile.

> *Dr. Arterio Stephen Sylvestri, II, originally of Hacerman, a small city in western Vermut, currently residing in Portwood, Magnestria.*
>
> *Calling: Practitioner*
>
> *Primary affinities, in order of strength (percentages currently unavailable): Death, Dark*
>
> *For more information, contact Dr. Sylvestri's representative, Vinia Kraft, by registering her quanticode on your mobile device.*

Her quanticode image is pictured below—a black and white swirl of lines. I scan it into my glossY but decide against calling it for now. Checking my messages, I see that Laura has responded.

From Laura: *I'm free tonight! What movie do you want to see?*

Since I have no idea what movies are out, I leave the choice up to her.

To Laura: *I'll watch anything. Surprise me! I'm free anytime after 7, so message me with the time, and we can walk over to the theater together.*

She responds almost instantly.

From Laura: *Great~ I picked something out. See you at 8!*

FORMAL

When I get back from the movie, Xander is in the room working on his glosscomp.

"Hey, what were you up to?" he asks.

"Just saw a movie with Laura." I shrug off my jacket and shoes.

He laughs. "She told me."

"Oh." Why is he asking, then?

His smile begins to grow strained. "Well, she told me you were going to a movie, not how it went. So, how was it?"

Xander, why do you try so hard? I know he's trying to be social, recognizing that this is my first date at Academia Hector. Does he feel an obligation to ask about the date? Does he actually care how it went? I can't tell.

I turn around and smile at him. "It was fine. The movie was alright, I think it was called..."

"Surgebreak."

"Right."

Xander grins. "She asked me what kind of movies you like."

Since when do I like action movies? Ian considered for a moment. *Maybe I used to like them, now that I think about it.* Action movies once allowed me to live vicariously through the lives of confident, cool practitioners. But after going through Menocht, something like Surgebreak seems almost boring.

Xander leans back in his seat. "So? Did anything *happen*?"

"We talked, we laughed, and I walked her there and back."

"Nothing else?" Xander has an expectant look in his eyes.

I roll my eyes. "No. It's just the first date, Xander—we're taking it slow."

"Ian," he exclaims, "you should live a little. Did you at least hold her hand?"

I feel a bit of redness rush to my cheeks. "No."

He winces. "Ian... She's going to think you weren't into her."

I sigh. It's not that I'm not attracted to Laura. I'm just...adjusting to normalcy, I guess. "I'm sure something more along the lines of what you're expecting will happen at the formal," I assure him. I'll give it my best effort, at least.

His expression turns serious. "Look, I know you're an introvert to begin with...but I don't want whatever accident you got yourself into to put a downer on the rest of the year."

I turn away. Xander has no idea what he's talking about—I can't just write off what happened to me. It's not like I want to feel distant, or antisocial.

"I'm fine, Xander."

"Alright, if you say so." At least he lets the topic rest.

* * *

As the week goes on, I find myself growing increasingly excited...not for the dance, but for the party two days after. I'm attending the dance because it's a good way to act normal, but coordinating and planning is a minor emotional chore. I'm glad I'm going but only because trying to be normal is good for me. Sylvestri's party, on the other hand, is genuinely intriguing. What does a gathering of ostensibly powerful decemancers look like?

I did end up contacting Sylvestri's representative, and even though she made me feel like a plebeian for doing so, I got answers to all my questions. From what the representative said, it sounded as if every primary practitioner of the Dark Art within a hundred miles had been invited.

She also answered my questions about the dress code: formal, suit and tie. She did hint that guests might spice up their wardrobes to display their decemantic prowess, but I wasn't able to discern exactly what she meant. She also gave me the address of the venue as well as the time that the gates open to the manor: 5:00 pm.

Wednesday comes and goes and with it the second decemancy class. It's just as disappointing as the first, and I'm happy to leave. I asked Professor Durning if I could observe what higher-level classes are working on, but she told me that such classes didn't exist. They're offered on the syllabus, but as nobody takes Death affinity as their primary affinity...nobody has progressed past Death Affinity I.

I couldn't fully mask my disappointment when she said that, and I'm sure she noticed. But she didn't say anything further, probably because, as a senior with only 30% affinity, I'd never get past Death Affinity I, anyway.

* * *

The night of the dance comes. Laura and I are in a group with Xander and a few other friends, and we've all planned to meet up outside the shuttle station at 9 pm. While I haven't donned formal clothes in a while, dressing well is one of the things that Mother beat into me at a young age, and I'd be hard-pressed to forget how to properly layer a dress shirt and how to knot my tie. I have to go under the bed to find my good pair of dress shoes in their once-opened box—a gift from my Aunt Julia last year. Altogether, with the suit, tie, and shoes, I look decent. I comb back my hair and gel unruly strands in place, and soon enough, it's 8:50.

While I had originally been planning to go with Xander, he hasn't come back to the room, so he must have gotten ready earlier. I'll meet him at the shuttle station with the others.

When I get down to the doors leading to the shuttle, it's almost 9, and I'm the only one there. Which is fine; I've been to a few dances, and the girls are typically a few minutes late. Mother insists it's just the way things are.

But none of the guys have arrived yet, either. I check my watch: Now it's officially 9. How am I the only one from our group here? I refer to the group message to make sure I have the meeting time and location correct.

I can't help but feel paranoid as the seconds tick by. What if someone knows about my real affinity and has kidnapped my friends as ransom?

That's so stupid, I tell myself. *Stop stressing out.*

Xander's friend Walsh is the first person to arrive. He's somehow pulling off a dark green suit and sky-blue suspenders, putting my mundane black coat and plain white shirt to shame.

"Hey," he says. "You look great."

I smile, unsure if he's trying to fish for the compliment he deserves or if he's just nice. "Likewise: love the green. Who are you going with?"

"Erica-Jane Sommers. You're going with Laura Benvolio, right?"

I nod. "Yeah. You have any idea where the others are?"

"Pretty sure a bunch of them are at a party on the Arts campus."

Really? "Oh, wow."

He reclines against the wall. "I went for a few minutes, though I didn't stay long. It's crazy over there—they have these insane ice sculptures, and a few of the pyromancers and Light practitioners have been putting on a fireworks show."

No wonder people haven't been answering their glossYs. Whatever—I'll wait.

Soon, twenty minutes pass.

"I think we should check on them."

Walsh looks up from his glossY. "They are pretty late...can you try calling Xander? He's the one that led the others over."

"Sure." I set up a call between the two of us. However, he doesn't accept it from his side.

"No response?" Walsh asks, unsurprised.

"Yeah," I sigh. "Can you wait here in case anyone else comes? I'm going to head over to that party and drag people back over here."

"Sure."

I turn away and shake my head, surprised that I'm the one trying to make everything go smoothly. It's dark enough—and crowded enough—that I levitate myself over the snow-covered path without attracting attention. Good thing, considering Aunt Julia would be disappointed if I ruined my shoes on the second wear.

I hear the explosions before I see them: bright, bursting spheres of flame that fill the central courtyard of the Arts Campus' residential area. As I get close, I see a few people standing at the gate leading to the central courtyard.

"Only practitioners allowed in after 9," one of the guys says. He holds up a flame in the palm of his hand.

I raise an eyebrow and hold out my own hand, manifesting black energy onto my palm. "We good?"

* * *

The vitality in this place is off the charts: I can't believe how many people they've managed to cram into the courtyard. It's not for nothing that they've decided to close the party off to non-practitioners—there's enough space for all of the practitioner students on campus, but regulars easily outnumber them. There's simply not enough space for everyone.

Blasts of fire and light mingle in the sky, bathing the party-goers in different hues. They're barely audible over the loud music pumping from a series of sound projection arrays set up on the walls of the courtyard. The students are largely dressed in formal wear, but a minority are dancing in T-shirts and jeans, unbothered by the cold. Some—likely Light practitioners—even sport translucent light projections that overlay onto their clothes. The projections vary wildly, giving some glowing angel wings and others neon articles of clothing.

Come to think of it, the warmth in the courtyard can't only be from all the warm bodies—it's cold enough outside for water to freeze. Sure enough, I spot a few symbols drawn into the court-yard's grass, metal stakes marking the node points—I suspect they're Sun affinity arrays providing steady warmth.

I'm at a loss as I consider locating Xander, Laura, and the others in this mess. If it were summer, I could just thrall insects and use them to search the party's guests. The winter night, however, is noticeably absent of small, inconspicuous living things.

A girl approaches me from the right. "Looking for someone?" she asks, smiling coyly.

"Yeah, a group of friends," I reply. "They're all regs."

She makes a face. "The regs are mostly hanging out by the living ice sculptures," she murmurs. "How'd you get in now if you're just a reg?"

I smile politely. "I'm a practitioner."

"I don't recognize you. Anyway, why's a practitioner like you hanging out with a group of regs?"

Perhaps I was being too charitable in assuming the only reason the practitioners closed off the party to regulars was because of capacity. I set off in the direction of the ice sculptures, ignoring her question. "Thanks for your help."

"Good luck, transfer student!" she replies, her words slightly slurred.

Nobody else tries to talk to me as I make my way over to the sculptures, probably because they assume I'm a reg. The Arts campus is small enough that most people know each other.

"Ian? You're here?" a voice calls out. I turn to the left and see Justin, my animancy-mentor, leaning drunkenly on another friend. "Nice!"

His friend turns and gives him a look. "You know this guy?"

Justin wipes his arm over his mouth. "He's a decemancer. Primary affinity decemancer!"

"Oh?" The friend, a tall guy with pale skin and slanted eyes, grins. "So you're better than this dummy, right?"

"He's just started!" Justin calls out.

I roll my eyes. "I'm better than him."

Justin seems too out of it to protest. "Well," his friend says, "I hope you have a better night than mine."

"Thanks," I reply grimly. I hope the others can at least walk. Even though much of the group are Xander's friends, and I'm not too familiar with them, I doubt that they'd willingly get hammered at a rave before the formal. A more likely scenario is that someone spiked the drinks.

My hunch is, unfortunately, verified a minute later: A pack of at least fifty regs are semi-conscious and leaning against each other, the smell of beer and vomit wafting around them. Some pyromancer is heating the floor of the entire venue, so they aren't going to freeze to death, but they look awful.

My mood isn't improved when one of the living ice sculptures knocks my shoulder, nearly sending me into a puddle of vomit. Shouldn't whoever is controlling them be more careful? In their defense, there are at least fifteen humanoid sculptures in the area, all of them larger than life and performing different dances.

When I find Xander and the others off to the side of the group, I raise my eyes to the sky and sigh: "Great."

* * *

I message the group chat first to inform the snazzily dressed Walsh of the current situation. Then, I approach my five incapacitated companions and gauge their collective ability to walk.

"Mmm...Ian...thanks for coming to get us." Xander coughs. "Someone must've spiked the drinks," he explains. "I'm totally out of it."

Xander seems the highest-functioning of the bunch, if that's any indicator of my chances of successfully walking them back to Campus Central.

It would be so, so easy to use decemancy to drag them back. There are so many ways to do it, too, ranging from directly controlling the bones in their bodies to creating composite bone skeleton minions to carry them back princess-style.

Instead, I resign myself to making a few trips.

* * *

With Walsh's help, we get everyone back in their rooms by 11:00 pm.

"So much for the formal," I say.

He shrugs. "They're never that much fun, anyway." He tugs absently at a cuff link.

I give him a look. "It's a shame they were all too out of it to appreciate your get-up." I'm no fashion expert, but even I can tell the man's wardrobe is on point.

He smiles. "There's really only one person I was trying to impress, and I think she'll appreciate me helping her more than a well-tailored jacket."

* * *

When Xander gets up on Saturday, he has a massive headache. "Shit," he moans from underneath his covers. "I feel dead."

"You're fine," I retort. "The worst has passed." *Passed into the toilet, anyway.*

"Help me to the nurse?"

"Sure."

He comes back an hour later with a less severe headache and a bout of fatigue, though he ends up sleeping the entire Saturday away.

Sucks for him. Finals start Wednesday. I'm not much better off—not using my practice is *killing* me—but at least I can sneak away and find some relief. Xander's just going to have to endure.

SYLVESTRI

It's Sunday evening, and I'm watching the Sylvestri manor from the boughs of a tree two hundred feet away. It's a large, private estate with a long yard lined by tall hedges. At the front of the property is an open gate that leads onto the off-track glossY landing circle—an area taking up half the front yard marked off by a bright-red rope strung between metal poles.

At 5:01 pm, the first of the guests start to arrive, private, off-track hoverglosses decelerating and touching down in the landing area. Each hovergloss deposits one or two guests, then hovers off the ground and takes off, departing the property. The guests cross over the red rope and make their way up to the property's front door where they exchange a few words with the two doormen before stepping inside.

After the tenth guest enters, I have a clear understanding of what Sylvestri's representative said about wearing something as a show of power.

I make a fist and draw out bones buried in the ground. Based on the wholeness of the bones and their...packaging, I think an owl must live nearby. Little bones are actually perfect for what I have in mind: something simple on the surface that will only attract the attention of people skilled in osteomancy.

While I know it's probably a bit reckless to publicly display power in such a way...I've been thinking a lot about my future as a practitioner, especially since Mother brought it up. Even though I've already sent out applications to programmatics corporations, I haven't built up any decemancer network whatsoever. This party might be the perfect opportunity I need to find my way into a position.

I head down to the front doors of the party, feeling somewhat inconspicuous when I realize I'm the only one to reach the entrance who didn't come on a hovergloss. The two doorkeepers smile and usher me in, expressions surprisingly warm. "Welcome to Dr. Sylvestri's manor!"

"The pleasure's mine," I reply as I step through the threshold. I follow a few other guests forward into a sizable parlor where the rest of the party-goers are sipping wine and sampling fine meats and cheeses.

What am I doing here? I wonder. *How did this Dr. Sylvestri even know to invite me?* Everyone else at this party seems to be wealthy and at least past the age of thirty. Based on the swirls of Death energy surrounding them, they're also fairly skilled in the Dark Art...especially in comparison to everyone at Academia Hector.

As I stand awkwardly at the center of the room, a woman in a patterned green dress approaches me from behind. She grabs my right hand and rubs her fingers over my bone gloves.

"Who is this young face?" she asks, giving me a coy smile.

"Julian Dunai," I say as I raise her hand to my lips, Mother's brutal lessons in etiquette surfacing. "Will you give me the pleasure of hearing your own?"

"Helia." She fingers a pendant hanging over her chest. "Helia Damas."

I haven't heard of her, though I didn't really expect to recognize any names here.

"How *ever* did you secure an invitation to this party?" she asks while she grabs a glass of wine from a passing waiter.

"One was delivered to my living chambers." Why, are the invitations difficult to obtain?

She lets out a dry laugh. "You do realize," she says, "that to even view the invitation, you need to have a Death affinity in excess of 65%." She takes a sip. "Did a parent or relative pass the invite off to you?"

Maybe coming to this was a *horrible* idea: Someone as young as me shouldn't have such high affinity, or at the very least, someone as *unknown* and as young as me shouldn't.

"My professor, actually," I say, pivoting. "Her primary affinity is Death, and she's good enough to secure a teaching position. However, she has no interest in parties, so..." I grab a wedge of dried salami from a passing waiter. "She passed her invite off to her best student."

Damas laughs. "So you're still in school? What year?"

"Oh, we have an academic amongst us?" another person calls out from ahead. A man in a charcoal pinstripe suit and a red tie turns and walks over, dragging two other gentlemen along with him. "Helia, who's this?" Though he says Helia's name, his eyes wander to my bone gloves.

"This," she says, gently placing a hand on my arm, "is Julian Dunai." Then she gestures to the man in gray. "And this is Antonio Cesar." She introduces the men on his sides as Bradley Lomefeld and Marcus Hoffmann. "I was just asking Julian what year he is in his studies."

I beam at them as I finish chewing. "I'm a fourth-year at Academia Hector."

"He says," Helia begins, giving me a knowing look, "that he's best in his class at decemancy."

"Oh-hoh," Cesar bellows. "Can we expect to see a demonstration later tonight?"

I raise an eyebrow. "Later tonight?"

Helia smacks Antonio's arm playfully. "Don't disorient our newest guest," she chides. "There's to be a dueling tournament in the pavilion after dinner."

I clear my throat. "What are the stakes?"

"Generally reputation and political standing," Cesar replies. "Though for a young, unheard of student like yourself, the duels may be the best kind of way to gain attention."

Suddenly, the man to Cesar's right, Marcus Hoffmann, clears his throat. "Julian, might I see your gloves?"

I hold out one of my hands. He doesn't seem particularly powerful, or he wouldn't be standing obediently at another's side.

"The workmanship," Marcus begins, "is exquisite. Where did you buy them?"

I give him a knowing smile. "What kind of decemancer do you take me for? I made them."

"So you specialize in osteomancy?" Helia asks.

"While I'm proficient in each domain of the Art, I personally prefer to work with bone."

"A rarity," Cesar notes. "You know who you should talk to..." He turns around and scans the crowd. "Therius Spiracor. Here, let me introduce you."

Cesar has a firm grip over my arm, and before I know it, I'm standing behind a thin, somewhat frail-looking older gentleman in a black suit with coattails.

"Terry," Cesar booms.

Therius turns around, wineglass almost touching his lower lip. "Antonio," he murmurs, his voice low and dry.

"I have someone I think you'll be interested in meeting."

Only then does Therius seem to notice my existence. He walks forward, grabs my hand, and begins to massage it in his own. "Lovely craftsmanship," he says, more to my hand than my face. "Your reagents...mammals of the forest, correct?"

"Correct." My face lights up. Someone who might actually give me interesting conversation...

"I'll leave the two of you," Cesar says as he backs away into the crowd, leaving Therius and me alone.

"How did you learn osteomancy?" he asks. Straight to the point.

"On my own."

He lets out a dry laugh. "What can you do?"

The kind of question I was hoping to avoid. "Do you have a challenge?" I ask, trying to get a gauge on the man's expectations.

"You made those gloves if I'm not mistaken," he says. "Can you form them into a mask?"

How difficult *should* this be? I don't want to make it seem too easy. "I should be able to manage it." I hold out my hands. Then, I bring them together and pull them apart. In between my two palms, I cup the bones, then turn my hands to the side to deposit the bones on my right hand. I bring that hand up to my face, then wave my hand in an upper diagonal swipe. The bones press to my face in a random, unpleasant pattern, but I feel like any more will be overdoing things.

"And you're self-taught?" Therius confirms. "Truly impressive. I figure you've already got potential job offers lined up by now."

I chuckle. "I've actually run into a bit of difficulty with my applications. Apparently, there was something wrong with my system connection and several of them didn't arrive by the deadline." I sigh. "I'm currently trying my best to find anything."

Therius' eyes flash. "Have you applied to the Rosemast Corporation?" he asks. I notice that he has a lapel pin with a rose made of white bone scapulas.

"No," I replied.

"Well," he says, giving me an amused look, "I'll see what I can do. Your name is Julian?"

"Julian Dunai."

* * *

I continue to mingle with guests, finding conversation increasingly more interesting as people get tipsy and begin to discuss scandals and politics. Before I know it, a bell sounds and we're herded into a dining room with three large, circular tables arranged for the guests. A glossY projector turns on and shows a list of names on the wall, separating people into their various tables. The tables themselves have little white cards at each spot with people's names on them.

I discover that I'm sitting at the same table as Dr. Sylvestri, who, to my knowledge, has not yet made an appearance.

Just as I sit down to dinner, the lights go out. All of them—the candles and the electric lamps—fall dark.

Nobody seems alarmed, so I figure this must be business as usual. Dr. Sylvestri's invitation did say that he had a secondary affinity in Dark.

I smell the scent of something burning that sets me on edge. Even though I can see the vitality of people around me, the space makes me feel claustrophobic.

When, I wonder, *is this dinner starting?*

"Welcome, guests, to Dr. Sylvestri's manor. He hopes that all have enjoyed the appetizers and company." A light emerges, shining on the form of a man at the front of the room. Is he at a podium?

"Welcome, all," he cheers. "It's nice to see you again in time for the holidays. In case we haven't before met, I'm Arterio Sylvestri, the man responsible for throwing all of this together." He pauses for light applause. At this point, I notice that the room is slowly growing lighter.

"Before we eat, I'd like to outline the evening's plan. First will be dinner, to be followed by desserts and duels in the pavilion. If you wish to enter a duel, you need only say so to any of the staff." He adjusts his tie and looks around the room. "Duels shall last an estimated two hours. Immediately following them shall be an exhibition in the parlor room, to be set up while others are in the pavilion. If you have any special requests regarding how your research or product is displayed, voice them to any of the staff. The open exhibition will last one hour. Finally, we will all gather on my terrace to watch a fireworks display."

He smiles and raises his hands, causing the room to assume its previous level of brightness. "Without further delay, dinner is served."

Applause follows, this time loud and spirited. I follow Sylvestri's form as he makes his way over to our table, smiling and clasping the hands of guests as he goes. Finally, he sits down and gives us all a look. "You didn't have to wait for me," he admonishes. "Let's eat!"

Thank you, Mother, for teaching me the mannerisms of a gentleman. I honestly never expected to use them.

I grab a fork and begin to eat the first course, a salad, while others engage Sylvestri in conversation. It comes as no surprise to me that the man is the table's center of attention. The spell he just pulled, bathing the room completely in dark, was powerful. That Dark is only his second-degree affinity implies that his decemancy must be comparably more potent. He's likely one of, if not the, strongest person in the room, excepting myself.

I listen in on the conversation but remain quiet, eating. They're currently discussing winter gardening—one of the least interesting topics I can possibly imagine in a temperate region like Magnestria. The food, at least, is delicious.

Somehow, the conversation leads to me. I nearly jolt upright in my seat as Sylvestri mentions my name.

"...Ignatius Julian Dunai, our newest companion. Still a student at the university," Sylvestri says, winking at no one in particular as his eyes rove around the table. "Tell us about yourself."

"Hello," I begin, unsure exactly what they're expecting me to share. "I'm Julian Dunai, a fourth year at Academia Hector." I fiddle with my hands under the table, though I keep my gaze sharp. Just like in the loop, my performance here is being watched.

"I grew up in a small city in Shattradan and come from a family of small repute." My nuclear family, at least. "I entered university after taking a gap year traveling, and I have been studying since." I smile politely. "Is there anything, in particular, I should expound upon?"

Sylvestri appears thoughtful. "How did you unlock your affinity?" he asks. "All of us have our own...unique stories, I can guarantee you."

The way he's looking at me...seems predatory. Sylvestri seems to be a dangerous man, or perhaps one with a voracious curiosity. Perhaps the two are one and the same.

I ponder what I should tell them. Sylvestri seems the type to not take no for an answer...

Maybe I'll just say the closest possible thing to the truth.

"I unlocked my affinity after the worst nightmare of my life," I say. "Horrendous things were done to me, and I did horrible things to others. For the first time ever, I felt no guilt over my actions." I give the table a half-smile. "When I woke, I had the affinity, just like that."

Every head angles toward Sylvestri, gauging his reaction before giving their own.

"What an interesting story," Sylvestri nods. "I've never heard of anyone unlocking their affinity in a *nightmare*, but as you said...whatever loosens the shackles of guilt, works. Confronting guilt is, at least for the majority of us, a significant factor in unlocking a dormant Death affinity."

The meal proceeds relatively smoothly, with only a few more questions aimed toward me. Soon enough, I'm following behind Sylvestri and the others to his pavilion—a dome-shaped, all-glass enclosure about half the size of a professional dueling stadium. I've since voiced my interest in participating in the duels to one of the waiters, who assured me that the dueling lineup would be projected for all to see before the first duel.

I have a sinking feeling that this is a bad idea, but I want to make a good impression on these powerful decemancers. I'll just have to be careful—perhaps using only osteomancy, to imply that I only have skill in one specialization, and even then, only controlling the bones making up my gloves. Certainly, no snapping people's bones from within their bodies or anything like that.

As we enter the pavilion, people begin to sit down at circular tables bordering the dueling ground. I find myself at a table with people I don't recognize and find it a relief when a waiter swiftly brings over a platter full of teacups filled with coffee. Sipping the drink is a welcome distraction.

"So, a new face," one of them begins. "How old do you think he is, Don?"

Another man seated at the table fiddles with his emerald tie before responding. "Late twenties, maybe?"

"What company do you work for?" the first man asks, his teeth unnaturally white.

I fake laughter. "I look older than I am," I reply. "I'm a fourth-year university student."

The entire table bursts out into laughter.

A woman takes a puff from her pipe and gives me a lazy grin. "And yet you've already managed to secure an invitation to old Sylvestri's yearly gathering." She shakes her head and chuckles. "You planning to duel?" She looks around the table. "We're all curious to see how fresh meat like yourself fares." The way her teeth clack on the word 'meat' strikes me as particularly aggressive.

"I did put in a word," I say, assuring them.

They begin to tell me their own specializations; in total, there are three animancers, two carnimancers, a thraller, a diagnostician, and an osteomancer (myself). Compared to the table I dined with, of which roughly half of the people were carnimancers, this distribution seems unrepresentative.

Somebody begins to say something else when, once more, the lights go out completely, save for the light shining onto a projector screen next to the dueling ground. A white light flashes, and in its wake, the screen is filled with a tournament-style lineup. *This is good,* I think, already planning how far I should go before intentionally losing.

I'll be participating in the fifth match against a woman named Erika Reinhart. I vaguely remember seeing her name on the list displaying dining table placements, but I haven't personally met her.

While others at the table talk, I try to decide how far to push things if Erika, or the next opponents, are too skilled. It might be smarter, in the end, to lose even the first match but do so while showing talent. The goal isn't to win but to position myself to secure company recruitment offers.

Just as the list goes up, Sylvestri appears in a dazzling flash of light that restores illumination to the pavilion.

"Now that everyone is comfortable, I'm going to outline some basic rules and guidelines. First, duelists can use whatever equipment and weapons already on them. Additionally, they may choose up to four items from the racks adjacent to the dueling grounds. Duels will follow standard Fassari protocol, in that they will immediately end upon incapacitation or forfeit of the match by one of the duelists. Remember: No attempts to permanently kill, maim, or dismember opponents are allowed. Any attempt to do so will be met with a swift intervention from myself, as well as expulsion from the premises. Additionally, the use of abilities that stand to threaten the spectators is completely forbidden." He holds his hands out to the sides of the podium. "With that, let the first duel commence!"

The two duelists make their way from their seats to the center of the dueling grounds. I recognize one of them from the table I sat at for dinner.

A minute passes as the duelists select various objects from the racks. It's difficult to make out exactly what the objects are from my angle, as most are enclosed in boxes and chests that mute Death energy.

Eventually, the duelists take their places, each standing at the midway point between the center line and their respective side of the grounds, such that half the field's length lies between the two of them. As they wait for the signal to begin, they don't seem particularly serious—probably because they're dueling purely for fun. Most of the people here seem to know each other fairly well, and based on the fact that so many people are over the age of fifty, I doubt they're that concerned about the outcome of a single friendly duel.

Me, on the other hand—I have a lot more to prove. I wonder if they paired me with someone who also feels pressure to win for a more exciting battle.

The person in a navy suit on the left makes the first move, holding up a sword infused with a soulstone on its hilt. The other person, a man in a cream-colored suit, waves a hand and a wave of pink flesh grows out from a chest by his feet to deflect the attack. Cream-suit steps backward and pulls out a bone whip, quickly coating it in pink energy. He then whips it at navy-suit, who deflects the move with the sword. Navy-suit ducks forward and kicks cream-suit's feet out from under him, causing the man to stumble backward. However, cream-suit rebounds quickly, pushing himself back up with the help of a fleshy arm.

The two continue to fight for a while. I can see that they must know each other well by the ways that they respond to one another's attacks. Sylvestri must have chosen them knowing that they would provide a good show.

I'm impressed by the display: Based on what I've seen at Academia Hector, these two duelists are gods. The confidence and expertise with which they execute attacks suggest decades of practice.

I find especially interesting the way the animancer uses a soulstone to empower his weapon—doing so gives it the ability to cut through flesh like butter. As the duel progresses, I realize that it's both severing the connection between the carnimancer and the flesh-construct as well as afflicting the flesh with necrosis, forcing the carnimancer to generate more—and sacrifice more Death energy—to offset the loss.

Eventually, the battle of endurance comes to an end, and cream-suit loses the duel with a blade pointed at his chest. The two men bow, laugh together, and then return to their seats.

Two more duels pass, though neither is as exciting or evenly matched as the first. Just as the fourth duel is about to commence, sirens blare outside of the house.

Sylvestri reappears on the podium. "We're going to take a small break while we deal with the disruption. Please remain in your seats for the time being."

Two minutes later, three guardians in riot robes appear, the sun and moon crests an indicator that each is an elementalist. One of them is holding a bulky black instrument in his hands. Sylvestri enters the room behind them, his face devoid of emotion.

One of the guardians speaks, her voice ringing out in the cavernous space. "High Death energy has been detected in this area over the past few hours," she says. She can't be referring to people's symbols of power—such as my gloves—can she? "We were dispatched to ensure that this event has no ties to a recent act of terrorism perpetrated by a decemancer."

Whispers quickly fill up the room.

"Please remain calm while we scan the room for the energy signature of the perpetrator in question. It should only take a moment, and I trust that no one at this gathering will find themselves implicated."

I notice that Sylvestri's countenance darkens. He must be incensed that these guardians have barged into his house and started scanning guests, all of whom are well-established and would never engage in terrorism against the state.

The man finishes scanning the room, then pulls his compatriots aside. They talk for a moment, then the woman nods.

"Like we suspected," she says smugly, "the perpetrator is here. We encourage them to surrender themselves now, or else we'll need to go scan each and every person present until we find them."

Seriously? As I look around the room, I can't help feeling that the person they're looking for is me. I don't think I did anything that could implicate me for terrorism, but honestly speaking...If I'm powerful enough to level a city, I'm a weapon and a potential threat.

But nobody knows I have 99% affinity beside Jasmine.

"Do you guys know what that thing they're carrying around is?" I ask.

The woman with the pipe levels her gaze at me. "It's one of those new ultraportable micropotentioreaders," she says. "Though I'm not sure how they're expecting to use it to cross-reference a terrorist's Death energy with any of our own." She takes a drag. "I don't trust it."

My gaze hardens. *So that's how it's going to be.* It's possible that someone detected a disturbance of Death energy caused by my bone construct. I do recall Sarah from my Death Affinity class mentioning the illegality of creating bone constructs, though I didn't think anyone would catch me if I created one over the open ocean.

So they might actually think I'm some kind of terrorist, and they might actually be here just for me.

What are my options? Go with them, clear up the misunderstanding...and then what? At the very least, I'll be convicted of misreporting my affinity—a crime punishable by up to a year in jail. The worst part will be the indelible stain of a criminal record. There's also a good chance Jasmine will be convicted of facilitating—or committing—potentiostat falsification.

Shit—I really screwed up.

I close my eyes and take a deep breath.

When I open them, I taste the salt of ocean air on my tongue and realize that I'm back on the dinghy.

CHAPTER

12

RINSE AND REPEAT

I lose myself to rage, sobering up on the boat an additional iteration later.

I squeeze my eyes tight, then sit up and begin to weep, my hands over my head. I'm angry, frustrated, relieved—my head is a tumbler of emotions. I take a few deep breaths.

The past months I've been trying to put on a calm face for the watchers, tried to beat them at their mind games, show them that this *loop* hasn't broken me. But I ruined that all when I ended up back in my room, when they tricked me into thinking I was free.

I ruined my facade even further in the last iteration.

I look down at my hands. I can't remember the last time an iteration has gone so poorly.

Fragments flash through my mind like shards of a broken mirror: ripping through the water and forming a bone construct around myself out of drowned bones; tearing through the skies like a rocket; digging the bones into my own skin and grafting foreign flesh around them; slamming into Menocht Bay like a hurricane and leveling half of the city with my speed and strength; thralling as many people as I could touch to stop breathing.

Me adding a city's worth of bones to my mega-construct, a four-legged lizard beast with me at its head, then doing as much as I can to decimate the entire province of Illuet.

I hang my head, staring off into the distance with a bitter taste in my mouth.

Somewhere along the way, I must have run into some trouble, or the watchers decided they'd had enough violence for one iteration. Regardless of why the loop restarted, I'm now back as myself, acutely aware of the normalcy of my arms and legs, the familiar bend of my ribs as I lean into the dinghy's side, all of it starkly contrasting with how it felt merging my entire being with a bone titan.

There wouldn't have been any way to come back from that, not in the real world. I intentionally warped myself into something *other*.

I sigh at myself in disgust: I've done this kind of *transformation* enough times to recognize it as one of my coping mechanisms.

But I'm back now, whole and calm.

I reassess my present situation. First, I've learned that the loop has layers: Menocht Bay must be the first, while my school should be the second.

I laugh at myself self-deprecatingly: *I clearly failed* that *layer.* I exhale and dip my hand into the water outside the boat.

How the hell did everything go so wrong?

I recognize that I know the answer, though I don't want to acknowledge it.

Everything went wrong, for the most part, because I couldn't keep myself from using decemancy. I went out on my own and made a bone construct. I wasn't thinking straight. Maybe I let the power get to my head, the fact that I had escaped the loop inflating my ego.

I don't even know.

Think, think, think. What could be the point of the next part of the loop, other than to teach me control?

Menocht Bay—this iteration—develops my power. Obviously.

Then the school iteration forces me to keep it truly hidden. No potentioreader. No telling anyone—not even a counselor sworn to secrecy like Jasmine. While that alone didn't set off the loop's restart, it's just one more potential avenue of suspicion: fundamentally, Jasmine was a counselor who saw *practitioners.*

If I'd woken up and realized that I didn't have to wait for the damned cruise ship to go to the city, I could've solved Menocht a long time ago. Perhaps there's a similar trick to finishing the school loop.

I think of the skills needed to kill the five-thousand-or-so people infected with ginger a few hours into the iteration. Considering the slow start I had learning decemancy, I needed...six months, maybe, to beat this layer of the loop. I wouldn't have done it as well, and I would've needed to kill more than twenty-thousand considering my slower traveling speed (sans bone construct), but I could've done it.

I frown and look up at the clear, blue sky. This time, I don't bother to wait for the boat, instead choosing to go straight to Menocht. I'm mostly convinced that the success or failure of this loop hinges not on my ability to deliver the ship to safety but on saving Menocht's people from a zombification. If I'm wrong, and the ship does matter, that'll be one more thing I've figured out, and I can just repeat the layer again.

I raise my arms and drag up a veritable graveyard of sunken bones to begin shaping the wyrm. The process takes only four minutes, even with non-human bones: I've grown faster with practice.

As I fly over the water, my mind wanders, and I think of life before the loop. I wonder about who the watchers are and what they're preparing me to do. *When I get out, will things ever be like they used to?* My lips firm into a thin line. *What will it take from me to make it so?*

I wonder if the watchers think that they can control me, or if they're regretting what they've let me become.

* * *

I kill the infected in the city again, though this time it's only two thousand. Given that most were still in the Flower District, it was a clean sweep. There were a few that were off in a more remote part of the city that were a slight inconvenience, but I found them eventually. If ginger wasn't so contagious, I'd deal with the issue by sending minions—either construed from bone or thralled—to find and kill all those with the signature low vitality caused by the pathogen. But because it spreads so easily by bodily fluids, I need to dehydrate at the least and at best burn the bodies before other people encounter them.

If the infected people number in the low thousands, this is totally feasible. But after twenty thousand...well, things fall apart. I can't kill the infected faster than the pathogen spreads. Hence why I was never able to exit the loop until now, when I entered the city two days earlier than before.

The boat never arrives, but all the same, I eventually blink and find myself in my dorm room. I sigh contentedly to myself and roll over in bed, grabbing my glossY off the bedside table to check the time. It's currently six in the morning, a solid two hours before I would naturally wake. I set an alarm for eight, then turn off the glossY's screen and fall back asleep.

I dream of being back in Menocht Bay, the city a ruin smoldering around me, red against a soot-black sky.

The alarm wakes me, and I silence it, lying in bed for a full half-hour. During that time, I resolve to absolutely refrain from using any decemancy while in this stage of the loop. What got me into trouble last time was making a flying construct and accepting the invitation to Sylvestri's party. If I never display any affinity, hopefully, I'll be out of the loop and back in the real world as soon as possible.

I have a sinking feeling in my stomach that it won't be so simple—especially considering how long it took to leave the first part of the loop in Menocht.

I eventually get out of bed, sighing and kicking off the covers as I change into a towel, slip on my shower shoes, and head out the door. I step into the shower and let the scalding water run over my back. I take deep breaths, repeating two words like a mantra: *be patient.* I have a clear direction to go in, and I can't afford to be hasty.

I get out of the shower and finish washing up, then return to my room and get dressed. Casual clothes, I remind myself, recalling that it's still the weekend. I grab my glossY and check my messages before I head out.

From Laura: *What's up?*

I sigh. Do I want to go down this rabbit hole again when nothing matters? What would my previous self do in this situation? Y'jeni, the me of before...was meek, completely unwilling to pursue anyone. I know I liked a few people in the past, so it wasn't from lack of interest. But I do think that if someone had reached out to me directly like this, I would've had the sense to at least flirt back.

As I formulate my response to Laura, I murmur that this is practice for when I leave the loop...whenever that is.

To Laura: *Nothing in particular. Have you already eaten breakfast?*

She responds five seconds later.

From Laura: *Yeah, a little while ago.*

To Laura: *Are you eating with anyone for lunch? We can meet up around noon.*

From Laura: *Nope, I'm free! See you at noon!*

I smile and shake my head slightly. "I wonder how long she's been waiting for me to ask her to the dance."

I shuffle downstairs and to the dining hall, giving Octavia a smile and a wave as I swipe my card.

"Nice to see you, Ian," she says.

"Likewise," I reply, beaming. "Have a great day."

I pile my plate with food, then sit down at a random, unpopulated table. I don't see any friends I should be sitting with—a small relief.

I scowl. *It's entirely possible I'll never leave this layer if I see friends as chores.* It all comes down to how closely I need to follow the behaviorisms of my former self and slip back into my old life.

While I presume that I'm supposed to act like my old self, it's difficult to hang around friends while fronting a flawless facade. It was even hard in the last iteration, when I thought that people were all real, let alone this iteration, when I know that any relationships I develop will be fast forgotten.

I tighten my grip around my glass of water. *This is nothing compared to saving Menocht. It's a calm vacation,* I reason, *especially since none of my test grades will matter, assuming I make it to the end of the semester.*

I finish my breakfast and head to the library to check up on the news, taking advantage of glosspads pre-loaded with subscription publications. In the last iteration, I dropped the ball in that department—I didn't care about what was happening in the grand scheme of things. Instead, I had just been happy to escape the loop.

I had been lost, I realize. I had felt isolated from friends, dissatisfied wasting time on classes decemancy rendered obsolete. I was unsure what the future held in store, unprepared for what came next. The reality is that I'm powerful enough to be classified as a national security threat anywhere I go. If I want to ensure my freedom outside of the loop, when I do finally escape...all the time in the world still might not be enough.

* * *

When I meet with Laura for lunch, she's cheerful and easy to talk to. I ask her about her studies and her family, learning that she's close to her parents and two younger siblings. I didn't even know she had siblings, nor did I know that the middle child has low-functioning autism.

Eventually, I cut to the chase. It's much less nerve-wracking to ask someone out to a dance when you know they'll say yes.

"Sure, I'd love to go with you," Laura says, eyes shining.

The week carried on exactly as I expected it to. Xander didn't seem to think anything was wrong, which was good, and nobody asked me if anything had happened. I wonder what factors have made the biggest difference between the last iteration—when everyone was constantly asking after my wellbeing—and now. I reflect upon my general state of mind: After the initial shock of waking up back in Menocht Bay, I've regained my composure. It's far easier for me to keep a level head in the loop than in real life where there are no restarts.

Later that week, Laura and I see *The Patient Lock*, a detective thriller. The date goes better than last time, and Laura and I end up holding hands toward the end of the movie. After the lights go up, we act as though nothing happened—fine by me. I walk her home, then return to my room. Xander's working on homework as usual, and I sit down at my own desk and get to work.

He turns around before I get the chance and shoots me a devious smile. "I heard the date went well."

I roll my eyes and lean back in my chair. "It wasn't a real date."

"You guys ended up holding hands," he adds. Did Laura tell him everything already? How fast can that girl send a message?

"It wasn't a real date," I repeat. "But it went well."

He proceeds to shake his head. "Also, I can't believe you saw *The Patient Lock* without me. How was it?"

"Alright; nothing extraordinary, but for a mindless action movie, it was pretty enjoyable."

We eventually settle into our work. An hour or so later, Xander brings up the topic of the winter formal.

"So, Laura also told me you asked her to the dance," he says. "Were you guys planning to join my group?"

I nod. "Sounds great."

"Also, just a note, we were all planning to head to a pregame on the Arts Campus. You're coming, right?"

I cringe internally. "Of course, I'm coming," I say, mentally adding, *to make sure none of you blackout.*

* * *

It's Friday, and I join up with everyone around 6:30 pm to eat a light, informal dinner. Then we head off to the Arts Campus. I know this time to bring a small bag with a spare pair of shoes, to the chagrin of everyone else around me ruining their dress shoes walking through the snow.

This early in the evening, the entrance to the main courtyard is unguarded. As we enter, everyone seems enthralled by the towering, bottom-lit ice sculptures and miniature fireworks overhead.

The group naturally gravitates toward the drinks table—a table that must be at least eighteen feet long. All sorts of alcohol line its length, and except for two people standing behind it near the center and scrolling through their glossYs, the table appears unattended. Anyone could probably slip something into any of the drinks here.

I think back to the previous iteration. In general, I trust Xander to be responsible—the guy has never returned home more than a little drunk. And yet he and the others all somehow got so intoxicated that they couldn't even move without help? Even when they knew they had the winter formal?

"Hey, guys," I say. "I don't think we should drink this stuff."

They turn back toward me. "Why?" Laura asks.

"I heard someone a day or two ago say that they were going to spike the drinks. I didn't think it would be a problem because someone would be watching to make sure that didn't happen, but"—I gesture to the inattentive people behind the table—"anyone could slip something into them."

Xander gives me a look. "C'mon, don't you think you're being a little paranoid?"

I give him a dry laugh. "These are Arts students," I say, shaking my head. "Don't you think it's a little...naive to trust that they've invited regs to this party for the sake of inclusivity?" While I might just be running my mouth, what I've said isn't untrue. It would also explain why it seemed like only the regs were moaning and passing out next to the ice sculptures.

Someone else in the party who I don't know very well speaks up. "It's possible," he mutters. "They'd never get punished for doing something like that, either."

Xander sighs, giving me a questioning look. "Fine, erring in the way of caution...did anyone else bring a flask?" Xander takes a steel flask out of his suit jacket. Two others hold theirs out. "Let's share what we brought to start off the night."

We all end up drinking a little—probably about a shot's worth of rum or vodka, depending on whose flask we drank from. The shot's got me feeling a little buzzed—an unfamiliar feeling given how long it's been since I've imbibed alcohol.

We dance for a solid half-hour at the pregame, enjoying the special effects put on by the practitioners. We gather everyone up and leave around 8:45 pm without incident, and to my relief. I definitely don't want to help clean people up again. We get back to Campus Central and head over to the buses, making the bus at 9 pm. Soon enough, we're spilling out of the crowded bus and into the open, walking towards the doors of the venue.

The noise of the inside accosts me. The way that the bass resonates with my body reminds me of Menocht Bay's cannons firing. I wonder if I should've taken some headache medicine beforehand. While the pregame also had music, the speakers hadn't been nearly as good—there hadn't even been a subwoofer.

Realizing that my attention was drifting, I shake my head and refocus on my current role, slipping into the shoes of a regular guy bringing a girl to the school dance. I plaster a smile onto my face, thinking of how convenient it is that the venue is so dark and nobody can scrutinize my expression too closely.

When Laura and I start dancing, I flush with mild embarrassment: I've long since been out of practice, and it shows. After a dance or two passes, however, I gain my bearings and get into the groove. The pulsing of the music no longer sounds like a Menocht cannon but rather like a heartbeat: thumping. Ephemeral.

"Ian?" she murmurs. I focus on her face, noticing a worried expression washing over her features.

"What?"

She blinks rapidly. "Never mind."

Eventually, we all stop dancing and head back to the bus. We all head back to our rooms, with Xander and I walking together.

"What did you think of tonight?" he asks, looking back at me as we pass through the underground hallway.

I run a hand through my hair. "It was great." Compared to the last iteration, it was paradise.

"Looked like you and Laura were having a good time."

I chuckle. "I can say the same for you and Elisa." The pair had been into each other, their bodies pressing together for some of the slower songs. They were classy enough not to grind at the formal while wearing their best clothes, but I could tell that things were really getting hot between them. I'm almost surprised Xander hasn't taken her somewhere...maybe even back to our room.

He sighs and shakes his head. "She's fire," he says.

"How long have you guys been dating now?" I ask. I genuinely don't remember.

He laughs for a few seconds. Then he glances at me with a seeking expression. "Seriously?"

It's been a while, I think, somewhat annoyed. At least I would remember for the next iteration. "My memory is crap," I say, shaking my head. "I'm also a little tipsy still." Not true, but whatever.

Xander's lips quirk. "It's been three months," he replies.

Right. "Okay," I reply, nodding. "You think the relationship is getting serious?"

He shrugs. "I really like her, but it's too early to tell." He suddenly laughs. "What about you and Laura? Are you guys going out yet?"

"Honestly, I'm not sure what's going on. There's definitely something happening between us, but we aren't official."

He knocks me in the shoulder. "She's hot," he says. "And she likes you. Though why she'd ever want someone as hopelessly inexperienced as you..."

I bump him back. "Funny, Xander."

* * *

On Sunday, I can't help but think of the decemancer get-together at Sylvestri's house. Though I know I haven't received an invitation, and that I need to stay low-key...I want to go. I'm still genuinely curious about Sylvestri and the other decemancers.

Instead, I keep myself busy hanging out with Laura. The two of us study together, working on some of our glosscomp classwork. I lean over to ask her about something, only to have her ask me something instead.

"Hey, I saw something back at winter formal..."

"Hmm?"

Her eyebrows scrunch together, then she turns away, laughing dismissively. "Just forget it."

What? "You can tell me," I say. "Now I'm curious."

She sighs. "Remember when we were dancing, and I looked at you like I'd seen a ghost?"

"Maybe?"

"Well...do you have any enemies or something?" she asks, rubbing her arm. "I don't know what family you come from, but..."

I chuckle. "No, nothing like that."

She looks into my eyes, expression severe. "I think someone's put a curse on you." She pauses to take in my reaction. "Ugh, I know this must sound a little paranoid, but..."

I shake my head.

"I saw a cloud of darkness around you," she murmurs, frowning. "It was only for a few seconds, but I know it wasn't a trick of the light. I could feel it."

A cloud? "What did you feel?" I ask, my voice filled with concern.

She shudders. "It made my skin crawl."

What she's saying...it shouldn't be possible. I couldn't have just circulated death aura like that without knowing...maybe a little bit I could believe, but enough for even a reg like Laura to notice? However, the idea that someone had hexed me was doubly laughable.

"Thanks for telling me," I say, voice low. "I'll keep an eye out for anything suspicious."

We finish up our study session an hour later. At the end, as she's about to go, I ask her out. It took absolutely zero units of courage given that I already knew she wanted me to ask her and that I was stuck in a time loop, but still...it *was* my first time.

"You don't mince words, do you?" She laughs.

"What?"

"I've never had someone ask me out by literally saying, 'Do you wanna go out?' There's usually some other kind of roundabout phrasing, something more...poetic."

I make a mental note to make things more "poetic" next time. "Well?"

"I'd love to go out with you," she replies, grinning. "When should we have our first official date?"

I cock my head. "How about Tuesday night? We can get dinner."

"Sounds good to me," she says. "See you in class!"

I wave goodbye, wondering to myself how much longer this layer is going to last.

* * *

The next two weeks pass without incident. Laura and I continue to meet, which is good, I guess. If this part of the loop is testing whether I can fit back into normal life, having a working relationship should be a boon. The strategy has been working well enough, considering that this iteration has lasted two weeks longer than the last.

With each day, the burden of abstaining from my practice weighs heavier upon me. When I lose my concentration, especially when I'm tired, sometimes, I start to practice the Art without thinking. People generally don't notice because they're just regs and can't detect Death energy except for when it manifests itself in large quantities, but I've had a few close calls: the dance with Laura, for instance.

Once I was going over a problem in my room. Xander was also working on something, but he wasn't paying attention. Before the loop, I had a nervous tick where I would scrunch my hands into fists over and over. I was doing just that as I thought over the problem, except that with each open and close of my fists, Death energy was circulating around my body. I snapped out of my problem-solving state only to realize that a cluster of dead insects and even a dead bird were either already in the room or try-ing to claw their way into it from the outside, be it the window, door, or vent.

I dispelled all the energy in an instant, breathing heavily, sweat dripping down my temple. I glanced over at Xander, expecting him to be looking at me and freaking out. Somehow, the scratch-ing at the window and the buzzing of insect wings hadn't been enough to seize his attention.

From that point on, I began to reserve private study rooms in the library. That way, even when I accidentally drew in Death en-ergy, nobody would see.

This week, though, I've resigned myself to the fact that com-plete abstinence isn't sustainable. If I literally cannot live without somehow exercising my incorporeal decemancy-muscle, I need to find a place where I can practice without drawing attention.

I intend to make a few soul gems. I won't bother with selling them—if they get traced back to me, it might trigger a loop restart—but I can hide them away. Moreover, unlike a bone con-struct, they aren't forbidden, and they shouldn't prompt any kind of investigation.

I end up taking a public bus to a forest preserve around twenty minutes away. I hike for about a half-hour until I come across a small cave. I don't sense anyone or anything larger than a mouse inside of it, which is good if unexpected—I'd expect a cave to be an animal's den.

I stretch out my arms, then begin to circle the ambient energy of the winter forest. The release is euphoric, like stepping into a pool of soothing, hot water after wading through a half-frozen pond.

It takes very little effort for me to spin the ambient energy of the forest into soul gems, so much that I churn out ten of them in half an hour. Some people might kill for the amount of auris the pile must be worth.

It shouldn't be this easy—making soul gems from ambient energy is difficult, even for me. It's far easier to make one from a whole animal's energy, like that of a recently deceased (or living) human. Even making soul gems from groups of insects, like that one student I met who was studying decemancy, is prohibitively difficult; let alone making a gem from the melange of lifeless leaves and frozen carrion coating the forest floor.

I smash the soul gems to pieces, scattering their oily energy back into the air. Their liquid pools like a viscous miasma, the concentrated energy needing time to dissipate.

"Damn it," I curse, crouching down onto my knees. I glare balefully at the energy in the corner. "99% affinity"—I sigh, looking down at my hands before standing back up—"what's the point?"

FORWARD

Within the cave, I concentrate on my breath, a rhythmic cloud of white smoke dissipating over my shivering hands, barely carrying any warmth. My lips thin into a line as I draw my hands together, dredging up the skeletons of nearby corpses. A family of mice died in a hollow outside of the cave, and I call them to myself. When they appear, their scampering forms trailing needle-point prints in the exterior snow, I wave my hand and send their bones into a flying tumult around me.

I sigh in contentment as the bones settle beneath my clothes and over my face, warming my body. Even after making soul gems and moving the bones, I feel an insatiable itch. Now that I've started practicing, the thought of stopping is almost unbearable.

So I continue to make soul gems. After making another ten or so, I cross my arms and shake my head. I'm feeling jittery now, but not in a good way. It's as though forming the most basic soul gems isn't satisfying whatever I'm feeling.

Nobody's monitoring Death energy out here, are they?

I shake my head, dismissing the desire to create larger, more energy-intensive gems. If the regional guardians measured my Death energy far off the coast, there's a good chance they have this entire area covered from top to bottom.

My mind wanders as I compress Death energy into gems. When I snap out of my thoughts, I'm confronted with a rather gruesome scene: The bones in my hands extend out past my fingertips, and blood from the exit wounds has dyed my forearm red.

This is something I used to do to ease stress closer to the beginning of my time in Menocht. Back then, I considered it good practice for manipulating my own bones and flesh, but in reality, it was just a bad habit—a perverse form of decemantic teething.

Did I really do this again? I wonder, sneering in self-deprecation. For all that that I tell myself I've adjusted to still being in the loop, my entrapment continues to wear on me.

I shake my head and decide to at least make use of my bloodletting. I sit down and crane my face until it's no more than three inches away from my hand, watching the blood drip into a growing pool until I start to feel lightheaded. Then I retract the bone and use a swell of carnimancy to close the wounds.

Finally, I manipulate the fresh blood into a tight, gyrating sphere. After a minute or so, a crimson pearl drops into my hand. I pocket it, then head out. While I don't necessarily feel like I've truly found release, I'm feeling better.

* * *

Before I know it, finals are over. I head back home on a train, thoughts of warming up by the living room fireplace making me drowsy. I close my eyes and rest my head limply on the seat. When I open them, I find myself shrouded in complete darkness. I can't see or hear anything around me.

I clench my fists, my entire body suddenly trembling. *I've moved on? The test was to make it successfully to the end of the semester?*

Tears stream down my face, spattering off as I convulse in a fit of humorless laughter. So that's how it was. Simple enough, right?

But where am I? In a cave? I stomp my feet on the ground, noting that the sound isn't producing an echo. I advance forward, hopeful that I'll eventually find the way out.

After a minute of walking, I sense a disturbance in the ambient energy. There's a kind of Death energy manifesting, rapidly assuming the form of a skeletal monstrosity with mismatched bones.

I grow genuinely confused. *Is it here to help me? I can't think of any other reason the watchers would place it here.* I wave my hand and beckon it over, replacing its fel-green eyes with soul-violet embers that crackle brilliantly in the dark.

Only seconds pass before another swirl of Death energy appears, heralding the arrival of a panther-like skeleton. It stands around aimlessly, solidifying my suspicion that the undead must be here for my convenience.

After an hour ticks by, I have a veritable army of skeletal undead around me, and I'm still nowhere close to figuring out where the exit to this endless chamber is. I know that there must be an exit...

Half an hour more goes by before an enormous energy disturbance rocks the area, causing the ground to tremor. A winged flesh-and-bone humanoid the size of an apartment building—I'll refer to it as a seraph—pops into being, giving me a better sense of my current location. Keeping in mind a lack of echo, I can only presume that I'm in an open space outdoors, though a space unnaturally devoid of light.

Like everything else in this space, the seraph would be completely invisible without my ability to see its turbulent vital energy. The most disconcerting part about the enormous, angelic skeleton is that its motion is *completely quiet*: I can only feel, not hear, a gust of wind riding off its wings unlike the other skeletons under my control whose bones click as they move.

"Come," I whisper under my breath, my voice hoarse. The seraph moves, its wings pumping it robotically forward until it towers before me. I can only see the green coals of its eyes as it stares down and the faintest wisps of coiling red outlining its bones.

I realize I've been holding my breath. I smile, then swipe my right hand down. The skeleton writhes for a second, but it only takes an instant for its eyes to glow violet. I wonder what—

I blink, and suddenly, I'm somewhere else. This new place is bright, and I close my eyes reflexively. As I slowly open them, blinking rapidly into the glaring light beyond, I become aware that this place is extremely loud as though I'm amongst a large, cheering crowd.

"Welcome, challenger," a booming voice announces. I now see that I'm on a field with a full stadium of people spectating around me.

What kind of layer is this?

"This is the Pit of Brutality. Your only job is to survive! Good luck!"

I snort incredulously. *What?* I look around at the frenzied spectators, wondering how this kind of thing could ever be legal. I suppose it doesn't matter if it's legal or not if it's in a dilation loop.

At least the instructions for this layer are refreshingly direct.

As I inspect the surroundings, I realize that the entire back quarter of the stadium functions as a giant sliding door. *Just what kind of stuff are they going to pit me against?*

The first monster to emerge is blue and scaly, with disproportionately large teeth and a misshapen head. I wonder how it's supposed to eat with all those overlapping teeth getting in the way.

The announcer said that my only job is to survive, I recall, frowning. *But then why are there so many spectators?* I have a hunch that part of the test in this layer is to provide the audience...entertainment.

When blue-and-scaly gets within twenty meters of me, I form my hands into claws and swish them across in an X, tearing the creature apart from the inside. It tumbles limp to the ground, already dead.

Oops.

I walk forward, ignoring the cries of shock from the crowd. I shuck the monster's skin away and fashion its bones into a set of armor, deciding that if I'm stuck in the equivalent of a gladiator ring, going along with the scenario and acting like a gladiator is the best way forward. I flay the hulking blue corpse's skin from its body until I only have dead, bloodless epidermis. Then I drape the azure skin over my shoulders like a thin cape.

I hope the crowd appreciates my showmanship. Before I have time to form a soul gem from the deceased monster, another one appears on the field, this time looking like a cross between a rhinoceros and a tiger.

I can't help but feel a rush of anticipation as the monster comes closer, its footfalls sending tremors through the ground. I wait until it's only a few meters away, then dash diagonally right. I'm not fast enough to avoid the monster completely, and it swipes at me with a paw. I laugh as I meet the strike with a bone-clad arm, stopping it cold.

As the rhinocecat makes contact with my arm, I use carnimancy to tear the muscles in its shoulder. I use osteomancy to force a stress break at the spot my arm contacts the monster's, then *push.*

The end result is that the rhinocecat recoils and screams furiously as it withdraws its disabled limb. It shakes its head and begins to circle around me, pumping its two horns up and down as it charges. When I run forward to meet it this time, I increase my speed, lifting myself off the ground and dragging myself forward by my own skeleton. I continue to run to keep up appearances; to observers, it should look as though my stride has doubled in length.

Even the monster seems a bit startled by my increase in speed, though it only lowers its horn and snorts as I draw closer. When we make contact this time, all it takes is a palm from me on its forehead, and its head caves in, sending blood and brain matter flying out over its back.

I laugh and grab one of the monster's horns, holding it like a scepter. As another hulking monster races out of the holding area, I separate and add a few of its bones to my set of armor. The rest of its skeleton I hover at my sides.

As my eyes scan over the blood-drenched field, I think to myself that this...this the first layer of the loop I can actually enjoy.

* * *

After who knows how long, the monsters stop coming. The announcer screams something that I tune out. I'm breathing heavily, my shoulders bobbing up and down as I stand in place.

The field is a swamp of gore. I clench my fists and relax them to relieve tension. I look up, wondering when—

I blink, and I'm in a pitch-black box.

Where the hell am I now? I push up against the walls of my enclosure. I'm encased in rough, splintery wood, long-since dead, its lamination stripping it of any vestiges of Death energy. I can't do anything with it.

Y'jeni. I'm not buried alive...am I? I elevate myself forward, only to find my efforts fruitless. There's something heavy and immovable surrounding the box on all sides, even the ceiling.

Right. So I probably *am* buried alive. Is this some kind of sick face-your-own-fears garbage?

I want to scream, but I shake my head and keep my composure. The damned watchers are no doubt watching how I choose to react.

What am I supposed to do? I must be buried really deep underground because I can't sense any vitality nearby, aside from a few worms. If I were closer to the surface, there would likely be at least a few buried skeletons or desiccated insect carapaces.

Kicking out at the box in frustration, I empower my limb with whatever Death energy I can muster. The wood splinters, but the action is fruitless: Behind the wood is a wall of wet dirt.

The key to this layer must be finding a way to dig myself out. If I try to claw my way forward with my hands, I'll run out of steam long before I reach the surface, and without dead matter to draw from, I won't have enough energy to reinforce myself for more than a few minutes.

A sinking feeling comes over my stomach. I may not have dead matter now...but where there is life, death follows. I stare down at my hands, flexing my fingers.

I really don't want to do what I think I need to do, but if this is a test of survival, I may have no other choice. I'd be better off acting decisively now than waiting around for rescue that will probably never come.

I grimace and clench my teeth, at once terrified and full of resolve. After deadening the nerves around my left wrist, I pop off my hand, severing the ligaments, tendons, and vessels. I seal off my new stump, snarling in pain despite my precautions, and direct my liberated hand up to the top of the box.

I avoid looking down at my stump, wondering if I'd be able—or willing—to cut off my hand in the real world. Just looking at it makes me light-headed: It's my first time self-dismembering.

I could reattach the hand now, if I wanted. *It's not too late.*

Ridiculous. None of this is real—any regret over my hand is irrational weakness. *No going back.* I strip off the flesh and condense it into soupy Death energy, then I surge the energy over the thin hand bones, empowering them. Finally, I sharpen the finger bones and secure them together so that they won't fall apart with my energy coursing through them.

There's only one question in my mind as the hand-drill begins to cut its way through the dirt: Will the Death energy yielded from a severed limb be enough to drill to the surface?

A few minutes after the drilling begins, the shock of losing my hand wears off. But as the drill approaches the surface, it's clear that it's not going to make it, the Death energy that once coated the hand like a glove frayed and dissipated.

I cut my arm and blood spills out into the air, held aloft by my practice. The blood's vitality turns from white to black. I send it up into the hole left by the drill, giving the whirring construct a final, much-needed boost.

Just thirty seconds later, a pinprick of light shines down from the surface, small enough to suggest I must be thirty feet underground.

Now what? I'm still stuck down in the box, and the passage made by the hand drill is small, not nearly big enough for me to fit through.

Cursing the fact that I'm not an earth elementalist, I call the drill back to me, then hold it in front and direct it into the wall, widening the aperture.

This is going to take much more energy than I anticipated.

By the time I make it to the surface, I'm barely conscious, my vitality gray and body withered. The drill falls apart as I release my hold on it and collapse onto the ground, breathing heavily. My remaining hand shakes with relief.

I close my eyes and find myself, *surprise*, somewhere else.

CORONA

I 'm sitting in a chair at a large, polished desk.

"What are your commands?" a voice asks from my left. I turn and take in his appearance, noting a military uniform and stringently formal bearing.

A soldier, and one under my command? Interesting. No need to keep up pretenses, then. I'd never attain an officer position in any nation's armed forces without being a practitioner. I must be here *because of*, rather than *in spite of*, my decemancy.

"Hand me the situation report," I say calmly. I have no idea what I'm doing here, but there should be some kind of report, right?

"There *is* no situation report...remember, Corona?"

Y'jeni, of *course* there's no situation report, but it sounds like it's a question I've asked before. Is there a reason no situation report is unavailable? And Corona, I've heard that title somewhere...

"You misunderstand," I reply, smiling. "How long has it been since I last asked for the situation report?"

I see him hesitate.

"It's been thirty minutes," he admits.

So I—or at least whatever stand-in existed before I appeared here—*did* ask for a situation report previously. "Isn't that enough time for one to have been written?" I murmur, standing up from my chair. The man recoils slightly; I notice a bead of sweat on his temple.

If I asked for a status report thirty minutes ago, there must've been a reason. Considering what the loop's put me through already, odds are something terrible is happening, and I'm going to be expected to deal with it.

I sigh and stand up from my chair. "Never mind."

The man stands there awkwardly. *Is there something I'm supposed to say to dismiss him?* I have limited knowledge of any military, let alone one with a rank called Corona. I have a feeling I'm going to be relying on false confidence to fake my way through my first few days here.

"Dismissed," I state, giving the man a loose salute.

"Sir!" The man salutes back, then about-faces and leaves the room.

The office is airy, with a vaulted ceiling and a large window looking out onto the ocean. The space is painted a tasteful cream that reveals the underlying material of the building—a kind of stone-stucco mixture. Two portraits depicting former officers hang on the walls in gilded, golden frames, and a knee-high table sits under the window, flanked by sitting cushions. *A tea table?*

The office, window view, and humidity suggest that I'm in Ho'ostar. Kester would be my second choice if I had to guess, but the language the officer used—Luxish—isn't commonly spoken there. Sere would be a third guess, but it's famous for its dry heat. The air here is far too muggy.

I make my way out of the office, inspecting the people and analyzing the characteristics of the military base. It doesn't match my expectations of stark, militaristic utility, its gilded halls and classical columns seemingly better suited for a government building.

"Sir!" a young brunette calls out from behind me, rushing as though trying to catch up. "While I don't have a full situation report, I have some new information!"

Oh, does she? I turn around and smile. "Excellent." I look at the name on her breastplate. *Sec. Schaeff.*

"It's already sent to your glossY, sir."

I check my pockets and retrieve the device, grateful that it's locked by my retinas rather than a random password. Sure enough, the first thing in my inbox is a short, encrypted document. I open an obviously placed decryption module on the glossY's applications pane and decode the message.

Soon, I have a much better sense of what's going on.

"Thank you, Secretary," I say, returning her salute. As luck would have it, a proper salute is one of those behaviorisms Mother thought important to learn.

The report confirms that I'm in Godora. I peruse it as I continue through the hallway, arriving at a door leading outside. As I step beyond the threshold, I'm immediately confronted by a wave of intense heat that's at least five degrees hotter than Menocht. At least it's not *that* humid...

I adjust the cuffs on my military jacket as I step into the building's courtyard, blinking into the sunlight and adjusting the brightness of the report's display. The missive describes the situation as thus: A fleet of armed combatants arrived from the West under the concealment of Dark and Cloud practitioners. Their numbers are unknown, but they've been sweeping through and setting fire to coastal villages, suggesting that the invaders count fire elementalists among their numbers.

The dispatch suggests that I take a unit of fifteen water elementalists aboard a hovergloss to investigate and, if possible, capture (or kill) the perpetrators.

I raise an eyebrow and launch myself into the air. I don't need to work with others to get this kind of task done. This just sounds like another test of strength like the previous layers. Really, after the first two layers of the loop, everything has seemed too easy.

I probably wasn't supposed to spend so much time and grow so strong in Menocht. I ultimately spent years there stuck on an arguably simple puzzle.

I narrow my eyes both in contemplation and to escape the sun's glare. *It's almost as though the past loop layers—this one included—haven't been specifically created to test a decemancer.* The dark room with the undead, for one, wasn't a challenge at all. And while the stadium fight had been fun, the greatest challenge it posed was one in restraint as I took care to finish opponents off slowly for the spectacle. While the buried alive layer had been painful and unsettling, it still hadn't been *difficult*.

Just what are my little watchers doing? Someone, or something, must be monitoring the loop. If this is indeed a dilation loop and time is sped up from my perspective, I wonder how closely they can track my progress.

I follow the curve of the beach, scooping up sunken bones as I do. Soon enough, I've managed to create a wyrm on the water's surface. While genuine flying bone constructs are forbidden, as long as I hold off from completing the wyrm with a flight focus and soul gems, there should be no problem. I focus my attention on manually propelling it across the water, its form undulating like a dolphin.

After a few minutes of 'flying', a small city with a burning high-rise building appears within my field of vision. I put on speed, spurring the wyrm toward the shore. As water melts into sand, the wyrm continues its spiraling squirm forward over solid ground. So long as it maintains contact with water or earth, the control strain it places on me is minimal. Trying to use it to fly without properly turning it into a flying construct and giving it a flight focus, however, would be significantly more taxing.

As I cruise over the ground, I track fluctuations in vitality nearby, trying to detect anything that might resemble a unit of mobile hostiles. To my chagrin, it takes me a full hour to track the invaders down. The only reason I'm able to succeed is that they're staying close to the shore to bombard more coastal cities. Had they gone further inland, the area to cover would be exponentially greater.

It's over as soon as I sense them, though: My bone wyrm is faster than their transport vessel, and I quickly run them down. After that, I wave my hand, and they all fall dead, their necks broken.

Easy.

I smile and chuckle. Whoever is watching, don't you see that this is just *too easy*? I run a hand through my hair.

"How long are you going to keep me here?" I ask. I blink expectantly...only to find I'm still on the wyrm. Why isn't the loop proceeding? I finished the challenge and closed my eyes!

I twitch as the sound of a massive explosion sounds out in front of me. Grim horror tears through my stomach, followed by disbelief. The world turns white, and I can't move and—

* * *

I'm on the dinghy.

Isn't that already saying enough? I laugh and bang my head on the boat's side, hysterical. "This is the worst kind of torture," I seethe. My countenance grows dark. As I step off the dinghy and begin to form a proper flying construct out of old sunken bones, I begin to contemplate how to speed up the next iteration of the loop.

What do I know so far?

I know that this is all the biggest bullshit—

No. Patience, patience, *patience*. What do I *know?*

The next loop layer seems to test whether or not I can blend in. But honestly, I never really verified that that was the purpose of the loop. Two run-throughs aren't enough to verify something like that.

I resolve myself to try something else in the next loop. I wonder...what would happen if I just left Academia Hector and went home? Sure, it'd be right before finals and everything, which would be suspicious, but I can think of some excuse. *A mental breakdown, perhaps?*

MOTHER

F inishing up the Menocht loop layer only takes a mechanical six hours after I forge an enormous bone wyrm out of human and fish skeletons and race to the city. *I almost can't believe how fast I'm able to defeat it... What was I doing the past few years? Muddling around like a fool? Lost in my own despair?*

I blink, and find myself back in the room with Xander.

I immediately set my plan into motion. I sit up in bed, breathing heavily. Xander, ever the light sleeper, wakes.

"Hey, you okay?" he asks, voice dry.

"No," I murmur. "Xander, I think I'm going crazy."

"Ian, don't say that," he mutters. "You just had a dream or something."

I look him in the eyes and give him my widest, most manic smile. Then I grab a pair of scissors from the drawer of my bedside table and proceed to rake the blade in a vertical stripe down my forearm.

I laugh as the blood drips down and wets both me and the sheets. Xander watches in mute horror, his mouth agape. He snaps out of his stupor and fumbles with his glossY.

I feign fascination with my bleeding forearm, outwardly paying him no mind. All the while I listen intently as he speaks with an Emergency Services operator and explains the situation in rushed, anxious phrases.

I'd feel bad if Xander would remember this for the rest of his life. *But, of course, he won't.*

Soon enough, two campus guardians come through the door. I ignore them until they address me directly, their voices surprisingly gentle.

"Ignatius," one of them says, "can you come with us?"

* * *

They first bring me to the nurse to stop the bleeding. She doesn't detect anything suspicious about me, which is good, considering her questions last time I visited her office. She heals me up and sends me on my way to one of the school's on-hand psychiatrists. I recognize the doctor's name from the list of counselors I'd been offered in the first school loop iteration.

I tell him that I'm surprised I haven't already been brought to a hospital or other institution. Didn't slitting my wrist vertically imply I was trying to kill myself, or had that been too subtle?

He gives me a warm smile. "Ignatius," he begins, "you weren't trying to kill yourself, were you?" His question sounds more like a suggestion.

I shake my head. "I was definitely trying to kill myself," I reply. "I'm still feeling quite suicidal, to be honest."

His face remains frozen in a calm smile. "You have no history of mental illness," he remarks. "And your roommate claims you were acting fine up until this morning." He crosses his arms. "Did something happen?"

I shake my head. "Nothing at all."

The psychologist sighs and shakes his head, letting part of the facade drop. "If you're serious, then we're going to have to send you home to recuperate. Campus policy. So close to finals period, this might seriously impact your ability to graduate on time."

I nod. "I couldn't care less about finals right now."

Of all the things I've said, that seems to concern him the most.

"I believe you," he says, giving me a level look. I can practically hear his unspoken thoughts: only someone actually ill would go home willingly just before finals his senior year.

Or, I think, *someone with nothing to lose.*

They transport me back to my house through the campus's transport array. It's typically only used by the wealthier practitioner students, so I'm flattered that the school chooses to send me through one. I've never taken a transport array before, so I approach the experience with curiosity, inspecting the glowing array inscriptions. Two guardians lead me up to the inscribed platform—a hexagon of slate gray.

"Remain still. Do not exit the transport platform."

A scarce five seconds later, the world flashes before my eyes, and my stomach flips. I'm overwhelmingly disoriented and nearly fall off the transport platform. When I look up, I realize that I'm in a different room than before, a cavernous structure filled with people and a series of equally spaced transport arrays.

This should be Jupiter's Center of Commerce.

I nearly drop to my knees when I see the form of a woman off in the room's corner. She's waiting to receive me, bleached hair hiding her face from my eyes.

"Mother," I whisper. It feels like it's been an eternity, but she looks the same. *Of course she would*, I think, berating myself. Time stands still in the loop. She's even wearing the same shawl that I last saw her in.

When she finally turns her head toward the transport platform, her hair parts and reveals her face. I see a small, gleaming drop of water at the corner of her left eye, but she's smiling as though excited to see me.

I take deep breaths to calm myself.

Mother has always been the focus I use to keep myself going. The pale image of her face in my mind is suddenly renewed by the live woman before me.

Why am I like this? I wonder in exasperation. *After everything I've been through, why is it that I can't move on? Am I that empty, that pathetic?*

"Ignatius," she calls out, walking toward the platform. The pair of guardians arranged to receive me escort me to her side, obviously watching for any sudden movements on my part.

"I've missed you," I murmur.

"Come along," she mutters, gesturing to the guards. "Let's get you out of this place." She sounds every bit the concerned parent.

She strides to a petite hovergloss, a basic variant with a clear, domed top and a heavy plastic underbelly. The guardians resist, arguing that Mother was supposed to be accompanied by a doctor to take me into custody.

"The doctor couldn't come," she replies, her voice decisive enough to cut metal. "I'll be taking him home. I've already collected his medication, so all he needs is rest and his family."

With that, she practically yanks me from the guardians' hands, pulling me by my shirt and into the hovergloss. When the glass lid goes down and seals us in from the outside, she shoots me a serious look.

"Whatever you're pulling, it's going to land you in trouble," she observes, blue eyes severe. "You've never been good at playing games."

JUPITER

The hovergloss locks onto the city's skyrail and glides forward. After the initial acceleration, it hardly feels like the hovergloss is moving at all; only the flashing of buildings and streets signals our rapid advance.

"I'm not playing at anything," I say. "I'm just...done."

"Done," she repeats without inflection, her mouth thinning. She rolls her eyes.

"Done," I repeat, crossing my arms. I feel the ebb and flow of vitality around us as we pass over rush-hour traffic.

"If you're done, what are you going to do about it?" she asks, staring deeply into my eyes, demanding my attention.

"Do about what?"

"You tell me."

I inhale deeply. "Mother..."

"You're clearly 'done' with something, Ignatius," she says softly, voice intense, eyes captivating and predatory. "What?"

"School."

"Why?"

"It's pointless, isn't it?"

Her face doesn't change. "No, it isn't," she responds. "It gets you a job."

"Why do I even want to get a job? Besides, you're the one who was so against me studying glossy programmatic in the first place."

Though I'm working to control my facial expressions to maintain a collected exterior, my heart is racing. I'm here, with Mother, talking to her.

For the first time in years, I actually have some sense of security. Even if the loop resets, the her of this loop is the same Mother I've always known—a flawless copy. Of anyone in my life, it's her that I trust most to help me sort this mess out. I don't plan to tell her about the loop and myself, of course—she'll never believe me without proof, and proof could reset the loop. But I can ask her other things.

"You want a job," she begins, "because without one you're nothing but a waste of space."

I laugh. "Why do I *really* want a job?"

"Because power is the only thing that matters," Mother replies, voice scathing. "And real power is something you don't have."

"What do I want to use power for?" I drawl, looking out at the bay peeking through the skyscrapers. "Why not live in isolation somewhere far from society?"

This is a mildly serious question; it's something I've been considering on and off for when I escape the loop.

"You're awfully argumentative today," Mother says, snorting. "It's because power exists to be used. And if it's not used willingly, well."

"Well, what?"

"Its use will be forced. Or it might just be destroyed."

"What do *you* want power for?" I ask. I stare at her expectantly, hands folded neatly over my lap. I know all about Mother's unfulfilled ambitions.

Her mouth twists into a frown. "I want to destroy this wretched city."

"Why?" I breathe. *But I know why.* Her single-minded purpose sends a shiver down my spine. *She wants to kill Vanderlich. She wants him and his tower to burn.*

"Because it is just," she responds, eyes steely.

"What then? After?"

"Nothing."

I blink.

"The best kind of goal is one that is simple," she replies, leaning back and closing her eyes. "I live to see Vanderlich die. I don't need anything more out of this life to be happy."

She's telling the truth. *She doesn't need me to exact vengeance for her.*

"What happened to your direction, Ignatius?" Mother asks, eyes still closed. "You were going to get a degree and join a company. A pathetic life, but a life, nonetheless. Better than no degree at all."

"You're right," I say. "I need something more. Something better than working for a company."

One eye snaps open. "You're too pathetic to reach for anything higher."

I chuckle. *Mother can be so...draconian.*

"Do you really mean that?" I know she does. Mother always says what she means. The me before the loop would have verified, however, futilely hoping that she'd take her words back.

"Yes."

"Isn't it pathetic to live your life for the sake of revenge?" I ask. I've always admired her for her resolve and devotion to Vanderlich's downfall, but seeing her now, saying that the only thing she needs to do in her life is carry out his death...it's more disappointing than I could have anticipated.

"It all depends on who you're taking revenge against," Mother replies, sitting up and giving me a serious look. "If a nobody like me dies to kill Vanderlich, I'd call that the worthiest of trades. If he dies killing someone like me, I'd call that the most pathetic of failures."

I think to myself for a moment. "What kind of goal is fitting of someone like Vanderlich?"

"Men like that no longer have goals beyond self-preservation," Mother spits.

"What if he tried to kill...?"

"We're home," Mother announces. "There's something wrong with you, and I'm going to find out what." She exits the hover-gloss, dragging my hand behind her in a vise-like grip.

* * *

Our building is, unsurprisingly, as I remember it: decaying, ornate, and palatial. The roof is spangled with crenellations, and a weathered, half-destroyed gargoyle grips onto the left wall, its head and wings replaced by curling ivy. While my great-grandfather owned the entire property, we now only hold title to a small sliver of the mansion-turned-multi-family-home.

Mother takes in the looming structure with a huff and leads me up the stairs by the hand like I'm an unruly child. The mansion has one door that opens into a gloomy hallway, its candelabras lit by undying flame. It's a luxury that the mansion inherited from its past—if the flames ever extinguish, I can't imagine the landlord replacing them with anything other than low-cost glow lamps.

We traverse the hallway, the floral designs on its dank, blood-colored carpet sinister in the low light. Mother pulls a key from her coat pocket and finesses it into the lock made finicky by age. After jimmying the key around a bit and twisting the knob, the tumbler catches, and the door creaks open.

She tugs me forward into the house as though I either don't know the way or am moving far too slowly for her liking. I shake my head and follow her lead, keeping with her aggressive pace.

"If you hate this place so much," I begin, "why do you still live here?"

As I wait for her response, I feel the energy of death circulating around the property. There used to be a private graveyard in the back, which I knew about and expected, but there are also several bodies buried under the property and one, suspiciously, stashed in one of the residences.

"It's the best property for the price," she snaps. When Father made the choice to sell the mansion before his untimely death, he did so only after securing a fifty-year agreement from the landowner to pay utility costs for the building, including our own privately owned sliver.

"But you hate it," I retort. "We have the money. We don't need this place." I gesture to the peeling wallpaper. Free utilities aren't worth Mother's angst.

After climbing another set of stairs, we reach the door to our house. Mother had our personal lock replaced a few years ago, so the key slides in without issue, and she unlocks the portal with a sharp twist of her fingers. The room is long and thin. A rectangular table spans its center, while an antique and cloudy mirror stands off in the corner next to an equally antique (and chipped) dresser. A patterned carpet lays across the floor, an heirloom of the past. It's too big for the room and curves up into the crown molding but is in pristine condition. I think Mother would rather die than let her 'priceless' rug fall into disrepair.

"What happened to Zefur?" I ask. I can't feel her vitality anywhere.

"Dead," Mother states, face devoid of emotion. "I wasn't planning to tell you immediately, given"—she gestures to my entire body—"the fact that you're back for *mental health* reasons, but since you asked, I'm not going to lie."

"How?" I ask. Zefur had only been six.

She shrugs off her coat and peels off her black heels. "Ate rat poison."

How unfortunate. I really missed Zefur. "What did you do with her body?" I know I'm not going to like the answer when I ask. I haven't detected a cat's corpse anywhere nearby.

"I threw her out with the trash," Mother replies. "What did you expect me to do? We don't own the backyard." She looks away. "I liked the cat too, you know. But it died, and I needed to get rid of it."

I sigh. No chance of getting the body back, then. But she's right: there isn't really anywhere else for her to put a dead animal but the trash.

I settle into one of the seven chairs along the dining room table, kicking off my shoes and draping my coat on its high back.

She joins me, sitting in the chair to my right, leaning up against the back and letting out a tired groan. "When you're old, your back is going to hurt too, you know."

"What have you been doing?" I ask. Her life is a series of schemes, circles within circles of deceit. Being in the loop and having to lie all the time has finally given me an awareness of how *exhausting* her life must be.

"Settling the accounts of Johann Orlief," she says.

"Why?" I lean into the table, clasping my arms on the wood. "How is he connected to Vanderlich?"

"Cousin," she answers. "A third cousin, but a cousin, nonetheless. He sees Vanderlich every so often, and sometimes, he does business for him."

"So, then. What's the end-game?"

Mother's eyes darken. "I plan to eventually work for his rival, Vanderlich's brother, Liam."

I shake my head. How could one family have business competition within itself? The wealth of the Vanderlich and extended family empire... Just thinking about it leaves a bitter taste in my mouth. Mother has beaten disgust into me like a reflex.

"Good luck with that," I say, voice hard though genuine.

As I take in her tired form, her wrinkles and creases, her declining vitality, and her worn-out cartilage, I feel pity wash over me. Though Mother is by all accounts a fairly brutal parent, I can't deny that I care about her.

"If Vanderlich were to die tomorrow, what would you do?" I ask.

"I would destroy this city."

"If the city burned to ash, what would you do?"

She gives me a cool look as though daring me to contest her. "I'd burn with it. If everything burns, why should I be the exception?"

I look away and roll my eyes. She believes what she's saying, but Mother has always been dramatic. If push came to shove, I doubt she'd really throw her life away so easily.

I have the sudden, unbidden impulse to give her what she wants. Even if it means restarting the loop, I'd only have to redo Menocht. I might never have the chance again: I wouldn't have the will and hatred needed to actually raze Jupiter to ash outside of the loop.

But...it could be a fun challenge, I muse. *Destroying Jupiter without triggering a restart.*

* * *

I settle into my room and change into an old pair of casual clothes. Thankfully, I won't have to wait long to receive my current wardrobe: Academia Hector said it would send over my belongings in the next twenty-four hours for pickup at a transfer station. I stare into the mirror, adjusting my collar and combing back my hair with a hand. I detect the slightest trace of faded energy on my bed—likely the place where Zefur died.

I fall onto my comforter, my head resting next to the darkened spot. I envision her in my mind, little Zefur...if there was more vitality to work with, I'd try and form it into a soul gem. Unfortunately, what's left of her is akin to the dust upon my dresser—thin and easily swept away.

After a moment of reflection, I head out the door. If I'm back in Jupiter, I might as well walk around the city a bit before I destroy it.

Mother's still sitting at the table when I emerge. "Where are you off to?"

"Nowhere in particular."

"I still can't figure out what you're planning," she admits. "Something must have changed for you to come home like this, though I sincerely doubt it's anything related to your supposedly attempted suicide."

I raise an eyebrow, pulling down my shirt sleeve. "You don't think I was serious when I made this?"

"You're too much of a coward to invite an early end," she says dismissively. "Besides, I was told that you cut yourself right in front of your roommate; you were never in any danger. This outcome was exactly what you wanted, but for the life of me, I can't understand what you have to gain." She shakes her head, lips curling into a slight grin. "Feel like sharing your plot with Mother?"

"*I* still can't figure out what I'm planning," I reply with a chuckle. "I might tell you, someday, when I know."

She gives me a wry smile. "I can appreciate you trying to be secretive, for once." She yawns. "Maybe you're finally learning. Or not."

I grab my coat as I swing past the dining table and open the front door. "I'll have dinner on my own," I call out from the threshold. Mother grunts in acknowledgment, and I close the door.

Soon enough, I'm out in front of the house. As I'm considering where to go, my train of thought is cut off by the sound of a familiar voice. *As if I could forget Vasil's obnoxious baritone.*

On a whim, I decide to give the watchers a small spectacle.

"Vasil," I call out, turning around. "Long time no see."

He sneers and straightens up at my calm demeanor.

"You're back," he says, folding his arms. "I can't say I'm surprised you faltered before the end. You made it three years, but..." He shrugs. "So close, my friend. So close."

I roll my eyes. "University is a waste of time."

His eyes narrow. "For you, maybe. If *I* went, I'd actually make something of myself."

Oh, Vasil, you can't even pass rudimentary math courses. Vasil is one of those people who is mean and bitter at the world because he hates himself. I have a better sense of what he feels, now. Menocht has, in many ways, forced me to confront my fears and flaws. But rather than turn me mean, Menocht has made me distant. Numb.

"Maybe I can help you," I say, smiling thinly.

He snorts and takes a step forward, puffing himself up like a lion. "Shut up, Ian," he bellows. "Like you could—"

I freeze Vasil in place, seizing control of his bones so that they remain stationary against his struggling muscles.

"Vasil," I say, false concern saturating my voice. "What's wrong?"

Vasil topples over, pupils constricting with fear.

"Let me help." I run over, dropping to my knees. I place a hand over his heart. "Oh, poor Vasil..." His heart jumps like it's been shocked by thunder. A shrill whine escapes his throat.

Noticing that he's trying to speak, I relax the bones in his jaw.

"Who are you?" he shrieks. "You're not—"

I seize the bones in his jaw, closing his mouth.

"Shh," I gesture. "Quiet, now. It's just me. Ian." I relax his jaw again, then give him a look.

"Of course," he replies hoarsely, his eyes filled with fear. "Yeah, Ian. Okay."

I smile to myself. Still no restart, and it seems like Vasil believes me to be an imposter, giving me leeway to act out of character.

"This city has pushed you down at every turn, Vasil. How would you like to push back?"

His eyebrows furrow. "Push back?"

"Can you do a few things for me? Hmm?"

"S-sure. Yeah, anything."

I give him a calculating look and caress his neck with a finger, tracing his carotid artery.

"Bring me to your brothers."

HOLLOW VENGEANCE

In retrospect, Jupiter was appallingly easy to destroy. Menocht Bay is a much sturdier city, equipped with cannons and a well-funded defense system. I failed to take into account that Menocht Bay is in a more dangerous part of the world, where outlaw practitioners ride around in naval vessels, periodically returning to the shore to raid for goods. Moreover, the Illyrian Ocean spawns all manner of creature from its depths, forcing coastal settlements to maintain defenses year-round.

Contrastingly, Jupiter is safely nestled in the highlands of Solar, framed by mountains and overlooking a calm lake. It's an elevated city, meaning its mass is predominantly buoyed by antigrav generators tapping into the magnetic ore under Lake Cyprus. Two hundred mighty legs, hundreds of feet in length, add greater stability, anchoring the city into the earth along its ovular length. Once, its stark white columns and obelisks reflecting over the lake perhaps evoked the sentiment of cutting-edge progress. A hundred and fifty years after its construction, it lags behind, lacking many basic protections standard in most elevated cities today.

The story of Jupiter's demise isn't particularly dramatic. After intimidating Vasil, I followed him to the den of youthful depravity known as Siren. I hadn't known much about Siren before Vasil brought me to its house, including the gang's name; I only knew that Vasil was involved in something illicit enough to pay for a large suite in our old mansion and that he often invited over 'Brothers' to partake in drug-muddled debauchery.

At least we live above Vasil's dwelling, or we might never get any sleep.

Siren's lair is a bit off the beaten path, located in the underhang of one of the city's support legs. Seedier buildings and stained pavement make for a fitting backdrop.

As I followed Vasil, I felt the graying vitality of the zone's inhabitants, as well as the darkened stains of death outside, spattered like oily paint over the patchy and overgrown grass. It didn't take much for me to stop everyone cold where they stood in the manner that I froze Vasil, locking their bones and muscles.

I was tempted to elevate the intimidation factor by wearing a mask shaped from bone fragments buried outside, but I kept the impulse in check. Holding people's bones in place leaves very little decemantic signature and mostly relies on the strength of my will rather than any actual energy exertion. By comparison, animating and shaping bones is far less subtle.

After seizing everyone's attention, I convinced the group to help me sabotage the antigrav generators. While they initially protested the motivation of such a plan, and what they'd get out of it, it didn't take more than a few minutes of squeezing their bones to get them to see the light. That, and I promised to help them steal the reactor engine inside the grav generator. That made them *much* more cooperative.

I wasn't content to stop with just Siren: their numbers wouldn't be enough for what I had planned. I ordered its members to bring me to other gangs, coercing four such groups to join our noble cause.

I think many of my recruits actually came to see our cause as noble, in a rebellious, stick-it-to-the-man kind of way. Vasil seemed especially in love with the idea of pushing back against the city that worked so hard to push him down. I like to think that his fervor arose out of pride for being my first follower.

The attack itself went smoothly. "Coincidentally", a critical mass of guards and janitors became incapacitated over the fifteen days leading up to the incident. I didn't anticipate that by the time I'd acquire the security keys to the generator room and seed a team of gang members into the building as temp replacements, I would inadvertently stir a revolution among Jupiter's under-classes.

Long story short, I destroyed the city's gravity generator in one of the more convoluted ways possible, and I managed to stay in the loop.

Since I destroyed the city, Mother and I have been taking refuge in the nearest town, putting ourselves up in a cheap motel. She's been despondent as though she isn't sure what she should do now that the city's crashed and sunk partway into the lake.

I was surprised at her reaction when the city jerked to the wa-ter's surface, its legs buckling one after the other under the strain of Jupiter's full weight. As we evacuated with the other citizens, I expected her to be happy, vindictive: the object of her hateful obsession, along with the property holdings and wealth of her nemesis, was sinking into the cold lake. It wasn't the fire-and-brimstone-like ending she probably wanted, but still, it was the *justice*—revenge—that she dreamt of daily.

Instead, her eyes were hollow, her hands white and shaking. I guess this ending wasn't what she wanted after all.

I remember asking her, "What's wrong? Angry you didn't de-stroy the city yourself?"

She seemed unable to respond, her eyes fixated on the city as it split down the middle and sank in twain, most of its legs having already collapsed.

Now, as we sit in an unfamiliar room, I ponder whether it's possible to fix Mother again. She ruined herself in her thirst for vengeance. Though she claimed that reaping revenge would be enough to leave her satisfied, I don't think she ever expected to actually *win*—her revenge was an unattainable goal that kept her ticking.

I spend the rest of the month helping her cope with the loss of her everything: her home, her community, and her ambition. When I'm greeted by the darkness of the loop's next layer, I sigh my relief into the stale air.

SWORD

As I make my way through the layers, Mother's empty gaze lingers with me. The adventurous enthusiasm I had the first time around has worn off, and I slog sullenly through the scenarios on my way to the Godora command layer. Even when it comes time to sever my own arm to use as a rotating drill, I barely flinch. No longer panicked by the shock of a claustrophobic buried-alive scenario, I dull my nerves and sever my arm with a painless gesture of my other hand.

While it taxes my body even more, requiring more Death energy, I find that I can keep the dismembered limb alive, reattaching it and recovering full motor faculties as I leave the wooden crate. The key is to insulate the wound site from Death energy, slowing permanent damage. Also important is not stripping the flesh from bone like I did the first time. The reattached limb initially felt a bit funny, but it was nothing a bit of carnimancy couldn't fix.

When I return to the Godora command layer, I proceed with far more caution than before. This time, instead of dealing with the terrorists personally, I keep my distance in a hovergloss, sending in two teams of fire and water elementalists: fire to resist and shape the power of an inevitable explosion, and water to contain and neutralize it. The original recommendation was for fifteen water elementalists, but I think my two seven-person teams make more sense.

My gaze is sharp as it peers out the window and into the surroundings. Suddenly, an earth-shaking boom resounds. My two elementalist teams, having been alerted to the possibility of an explosion by yours truly, return to their hovergloss unscathed. The sand, scorched and crystallized by the contained fire, is the only casualty of the fight.

I clear my throat, then lead everyone back to HQ to discuss strategy against our western invaders. When I get back, one of my subordinates passes me a report with more details on the attacks. The document presents conclusive evidence that practitioners of Dark and Cloud enabled the terrorists to enter the country undetected. It also points out that any attempt to address the threat will require us—that is, the government of Godora—to at least *attempt* formal communications with the Selejo Prince's Union (SPU).

I frown at the missive. I'm not particularly familiar with Godora or the SPU, but I recall that they had a bloody war two decades ago. While tensions have faded, I can't imagine the two countries are on good terms. I wouldn't even be surprised if the terrorists were *supported* by the SPU. If the SPU was behind the attacks, *talking* to the SPU about them wouldn't be helpful. And even if the SPU *wasn't* behind the attacks, it has no incentive to offer assistance.

In short, the report doesn't seem to have any idea how to address the current situation.

* * *

I lean back in the chair of my quarters, trying to figure out what I'm supposed to do to escape this layer of the dilation loop. A pen and a pad of paper lay at my otherwise spotless desk; sunlight from the window dapples the imported oak and draws out its red hue.

I start to think back on what I've learned since entering the loop. Despite my own research, I've never heard of a dilation loop with the ability to create such a vivid and long-lived simulation. "Moreover," I murmur under my breath, "I'm convinced that I'm *not* the first person to ever use this loop technology." It's oddly refreshing to voice my ideas out loud rather than just keep them in my head. I pause for a moment, thinking of ways to justify my observation.

"The simulation is too polished to be in an alpha stage of development. Others must have tested out the technology to help refine it, at the very least."

A sudden thought comes to mind: is it possible that I signed up for this damned loop and just don't remember it?

"It's true I don't remember where I was and what I was doing before waking up on the dinghy," I concede. This thinking leads me down a new path of inquiry: the design of the loop. *Fundamentally, what is the purpose of the loop?*

I write down *Purpose of Loop* on the first line of the notepad page. Before I escaped Menocht, I theorized that the loop was a kind of torture, a stage of hell where people relived a nightmare over and over again.

But it's clear there's more to the loop than the psychological torment it's put me through. The watchers, whoever they are, they've been trying to forge me into some kind of weapon. I'm sure of it. After all, when I finally break out of this loop, they'll have *me*.

Though it's presumptuous to assume that I'll willingly cooperate.

But assuming that the purpose of this loop is to awaken and hone my decemancy...I can think of a few key questions.

The first loop layer was wholly sufficient to awaken and hone my affinity. Since that's the case, why am I forced to endure these other layers?

Moreover, I think caustically, *if I were developing a loop with the sole intent of developing someone's affinity, I would include a case releasing the looper in the event that their affinity reaches a certain threshold.* Or, alternatively, if the looper never made any progress at all.

And it's impossible that I've failed to meet an affinity threshold: I've developed 100% Death affinity within the margin of error. It's important to note that perfect affinity is impossible to obtain. As far as I know, affinity approaches an asymptote around one hundred percent.

"So there must be something else," I murmur. Something this loop is supposed to do aside from solely develop my power as a practitioner. There has to be some way to explain why I haven't yet escaped the loop.

I cover the notepad page with my rhetoric and conclusions, pausing before standing and walking towards the room's entrance.

"I'm heading out to get some fresh air," I explain to the two guards bookending the door. They stare at me, then give crisp nods. I stride forward into the hall, admiring its open corridors and classical columns. The compound is half exposed to the elements, probably because of year-round high temperatures and the abundance of hydromancers on-site to prevent water damage. Tropical is a welcome change from the temperate lands bordering the Illyrian Ocean.

As I begin my walk, I notice for the first time just how *busy* the compound is. Uniformed personnel are swarming around in groups of two and three, likely spurred to action by the attacks. They give me a fair bit of distance—I'm not sure if it's because of my rank or because they know that I'm a peak-affinity dece-mancer.

A few minutes into the walk, my thoughts begin to wander once more. One point that comes to mind is how the watchers plan to get me to cooperate once I exit the loop. I can think of a few ways:

1. I really did sign some kind of contract before entering the loop—one that will kill me (or have other severe repercus-sions) if I break its terms. If a bunch of scientists contacted me about an experimental opportunity to unlock my affin-ity, I doubt I'd hesitate to hear them out, and if they gave me seemingly reasonable terms, such as, if the treatment is successful, entering into an oath to work for them for a cer-tain amount of time, I can see myself agreeing to it.
2. Blackmail. I'd probably go along with their demands long enough to ensure that nothing adverse happened to myself or my family.
3. The watcher organization has a persuasive justification for everything that's happened so far. I.e. it needed to unlock my affinity to accomplish an important task, one I also be-lieve in (though now have no memory of).

The only truly feasible option is the first. If the watchers had any inkling how powerful I would become, I doubt they'd decide to use blackmail to get what they want. They wouldn't want me as an enemy. And the third option? If I were them, I'd still just go with option number one, unwilling to leave something as crucial as voluntary cooperation to chance.

"I need to prepare for when I get out," I mutter. Taking out my glossY—a similar model to the one I have in the school loop layer—I look up binding contracts on the distributed network, such as the life-death oath that Jasmine made when I entered her office. There are a few different contract options, ranging from the most severe (life-death) to low-severity collateral oaths.

The life-death oath is fairly simple: if you break the terms of the oath, you'll die. Thankfully, most oaths also have safeguards to prevent accidental oath-breaking. For instance, if you take an oath for patient-client confidentiality, and you are about to disclose confidential information, it will initially prevent you from doing so. More than that, usually there will be some physical indicator of imminent oath-breakage as well, such as a red chain appearing around the neck.

Thus, it takes deliberate will to bypass the oath's safeguards and break its terms. It's still possible to do so, though, in the event that the oathbreaker values their life less than breaking their oath.

Collateral oaths are probably the most common kind of oath. They work like life-death oaths, except rather than using the oath-taker's life as collateral, physical objects are used instead. For instance, breaking the oath might result in the destruction or transfer of property.

There are a few more specific kinds of oaths, but they all work in the same general manner.

The key question that I'm mulling over is: would I have agreed to a life-death oath? I feel confident that I can handle the loss incurred through just about every other type of oath. Moreover, I would likely be able to secure the services of an End practitioner to get any outstanding oaths broken by force...all except for the life-death oath with its unbreakable bond.

I would've been wary of signing such a serious oath. But it's possible that if the terms of the oath *seemed reasonable*...

I sigh as I search the Distributed Network for any information about people who have escaped their life-death oaths. I figure there have to have been some people, especially considering the varied abilities of practitioners.

I'm mildly astonished to find that there actually *is* someone who got out of their oath.

Dorel Lemon escaped from her life-death oath around sixty years ago, during the Minoan war between Kester and Corneria. A native to Northwick, Corneria, Lemon was apparently sent to Kester, serving as a Light-affinity healer on the Gnoste battle-front...for the other side. Lemon was a spy.

Lemon was ultimately caught and subjected to a mandatory life-death oath requiring her to work as a double agent. The terms were strict, leaving her no room to alert any superiors that she'd fallen under the influence of the enemy.

At the height of the Minoan War, she was tasked with feeding potentially disastrous intel to the Cornerians. Even if Lemon wished to break her oath, she'd only get a few words into a sentence before red chains would constrict her throat and asphyxiate her, growing increasingly tight around her neck. If she didn't die from asphyxiation, the chains would squeeze so tight as to crush her throat and cut through it altogether.

"...But she discovered a way to escape?" I read, annoyed. *What an insufficient description.* I read another paragraph ahead, but after that brief entry, the document steers toward her successful political career as a war hero.

I'm sure *many* people have 'prepared' to weasel out of an oath, but few (one on record) have actually survived breaking something so stringent as a life-death oath. There must be a trick to it—one that possibly died with Lemon.

As I continue my walk along the shore, I squint into the glare of the sun, low in the clouds, casting a golden haze in all directions. Seagulls croon from their perches atop a rocky outcrop framing the ocean to my right, while the shore stretches on endlessly to the left.

I take off my dress shoes with a contented sigh, leaving them by the grassy embankment bordering the path. I next roll up my trousers and deposit my military jacket on the ground, forgiving myself for soiling its perfectly pressed, spotlessly black surface.

Getting the jacket blown up is far worse than getting it dusty, right?

The sand is light tan and covered in all kinds of shells. Menocht is situated on a much rockier bay, bereft of the soft grains now squeezing between my toes. Menocht does have plenty of similar shells, but they're usually buried tens of feet underwater.

I try not to think of Dorel Lemon or the life-death oath as I walk along the shore, instead choosing to bask in the dying light and cool ocean breeze. *There's nothing else I need to do today,* I tell myself. Unlike the past few loop layers, I feel like this one will go on for a more extended duration. Perhaps not as long as the school layer, but it should persist at least a week or so until I figure out how to deal with the threat at hand.

I'm admittedly at a loss for how to proceed. I'm not the most social type, which is, of course, one source of Mother's lamentations. Sure, she's taught me all the knowledge necessary to fit into aristocratic society, and I can fake my way through most things sufficiently, but I never developed the finesse required to wield charisma to worthwhile effect. My actions speak clearly in that regard, considering the years stuck in the Menocht bloodbath.

"It's your own fault I'm so indecisive, Mother," I state wistfully, lips curling into a smile. Her deciding everything for me as a child couldn't be considered helpful.

"*Who?*" a voice says, oddly...synthetic.

I whip my head around. I don't sense any vital signatures nearby.

"*I'm here, er, sorry, sir. Here, on your waist.*"

My head snaps down. *What?*

"*Are you okay? It's just me.*"

I remove the scabbard from my waist and hold it up, inspecting the sheath. A Pardus panther logo stretches across its length, claws long and threatening, body sinuous and muscled.

I have a glosSword? Really? Is *that* what the Godoran military spends its money on? I've never seen one in person, the weapon rare outside of Ho'ostar and Sere, though I've heard that it's powerful. I recall reading about how its ban in Shattradan has been a sore point during the annual Fassari Summit, with Godora and Brin, in particular, protesting the allowance of similar energy weapons developed in the East.

"What's your model number?" I ask.

"You don't need to talk aloud," the sword responds.

How is it even responding?

"Just keep the scabbard close at hand. That's how I'm responding to you, by the way."

It's responding mentally? But it sounds just like someone's voice.

"You have the voice emulation module active," the sword adds. *"It makes for a more natural dialogue."*

Huh. "So...what exactly do you *do?*" I ask, intrigued by the seemingly intelligent blade.

"I am model number 300x, specializing in amplification."

I slowly draw the sword from its sheath. I note that the blade has an identical image of a panther across its length and that its blue translucent surface seems to absorb, rather than reflect, sunlight, blending in disconcertingly with the open sky. I don't know exactly what type of sword it is, but it seems to be of medium length, symmetrical with two sharp edges on either side, and a wickedly sharp tip. Just caressing it is enough to draw blood.

"Are there any practice grounds nearby?" I ask the sword. "The more private, the better."

"The closest is currently occupied by twenty-three individuals, with no other practice grounds within a ten-mile radius."

I raise an eyebrow, then look around the beachfront.

My decemancy seems to be accepted here; otherwise, I wouldn't be an officer, nor would I possess an expensive asset like the glosSword. It should be fine to do a little...*experimentation*, shouldn't it?

I step toward the rhythmic lapping of the tide, firm wet sand crunching beneath my toes. When I reach the water, my foot finds purchase on its surface. Well, it perhaps *looks* like that, but I'm actually just levitating. It's fun to think of it as walking on water, though.

By the time I'm fifty feet or so from the shore, I've channeled a good deal of power into the sword. Now instead of a matte sky blue, its surface is clouded by a dark nebula interspersed with violet specks of light.

"Yes, I do look quite badass, thank you," the sword states.

I glare at the shining blade. "I didn't think anything *close* to that."

"I'm almost charged," the sword announces, practically cutting off my response. Then, about fifteen seconds later: *"The next spell will be overcharged!"*

"How do I use you?" I ask, unsure of how to actually use the charged energy to amplify my own casting.

"Use me like you would any other focus," it instructs. *"And yes, I know that seems very simple! But you're in good hands with a model 300x like me!"*

I begin to collect bones and shells around me and am surprised to find that I'm able to reach much farther than usual.

"Your range is increased by the amplification effect," the sword volunteers, answering my question.

Next, I try bringing all the collected pieces together into a white mosaic above the water. It's not any easier to do so, nor is my control better, but I find the amount of energy required is less than usual.

"Approximately forty-percent of energy cost recouped!" the sword announces.

As I return the bones and shells to their original locations, I assess the utility of the device. Honestly, it's not bad. I'm not exactly desperate for greater range, nor am I ever in danger of depleting my energy stores...but it's nice to be more powerful than usual. It's overkill, but I've gone far past overkill at this point with my decemancy alone. I'll take all the power I can get.

"What else can you do?" I wonder out loud, turning the sword over in my hand. "Why are you so damned sharp if you're just a focus, anyway?"

"Ah, good question! As a glosSword model 300x, my added feature is amplification; however, I still come standard with all base model glosSword features as well." The sword pauses for a second before continuing: *"I see you're also unfamiliar with those features! Not to worry, a demonstration is in order. Hold me in your hands."*

I adjust my grip to hold the sword with both hands, rather than just one.

"Like this?"

"Your hands are the wrong way," the sword replies. *"The left should be behind the right for proper activation."*

What kind of dumb programming is this? I grumble to myself.

"The ordering of your hands is important to form the proper energy circuit. If you were left-handed, you'd have been issued a different sword entirely."

Fine. "Now what?" I ask, my hands finally in the right position.

"Now just use me like you would any other sword!"

Great advice, considering I have no idea how to use *any* sword at all.

"Ah, if you aren't a swordsman, even though your profile says you are, you can turn on one of eight auto modes."

Y'jeni, I'll just take the sword as an amplifier at this point. "What eight modes?" I sigh. "Is there some kind of instruction booklet I can read?"

"GlosSwords are highly regulated confidential weapons of intermediate destruction capabilities, and as such, any information available to the public is either basic or incorrect. That's why you have me, your weapon guidance system!"

"The *eight modes,*" I repeat, swirling some shells idly around myself. "What are they?"

"Detector mode, discrete mode, flight mode, auto-attack mode, aegis mode, sniper mode, defender mode, and companion mode!"

I frown. The last mode doesn't sound conducive to combat. "What's companion mode?"

"Companion mode uses fifty-percent of your energy to manifest an energy companion that acts independently of yourself, to be used with a soul gem. Energy amplification amount is diminished based on the distance of companion from the user."

I stare unblinkingly at the sword.

"So, what do you think?" it asks, seemingly proud of itself—if an inanimate object can be proud. It must've sensed my disbelief at the eighth mode. I can feel my heart hammering with anticipation.

"The eighth mode can use a soul gem?"

"Yes."

"Can any of the other modes?"

"No, only companion mode makes use of soul gems."

Unfortunate, but that only makes choosing which mode to use easier. "Can it use multiple soul gems?"

"It can use up to seven soul gems: two eye sockets, a heart socket, a liver socket, and three other sockets of your choice. The only mandatory option is the heart socket, with a minimum grade soul gem of high-grade. Auxiliary sockets can be filled by mid-grade

gems. Up to ten additional soul gems can be added with a battery pack extension."

I pause, tilting my head. I have a general sense of what soul gems are considered *good*, versus *bad*, but I don't have an accurate way to classify them by grade without a reference. I give the sword a moment to provide any relevant information, but it remains silent. I suppose it isn't an encyclopedia.

Instead, I take out my glossY and trawl through the distributed network for information on soul gem grades. I select the first source, a soul gem supplier I recognize even though I'm from the northern continent of Shattradan: Thakka Imperial Soul Gem Co., situated in the southern Adrilli Isles.

Soul gems are classified based on homogeneity and size. The most expensive soul gems generally come from a single powerful entity. These are homogenous (as they come from one creature), large (as they come from a powerful source), and are easier to market. It's also more glamorous to buy an elder rift dragon soul gem than a million-beetle soul gem, even if the latter is technically homogenous and large.

Thakka's page indicates that each soul gem must be individually appraised to ascertain its quality, however, due to the importance of a decemancer's respective animancy skill. But if even a low-grade gem goes for 4,500 auris...and a high grade for 25,000 auris...

Due to the glosSword amplifying my range, I can sense the presence of numerous aquatic creatures around me—most of them fish. I have a feeling that, despite the non-homogeneity of the individual fish, I'll be able to make a soul gem sufficient enough to create a glosSword companion.

I spread my arms wide, killing fish within my sensory range, then slowly bring my arms together. As I do so, I concentrate the Death energy into a deep violet soul gem, taking care to make the energy as uniform as possible for a clean crystallization process.

In twenty minutes, after distilling and re-distilling the energy, the gem is complete.

I turn to the glosSword hovering gently next to me and ask, "Is this soul gem sufficient to create a companion?"

"Scanning...soul gem of peak-high grade detected. Would you like to proceed in activating companion mode?"

I nod.

"Commencing mode eight!" the sword declares, its form soon engulfed in black radiance. *"Companion forming around gem. Please wait. Please wait. Please wait."*

I'm waiting.

"Please wait...please wait..."

It's been ten minutes at this point, and I'm impatiently tapping my foot on the water. Or would it be more accurate to say splashing?

"Please wait. Please wait..."

I scowl. *It would be bearable if it didn't say "please wait" every 10 seconds. Seriously, who programmed this thing?*

"Companion complete!" the sword suddenly announces, releasing a final flash of inky brilliance. I squint into the harsh light, unable to see anything but the glow of my soulstone within. As the light fades, I see the soulstone's violet pulse like a heartbeat through a network of nearly transparent, blue, square plates.

"It's a fish," I observe, deadpanning. "Am I stuck with a fish?"

"My soul gem is made of fish souls, so I am a fish companion?"

"Is that a question?" I reply, confused. Did becoming a companion make it less intelligent? "Can you become something else?"

"Do you? Have a vitality template?"

Curious, I decide to give the spectral fish a small sliver of my own vitality.

"Error — human vitality detected!"

Fine then, I murmur under my breath. "How about this?" I say, offering the fish the vitality of a seagull just plucked from the sky.

"Vitality signature accepted...transitioning...transitioning."

Not this again...

Two minutes later, the fish explodes in a shower of black sparks. In its place is a seagull made of similar blue plates with my soul gem at its center. It looks almost like an angular origami bird.

"So, what can you do?" I ask.

"I can do?"

I roll my eyes and smile. "Just...never mind." *The companion probably just needs time to develop*, I assure myself. At this point, the sun is low over the water, indicating that it's about time I return to the shore and collect my belongings.

The bird perches on my shoulder, its three-pronged feet digging in with surprising strength. *I guess we'll see what you can do.* I smile. *50% of my power is nothing to balk at.*

* * *

A week has passed, and I have nothing to show for it. I've mostly spent my days playing with the bird-shaped glosSword—descriptively named Bluebird—while waiting for the SPU ambassadors to arrive. There have been no new attacks, and the military base has functioned fine without my interference.

The ambassadors are slated to arrive any minute, hopefully breaking the monotony of the past few days. Maybe they'll have interesting intelligence to relay about the Godoran beach attacks; who knows?

My intuition, however, says that asking the SPU for anything is a waste of time.

I sense the ambassadors' arrival before anyone comes to alert me, the glosSword amplification feature proving its utility. The two ambassadors are coming by way of an armored hovergloss, escorted by six guards. It takes them a near eternity to arrive, their bulky hovergloss maintaining the minimum speed limit for the transit line. Seriously, what do they have on that thing to make it so heavy?

Bluebird, can you do a bit of investigating? I ask, giving the construct a soft pat on the wing. *Do a search for weapons.*

Bluebird darts off my shoulder in a flash, disappearing through the open window of my office. It only takes a minute for the bird to return, its violet eyes glinting in the midday light. At this point, I've outfitted Bluebird with seven soul gems, filling each of the spots with a peak-high soul gem: two for the eyes, one for the heart, one for the liver, one for each wing, and one for the tail. I found that with each soul gem, Bluebird's power increased by about 7%, compounding. So, 50% of my power with the first gem, multiplied by 1.07^6, is nearly 75% of my power. In practice, the number is slightly less, but I have a feeling that with prismatic soul gems, I'll be able to get Bluebird's power over 90%.

I wonder if the people watching this loop are terrified at the implications. I would be if I were them. One of me is more than enough to deal with, not to mention a version that looks like a paper seagull.

No artillery but eight explosives, Bluebird reports. *At these locations.* Bluebird relays to me a rough map of the hovergloss, along with pinpoint locations of the bombs stationed within it. It's impossible not to notice that the bombs are in very bizarre locations, such as in the air ducts and the waste tank.

I shrug. "Well, I guess we should do something about the situation. Maybe the SPU delegation can shine some light on what happened." I stretch my neck and shoulders, then stand up. "I'll go greet our guests myself."

INTERCEPTION

Like Bluebird, I decide to leave out the window to avoid alerting anyone to my absence—I can't rule out someone at the base feeding information to those controlling the explosives. While I'm not as fast as Bluebird—the little guy is at least twice as fast due to his small size and weight—I get to the hovergloss in under a minute.

Now, how to handle this delicately? I ponder, realizing that I'm not sure how to evacuate the hovergloss. From my vantage point one hundred feet away, I perceive six guards, two ambassadors, and an armored hovergloss. I give Bluebird a look, its violet soul gem eyes staring emotionlessly back. *Not going to find any help there.*

I have a feeling that if I do this poorly, I'm going to find myself quickly waking up on the dinghy. Explosives are no joke: Last time, I was taken out before I knew what was happening. Unfortunately, I don't have very long to think of a new plan. I'm loath to take Bluebird out of companion mode, but I think in this circumstance aegis mode might be a better strategy.

Bluebird, the defensive aegis mode...can you go into that right now?

"Switching modes will take fifteen seconds and require a twenty-second charging period. Commence?"

Do it. The defensive aegis is supposedly able to use up to one hundred percent of my energy to create a shield; it might keep me safe if one of the explosives goes off. I'm not sure how much energy is required to defend myself fully, nor do I have an exact metric by which to quantify my ability to draw Death energy. While decemancy doesn't naturally provide the best defense against sudden burst attacks, being able to funnel my energy into a shield like the glosSword aegis should offset that weakness.

Feeling slightly less vulnerable, I decide to go forward with the first plan that comes to mind: ripping the hovergloss's metal chassis with a few whirring blades of bone and extracting the people out the front of the hull. I have a few pieces of bone lining the inside of my officer's uniform, providing me with all the ammunition I need.

I send the bones out without delay, their slender forms whipping through the air like bullets. I begin to rotate them like spinning tops as they approach the hovergloss, allowing their empowered edges to cut through the hull like knives through butter. Before the hovergloss occupants realize the hull has been breached, I seize hold of their bodies and launch them out of the hovergloss.

When they realize what's happening, they begin to panic, muscles rebelling futilely against my control. The hovergloss continues unimpeded while I drag the contingent back to my location in the air until I use my bone shards to derail the car and hold it in place.

Soon, the party is close enough to me that I can send out the glosSword aegis around all of us.

I guess we're as safe as we're going to be.

"I have to apologize for the unfortunate circumstances of our introduction," I begin, addressing their unnaturally still forms. "I am Corona Dunai—the one who requested your presence here. It seems that you were all unaware that your hovergloss was filled with explosives."

I let the words sink in.

"I've taken the hovergloss off the rail. It hasn't exploded yet, obviously, but you can test it remotely for bombs if you doubt my honesty. Now, after finishing this sentence, I'm going to bring us down to the ground and relinquish my control over you; if you make any hostile movements, I'll control you again, so I'd advise against it."

I levitate us down gently. As I let my hold over their muscles relax, the two ambassadors keel over panting while the six guards groan and immediately take up a defensive position.

I smile. "Thank you for your understanding—that couldn't have been comfortable."

The ambassador with pale, yellow hair on the right speaks up: "It was certainly less than comfortable, but" —he pauses for a second, giving me an appraising look—"better that than dead."

* * *

The rest of the base was quick to respond to the bomb threat, swiftly isolating the hovergloss and sending in a team to disarm the bombs. While they did that, I took the ambassador party on a slow tour of the base.

Eventually, the ambassadors—Evelio and Yeka—are seated in cozy wooden chairs facing my own, their hands folded in their laps. They seem nervous, their movements twitchy and different from before.

"Getting straight to the point, do you have information on the group carrying out the Godoran coastal attacks? This room is warded against any listening devices, so speak freely." I have no idea if that's true, but it shouldn't matter. None of this is real.

"The attacks are likely carried out by the group Hashat, a cult of Dark and Cloud practitioners," Evelio says, his blond bangs sticky with sweat.

"What are their aims?" I ask. "I can't see too much point in blowing up our scenic coastline."

"That's just the thing; it's a bit of an embarrassment. For a group to have so many practitioners—"

Yeka gives his partner a scowl. "Slow down, there." He gives me a pointed look. "The cult believes that there's something...hidden off the Godoran coast. Some kind of *entity*, and they seek to empower it, awaken it. What Evelio means to say is that many of our society's elite have gotten *caught up* in this conspiracy."

I get it now. Every practitioner is valued and considered a national asset. The SPU would know if hundreds of them suddenly disappeared into a cult. That means Hashat is being run covertly, its members keeping their day jobs while committing acts of destruction on the side.

Now that I think about it, they did attack Godora on a weekend...

"So that's why the SPU is also interested in dismantling Hashat," I say. "Can't have a number of your elite romping around trying to awaken some kind of monster."

Yeka nods. "That's an unfortunately accurate summary of the situation. Essentially, what we ask of you is the ability to interrogate the captives and try them in our own courts. Our aim is to find the root of Hashat and shut the cult down."

"So you want us to catch the cultists...and just hand them over to you?" I'm not exactly an expert, but considering Godora's subpar relationship with the SPU, handing practitioner 'terrorists' over to their courts would be political suicide. "You must see why I can't agree to those terms."

Evelio smiles. "We understand your position. While in that case we won't be able to offer any assistance, do tell us if you change your mind. The only way to actually disrupt this cult, after all, is to cut it off at the base—something that can only be done from within the SPU."

I smile back. "It's been a pleasure talking. Now, I have other business to attend to, but while you wait for a replacement hovergloss, Secretary Schaeff can give you an extended tour of the grounds."

"That would be excellent," Evelio says, his eyes filled with palpable relief.

The two ambassadors still seem quite jumpy and unnerved. My eyes narrow as I ask, "With everything you've told me, I still have a question: Why were there bombs on your hovergloss?"

The ambassadors look at one another. "We...we honestly have no idea," Yeka says. "There's no point in killing us."

"It's also odd that the bombs haven't gone off yet," I observe. "Almost like they're connected to a remote trigger—one that has yet to be engaged. For some reason, I think that there's something you're hiding."

I only realize when Evelio swallows and falls backward that I've left my seat: I'm leaning aggressively over the table, my face less than a foot away from Yeka.

"Well?" I ask.

"We aren't powerful practitioners," Evelio sniffs. "It's in poor taste to intimidate us with your practice."

Intimidate them? With decemancy?

I lean back and stand up, arms planted on the table. "You're wrong," I say. "This isn't my *practice*. It's my *experience*."

They don't know how many times I tried to warn the Menocht people. How many times I tried to tell them, get them to listen, get them to do *anything* other than sitting around and letting their city turn to shit. I stopped trying to work with them years ago. You can tell them the city is going to fall in the next two days all you'd like, but they won't ever believe you.

I continue: "I've been on the frontlines of calamity for years. You don't think I've had to deal with my fair share of treacherous information brokers?" I think back to when I first made it to the city, after I learned how to take control of the cruise ship. I think back to the countless iterations that I stumbled around blindly, following false trail after false trail, often murdered for my curiosity.

"We really don't know anything about the explosives," Yeka spits. "I wouldn't have agreed to ride an explosive-filled hovergloss to diplomatic negotiations, even if I knew I wouldn't be caught in the blast. It's dishonorable."

Evelio clears his throat. "Moreover, it wouldn't have accomplished anything. Think about it: What would the SPU have to gain from sending a diplomatic envoy, only to attack in bad faith?"

They aren't wrong, but I do believe there's something they aren't telling me.

"But?"

The two are silent for a moment.

"This room, it's definitely soundproof?" Yeka asks.

"Yes," I state unhesitatingly.

He sighs and folds his hands. "We personally believe that whoever is at the head of this cult also holds a high place of power."

"Like who?"

Evelio replies, his voice like ice: "Like one of the twelve princes."

"Why do you think that?" I ask, intrigued. This is the kind of information I was looking for.

"They all *hate* each other."

Yeka gives Evelio a look. "That's ridiculous." He then turns to me. "Only *five* of them hate each other—the Prime of Fives, unsurprisingly."

"But I think whoever is behind the cult isn't one of the primes," Evelio protests. "Besides, you see how the princes treat one another during the council meetings. Though *some* of them get along—"

"Stop gossiping to the Godoran," Yeka snaps. "With all due respect, Corona, I think it's time we accompany your secretary. Be careful, and...thank you for taking us out of the hovergloss, even if your methods were uncomfortable."

I give the two a curt nod. "Secretary Schaeff is just outside the door. This meeting was more useful than I expected, so thank you for helping with my investigation. Have a good day, gentlemen." This isn't saying much, given my low expectations going in, but I really did get some good information.

I decide that it's time to gather information myself. If I play it safe and send professional spies, it might take months before obtaining any conclusive information. Besides, it's not for nothing that I'm a high-affinity decemancer. Thralling and diagnosty, while not my preferred specialties, are perfect for what I have in mind.

CHAPTER

20

SHADE AND LUX

I awake in a cold sweat, hand raised over my face, groaning as I sit up. Another nightmare, this one a rehash of the first one I had after waking in Academia Hector—a memory of the beginning.

My dreams haven't strayed back to the start of the loop for a long time. I feel for vital energy around me, suspecting that someone has been affecting my dreams.

Found you, I think, locking onto an unfamiliar energy signature on the roof. I freeze them in place, locking their bones in position. My living chamber is an open, breezy room whose one large window is covered by a sheer curtain enchanted with obfuscation. It should've been enough to keep my dreams interference-free.

I dart out the window and fly to the roof. There I see the source of the vital signature: an individual wrapped in dark layers of cloth such that few distinguishing characteristics are visible.

Hmm, what to do... I need to take this person somewhere secure for questioning, somewhere that won't invite meaningless attention. *But where?* My eyes scan the area around me, eventually settling on the reflection of the moon on the water. *Seems like the only private place in or around the base is the open ocean.* How ironic.

I walk over and place a hand on my captive, giving them a chastising smile. Then I take off, dragging them behind me through the air. I stop my flight above the ocean, creating a platform of shells to stand on two feet above the ocean's calm surface. Finally, I relinquish control.

They immediately keel over, panting and darting to the side of the platform.

"There's nowhere to go," I say.

"You..."

"How much did you see?" I ask. "Remorse practitioner, correct?"

The wrapped individual turns in place, seemingly uninterested in answering my questions.

I sigh. "You and I both know there's no escaping from here. Now tell me: How much did you see?"

"You think you're living in an illusion." From the timbre of the voice, I'm fairly certain the practitioner is a woman.

I spread my arms to the side. "Guilty as charged. But based on what you saw, aren't you the least bit curious to know whether I'm actually right?"

The practitioner sighs. "How could you be right? I'm supposed to believe that none of this"—she gestures towards the coastline— "is real?"

I nod. "Exactly."

"It's pointless to entertain that kind of presumption," she asserts.

"Believe what you want." Based on her indignant reaction, it doesn't seem like she got very far into my memories. If she saw me at my most powerful in Menocht, I don't think she'd be talking to me so casually after intruding on my dreams.

"Who sent you?"

"I won't tell you, and respectfully, I ask that you let me go. I'm not a member of Hashat, and I know you won't believe me, but I meant no harm by viewing your dreams. The two of us, I suspect, are working towards a common cause."

I take a deep breath. It's chillier than I would have expected; my standard-issue Godoran night robe exposes the rise of my chest to the ocean breeze.

"Look, I can be reasonable."

"Then let me go," she says, kicking her foot lightly on the column of shells.

I chuckle and shake my head, amused by the practitioner's stomp. "You violated my mind while I slept; I'm not just going to let you go," I point out. "But I think maybe you can give me something worth your free passage. If I'm not mistaken, you're someone's pet practitioner from the SPU."

"What makes you so sure?"

"You're too naive to be a mercenary."

"You—"

I silence her with a sharp *shh*. "I will soon be leaving the Opascal Base to take a diplomatic trip to the SPU. In one or two days, depending on when the final paperwork is approved." I assume she knows of this plan already if she really is an agent of the SPU.

"The purpose of the trip is, of course, to find more information on Hashat. From what you said before, I can infer that you're also in the area to investigate the cult's activities. What would your superior say about assisting me in my endeavors?"

"That is..." Half a second goes by; though the practitioner's face is largely covered by black cloth, her eyes narrow as though in consideration. "That is acceptable."

It suddenly hits me: Is it possible that this Remorse practitioner is currently in communication with her superior? That kind of communication channel isn't necessarily expensive or anything—it could be the same kind of quantum channel that

Jeremy established with Captain Conningway back in Menocht Bay—but what person has enough time on their hands to be up in the middle of the night, tailing their underling?

I shake my head, feeling as though the conversation brought with it far more questions than answers. "Then it's settled."

"Excellent. I'll deliver more information tomorrow—discreetly, of course."

I have no way of making sure she'll follow through, but I don't think I have any other options. I turn away, facing the moon. "What's your name?"

"Call me Shade."

Definitely not a pseudonym. "Sure. As long as you call me Iggy."

* * *

I wake up irritable and tired from yet *another* nightmare. I chuckle darkly at the absurdity: a nightmare within a nightmare.

I wash and dress, then I busy myself with the paperwork that unsurprisingly accompanies my last-minute decision to take a diplomatic trip to the SPU. My justification is sound, however: a foreign agent, likely from the SPU, tried to blow up a hovergloss on the grounds of this military base. Moreover, we are currently stonewalled with respect to our investigations on Hashat's plans and operations.

Rather than give the enemy time to continue plotting, striking while the iron is hot is a solid strategy—and it is one I plan to fully take advantage of. I'm also looking forward to working with Shade, though for my purposes, *working with* may as well mean *investigating* the woman's shadowy background.

In the spare time between meetings and doing paperwork, I give greater consideration to how I was in the past, before the loop.

Wasn't Xander always telling me to go and do things, like attend the winter formal? In the second pass through the school layer, I asked him about this point directly. He admitted that he had always suggested those kinds of things, but it was only very recently that I started to actually say *yes*.

If this loop is a test of some sort, or it's trying to turn me into some kind of weapon, it would make sense if it prioritized lessening my social anxiety. Likewise, learning how to hide my decemancy and acting like a typical regular are also no-doubt useful skills for post-loop life.

I pull open the drapes in my office window and peer out at the bustling courtyard below. Uniformed staff patrol throughout, carting documents, supplies, and water every which way.

I wonder where Shade is, and I imagine her hiding out in a secret cavern or in the northern foothills. More likely, she is taking refuge in a nearby town as a common traveler.

In the evening, I find a small note on my bed with an attached map of the nearby area. A small cave is marked and circled in red.

> *Come to this location at midnight tonight.*
> *-Shade*

* * *

I knew she'd be hiding out in a cavern, I think smugly as I reach the mouth of a small, partially obscured cave. Tropical foliage has overgrown around a few sheets of tapered stone that lead inside. I touch down a few feet from the entrance, breathing in deeply and savoring the area's saturated vitality.

It's no wonder necromancy, the spurned root of decemancy, first developed in equatorial regions: There's abundant life for the taking.

I sense two individuals inside, about thirty meters deep. *Shade and someone else—perhaps her contact from the previous night?*

Earlier today, I spent some time downloading a voice registry of officials and nobles in the SPU—along with their known subordinates—courtesy of the Godoran intelligence service. The glosSword's discreet mode *should* be able to use the information to identify people based on their voice. According to Bluebird, the discrete mode glosSword can disassemble to look like armor or jewelry while recording the surroundings from a minimum of 3 vantage points. I gently pat what used to be its hilt—now a thick chain on my belt—in encouragement.

I round a bend and find myself in a hollowed chamber, the rock face shimmering in the glow of a torch. Next to the torch are Shade and a masked individual, both sitting on small cushions. Between them is a thin, short table common to the Ho'ostar peninsula.

"Hello," I say, announcing myself.

Their eyes track me warily as I proceed forward.

"How did you find your way here in the dark?" Shade asks. "Lux would've sensed any light sources within the cavern."

I cock my head. "Light?" I flash my eyes violet for a moment. "I do fine without it."

"Decemancer," Shade's companion murmurs. "As you know, this is Shade. As for myself...you can call me Lux."

I smile in response. "And what are you, an elementalist?"

His eyes—the only part of his face visible—narrow. "You know that Shade has Dark affinity. Can you guess mine?"

I nod slowly. I actually hadn't noticed that Shade had a second affinity besides Remorse, but I'm not surprised. Based on Lux's name, I can venture forth a guess.

"Light affinity?" I ask. "An elementalist?"

"Light affinity is right, but I'm not a fire elementalist," he mutters.

I'm honestly not really sure what Light practitioners do. Aren't most of them elementalists?

"According to the Practitioner Basics guidebook, Light practitioners control the presence of radiance, just as Dark practitioners control the presence of void," the glosSword chimes in, answering

my unspoken question. *"Unlike Sun practitioners, the majority of Light practitioners have no talent for elementalism."*

"So, then, what skills do you have?" I ask, genuinely curious.

Shade shoots Lux what can only be interpreted as a withering look. "Just tell him." She looks back at me. "It's not like he'll need to use the knowledge against you."

Lux does half an eye-roll.

"I'm an illusionist," he says, arms crossed over his chest.

I blink. "Huh."

"What?"

"Can you make some kind of illusion now?" I glance at the torch. "Or is that an illusion, there?"

Lux shakes his head. "The fire's real. It gets a little cool in here without sunlight."

I nearly balk at his words. Even though this is a cave, its location is right on the equator. It's *hot.*

Maybe these SPU people are just used to this kind of heat. It's not the dry heat closer to the eastern coast of Godora, but that of northern Godora and the eastern SPU. In other words, wet, hot, and oppressive, even in autumn.

Lux makes a gesture with his right hand, and an orb of pure brilliance hovers over his palm. *"This* is radiance." The orb shifts and deforms, scattering. A moment later, a life-like bull paws the ground in front of me, its nostrils flaring.

"Understood," I say. "But why can I also *hear* the bull?" The sound aspect shouldn't be related to Lux's Light affinity.

"I also have Cloud affinity," Lux says, scratching his head.

"So you *are* an elementalist," I counter. "You use the wind to create sound waves?"

Lux sighs. "Something like that."

Now I turn to Shade. "I get his role in our operation, but what do *you* do?" I know that she's able to sneak around using her Dark affinity and that she is able to intrude in dreams using her Remorse affinity, but I know little else.

She smirks. "I go places I shouldn't, and I take things that shouldn't be touched. That about sums it up."

Nothing new there, but her skills seem reasonable enough. Not everyone has a vast portfolio of abilities like myself. My own experience gives me confidence in her ability to trespass and steal both physical objects and incorporeal intelligence.

I suddenly hear a small *click*. By now, the glosSword's discrete mode has recorded and analyzed about a minute of dialogue.

Have you discerned their identities? I ask nonverbally.

"Yes," the glosSword replies, its voice ringing in my mind. "*The one on the left has been subtly changing the sound of his voice and that of his companion. Nevertheless, the Pardus 300x's discrete mode comes ready with a sound-reconstruction suite!*"

My lips quirk. *So who are they, then?*

"*The one you think of as 'Lux' is Jairinka Selejo, the son of the eleventh prince of the SPU, and the one you call 'Shade' is the lesser noble Ajun'ra Iffis.*"

Hmph. A prince's son? Eleven isn't very high; not one of the Primes, I muse. *And the son of a low-ranked prince must not hold too much influence.* Jairinka's affinity doesn't seem weak, though; moreover, his Light and Cloud affinities complement each other well, amplifying their overall effectiveness.

Now, *Iffis*...I feel like I recognize that name. It was probably in some intelligence report.

"*House Iffis is largely in charge of the SPU's border guard, having historic claim to a long—but thin—strip of land up against the Ho'ostar river,*" the glosSword interjects.

Oh, I remember now. It was Iffis's office that agreed to clear me—and a small diplomatic entourage—to pass over the border between the SPU and Godora the day after tomorrow.

So: a Selejo and an Iffis. Both fairly powerful practitioners, and both working covertly to solve the Hashat problem. They must have their own motivations for wanting to take down Hashat. Otherwise, I can't imagine why they'd take the matter into their own hands.

I'll feign ignorance for now. "Lux and Shade, what is the plan to aid me in my investigation of Hashat? You must understand that as a Corona, my time is valuable, and to be seen cavorting with agents of the SPU is a serious risk."

Shade—Ajun'ra—nods to Lux—Jairinka. The young man gives her a look, but begins to speak: "We've prepared a list of people for you to meet when you arrive. Circumstances being what they are, we suspect that these contacts may be unwilling to share what they know with SPU officials such as ourselves. Anyone could be a member of Hashat, you understand. But to you, a Godoran Corona...I think they'll be willing to share more sensitive information."

It seems somewhat ridiculous that they intend to use a foreigner to obtain intelligence from likely high-ranking officials. Godora and the SPU definitely aren't *friends*—to involve a Godoran in an SPU investigation would have terrible optics. What are the other motivations they could have, if what they're telling me isn't true? Could it be a test of loyalty, using me to see which officials will spill the SPU's secrets to a Godoran?

I honestly can't think of a better justification than what they told me, though. If Hashat has members at high levels of political power, and Ajun'ra and Jairinka are two young officers tasked with dismantling the organization, they might be forced to resort to unorthodox methods.

"Are you allowed to meet with me?" I wonder, "or is this off the record?" I'm certainly not mentioning it to the Godorans.

Jairinka's pulse begins to increase. Ajun'ra takes the lead, saying, "We're in contact with a superior who has approved all of our interactions. Now, to return to speaking about the plan... Aside from the list of officials, we would like to rendez-vous with you on the night of your arrival. We may be able to cooperate to find Hashat while you're in Zukal'iss. Would you be able to sneak away to meet with us?"

Part of the purpose of this trip, at least from my end, is to try and find Hashat in the SPU. I was planning on sneaking away anyway—Jairinka and Ajun'ra helping shouldn't hurt, especially since they'll be familiar with the city.

"That is acceptable. How will you find me?"

"You're a Corona; you should have a glosSword. If you agree, we can connect a small tracker to your sword. To be clear, the tracker will remain with us, and won't tell us any information unless the sword establishes a connection to it."

"And what will that do, exactly?"

"It will allow us to find you; the tracker is like a compass." Ajun'ra holds up a small white sphere. Within is a single cyan dot at the center. "The tracking dot will press up against the sphere's wall to indicate your location; it'll even inform us if you're underground or in a tall building."

Is there any way to verify what they're saying is true? Connecting the glosSword to a tracking device doesn't sit well with me.

"The glosSword model 300x has a full suite of security functions to ensure resilience against adversarial technologies. If you connect to their tracker and I am compromised despite these protections, I will enter a locked-down state."

Perhaps if this was the real world I might still hesitate, but the risk sounds minimal enough to be worth the reward of having the assistance of two SPU officers. "Let's do it."

THE PALACE OF FORTITUDE

Since the meeting with Ajun'ra and Jairinka, I've been filling out a mountain of paperwork and preparing the Opascal Base for my absence.

I've also been working on familiarizing myself with the capabilities of the glosSword—and notably, its companion mode. Bluebird can shift from its avian form into the glosSword's standard blade, its soul gems automatically socketing themselves in the hilt. Moving between the two forms requires only a little energy from myself.

The best part about Bluebird is that it's able to use *my* power, functioning like an inferior, bird-shaped clone. Since its energy is taken directly from me or from soul gems, rather than filtered through the sword's internal energy source, Bluebird can carry out commands such as thralling or diagnosty. This allows it to covertly surveil an area without my direct interference. However, Bluebird can also complete tasks like propelling itself through the air or deploying non-Death-aligned energy missiles.

"How do you do it?" I mutter out loud.

"How do I do—"

"Shh," I say, cutting the glosSword off. The question was rhetorical: I know how the sword is using Death energy so flexibly. It mixes Death energy with pure, filtered energy coming from a generator built into the sword itself. It's obvious just from looking at Bluebird's abilities. They're somewhat muted, like something is diluting their decemantic potency, but rather than detract from Bluebird's power, the diluting energy gives the sword construct much more flexibility.

If a bird can do it, so can I, I think sourly, manifesting a globe of simmering energy on my palm. *If only I weren't so talentless in every other affinity.*

I think of the decemancer Sylvestri, a man who has both Death and Dark affinities. Though I didn't interact with him for very long, I don't remember him using the two energies together.

I tilt my head slightly, my eyes continuing to follow Bluebird as it swoops and darts through the air. *That's the point, though,* I realize. Bluebird isn't using *Dark energy.* It's using some kind of...null affinity energy. *Un-aligned.*

"How," I begin, feeling like I have a better sense of what to ask, "do you generate un-aligned energy?"

"A reactor," the sword-bird replies. *"Stored in a void chamber to deal with excess heat and its large size."*

I frown. "A what?" Reactor is too general a word to mean much.

"A natural, autonomous energy bank. A fusion reactor."

I frown. "So not like what's used to power cities, then?" Those, too, are often called reactors.

"No, it's not practitioner energy but natural energy. Energy from the world."

"Can I get one?" I ask. "How do you *obtain* a fusion reactor?" It must be built into the sword somewhere.

"They are quite easy to construct if you have a high-affinity team of Sun, Earth, and Moon practitioners, as well as Beginning and Regret practitioners. Three Sun, one Moon, three Beginning, and one Regret, ideally. And, of course, you need at least five masters of Dark spatial energy to anchor the reactor to a pocket dimension and a

Light-affinity fire elementalist to form a one-way energy transfer channel."

I swear the sword seems *smug* listing off all those requirements. Gathering a team of practitioners with the aforementioned qualifications is utterly prohibitive. Pardus—the company behind the glosSword—must be paying a fortune to keep such a team employed and steadily producing them.

"What else can the energy be used for?" I ask. "Can I draw out energy directly through you?"

"You are advised not to do so. The energy tether is configured to provide only the smallest trickle of power at any time. This trickle is smaller than what is perceptible to humans; if you try to draw on the energy, you may enlarge its channel, destroy the channel bindings, and take in enough energy to instantly incinerate everything within four meters, including yourself. Also, all my functionalities may be permanently destroyed."

I stare at Bluebird for a second. "Got it."

I'm tempted to give it a try, just to see, but my self-preservation wins out: It's not really worth dying and starting the loop over again, wasting a month or so on the school layer, and then redoing all the political finagling and paperwork I've done to plan this trip to the SPU to find the root of Hashat.

* * *

The SPU's capital city, Zukal'iss, is typically translated into Luxish as "New Hope." The name itself derives from an archaic, obsolete dialect of Swellish.

It's a fitting name based on my knowledge of the hawkish country. There's a reason why the *Selejo* Prince's Union lies just across the Bay of Ramsay from the *Selejo* continent-state, with relations between the similarly-named countries contentious. About 80 years ago, Selejo's kingdoms faced off against every form of natural disaster and plague. The rulers blamed the island of Koro for their woes but also didn't have the power to stop the endless storms or rampant disease.

Royalty from the fragmented Selejan kingdoms fled Selejo to preserve their own lives, quickly seizing Ho'ostar's northwestern edge before expanding out to fill half the continent.

Success in Ho'ostar didn't erase the fact that the rulers of Selejo had abandoned their people to die. Only five years after the rulers' exodus did the storms and disease come to a sudden halt. But the new Selejo returned with a vengeance, its fallen kingdoms reforming themselves into provinces under one despot: the Sezakuin. The woman had a personal vendetta against the newborn SPU, and the region was perpetually at war until her natural death seventeen years ago.

While Selejo rained hell from the north, the other kingdoms of Ho'ostar—Godora, Kyeila, and Brin—were also openly hostile, viewing the SPU's seizure of land as a declaration of war. Accordingly, for the past seventy-five years, the SPU has faced hostility on all sides.

Now the Sezakuin's daughter, the Eldemari, reigns over Selejo. Around the same time that she took control, Huron Selejo became Crowned Prime of the SPU. He's the one who brokered the current peace accords within the Ho'ostar peninsula and Selejo.

Unfortunately, since Huron's death twelve years ago, the peace has been fraying from all sides. And based on the growing militarization of the Bay of Ramsay, my intelligence officers believe it will soon end.

"Corona," a voice says from behind me. I take my eyes off the land beyond the hovergloss window.

"Yes?"

Secretary Schaeff's finger hovers over her glosspad. "What are the chances that the SPU's officials sincerely help us?"

If I didn't have the connection with Jairinka and Ajun'ra, I'd be more pessimistic. "The odds are low, but all we need is for one person on our meeting list to be sincere."

She frowns. "But if it's true that the primes are involved in Hashat...well, take the Crowned Prime as an example. He's able to use Regret to scry into the future and End to see threads of fate."

I nod. The SPU's first prince is lucky, having two high affinities and the resources to develop both.

Schaeff continues: "If he's connected to Hashat, he has the means to prevent us from getting the information we need."

"If he's connected to Hashat, we have bigger problems."

She bows her head, her brow still furrowed in concern. "Fair enough."

As the conversation dies, a question comes into my head: Would I defeat the Crowned Prime if we came to blows? I'm certain he would be unable to defeat me in a direct confrontation, but with his ability to see into the future...

I could theoretically kill and thrall the inhabitants of his city, creating an army of dead, allowing me to box him in and end him. Likewise, if the prince wanted me dead, all it would take was a well-placed suicide bomber—like those Hashat zealots.

Despite having such high Death affinity, I have to admit...it's easy to kill me with a surprise attack. I glance over at the glosS-word resting against my seat. *At least with aegis mode, I have some form of automatic protection.*

Three hours later, the hovergloss hums to a stop outside of a military convoy checkpoint. The plan is for us to disembark and then be led by SPU officials into Zukal'iss. Everything passes uneventfully, and within two hours of leaving the hovergloss, we are delivered to the steps of the Palace of Fortitude, Ichormai. It is in this massive palace that we are first received by diplomats, then directed to our guest living quarters.

Everything continues to be uneventful until the evening, when I am invited to privately dine with an unnamed individual.

The letter is delivered to me as I conclude the last of three meetings with people off Jairinka and Ajun'ra's contact list. The meetings contained no shocking information, just suspicions and unproven theories.

I was originally planning to have a small dinner with my entourage at a recommended local restaurant, but the letter's invitation doesn't seem like something I should refuse.

> Corona Dunai,
>
> I invite you to dine with me this evening, in my quarters.
>
> I am filled with questions, such as why the entire world seems centered on you. Investigating this mystery has been trying my patience and pushing my curiosity to new heights.
>
> Someone will come to your quarters at 7:00.
>
> Best regards.

The letter is unsigned, but I have a suspicion that it is the Crowned Prime. I'm not sure how threads of fate would work in this loop, but it would make sense for all of them to be tied to myself. I wouldn't be surprised if such a phenomenon incited the prime's curiosity.

TANGLED FATE

J ust as the letter said, at 7:00 pm, a young guardswoman comes
to my room to lead me through the winding palace.

Ichormai is a palace with three layers: the outer palace, the inner palace, and the kernel. Lesser officials and foreign dignitaries
stay in the outer palace. The inner palace is populated by bloodline nobles and high-ranking officials, and there is also a combat
school for high-blooded scions.

The kernel is reserved only for the princes, their families, and
specially invited guests.

First, we pass through the outer palace, filled with innumer-
able paintings and sculptures and with floors of marble and walls
of filigreed white, black, and crimson accents. Entering the inner
palace feels like stepping into a different world: It's more garden
than palace, filled with colorful plants and grassy courtyards.
Open wooden hallways stretch throughout, and beautiful stone
and metal statues peer out from foliage and flowers. Where the
outer palace felt echoey and almost unpopulated, the inner
palace is fecund—vitality is everywhere, and people are found
in every hall and manicured plot, conversing, meditating, reading...even sparring.

I can't help but smile seeing all the energy and exuberance. The inner palace...it's idyllic, tranquil, but also full of humanity.

But we don't stop there. The guard leads me through a winding side corridor until we come before an imposing, vault-like door. The immediate vicinity almost feels like a servant's passage. Dust and dirt gather in the corners of the hall, and the floor looks obviously more weathered, its stone discolored in areas and marred by scratches. The marble even dips down in one area as though enough people have walked on it over the years to press the stone down.

"We will wait here," the guard says, her voice stoic and posture stiff. "The prince will come when he is ready."

He must know we're here with his ability to see the future and all. Sure enough, about ten seconds after we've stopped, the door opens. The guard looks at me, face expressionless.

"He's ready to receive you," she explains, tilting her head towards the empty doorway.

I nod my head. This entire wing of the palace has been understandably warded against detection magic, including my ability to sense vitality and Death energy. I can't sense anyone on the other side of the door.

I walk forward into the portal, leaving the guard behind. The door shuts behind me, gasping air as it closes, reminding me of the entrance to a vault...or tomb.

I find myself in a long hallway that naturally expands into an open, many-windowed room. The room's tiles are ornate but also rustic—nothing like the expensive marble outfitting the outer palace. The walls also convey a sense of age. They are a gentle off-white like the pages of an aged book or yellowed teeth. Tied to support pillars near the walls are expressive tapestries depicting epic scenes, filled with people bearing weapons, offering tribute, and riding horses. The tapestries are a dark navy, giving the impression of a night sky bearing the imprint of human history.

I hear the calls of birdsong and notice a pair of uncaged parakeets hanging from the tapestry on the right wall, one green, one blue. Underneath them is a small vessel of water filled with small toys. One of the birds appears to be wearing a cloth diaper of all things.

And there, at the very back of the mostly empty room, body mostly concealed by an old divan, is a figure shrouded in sunlight. His head is tilted to the side so that I can see one eye and the profile of his nose and jaw. Cornsilk hair shines white, his sun-kissed eyelashes like the points of stars. His hair is long, obscuring his forehead and ears, stretching down to his shoulder blades.

"So you're the one," he says, turning so that I can see both blue eyes. His arms drape over the intricate wood of the divan, casting short shadows on its dark, floral cloth. His face and figure are androgynous, lanky, and well-toned, his features sharp and classically aquiline. A small but ornate hair ornament lies next to his right ear, its gems casting little blue shadows on his beige robe.

"Hello," I say, wondering how there can be so much bright sunlight in the evening. "I am Ignatius Dunai, Corona of Godora." I wait for him to introduce himself, but he remains quiet, the corners of his mouth curling up ever so slightly. "I presume that you are the Crowned Prime."

He snorts at that. "Call me Euryphel."

"Not Karen?" I ask.

"*Never* Karen. Though if I'm not mistaken, you ask people to call you Ian—a shortening of your middle name."

I nod. "It's true. So, His Majesty Karen Euryphel Selejo...thank you for inviting me." He technically invited me for dinner, but I don't see any tables or chairs, nor do I detect any food. I feel a bit awkward standing in the middle of the room.

"I have questions for you," he says, hands fiddling with a stray thread on the divan. "Why," he begins, inclining his head, "are you the center of everything?"

I chuckle. It's the same question from his note. "Do you want to guess?" I'm still unsure whether I've correctly guessed that being in a dilation loop interferes with End practitioner fate-sight.

"Everything is tangled...and points to you. Every arrow of fate points...toward...*you*." He pauses. "Even mine. None of this is real, is it?" His tone is suddenly playful, his expression like that of a cat playing with a mouse.

I cough out of shock, swallowing air the wrong way. "It's real for me," I retort. "But for you, no." How did he come to that conclusion so quickly? Even after seeing my dreams, Ajun'ra was quick to deny the possibility.

He closes his eyes and basks in the sun for a moment, his face serene. *Quite unlike how I would expect someone to act if they found out that they're not actually real.*

"Why are you stuck, here, in an unreal world?" the prince asks. "I can tell by your accent that you're from eastern Shattradan, though you aren't from house Gilly or Illalios." The most powerful families in Gent, Solar, and Koria, the eastern provinces. "How did you come to the Ho'ostar peninsula?"

I smile. The SPU primarily speaks Swellish—the language dominant in Shattradan. As a Solar native, my Swellish is more lilted and has harder consonants than the SPU pronunciation. In Selejo, where Academia Hector is located, the vernacular tongue is Luxish, which is also the language of Godora and Menocht.

"I am just as baffled as you. One day, I woke up in a many-layered temporal loop—one I have yet to exit."

Euryphel's only sign of emotion is the slight inward pull of his eyebrows. "You woke up in a dilation loop without any recollection of how you entered?" He pushes himself off the divan and walks over to one of the windows, proceeding to sit on the sill. "Then you don't have an escape word?"

I chuckle dryly. "If I did, I would have used it by now."

His gaze is thoughtful. "How long have you been in the chamber?"

I exhale a sharp breath. "A few years. I lost track for a while in the beginning."

The prince chuckles darkly. "What a nightmare." He shakes his head. "Whoever did this to you... What they've done is deeply immoral." He points to the now-vacant divan and says, "Do sit."

I recline on the old divan, its well-worn fabric soft and comfortable.

"The worst part is," I say, expression dour, "that I probably *agreed* to do this."

"Why do you say that?"

"Before the loop...I had not awakened my affinity."

A look of understanding enters the prince's eyes. "I see. Some people would do anything for the hope of awakening."

There is silence for a moment.

"This is the first time we've spoken, isn't it?" he asks.

I nod.

"When I used to use the royal dilation chamber as a child," Euryphel explains, "I hated interacting with people in it. I could never forget that they weren't *real*, that their memory was temporary."

"Before the loop, I was afraid of people," I confess. "At least, inside of it, I've learned that what others think is largely unimportant."

The prince laughs, his eyes bright. "You don't really believe that do you?"

I wave him off. "Regardless, like you said, I too try to avoid any unnecessary social contact. Though as the loop has worn on, I've found myself growing increasingly desperate for someone to talk to."

"Someone who will remember." Euryphel nods.

"Or, at the very least...someone who knows."

"I guess I'm better than nothing," the prince says, his mouth quirking. "This has been a refreshing conversation." He walks over to the divan and sits on the left armrest. "Now, tell me *everything.*"

* * *

By the end of my brief recounting, the prince has an inscrutable look in his eyes.

"You know, I thought *I* was lonely," he murmurs. "But you are, by far, the loneliest creature I've ever met."

I turn away. "You're overstating it." Surely prisoners in isolation cells are lonelier, aren't they? My ordeal is nothing compared to theirs. "But why are you lonely?" The Crowned Prime is surrounded by people: attendants, nobles, and family members. He is young and handsome, something like twenty-eight years of age, and I can imagine his quick wit and even temperament are an easy addition to social gatherings.

"When you're as powerful as us," he begins—I'm not sure if that's a royal "us" or he's referring to me as well—"people see you as more than what you are."

I understand immediately. How do you treat someone with the power to kill millions, someone like me? You can't help but distance yourself, conceal yourself...pretend that nothing has changed. Too little power and you're helpless; too much and you're a threat.

At this point, it's quite late, and I have yet to eat anything. Unsurprisingly, my stomach growls.

"Oh, we were supposed to eat dinner, weren't we?" the prince says, massaging his jaw absentmindedly. "Hmm, most of the servants are likely home to their families by now, including the kitchen staff."

"I'm fine," I retort. It sounds like the prince has already eaten.

"You know," he murmurs, ignoring me. Eyes glinting in the light of the ever-sunny windows, he says, "We could go out and eat." The way he says 'go out' makes it sound like he's planning something scandalous.

I give him a look. "Wouldn't someone recognize you?"

Euryphel shrugs. "Possibly. But it's not too difficult if you're wearing the right thing and aren't trailed by an entourage of guards and sycophants."

I nod slowly. "Alright."

"Besides," the prince says, "I have an inkling that there's a place we can go that will help you solve this layer's puzzle and get you one step closer to leaving the loop." He waves me on with a hand as he slides off the windowsill and onto the floor. "First, follow me out of the sunroom."

The room sure is aptly named.

He walks to the back of the room, following the hallway in the direction I came from. He even walks to the vaulted door I used as an entrance. But when he gives the door a light tap, it opens like it weighs nothing, and the room beyond its threshold is not the dingy hallway I expected. This room looks like the proper bedroom for a prince: massive, lit by an overhead chandelier, and outfitted in tasteful furniture. The prince walks confidently to the smallest of three large dressers and pulls the second drawer from the top. He immediately begins to compare three plain, brown tunics.

Is that entire dresser just filled with nondescript reg clothes?

The prince turns back to look at me, then shakes his head and places the tunics back in the drawer. He closes it and instead opens the drawer on the bottom, withdrawing a white linen shirt and a pair of black trousers.

He tosses these onto the floor, then walks over to a different dresser and takes out a red jacket with gold embroidery. He carries this jacket to his bed, grabbing the shirt and pants on his way with his foot and punting them onto the massive bedframe.

"I can't dress down *too* much," he explains, grinning. "I need to match with you."

The prince faces away from me toward his bed, then undresses. I turn away out of politeness. I wait about a minute, then peek over. The prince has transitioned from dressing to applying some kind of makeup to his face. He sits at a small wooden vanity, his hands controlling a fine brush with practiced ease.

After another five minutes of makeup, the prince wipes his hands on a heavily discolored rag and opens a jar of brown mud. He sticks a finger in it, then dabs some onto his closed eyelids. The mud quickly absorbs, and when he opens his eyes, they are no longer blue, but brown.

I must admit, Euryphel is skilled in disguises. He has his long hair in a tail, tied with a leather strap, a few strands framing his face. His features are even sharper than before, the shadows of his cheeks and nose enhanced, making him look older than he is. His eyebrows are thicker and slightly darker, matching his butterscotch-brown eyes, and the combination of jacket, shirt, and pants gives him the air of a wealthy bachelor.

"You must have a lot of practice sneaking out," I comment. "I'm impressed."

"Not as much as you'd think," he says, sighing. "You know, I have about a billion things that need doing, and I'm neglecting all of them. It's making me antsy, even if none of them actually...well." He arches an eyebrow.

"I still can't quite wrap my head around how willing you are to believe none of this is real," I murmur as the prince leads me from the room.

He steps into a pair of boots, tugs them on, and opens the vault door. This time, I see him struggle a bit like the door is heavier. When it opens, we're standing in the outer palace, in some kind of small, empty salon.

I turn back and laugh when I see the door has a "SERVANTS ONLY" sign hanging on it. The prince grins and chuckles back.

"I wouldn't believe it if I hadn't experienced it before myself," he explains. "I've been in a dilation chamber loads of times, and it's always the same, except all the arrows point at *me*, rather than someone else."

The prince hasn't moved since we emerged from the door.

"I suppose that makes sense," I reply. "Where are we going, by the way?"

"Oh, apologies; we're just waiting a moment." He walks back over to the "SERVANTS ONLY" door—the one we just came from—and opens it without any issue, revealing a passageway intended for servant use. "Our exit to the street is just through here."

We navigate the dimly lit hallway, eventually arriving at a green wooden door that the prince opens with a kick.

"Ah, finally, fresh air," he exclaims, breathing in deeply and laughing. He turns to me and puts a hand in his pocket. "What kind of food do you feel like? My treat!"

STAKEOUT

"You know," I whisper as I crouch on the side of a gritty residential highrise, "when you said you knew a place that might help unravel Hashat's plot, I thought you were still talking about a restaurant." Thankfully, we did at least find somewhere to eat before heading here.

Euryphel chortles quietly, his teeth flashing. "Shh..."

"How do you even know about this place, anyway?"

The prince appears thoughtful. "Before you arrived, I was able to see a convergence of arrows on this area. Specifically, I noticed that many lesser nobles had nets of intrigue around them—and that those tight nets of arrows all cinched together at this location. I also admittedly received intelligence from a few trusted officers I've personally tasked with rooting out Hashat."

Is it possible he's talking about Jairinka and Ajun'ra? "But when did you ever come here to see the arrows' convergence?"

He smirks. "I can see the entire city from the palace. Threads of fate don't stop at physical walls."

Something—or someone—stirs below us, and we fall silent.

The surrounding area is quiet, and a few dim street lanterns cast yellow light on rustic cobblestone and smooth rock cast by earth elementalists. In contrast, the buildings are grindingly close together and poke up like rotted teeth: black, gray, and spotted with dark windows. Utilitarian, without much style, and intended for poorer residents. Shattered pieces of glass bottles and a few people hunkered in damp alleyways add to the grim aesthetic. Even though the neighborhood's infrastructure is well-maintained, everything else *screams* poverty.

We are currently hanging from the narrow fire escape of one of the featureless buildings. Euryphel cautioned against using any kind of energy manipulation, and so instead of comfortably floating in the air via osteomancy, I am *physically* hanging, my muscles starting to strain with exertion. I am tempted to use my glosSword as a hovering chair, but the glowing implement is the opposite of covert. I currently have the glosSword set to discrete mode, allowing me to wear it as a watch and a belt. The belt has a front and back-facing camera. The watch face, too, has a hidden camera, allowing me to record the surroundings in three directions.

The way the loop works, it's impossible for me to improve my physical capabilities, as my body resets whenever I die or transition layers. Well, technically I can improve during a single loop layer, but there's a limit to how much I'm willing to work on physical fitness when I can do everything with decemancy. I *can* use carnimancy to artificially stimulate muscle growth, but it's a little late for that. I didn't foresee myself in this kind of situation, hanging twenty stories above the ground.

Euryphel appears strangely calm, his body lax and breathing slow and regular. I guess it makes sense if he can peek into the future and know that he probably isn't going to fall and die.

One plus of being a decemancer is that even when I'm not using Death energy, I can still see vitality, allowing me to see in the dark. Dead objects are like translucent layers of black, with people showing as varied shades of gray behind them. It gives me a general sense of how many walls are within the building, how thick the walls are, and how many lives lie within. I will admit that it's difficult to create any kind of comprehensive map from the walls, given that they lack luminosity and shading to indicate where one pitch-black wall begins and ends.

I figure that Euryphel must have some similar kind of passive skill that allows him to see—probably something to do with his wind elementalism. Perhaps he can passively sense air currents. That, combined with his ability to see threads of fate—arrows, in his words—would give him a good sense of both the environment and the people within it.

The noise we heard below turns out to be nothing more than a small mouse skittering among the refuse.

"Do you do this often?" I whisper.

"Never," Euryphel replies, "but I've always wanted to."

"You said you spent some time in a dilation chamber," I point out. "Why not do it then?"

Euryphel shrugs his shoulders as much as he can while holding onto the fire escape. "That was a long time ago. And usually, you don't spend more than a few hours in the chamber at a time, completing small objectives and challenges. The kind of loop you've described to me, lasting *years*...it would take an extreme amount of energy to power it. It's far too extravagant."

I nod. "They probably would've been happy with the result after just a month. By then, I'd already awakened my affinity."

"It almost feels like a stress test. Like..." The prince pauses. "Like they're trying to see what the limits of their technology are. Sure, they could awaken you in a month, but in a year? In five years? What would happen then?"

"At what point," I continue his words, "does the improvement halt? What is the optimal length of time?" I shake my head. "It's plausible. I can tell you now that all it took, for me at least, was about a year."

Euryphel shifts position. "A year for what?"

I snort. "A year to learn decemancy."

He appears perplexed.

I sigh. "It doesn't matter. But I stand by my assertion that a year would've been enough. I'm tired of this loop, of this stupid experiment, of whoever is watching us even now for the sake of entertainment, research, or whatever."

"Surely you have a plan for when you get out," the prince says lightly.

"Nothing concrete. What would you do, in my position?"

"Hmm," Euryphel intones, his expression contemplative. "I would probably thank the people who put me in the loop. That would be my first move." Seeing my expression, he moves to defend himself. "Whoever these people are that have placed you here, it has certainly cost them a great deal. At the end of the day, the one to profit most will likely be you."

"And what if they've roped me into some kind of life-death oath or another kind of binding contract?"

"If that's the case...come and find me."

I blink, surprised by his answer. "Find you? Why?"

"I'd like you. The real me, that is. That aside...I could leverage your release from the oath."

"That would be nice and all, but what could you give them in return?" I doubt much would be worth the servitude of a peak decemancer.

The prince's expression freezes, his eyes uncharacteristically cold. "Oh, I have my ways. I think the real-world me would consider it worth the effort to release you from an oath."

My eyebrows furrow. "You say that, but you haven't even seen what I can do. All you know is what I've told you..."

The prince's mouth opens slightly, as though he's been caught off-guard. "Huh. I suppose that's true, for you."

Has he seen some kind of future in which I've displayed my power?

"Did you entertain attacking me to see what your Regret affinity's future prediction would show you?" I ask, my mouth curling up into a smile.

Euryphel gives me a pained look. "Maybe."

I suppress laughter. "Fine. I actually feel much better knowing you have some idea that what I've said isn't all hot air."

"If you're really as powerful as you say, and you enter Zukal'iss in the real world, all the arrows may not point to you, but I would be unable to miss your presence. When powerful people walk, the world shifts around them like flowing water."

"Is that so?"

"It is."

We fall back into a comfortable silence. I can't help but wonder where these Hashat people are, and if they're even coming. It's already nearing midnight.

Suddenly, both Euryphel and I sense a presence coming from the right, seeming to dance across the buildings at a rapid pace.

It's Ajun'ra Iffis, without a doubt. And is that...Jairinka strapped to her back, along for the ride?

I suddenly remember that we were supposed to meet tonight. Jairinka and Ajun'ra must be using their tracker to find the glosSword, and by extension, me.

But them joining us should still be fine. Even if Jairinka isn't one of the officers that Euryphel mentioned earlier, he should know the Crowned Prime; Euryphel is his uncle. I recall that the first and eleventh princes—Euryphel and Jairinka's father—get along with each other; there's some kind of rule that all the princes with ones in their rank—the first, tenth, eleventh, and twelfth princes—form a block together. It's not a coincidence that these lower-ranked princes are also older and less personally ambitious. Jairinka's father, for instance, has been at rank eleven for fifteen years, falling from rank seven in his prime thirty years ago.

The exception to the rule is the third prince, Ezenti Demetrius Selejo. The man is seventy and has stayed at rank three for his entire life since taking the seat of the third at the age of fourteen. I wonder how long Euryphel will last. The Crowned Prime he replaced, O'osta Kestrelius Selejo, lasted eight months.

If I remember correctly, Euryphel has held his seat for eleven years.

"Who is that?" the first prince asks, glaring at the oncomers. It must be frustrating for him, half-blind with people's arrows pointing to me. *He'd normally be able to tell if these people are coming after him, someone in the building, or if they are off doing something completely unrelated.*

"It's a *them*," I say, correcting him. "Specifically, it's your nephew, Jairinka, and his companion, Ajun'ra Iffis."

"What?" the prince mutters, seeming completely baffled. "I didn't see this coming."

"They're here for me," I reply under my breath. And based on Ajun'ra's fierce expression, they seem upset. They probably came looking for me near the palace, only to find me disappeared.

"*Why?*" the prince asks, gritting his teeth.

"Well, to figure out this Hashat mess."

Euryphel blinks. "Fine, then. I am personally unfamiliar with Ajun'ra, but House Iffis has strong bloodline Dark affinity."

I nod. "She's a Dark and Remorse practitioner."

"Interesting. Jairinka I know to be quite proficient in illusions. Alright, let's give it a go with the four of us."

"Do you want to tell them your identity?" I ask, uncertain how to proceed. "They are unaware that this is a time loop." How would I explain that I've enticed the Crowned Prime to join me in a stakeout?

"No, no...hmm...tell them that I am just a wind elementalist, loaned to you from one of the noble houses also interested in uprooting Hashat."

"Tell us what?" hisses a panting Ajun'ra, her chest heaving and temples dripping sweat. Jairinka swiftly pivots from her back and grabs onto a lower section of the fire escape.

"Hello, there," I say, voice cheerful. "Glad you two could make it. This is Eury, a wind elementalist given to us from House—" Who were the people I spoke with today? Something like house...

"—House Claremeon," Euryphel interjects, gracing me with a sharp smile.

Ajun'ra looks around. "So you're the one who found this place, huh?"

The prince smiles. "That's right. I've been investigating for a few weeks now, and I've come to the conclusion that a number of nobles periodically meet in this building. Odd, wouldn't you say?"

Jairinka is staring at Euryphel with a complex expression, his eyes narrowing as though trying to work out a puzzle. Suddenly, he exhales deeply and puts a hand over his face.

"Uncle!" he groans, shaking his head. "You have infinitely more important things to do than be my babysitter. I'll be *fine!*" He bangs his arm against the fire escape in protest. "I'm only five years your junior. This... Just let me do this on my own."

Well, so much for disguising Euryphel.

It only takes Ajun'ra a millisecond to infer "Eury's" real identity, and she immediately drops to her knees—or at least tries to side-kneel on the metal.

"My Prime," she says, her voice submissive. "I apologize for my earlier lack of polite address. Please do inform me why someone of your august stature has deigned to help us in our humble task."

Wow, Ajun'ra can spew noble-ese effortlessly. An impressive skill. If Mother were here, she'd ask me why *I* can't talk like that. I resolve to never, ever let the two of them meet.

"Y'jeni, Jairinka...I'm not babysitting you."

"But, Uncle...why are you here? With *him?*" Jairinka suddenly grimaces, likely realizing that if I didn't already know his identity, I sure do now.

"The threads of fate indicate that Hashat is going to unleash calamity on the continent. Thus, I've decided to help Corona Dunai in his endeavors since the other princes and the assembly have been dragging their feet."

I wonder if what the prince says is true, or if he's inventing an excuse. Regardless, both Jairinka and Ajun'ra blanche, taking the prince's words as unassailable fact.

"So that's how it is," Ajun'ra whispers under her breath.

"Hashat members are going to meet here tonight?" Jairinka asks, his expression grave.

"Any time now," Euryphel clarifies, motioning for everyone to be quiet and wait.

And so we wait.

And wait...

I look at the glosSword watch on my wrist. It's past midnight. Where are these Hashat nobles? Did they all accidentally sacrifice themselves to whatever is supposedly slumbering under the ocean?

"Shh..." the prince whispers, gathering everyone's attention. "They're coming in a little under a minute. Steel yourselves and make sure you aren't visible from the vantage point of the entrance."

We all wait silently. Jairinka casts a small illusion powered by a precious stone—the kind sold by Pan's, its surface slightly irregular, betraying that it isn't a product of mass-production. Unfit for elementalism, but based on the obscuring fog twisting around us, excellent for Light and Moon manipulation. The use of the stone, as well as the naturally deceptive nature of illusions, greatly mitigates the risk of someone detecting an energy signature.

For contrast, if I let out a small tendril of Death energy—one any decent Life practitioner would probably notice. Illusions are good at fooling the subconscious, and thus are much more likely to go undetected.

I can't help but feel jealous that Euryphel's most salient abilities—namely, seeing threads of fate, sensing people and structures through the wind, and peering into the future—go completely un-neutered: They're all either passive or internal to the mind.

Ajun'ra blends naturally into the darkness, likely due to some kind of enchantment on her robes. She doesn't need to expend energy to conceal herself.

It's funny to find that in this kind of situation, I'm the least useful, relying on Jairinka's mist and Euryphel's future vision to go undetected. That and the building's natural cover, of course, but it's good to have redundancies.

The first group shows up just as Euryphel predicted—five individuals in heavy, concealing robes. It's difficult to tell any details about the newcomers with them being on the other side of the building. When they enter the building, everyone looks to Euryphel for the next order. The prince looks around and shakes his head, bringing a finger to his lips.

Over the next twenty minutes, over thirty new people arrive in small groups, all wearing similar dark, concealing attire. As a group of panting stragglers enters the building, the prince lets out a breath of air and softly clears his throat.

"That's the last of them that I can tell," Euryphel says. "Given that it is 1:07 am, I'm inclined to believe that the meeting was scheduled to commence at one." He looks around. "What were you originally planning to do once you caught Hashat?"

Now that I think about it...if I am able to kill the people in attendance, would the loop progress? Or will I have to kill *every* member, not just those there tonight? From all the intelligence

I've gathered, it's likely that there are far more members of the organization who aren't present.

I glance at Ajun'ra and Jairinka. My understanding is that they want to stop Hashat the *cult*, not Hashat's individual members. An ideal win for them would be destroying the cult and consequently liberating its ensorcelled members to once more be fully productive members of society. I recognize that following out their plan would be sufficient to advance the loop, but I also know that it should be much easier to just murder everyone in the cult rather than try to upend the cult from the inside out. The former requires power, the latter finesse...and I know my area of strength.

Euryphel waits a moment for us to respond, but none of us offer up a plan. Euryphel looks at me and raises an eyebrow.

"We should capture and imprison them," he states, taking charge. "I have a feeling we can use them as bait to root the rest of them out."

Jairinka frowns but nods, and Ajun'ra inclines her head in supplication.

"What do you want us to do?" I ask, inclining my head toward the building.

He gives me a look. "You can capture all of them; go do it."

I snort and give him a wry smile. We're close enough to the building that I can just manage it. "Alright then." I wave my hand and all the thirty-two Hashat members freeze, their tendons and muscles futilely straining against immobilized bone. "But how were you planning to get them from here to a holding facility?"

"What happened?" Ajun'ra asked, eyes narrowing at me in confusion.

I smile, my eyes flashing violet. "I took care of them. They're not dead, just immobilized. If you were watching me when the SPU ambassadors came to the Opascal Base scarcely a week ago, well, I gave them a similar form of welcome."

Ajun'ra crosses her arms and uses Dark energy to affix the soles of her shoes to the shadows covering the fire escape. "I wasn't watching."

"To answer your question," the Crowned Prime butts in, raising an eyebrow, "I'll simply let the Guard take care of it."

"What Guard?" I ask.

"The Prime Guard," Euryphel explains. "My personal entourage."

"I haven't sensed any sort of guardsmen nearby."

"That's because they count skilled Life, Dark, and Regret practitioners among their number, allowing them to evade detection. Apparently, even from someone like you at sufficient range."

"And how do you see them?" I ask.

"They can't evade the sight of a high-affinity End practitioner. I see them just fine." He tilts his head. "They've closed in on the building. One moment... There, we can go."

"I see them now..." I murmur, frowning. "I had to really focus: They blend in like chameleons. You're right, though, that they're already inside putting people into restraints. We can leave."

Jairinka meets Ajun'ra's eyes, fear and awe present in equal measure. Her matching expression says it all: *perhaps we've bitten off a bit more than we thought.*

BAIT

I can't deny that I'm tired when I wake in the morning. The accommodations provided to me are excellent, and the bed is plush like a cloud, but by the time we returned to the Palace of Fortitude, it's after two in the morning, and I find it difficult to fall asleep.

I cannot, however, renege last-minute on my morning appointments with people off Jairinka and Ajun'ra's list, so I get up at half-past five to take a shower.

When I return to my bedroom, a folded note lies conspicuously on the bed. I pick it up and read:

> *I've liberated you from your tedious meetings.*
> *Come join me for breakfast in the inner palace.*
> *A guard will escort you at 7:00.*
> *-E*

So much for keeping my appointments. But if Euryphel says that my meetings have been dealt with, I'll take his word for it.

I look around the room, trying to detect any traces of vitality, but I find none. Perhaps Euryphel uses his Prime Guard to discreetly deliver small correspondences within the palace.

I go back to sleep for a bit, then wake and wait for my escort. It turns out to be the same guardswoman from yesterday, and she leads me down a set of different corridors stretching through the outer and inner palaces. We end up before a small, white, wooden door in one of the open hallways of the inner palace. If I have to guess, I'd say that the door belongs to a service closet.

As before, the door opens on its own. I pass through, only to find that Euryphel is standing behind the door. We aren't in the sunroom, nor his bedroom, but rather a rustic-looking salon connected to a kitchen operated by a crew of four. The room smells divine.

"Welcome to my salon," the prince says as he gestures for me to take a seat on a large loveseat. He lays on a nearby couch.

"How do your doors work?" I ask, interested in finding out how the prince controls space in the palace.

The prince calls out to the kitchen for a pot of tea before replying, "The doors employ sophisticated Dark enchantments, like the kind you might use to create dimensional storage."

I look at the glosSword in the scabbard on my waist and recall its use of a reactor: an energy font stored away in some other dimensional space and carefully tethered to the sword. That must be the kind of Dark enchanting the prince is talking about.

"Sounds expensive," I reply.

"Undoubtedly," Euryphel says. "The palace was constructed a long time ago, though. I think one of the former princes had talent in space manipulation—one of the rarer subdomains of the Dark affinity."

The tea comes out, already steeping in a glass pot with aged copper accents, and the prince pours us each a cup.

"So, what's the plan?" I ask.

"The plan," he says, taking a tentative sip, pulling away from the too-hot cup, "is to use the bait to catch a big fish."

"That's not quite a plan," I chide, grabbing my own teacup to warm my hands. "How do you think to use our bait?"

"Like I said, before you came, I had already been investigating Hashat, inspecting the arrows of fate winding about the city for troubling patterns." Euryphel blows on his tea and stirs in a sugar cube. "The members we captured are now a lost cause. They're unmasked, captured, and completely vulnerable to the punishment of the state. There's nowhere to run."

I frown. "Unless?"

"Unless the group manages to prove its worth."

"You mean...unleash a monster on Godora?"

The prince fingers his porcelain cup. "Not quite. The beast they hope to awaken lies under the Illyrian Ocean, on the Godoran coastline, but they plan to use it on Selejo. Their thinking, I have come to understand, is that the SPU must prove its superiority by ending the farce of ceasefire and neutrality." The prince smiles, his lips thinly pressing together. "They're a prideful bunch, the nobles who have joined Hashat."

"I'm still unsure what this has to do with the prisoners."

"It's simple. We tell Hashat that they have one week to raise the monster from the depths of the Illyrian ocean and turn it on Selejo. If they complete their task, we will release the prisoners." The prince smiles. "Though I don't think that will be necessary."

"Won't this put Godora in danger?" I ask, sipping from my teacup. "I believe that I need to *protect* Godora, not let it suffer terrorist attacks."

"That's why you, Jairinka, and Ajun'ra will return to Godora and wait for them. My intelligence suggests that they actually *do* have the capabilities to raise an abyssal monstrosity from the ocean—believe it or not. Destroy the monster, and the cult will naturally dissolve, its purpose extinguished. Then you should move on to the next layer of your loop."

The prince says this calmly while sipping his steaming cup of tea, his right hand simultaneously fidgeting with an ornate little teaspoon.

It sounds like a shallow plan. It relies on a lot of uncertainties, and the prince hasn't suggested any contingencies. What if the metaphorical bait isn't taken, and what if Hashat's members don't embark on a wild quest to free the monster slumbering in the Illyrian deep? What if the monstrosity refuses to show? What if it's too powerful to be stopped?

But this is a loop, not real life: if something goes wrong, there's always another attempt. Even if I, as a Godoran Corona, would refuse such a risky plan in a world with consequences...but here?

"Just give me notice when they'll be coming, and where, and I'll figure out the rest."

* * *

The prince and I spend the rest of the day exploring the city, continuing our pre-stakeout fun from the previous evening. I have a feeling most of the things we're doing he's never done before but always wanted to do. We've gone into all sorts of random shops and ventured down random alleys in all manner of neighborhood, touring colorful residential areas, an open bazaar, and three different public gardens.

We're currently strolling in a busy part of the city with a public water fountain—the ideal place for parents to leave their children while they work a market stall or browse for goods. A veritable series of geysers jet up from the ground, misting onlooking children and blasting the ones who wait directly over the geyser hole. One child squeals and falls over, the geyser hitting him squarely in his unclothed unmentionables.

The fountain is really just the front yard of a massive building with an ancient appearance. It feels distinctly out of place, with old stone and classical pillars holding up its squat girth. The trend these days is to build up, rather than out, but this building embodies an opposite principle of design.

"What building is that?" I ask, unable to get a good look at the letters engraved over the entrance.

"The public bathhouse," Euryphel replies offhandedly. "As you can tell, it's an old building. Actually predates the building of the capital." He snorts. "Legends say the first princes built the capital here because they couldn't bear to part with this bathhouse."

"Is it any good?" I ask.

"It's supposed to be excellent," the prince replies.

I frown. "Have you been?"

The prince's stride falters for a moment. "No. I don't have time for bathhouses."

"We have time now," I reply.

Euryphel gives me a sideways glance. "I don't go to bathhouses."

Why not? I wonder, surprised. The prince is attractive, confident...I can't really see him being *shy* about visiting the baths.

"Is it because you're the CP?" I ask, acronyming his title. "Too conspicuous?"

Euryphel sighs, turning back to face me. His expression looks thoughtful like he's trying to decide whether or not to tell me something.

"It's not because I'm the 'CP,'" he finally says, clearly entertained by the acronym. "It's...a personal affair."

I can't help but be curious—the prince is normally content to answer any question I ask regarding his life as Crowned Prime and the workings of the SPU. Still, I decide to let the matter go. If he doesn't feel like telling me, I wouldn't force it.

We conclude the day with another excellent dinner, this one apparently suggested by one of the Prime Guard ('a little bird told me,' being the prince's exact words). The cozy shop offers Sereish cuisine: delicious curries over sour, thin dough and flakey, savory scones. We eat our fill while exchanging stories and discussing the things we've seen throughout the day.

Somewhere along the way, a bottle of white wine comes out, and we start to discuss other things, like our general hopes and dreams for the future. What I want to do when I leave the loop. What he wants to do to build up the SPU. Ways we can think of working together in the future, collaborating to build a better world, and methods to stabilize the region and safeguard the SPU's recovering relationships with its neighbors.

We start the second bottle of wine, and at this point, we're asking each other all sorts of inane questions. We talk about our astral alignments, discuss the futility of truly understanding people who aren't ourselves, and balk at the meaninglessness of life and the reticence of the gods to do anything productive. The questions continue their downward spiral until we're asking each other our favorite color, our favorite animal, our *spirit* animal, about our first crushes, about the exact moment our voices decided to unexpectedly drop...we ramble on and on.

I check my glosSword watch for the time and recoil dramatically when the time reads as a quarter past ten in the evening. We've been talking for nearly four hours.

"We should go back," I say, yawning. "It's late. I bet the entourage I came with are confused out of their minds where I keep disappearing off to."

The prince winces. "Yes, we should go back. I'll have a guardsman call us a coach." Whatever method the prince uses to communicate with the Guard, it certainly works. A few minutes later, an extra-large hovergloss—almost the size of a small bus—arrives at the nearest hangar point, a tower-like building jutting up into the network of spider-thread hovergloss wires. Thankfully, the hangar point has an elevator platform, and we don't have to climb ten flights of stairs in our...*impaired* state.

"We're going to feel this tomorrow." The prince chuckles softly as he settles onto the bench of the hovergloss, spreading out on his back and bringing his feet up. I sit on the opposite bench, leaning my head against the side of the wall.

"What was in that wine?" I mutter.

"Well," the prince replies, smilingly dumbly, "we finished two bottles. That's one bottle for each of us."

"Just one bottle!" I exclaim in mock indignation. "I feel like I've drunk ten." I sigh and lean a bit farther back, practically already feeling the headache of the hangover I'll have in the morning.

"Well, this is what one bottle will do to you," Euryphel grunts, adjusting his position. He keeps slipping, and his alcoholic inco-ordination prevents him from properly fixing his position. Every little adjustment is made clumsily as though his limbs are lined with lead.

I'm similarly impaired, but at least I'm in a more secure po-sition nestled in the corner. Poor Euryphel almost rolls off the bench with every acceleration of the hovergloss coach. Envision-ing the SPU's Crowned Prime, this is definitely not the image I'd think of.

"Speaking from experience?" I ask, tilting my head toward the back wall.

"The experience of others," Euryphel quips. "I'd never do this normally, you know. Too many things to do."

"I wish the real you could do things like this," I murmur. "Why not just rent out a dilation chamber?"

Euryphel frowns. "People would watch the footage later. They'd wonder why I wasted a national resource on loafing around like a common man."

That gets a rise out of me. "Hah! I knew it! I knew people would be watching this...me!"

"Well, they're not watching you *now*, whoever 'they' is. The di-lation factor is too strong. They'll use a team of experts to parse the recording into a reel of highlights since nobody has time to watch all the footage—years of footage in your case—on their own."

I deflate like a popped balloon. "So they're not really watching me."

"No."

I hiss softly. "There's a way to destroy the recording after I exit the loop, isn't there?"

The prince nods or rather rolls his head horizontally across the seat. "I've been debating whether it's best to destroy it."

Suddenly, the coach decelerates, marking our arrival at the Palace of Fortitude's hovergloss hangar. It's normally used by tourists coming to tour the outer palace, but this late at night, it's deserted. The prince and I stagger to our feet, our limbs like gelatin as we exit and make our way into the elevator and down the street. The prince squints his eyes and flails his arms, picking up a small gust.

"This door," Euryphel grunts, ambling forward towards a random door in the alley. He rests on it for a second, then turns the handle. The door leads directly into his bedroom. He breathes a sigh of relief and ushers me in behind him. The two of us kick off our shoes, strip off our outerwear, and collapse onto the bed and couch, respectively.

When we wake in the morning, the sunlight reveals that we're both in the clothes we wore last night. I'm surprised to find no sign of a hangover, the sun shining through the prince's window calming rather than disorienting. *And here I was worried I'd have to do a few "modifications" to get my body functioning normally again.*

I check my watch and grimace at the time: 10:15 am.

"Eury," I bark, eyeing the mountain of covers on the bed. "Get up."

I walk over to the side of the bed, surprised that the prince is in such a deep sleep. Sure enough, his head is poking out of the covers, his eyes closed and a bit of drool pooling onto his pillow.

"Hey," I say, leaning in. I reach my hand out, stopping just before the prince's covered shoulder. I'm not sure how the prince will react to being woken up. What if he lashes out with his elementalism? At this range, wind blades would be difficult to stop completely. I decide to step back a few paces, then look around for something I can manipulate with decemancy. I see a leaf on the ground, probably tracked in by one of us last night. At my command, the leaf whips through the air and lands on Euryphel's face, brushing against his nose.

The prince awakens with an explosive sneeze, drool flying off his jaw and onto his comforter, the comforter subsequently blowing off the bed and onto the ground. The force of the sneeze almost knocks me over.

"I've never seen a wind-empowered sneeze before," I say dryly. "Good morning."

"What time is it?" the prince asks, frowning even as his cheeks turn red.

"Just after ten."

He rubs his palms into his face. "It's possible to salvage the day. Y'jeni."

"Why don't I feel hungover?"

Euryphel waves his hand dismissively as he gets out of bed. "Life enchantments in the ceiling." He turns around to look at me, giving me an appraising look. "I'm going to send you back to your room directly."

I shrug. "Alright with me."

"It's ready for you now," Euryphel adds, gesturing to the door.

"I'll see you...when?"

The prince looks thoughtful. "When?" He raises an eyebrow. "When the bait has been swallowed."

ORIGINS

The diplomatic trip ends the day after I last have direct contact with Euryphel. It is only on this last day that I am able to meet with most of Jairinka and Ajun'ra's contacts, but none of my meetings significantly change my view of Hashat.

That is until I speak with General Hor'well.

The general is a middle-aged man with thick, bronze hair and a firm jaw. He has a strong Sun affinity, and the seven scarlet stripes on his uniform speak to his proficiency as a fire elementalist.

The first thing that most people probably notice about him is his missing right eye. A large scar crosses from his nose to his eyebrow, leaving no question that his eyepatch isn't for show.

The first thing that *I* notice about him is the swirling orb of Death energy behind the leather eyepatch. *Very* interesting, that. Who gave the general his artificial eye?

I sit down on a plump silk cushion at the quarter table in the general's office. General Hor'well joins a few seconds later, sitting across from me after setting down a pot of tea and two teacups. He pours us each a cup of tea in silence, his movements deliberate and controlled.

When we each have a steaming cup of tea, the man speaks: "It's not often I get the chance to speak to a Godoran, much less serve one tea."

We say a few pleasantries. Eventually, I just have to ask, "I don't mean to intrude, but what happened to your eye?"

Hor'well blinks once, then frowns. "That's an oddly relevant question. When I was much younger, about your age, perhaps, I went on a campaign in Luxelles. What do you know of Luxelles?"

"I know the province is in Sere." Luxelles is a distant province with little global relevance.

He nods. "It's a remote province. Lots of land, but most of it is desert. Do you know why we campaigned there?"

I wait in silence, feeling that speaking would only emphasize my ignorance of the region's politics.

"To put it bluntly, we were there to interfere with negotiations between Selejo and the Adrilli Isles. From what I understand, Selejo was interested in borrowing one of the Adrilli Isles' governors to complete a task. The governor of Thakka, to be precise."

I ponder this bit of information. The governor of Thakka, a few decades ago, before I was born. *I have absolutely no idea who the general is talking about.*

"The Adrilli Isles thought the request was overreaching and didn't agree to send their governor. However, we were unaware of this falling-out and continued with plans to destroy the diplomatic convoys from both Selejo and Adrilli. I lost my eye to one of the Adrilli guards."

"It sounds like you believe the engagement to be a mistake," I say quietly.

Hor'well nods slowly. "Oh, it was a mistake. Attacking the Adrilli caused them to change their position on aiding Selejo. While the assembly never sent over the Thakkan governor, they did send some of his pupils. It was *almost* good enough."

"Almost good enough for what?"

"You're here to talk about Hashat, aren't you?"

I nod.

"They're trying to succeed where the governor of Thakka's students failed." The general sips his tea, then looks out the window.

"There are tales of a monster lurking between the Adrilli Isles and Selejo, as well as a monster just past the banks of Godora, in the depths of the Jermal Trench."

"Monster, General?"

Hor'well grimaces. "After five years, the Adrilli took back their students and called the attempts to wake the western monster a mistake." His lips purse into a sneer. "Or rather, they failed to find the rift that supposedly spawned it."

"You think they were after a rift, rather than a monster?"

"A monster has little value on its own unless it can be controlled. What better way is there to control a riftbeast than with energy stolen straight from its birthplace? Moreover, as the esteemed Corona would know, the rift itself would have other valuables."

"So you believe that Hashat is trying to wake a monster in the Illyrian Ocean?"

"I do."

"And you also believe that the Selejans and the Adrilli tried something similar in the past but failed?"

"That is correct."

I narrow my eyes in contemplation. "Why does Hashat believe it can succeed where both Selejo and Adrilli failed? Have they discovered a rift, giving the riftbeast theory credence?"

His expression turns guarded. "I don't trust the wards on this room. The problem with Hashat is that they have members everywhere, at *every* level of power."

This doesn't feel like new information, though I can't ignore the intensity of the look the general is giving me.

I ask him a few more questions, but I don't receive anything more than cryptic replies. He sidesteps around answering whether a rift has been discovered, shaping the conversation instead toward the intricacies of military officer politics.

"I want to pivot and return to my first question, General Hor'well. I originally asked you how you lost your eye, but I am quite curious... Who gave you a new one?"

"You *are* a practitioner of the dark art," the general says, lips curving into a slight frown. "I suppose you would be able to sense this eye of mine." He takes a sip of tea, only to find his cup empty. Pouring himself more liquid from the pot, he states, "The person who gave me this eye died eight years ago."

Still, not really what I was asking.

He narrows his good eye. "Thank you for joining me," General Hor'well says curtly, "but I think I've said all there is to say."

LEVIATHAN

A fter returning to Godora, the days pass slowly. I can't help but wish I had someone like Euryphel to pass the time with.

Five days later, I'm not sure whether or not to feel surprised when one hundred Hashat acolytes in dark robes appear on a remote beach in Godora, just as Euryphel promised. I watch them congregate from the concealment of tall grass and palm trees, relying on my practice to glean the fine details of their movements.

The Hashat cultists write a series of symbols and geometric shapes in the sand in a dark, sticky crimson. Seven cultists do all the writing, followed by underlings holding black buckets. The seven frequently dip their brushes into the buckets, the coagulated liquid proving a poor medium for writing on sand.

It takes the seven cultists a full hour to finish their work, an array of different geometric nodes nested within one another and filled with illegible, cursive-like scrawl. Even from a distance, I can tell it's unlike any language I've ever seen. Hashat's creation is at once beautiful and hideous, its sinuous lines and shapes offset by ugly globs of dark tissue.

The array having been finished, the cultists mutter amongst themselves before taking their respective places along the circumference of the circle encompassing all the other shapes. The cultists hold out their arms, then each takes a dagger hidden in their robes and cuts their wrist. Blood immediately pools out, but instead of dropping to the ground, the fresh blood moves toward the center of the array, where a pit has been dug into the sand. The blood fills the pit quickly, the small trickle from each wrist compounding into a steady flow.

When the pit is full, the cultists all pull their arms back and wrap prepared bandages around their wrists to staunch the flow. The seven cultists who drew the array then come forward, walking carefully along seven paths of sand devoid of writing. As they reach the edge of the pit, they each pull out a small sheet of paper and chant in unison. As they speak, the blood pit begins to roil, bubbles churning the surface. When the seven utter the last syllable, the blood pit explodes upward like a geyser. The blood falls back down slowly; it almost looks like someone has poured a bucket of viscous red paint over a dense column of air.

The ground subtly moves underfoot. Then it moves again with greater force. The water off the beach grows preternaturally placid and still. I realize that it's being sucked down. The water appears still only because it is no longer moving under the force of the tides, but instead, some other force is funneling it down.

A minute passes. By now, the water has formed into a strong whirlpool. The cultists lie prostrate around the blood array, while the seven leaders lock hands and chant in low voices around the half-empty central pit.

"Just how big is this monster?" I murmur to myself.

When all the blood oozes downward from the air into the pit, the whirlpool violently explodes outward, and a nest of writhing tentacles stretches in every which direction into the air, filling the entire field of view from our vantage point. More and more tentacles erupt from the water every second, uncountable in their number.

The chanting stops. The tentacles are all still for the smallest of moments, like the beast they are connected to has involuntarily shuddered. That's when a tentacle as thick as a man and several times taller than the Palace of Fortitude shoots vertically out of the mass, dwarfing the other tentacles. The smaller tentacles now look like the kind of hair that might cover a wild boar, while the enormous tentacle appears like a naked leg. Or, perhaps, like a worm-like parasite lunging from an animal's corpse.

Soon, another giant tentacle joins the first and is, in turn, joined by several others. Eventually, seven tentacles wave calmly above the water like eyeless serpents—one for each of the head cultists.

One of the seven leaders removes his hand from his neighbor and holds it out high. A tentacle immediately begins to surge upward.

The Hashat cultists have absolutely surpassed my expectations. Summoning this kind of monster and finding a way to control it is impressive. Unfortunately for them, I'm here to cut the leviathan down.

The cultists suddenly freeze, their limbs locked against their will. I smile grimly, moving forward out of concealment and onto the open beach.

The monster in the water immediately begins to move its seven large tentacles as though greatly agitated. I kick off the ground and fly over the sand, stopping when I reach the blood array. I peer down at the seven cultist leaders and notice that each wears a manic grin, their eyes filled with challenge as they meet my own.

I feel a strong sense of foreboding, but I glide toward the thrashing leviathan. The monster is a powerful flame of vitality, its many arms surging outward from some spherical core under the water. Dealing with the tentacles is futile: I need to kill the monster, not play with it.

The size of the monster is a problem, however: I won't be able to act effectively at a distance. Steeling myself for the chill of the ocean, I strip off my jacket and trousers, revealing an amphibious suit and an intricate harness of protective bone, then dart into the water. I use the harness to drag me forward into the murky water and close my eyes, sensing the vitality around me rather than relying on sight to make sense of the gray fathoms. The glosSword at my side hums as though it, too, is filled with adrenaline.

Suddenly, an enormous tentacle breaks through the surface and swings down at me like a butcher's cleaver. I dodge to the side and continue moving toward the tangled mass of vitality. The limb is persistent, however, and follows me like a maddened snake, striking ceaselessly from behind.

I grit my teeth in anger, unsure of how to disable the boneless limb. The entire thing is filled with muscle, proving difficult to ruin completely in one go. Even so, each time it passes by, I sever more and more of its muscle sinews. After about thirty seconds, the tentacle is noticeably less responsive.

But then it is replaced by *three* tentacles, which all dart in the same snake-like matter from three different angles.

I dodge the two coming from the sides, but the third strikes me from behind. I use all my power to shield myself from the blow and try to move in the same direction of the force towards the leviathan. The strike is still incredibly jarring, and I instinctively begin to cough and open my eyes. Even the glosSword's defensive aegis is unable to adequately cushion the blow.

I've come far enough at this point that I can see the shadowy, impossibly huge, writhing mass of the monster. A single enormous eye stares at me, unmoving, almost completely black except for a ring of solid, glowing yellow around its rim. What can only be described as an equally large beak extends from the creature's underside. The beak opens and closes suddenly with an audible *clack*, sending a powerful ripple through the water.

Hair-like tentacles stir all along the creature's body like maggots on a corpse, some even curling over the rim of the eye.

I don't sense any kind of malevolence, but rather indifference. Staring into its eye that is at least twenty times larger than me, I begin to feel a powerful, deep-rooted fear. Before this leviathan, I am small and insignificant, hardly able to disable a single tentacle or three coming toward me at once, let alone seven cornering me from each direction.

I am struck by powerful indecision: What am I supposed to do? Me, the all-powerful decemancer, invincible against anything alive, able to sever vessels and stop hearts with a single gesture. What can I do against a city-sized—

A tentacle swats at me from the left, punching me through the water diagonally, closer to the beak. And still, I am struck by indecision.

It's only a game, I remind myself. *None of this is real. You* must *win.*

I can't run away. I need to face this thing—face it...and destroy it.

I sneer at the beast, then dart forward in an erratic path toward its beady black eye. As I come close, the ten-foot-long tentacles covering the monster's surface strike from every direction. These, however, are small enough for me to deal with in one gesture, and I tear the muscles of each tentacle with impunity.

In a second, I am at the rubbery surface of the beast, but I don't stop my forward momentum; instead, I bring my arms together, then rip them apart like I am tearing a piece of paper. The skin parts, and I strain to kill off as much surrounding flesh as possible and dig my way in. A large tentacle is a second behind, its head trying to follow me into the lengthening wound.

I grin savagely, victoriously: the torn hole is deep enough to conceal me and too narrow for the large tentacles to fit.

I begin to carve a path through the beast, using the glosSword as a conduit through which to channel blasts of necrotic energy, rotting away flesh and allowing me to tear it apart. I continue like this for several minutes, cutting ever deeper toward the center of the monster's vitality. Inside the beast it is quiet and wet, suffused with the smell of the ocean.

Eventually, I reach the thick wall of a pulsing, dark object. I can only see a small part of it at once, but I have the impression that it must be the size of a residential high rise when viewed in its entirety.

The heart.

I begin to siphon off vitality, forming it into a grand stream of energy that wraps around me like a thick web of strings. It's more vitality than I have ever seen in one place. I wonder if I'm up to the challenge of controlling that much power at once, of condensing it into a single point. What kind of density would such a soul gem have if it was made out of vitality so potent as to be viscous and sticky rather than mist-like?

We'll just have to find out. I grunt, closing my eyes, letting well-honed instinct and technique take over. I lose myself as if in meditation, threading the surging vitality into a hex-weave tapestry, then folding that into numerous shapes, letting the vitality flow organically. I feel it surge around me like a vortex, its manifold strands warm and comforting like a cocoon. Like a womb.

Despite my state of intense concentration, I retain a vague awareness of my surroundings, and I notice that the heart has begun to beat with greater intensity. I wonder what the creature is doing on the surface, whether it has thrashed the beach to ruin or whether it has dived back into the Jermal Trench.

And still, I pull the stringy vitality out and continue to layer it around me, slowly condensing it down, kneading it together, organizing it, crystallizing it, then crushing it. My breathing is calm and in sync with my animancy.

I lose track of time; at some point, the heartbeat begins to slow, and then finally, it stops with one great, last pumping heave. At that point, I open my eyes, then look down, almost surprised to find a gem the size of a human skull floating between my palms.

I blink, and my surroundings shift.

INTERLUDE — THE PROPHET

One hour before the start of the loop

Lisandro licked his lips and turned around. "I almost can't believe we're doing this so soon after the last one." He sighed and typed a few final notes into the glosscomp.

The woman standing behind him, Dedere, smiled thinly, her red lipstick vibrant against her otherwise colorless complexion. "It's what the *Prophet* says will work," she said, rolling her eyes.

Lisandro made a small groaning noise. "I don't think we've researched this subject thoroughly enough," he noted, exasperated—not that his complaints would change anything at this point. "People with dormant affinities might never unlock them except for in an exact, specific scenario. I'm not confident the Infinity Loop dilation chamber will be configured for the right scenarios..."

Dedere placed a hand on his shoulder. "That's exactly why ol' Prophet had a direct hand in constructing the logic and scenarios of the infinity loop."

"I don't like it. The fact that the loop is set to use places that we've recorded with the tempFix only this past month means that it won't be perfect. For instance, in the first layer, that godfor-saken boat." He shook his head.

"Not all of the loop is tempFixed," Dedere remarked, looking over Lisandro's shoulder. "And of the parts that are, many of them are carried over from some of the past experiments."

"What if this doesn't work, Dedere?"

"What?" she said, turning around.

"What if the loop comes to nothing *again*?" he asked, shooting her a blank expression.

"We'll just find another person, I suppose." She grimaced at the thought. They could—and would—do it if they absolutely had to, but the energy cost of running the Infinity Loop again...and with-out any results to show for it...

"Did the Prophet ever say anything about why this guy was chosen?" Lisandro asked, eyebrows sagging in defeat. "It seems pretty arbitrary to me; he's just a university kid over at Academia Hector."

"Wouldn't matter," Dedere replied, eyes distant. "At this point, he doesn't need to give reasons." Their mentor was known for his uncanny intuition.

"He didn't say anything at all?"

"Not that I've heard, at least." She brushed a strand of hair be-hind her ear. "We should make our way to the launch room."

Lisandro pulled away from the computer and stood, brushing off his knee-length steel-gray coat.

* * *

Dedere leafed through the packet of Beginning, End, and Re-morse augury results. At the top of each page was the phrase, "Dunai, I. J. CONFIDENTIAL PATIENT RECORDS," along with the date and the page number. She'd printed it fifteen minutes ago, just as the patient was entering the dilation chamber. Due to the nature of their experiment, they could only conduct the full augury after a participant formally signed their name and agreed to the joint-fulfillment oath.

"There's a lot coming up on the fears index," she exclaimed. "He has a score of *320*. Hey, Lisandro?"

"Um, 320? On the fears index?" he echoed, bringing himself back into the moment with a small shake of his head. "Wait, what?"

"I know!" Dedere continued. "This guy...he's afraid of all the major categories. Hates dark places, cramped spaces, fears being buried alive, doesn't like heights, *hates* dead things, fears giving any kind of public performance, fears failure, fears dropping out of school, even fears his *mother*... The one major thing he doesn't seem to mind is spiders. Huh."

Lisandro frowned. "And the Infinity Loop is going to generate a trial configuration based on *that?*"

"Apparently."

"How many layers deep is required to address 320 fears?" he asked, getting up from his chair. "We need to check the machine. It's already been calibrating for five and a half minutes. Maybe Dr. Prophin made a mistake." Lisandro winced at his own words.

Dedere checked the informational glossComp screen on the exterior of the simulation machine. "Somehow, the trial managed to combine 320 fears into eight layers. Maybe the layers will be more challenging, trying to fit so many fears at once?"

Lisandro brought up the results of the fear index on his glosscomp, juxtaposing them with the trial configuration. "Why did the glossproggers index the fears as hex numbers?" he asked, exasperated. To see which fears were included in which trials, he needed to consult a lookup table.

"But look," Dedere said, pointing at the screen, "even without knowing which fears, we can still see that the first layer of the loop incorporated *268 fears*." She took in a shallow breath. "Y'jeni."

She and Lisandro shared a pitying look for the unfortunate, likely unsuspecting trial-goer.

"Well, it's too late to change anything now," Dedere said, fists tightening. She turned her head absently toward the room's exit, thinking of the man who had quietly strong-armed the project to actualization: Dr. "Prophet" Prophin, a man so busy he left his two researchers to oversee a multi-million auri trial while he planned his multi-billion auri experiment.

I hope his faith in us isn't misplaced.

GERMAINE ON A TRAIN

I am sitting with my sister on a train. We're in a spacious cabin with a table situated between us. We each take up one side of the cabin's benches, various bags and belongings cluttering the area.

"Ian?" she says, looking out the window. She turns toward me. "Hello?"

I shake my head. "Sorry, what?"

I haven't seen Germaine in years. *I'm older than her now*, I realize with a start. *Mentally, at least.* Germaine is—was—only two years older than me.

She positively glows with vitality, to both my eyes and my decemantic senses. But why is she here and in such good spirits?

"'I'm so proud of you,' is what I said, you dummy." She snorts at my uncomprehending expression.

"Why?"

She smiles. "Mother's proud of you too, you know, even if she won't say it out loud."

"...You can believe that if you want," I reply.

"She told me." Germaine sniffs indignantly. "She would never say it to *you* out loud, but she said it."

"Why would she say that?"

Germaine's eyes grow soft. She turns toward the window again, raising one leg onto the seat. "At one of those parties she so often attends, someone commented on your graduating." She sighs. "I was at the party, too, for the record. 'Spying' for Mother, you know."

I knew.

"They said that she must be proud, having a son graduating at the top of his class. You should have heard this person—her voice was so sarcastic and cruel, Ian. It was really unbearable."

I understand immediately. Whoever the person was must be familiar enough with Mother to know her eternal shame—that despite inheriting the bloodline of their father, neither of her children had an ounce of practitioner potential.

Germaine continues. "But Mother only smiled." Germaine's voice turned warm, and she faced back towards me. "She said that anyone would be proud to have a child at the top of the class."

I blink. "Is that it?"

Germaine sighed once more. "Yep."

I snort. "It's not really the same as saying she's proud of me, you know."

She gives me a look and crosses her arms. "You weren't there, Ian. But she meant it. You know how I know?"

"How?"

She walks her fingers across the table, then flicks my chest. "I just do, alright?"

I laugh for a solid few seconds.

"Hey," she says. "It wasn't that funny."

"I've missed you, Germaine."

She smiles. "I know. I'm just too cool, right?"

"Right."

There's silence for a moment.

"What's our stop again?" I ask, fishing for information.

"It's the last stop," she states. "Don't you remember?"

"No."

"It's literally the name of where we're going."

I roll my eyes. "Whatever."

Germaine takes out a pencil and begins to work in a notebook. I take in a deep breath and think about where the train could be headed. I extend my senses out, trying to see if I can detect any insects nearby. Unfortunately, this train has vermin filters at its apertures—a protective measure against transferring invasive species between provinces. That means that, at the very least, we're going somewhere far off. Not so far as to require a transport array, but far.

The conductor suddenly shouts a destination, his voice magnified throughout the train's length. "Approaching Brin City! Approaching Brin City!"

"Brin City?" I mutter under my breath in surprise. Brin is quite far from home, almost on the opposite edge of the world. *Close to Godora and the SPU, actually.*

"Ugh, we still have a few more hours to go."

"How many hours until we arrive, you think?" I ask innocuously.

"To Menocht? Oh, maybe three."

I nod.

Menocht!?

"Germaine...remind me again why we took the train all the way here."

Fixated on her notebook, she replies, "Transport array was too expensive. Besides, I found a discount on high-speed train tickets. This kind of train uses a new kind of hoverail. It glosses along almost twice as fast, so stop complaining."

"And why are we going all the way to Menocht, though? Why not somewhere closer?"

Germaine finally looks up from her notebook, placing her pencil down on the desk. "Well, you're sure full of questions today. Did you lose your memory or something?"

"...No."

"It's only three more hours, Ian. We're almost there."

Germaine resumes her work. I peer over, looking at the beginnings of a sketch.

"Hey, why are you sketching me?" I ask. It's a stylized representation, but I can pick myself out easily, if only because she's drawing me in my current position nestled between a cherry red suitcase and a dark green jacket.

"Maybe I'm not sketching you. Ever think of that?"

I scoff. "What are you, five?"

She rolls her eyes and shakes her head slowly. "I'm drawing you because I want to. Good enough?"

I snort and give her a crooked smile. "Guess I can't complain."

"Finally. Just...read on your glosspad, or look out the window if you're bored."

Instead, I look at her from the side, fixing my eyes on the edge of the window. A part of me wants to cry, seeing Germaine after so long. There's a kernel of tension in my stomach that's been churning ever since I found myself on the train with her, the kind of tension that demands release.

It's not that I never thought I'd see her again, but I genuinely missed Germaine. I missed her in a different way than Mother. My whole life seems—or seemed, I suppose—to orbit around Mother. It was always her metric of success that I needed to care about, and it was always her that I disappointed. For me, missing Mother is more like missing the feeling of pain. Pain hurts, but it anchors you, it reminds you who you are and that you can feel. Better to feel pain than nothing at all, moorlessly adrift.

Missing Germaine is like missing the sun.

After you've lived without the sun for a while, you get used to it, even think you don't need it. The dark becomes a friend. But when the sun returns...you realize everything you told yourself was a lie. You need the sun after all.

"Germaine," I begin suddenly. "Germaine."

"What?"

"I'm a practitioner."

She pauses, looking up, pencil in hand. "What?"

"I'm a practitioner."

"I heard you the first time. What?"

"Don't you mean, 'when'?" I lean back in my seat. "I'm serious, you know."

"Ian, I—since when?"

"Since now," I reply sadly. "Since just a moment ago."

I can tell that Germaine is getting both confused and worried, her eyebrows furrowing together. I consider telling her that we're in a simulated loop outright, but doing so seems futile.

"Germaine, I really can't explain, alright? It's too complicated."

She looks at me with a stunned expression. "Too...complicated?"

Y'jeni, I've already misspoken. I'm doomed unless I tell her everything.

"Sorry, sorry, I'll tell you. We have three hours, I guess..."

"Prove it," she interjects as though coming out of a trance. She grabs my arm and gives me an intense stare. "Show me."

I open my mouth, then close it. "What should I do?" I ask helplessly, my voice low. I feel like I'm about to show something illicit. Isn't it easier to just keep my mouth shut?

Maybe around Mother, I think. But...I want to tell Germaine.

But what to *show* her?

I think back to when I first sat in Jasmine's school therapist office. I convinced her by levitating myself. I could try that again. But a feeling comes over me, and I want to try something else.

Germaine is wearing leather boots. Animal skin is one of the few materials that, even when cured and processed, retains enough of its original structure and energy to be controlled, albeit with great difficulty. What remains of its energy is akin to a lump of dying coal, but with the right amount of finesse and control, it *is* possible to control it.

As Germaine's right boot slowly drifts into the air, she recoils and falls back onto the bench, eyes wide. Her boot is still elevated, and she looks at it like it's some kind of foreign object. She worms her foot out and sits cross-legged.

"Ok then."

"So?" I begin, trailing off.

"What kind of affinity lets you do that?" she asks, still staring at the boot. I let the leather drop down onto the seat. "It didn't look like wind elementalism."

I direct my gaze on the rugged ocean-side scenery outside the window. "Death."

I see her smile falter out of the corner of my eye. "Death...affinity?" She pauses. "That's...that's great!" she exclaims.

I raise an eyebrow and turn back to meet her gaze. "Really?"

"They make a lot of money," she replies. "More than a glossprogger."

I nod.

"Also," she continues, her forehead lining with thought, "it's one of the least dangerous affinities." She smiles. "Decemancers usually work in factories or in closed rooms as security specialists. Now, if you were an elementalist..."

I understand Germaine's perspective immediately: Most with Death affinity could never participate in the kinds of duels I saw at Sylvestri's party. Most are like Professor Durning's students, barely able to condense energy into a low-grade gem, or struggling to manipulate even the freshest and most intact of corpses. With practice, such people can master a small niche, using their affinity to do monotonous, but profitable, tasks. The most common such professions, as Germaine mentioned, are those who work in slaughterhouses or those who keep an eye on all vital signatures within a guarded area. If talented, the latter might even use thralled insects to keep an area under watch.

Contrastingly, an elementalist of even low affinity would be expected to work as a guard, soldier, or duelist. It's actually the high-affinity elementalists that leave these more dangerous professions behind. Those people serve as deterrents against conflict, usually waiting calmly on standby to be sent out, often even occupying political seats. For instance, even though he's a wind elementalist, the Crowned Prime spends his days in the well-defended walls of Ichormai.

"Germaine," I butt in. "You're talking about decemancers of low affinity." I give her a cool smile. "What of those with high affinity?" I see her jovial expression freeze on her face. And I tell her the truth: "My affinity is over 90%, Germaine. What about someone like me?"

She chuckles lightly. "Come on, Ian. Over 90%? People don't just develop 90% affinity overnight, you know. Now seriously, what's your affinity?"

"You caught me," I say, holding up my hands. "It's over...99%."

Now she laughs boisterously. "Not going to tell me? Fine."

I sigh. "Germaine...I need to tell you a story."

And so I tell her about the loop.

* * *

"And you think you're still stuck in a loop now?" Germaine says as we walk through the train station. The two of us have our hands full with suitcases and miscellaneous bags. "But there's no way to prove it."

"Yes."

"Unless you're like Euryphel, and you have End affinity." Germaine sighs. "I wish I had End affinity. It'd be cool to see threads of fate everywhere." She grunts as she hauls two stacked bags over a bump. "Wow."

"Do you believe me?" I ask.

"Well," she starts, giving me a look, "you're a practitioner now, so something must've happened. Your explanation of being stuck in a...what did Euryphel call it?"

"A dilation loop."

"Yeah, that. It seems plausible, though I'm not fond of the idea that I'm not *real*, if you know what I mean."

"You're real to me," I reply unhelpfully.

"Mhm. Man, really 99% affinity?"

I nod.

"But...what about when you leave the dilation loop? Are you still going to keep that affinity then?"

"Why wouldn't I?"

"Well, if none of this is real, why is your decemancy real? It could be all in your head."

"I see what you mean. But what would be the point of sending me here if I came out without any kind of power?"

Germaine pauses. "You said that this entire thing might just be a big experiment, and you a single trial. What if it fails?"

What if it fails? What if, when I wake up, this was all for nothing?

"I'll deal with whatever happens when it happens," I mutter in response. "There's no use speculating when all I'm doing is guessing. Where are we going, Germaine?"

"It's a place called Hotel Denochs."

I nod. "I know how to get there." It's a fairly nice hotel that overlooks the water. I've been there a few times since it's close to the docks. To be fair, since it's adjacent to a defensive artillery station, the hotel was often a casualty of conflict.

We arrive at the hotel a few minutes later, the two of us sweating from lugging heavy bags in the city's afternoon heat. Thankfully, the building is almost as close to the train station as it is to the docks.

"I believe you," Germaine says as we deposit the bags in our shared room. She walks over to the room's sole window—a wide, glass pane with a view of the city's right-most pier. "I can tell that you've spent a lot of time in this place." I come over and join her. In the reflection of the window, I can see that her lip is trembling.

"I appreciate your faith in me," I murmur.

"You've changed a lot, you know?" she says, her voice constricted. "What's happened to you"—she opens her mouth, closes it, then opens it again as though trying to find the right words—"is nothing less than torture. Stranding you here without any directions, without any idea why, and not pulling you out when it was clear that you were struggling. I'd kill those bastards if I could."

I mull over her words, then think of Euryphel's perspective. "I shouldn't be thankful at all if I wake up a practitioner?"

Her expression morphs into a grimace. "Being a practitioner won't make you happy. In your case, it's more likely to get you killed. Am I wrong?"

I shake my head. "You're not wrong."

"So why be thankful?" She snarls, finally turning toward me. She grabs my shoulders. "It's not okay!"

"But Mother..."

Germaine lets out a strangled sound. "I wouldn't be surprised if this is somehow her doing. Y'jeni, that woman..."

I pull Germaine into a hug. "Germaine. It's alright. I'm happy, okay?" I stroke her back. "When I get out of here, I'll keep out of trouble, okay?"

She begins to sob. "You're such an idiot." She breathes shakily. "You can't keep out of trouble if you have a 99% affinity."

"Just what am I supposed to do?" I ask quietly. I never thought Germaine would have a meltdown over this. I thought she'd be...happy. Perhaps even relieved.

"I don't know," she says after a moment. "I don't think there's anything you *can* do."

We remain there for a time, me gently stroking her back, her arms wrapped around my shoulders. Eventually, we each take a seat on the bed.

"I never told you why we came to Menocht, did I?" Germaine says, changing the topic. "It's for one of Father's cousins."

I narrow my eyes. "Who?"

"His name is Marcus Adricaius. He decided to host a family reunion to celebrate the marriage of his daughter, Festina Adricaius, to Beirut Helvelium. For some reason, that meant inviting us."

"Mother?"

She shakes her head. "Not invited."

"Really?"

"Really. She's been disowned by the family, after all."

"Why us?" I ask. "And when and where is this reunion happening?"

Germaine takes out her glossY and pulls up an elegant invitation. "Look for yourself."

> *Germaine and Ignatius,*
>
> *It is my pleasure to invite you both to the wedding of my daughter, Festina, to Beirut Helvelium. It has been years since I have seen the two of you, and I would be pleased to pay for your travel to Menocht Bay to attend the ceremony. I believe that it is time for you to reunite with the better half of your family.*
>
> *Fondly,*
> *Uncle Marcus*

After Germaine's RSVP is another message:

<u>ITINERARY</u>
Thursday
Arrival: check-in at Hotel Denochs between 2:00 pm and 5:00 pm.
Proceed to dinner and festivities at Sunset Winery, taking a shuttle from the hotel at 5:00 pm or arranging other means of transportation.
Shuttles will be running at 10:00 pm and 12:00 am back to the hotel.
Friday
Brunch at the Glass Palace at noon.
Rehearsal dinner in Bridoc Yacht Club at 6:00 pm for immediate family.
Festivities and entertainment at the estate of Zebede Dunai, 1283 Grand Vista, from 8:00 pm until 2:00 am.
Saturday
Wedding ceremony in Gosophal Orchard at 3:00 pm.
Reception immediately following at Bridoc Yacht Club. Transportation shuttles provided at wedding.
Shuttles will run between 10:00 pm and 2:00 am on the hour to return to the hotel.
Sunday
Departure, with check-out by noon.

I shake my head. What a schedule.

"Any idea how many people are coming to this thing?"

"All I know is what's in this invitation."

I look at the time on the glossY. "It's almost 4 pm now. Other relatives should have already arrived at the hotel."

"Probably."

"What do you think is the purpose of this layer, Germaine?" I ask, leaning back on the bed. "A family reunion X wedding...seeing you...it's odd."

"Sounds like something unexpected will happen. What are you planning to do, huh? Are you coming to the reunion as a decemancer?"

I close my eyes. "How about you choose."

"You know, this is the family that cast us off for the past fifteen years, ever since Father started having difficulties. I couldn't care less about them, except that they offered us a free trip to Menocht. I know that they've looked down on us. They made it even more difficult for Mother." She lays down next to me. "If they had just given her some help, treated her like part of the family, maybe she would be different."

"Maybe."

"I kind of want to get back at them..." Germaine says, voice small. "But we're here for a wedding, not a competition."

I nod. "Got it."

WINERY

G ermaine and I rest up in the room until just before 5 pm. At that point, we head downstairs to the hotel lobby. There are at least fifty people already present, milling about in fine clothing. Germaine and I take one look and head right back up to our room.

"They just said that we were going to a winery..." Germaine grumbles, rummaging through a suitcase. "I don't think I brought enough fancy clothing. Damn it."

"Germaine, we're going to miss the shuttle."

"That's easy for you to say! You can wear the same jacket and pants and just need to change your shirt and tie."

I roll my eyes. "Forget about the shuttle. I'll get us there regardless."

She turns around. "Oh, really?"

"Yep."

She laughs. "Fine then. You know, the itinerary didn't say when festivities at the winery would begin. It just said that a shuttle would bring people around 5 pm."

"There must be at least three different shuttles leaving around 5 pm," I conclude. "There's no way a single shuttle could fit everyone." I take out my glossY and conduct a search on the location of the winery. The winery is located on the opposite side of the Zimbadi River, which flows from Lake Kaspar into Menocht Bay. It's about a thirty-minute shuttle ride away, I reckon.

"Just pick one of your dresses; we can go shopping for another tomorrow, during the rehearsal dinner."

"I know, I know…" She grabs a teal dress and runs into the bathroom. She comes out a minute later. "How is it?"

"Perfect." Germaine is a naturally tall, slender person. The dress is simple but flattering.

At this point, it's a few minutes past five. There's a good chance that we could make one of the shuttles still, so Germaine and I hurry down. Like I thought, there's still a large group of people standing around chatting. A line-of-sorts stretches from the lobby through the door and outside.

"You know," I murmur, "we could still go another way."

"Oh really? By what, bone wyrm?"

I chuckle. "Nothing so pretentious. Let's get out of here, first."

We arrive on the street. I walk with Germaine over to the docks, eventually leading her into some tall grass and a rocky embankment with a "Dangerous — No Trespassing" sign.

"I feel like a naughty child," she says, giggling as we step on slick rocks. "Where are we going? Wait, what are those?"

I lead her around to a small, protected cove. "Let's go down. Don't struggle."

Germaine lets out a small scream as I levitate the two of us down. We touch down on the beach, Germaine's high heels immediately sinking into the sand. She kicks off her shoes and pulls up the hem of her shin-length dress, then bends down and peers at a large turtle resting on a rocky outcrop.

"I know you like turtles," I say, beaming.

"Ian, they're tortoises, but yes, I like them!"

Tortoises? Really?

"What did you do to me back there, though? It felt like I was a kitten being grabbed by the scruff of the neck—except rather than localized to my neck, the feeling was everywhere."

"I grabbed your body," I say. "And I moved it."

"I thought decemancers could only move dead things," she mutters as she walks over to another tortoise.

I scratch my head. "It's more difficult to move things that are alive, but it's possible. There's a thread of death in everything."

"You know, that's one of the wisest things you've ever said."

I burst out laughing. "Funny. *Very* funny."

I'm suddenly overcome by an acute feeling of loss. No matter how much I want this to be real...it isn't. This isn't really Germaine. She won't remember any of this.

I'm in the loop. I'm not here to have fun: I'm here to escape. Which brings me back to the issue of the moment: What is the point of this layer of the loop? I highly doubt it's like the school loop layer, forcing me to restrain my practice to evade detection. For that reason, I'm willing to risk taking Germaine on a little adventure.

"Let's go," I exclaim, gesturing for Germaine to come over. She comes to my side and gives me an expectant look. I point at the water. "Watch carefully."

Shells churn up the surface of the water like white and brown bubbles, drifting into the air. I form them into a solid platform complete with a small bone railing. I move the platform over to us and gesture for Germaine to step aboard.

She does so without hesitation, her sandy, bare feet meeting jagged shell. She doesn't complain and is soon leaning against the bone railing. As we begin to pick up speed, her hair streams across her face, her high bun starting to get messy and windswept.

"This is amazing," she says, sighing and leaning even farther over as though trying to dip her fingers into the ocean's spray. "Just incredible."

We follow the coastline down until the Zimbadi River. At that point, the winery vineyard is in sight, and I disassemble the platform into shells. Germaine walks beside me, heels held in her hands.

"Let me wash my feet quickly." She bends down and puts her feet in the river, its languid current stripping them of any sandy grits. She stands, then saunters over to a stone pathway, high-kicking her feet as she goes as though to dry them. Feet properly dried, she hops in place as she slips one shoe on her left foot, then the right.

Sometimes, it's easy to doubt that Germaine is twenty-five.

I take her arm and lead her through the winery path. Around us lay weeping willow trees—an out-of-place species when compared to nearby palm trees and tropical flowers—and their sinuous branches drape elegantly into a series of shallow pools lining the path leading up to the winery.

We hear the festivities before we reach the winery's back gates. Music from a live ensemble plays in the background, while the chatter of at least one hundred people fills the evening air. It's nearly 5:45 pm, but the sun is still high above the horizon and likely won't set until after seven.

The atmosphere is markedly different from Sylvestri's decemancer get-together. I give Germaine's hand a squeeze. "Ready to go in?"

She smirks and rolls her eyes. "I don't know if I'll ever be ready to meet this half of the family." Still, she's the one who takes the first step forward to knock on the unattended gate. It opens shortly after.

An attendant dressed in servile black robes peaks out, holding a platter of shrimp. "Excuse me?" He sounds perplexed. "Can I help you?"

I look to Germaine, then look back.

"We're here for the party," she says, smiling. "We took a scenic route up to the winery."

The server nods slowly in understanding. "Go around to the right and follow the side trail to the main entrance. They're strict about letting in only those who have been invited, so I'm afraid I can't let you in here."

We nod our understanding.

"Thank you," Germaine says, smiling. The door shuts, and we're left to find our way to the main entrance. Like the server said, the side path winds up and around the perimeter of the winery. The winery grounds are quite large, but before long, we spot a fast-moving line of people before an ornate wrought-iron gate. The two guards heading the queue attend to their glosspads, likely checking off names from a guest list. Germaine and I walk over to the back of the line and wait.

The contingent of five in front of us are involved in a spirited conversation and pay us no mind. However, a few seconds later, a group of three moves into place behind us. It appears to be a family, with two aged parents and an adult son, who looks to be around our age.

"And who is this lovely lady?" the older man behind us says, beaming. Germaine and I turn around. "You look absolutely stunning in that dress."

The man in question looks quite good himself, a veritable silver fox. His wife, too, is attractive and slender, fitting into a silvery cocktail dress. Their son rolls his eyes, as though trying to mask his embarrassment.

"Hello," Germaine says, bowing her head slightly. "I'm Germaine Artemis Dunai." She gives me a look, as though suggesting that maybe I should introduce myself.

I cough and say, "And I'm Julian Ignatius Dunai."

"Ah, so siblings," the woman says, matching her husband's smile. "And with the Dunai name, though I can't say I recognize either of you."

"We're distant relatives of the bride," Germaine explains, smiling gently. "And what are your names, if I might ask?"

The woman replies, "I am Rosa Lisandra, and these are Felix Ronaldo and Matteo Vero, surnamed Clavicelli." She indicates first her husband, then her son.

"A pleasure to make your acquaintance," I say politely. "And what is your relationship to the bride?"

Felix replies, "Rosa is a cousin of Marcus Adricaius."

Germaine and I share a small look of understanding. If Rosa is related to Marcus as a cousin, it's possible that she is directly related to Father. Of course, she could be a cousin on the other side of Marcus' family.

"Do you by any chance know a late Demetrius Dunai?" Germaine probes.

Rosa's face twitches. "Demetrius...why?"

"Just curious," Germaine says, letting the matter drop. "Do you know a Julia Verina Dunai?"

"Aunty Julia's a slut," Matteo murmurs under his breath, giving us a look.

So we are related directly, I realize. *Though from that comment, I'm not sure if that's a good thing.*

Rosa gives her son the stink eye. "We're familiar with Julia. Why?"

"Well," Germaine says, "she's our aunt."

Rosa's eyes narrow as though she's starting to put the pieces together. "Y'jeni, you're Demetrius's children, aren't you?" This statement seems to arouse the interest of the young Clavicelli.

"We are indeed," Germaine says, still smiling. She shoots me a look, and I realize it's because I have dropped my own smile. I take in a resigned breath and plaster a polite expression onto my face.

"The two of you seemed to have grown up well," Felix states as though trying to diffuse the slight tension.

"Julian recently graduated from Academia Hector at the top of his class," Germaine says proudly.

"In what field of study?" Felix asks, eyes bright with genuine curiosity. I can tell that he has no idea where his unfortunate question is going. Anyone who knows of the Demetrius scandal would also know the shame of his children. Felix, for better or worse, seems wholly ignorant.

As though sensing my own reticence, Germaine continues unabashed: "Glossy programmatics."

Felix keeps smiling, but he looks confused as though waiting for some other answer.

Germaine and I decided to keep my decemancy under wraps—at least, for the time being. Outing me now would cause no small stir, and without having a better idea of the purpose of the loop, it might be contrary to our ultimate purposes.

I look over at Germaine. "Germaine is a professional artist," I explain, pivoting the conversation's focus. "She has a successful studio in Gent City, even though she's only twenty-five." Germaine being labeled an artistic prodigy as an adolescent was what shielded her from the bulk of Mother's ire. Mother's son, on the other hand, while bright, was no genius, nor was he talented in any of the disciplines appreciated by high society. Utterly disappointing.

"Oh, how excellent!" Felix says, nodding excitedly.

I look off to the side while the parents inquire about Germaine's artwork and studio. The young Matteo soon fills my vision, his arms crossed against his chest.

"Isn't this party really something?" he says, smirking. "Over two hundred attendees to the winery alone. I hear the wedding reception will have over five hundred in attendance."

It's quite the show of wealth, I'll give him that. "It's an honor to be invited," I reply. I don't particularly want to converse with someone who called Aunt Julia a slut.

"I apologize for my comment earlier," he says suddenly. "Julia offended my parents a few years back. She refused to help them with an important task. Their resentment has trickled into me over time."

I cock my head. *Why the apology?* "And what kind of practitioner are you?" I ask.

"Sun," he replies. "Before you ask, I'm not an elementalist."

Unlucky. Not nearly as unlucky as to be born without any affinity, but unlucky all the same. Sun practitioners, while lauded elementalists, flounder outside of combat. I know that those with Sun affinity have some ability to influence plants and light, but they're outshone by both Light and Life practitioners.

"Wasn't going to ask."

"What's it like?" he asks suddenly.

"What's *what* like?"

"Growing up in this family as a non-practitioner."

I snort indignantly. "*Exactly* as you might expect."

"I guess that's why I've never seen you at any family functions."

"Name?" a deep voice asks. I turn around, startled to find that we've reached the top of the line.

"Germaine Artemis Dunai and Julian Ignatius Dunai."

The rightmost guard makes a scrolling motion with his finger, then taps the glosspad screen twice. "Go on in."

As we move past the gate, the sounds of music immediately intensify. I once again take Germaine's arm as she leads us into the crowd.

Most places have only trace, ambient levels of vital energy, but the winery is saturated with it. I sense vitality all around me, as plentiful as the partygoers. There is so much festivity and merriment that vitality is misting off the crowd and saturating the air itself.

I could practically get drunk off the vitality alone. I feel it ebb into me and fill my body, suffusing me with power. This kind of vital energy isn't natural; is it possible the winery has a special life array it activates during private events?

I look over at Germaine as she jerks my arm in a new direction, having spotted some food.

"Appetizers..." she grumbles under her breath, wheedling her way between other attendees.

Laughing at her determination, I ask, "How do you feel?"

"Good. Why?"

"This place is bursting with life. Literally bursting." I laugh. "I never expected this," I murmur furtively, with a grin. "I expected a gathering of conniving, politicking schemers. But instead it's a carefree, happy—"

"Hold on there," Germaine says, raising an eyebrow. "You okay?"

"I'm fantastic."

"Now I'm really concerned." She inspects my face as though trying to see if I'm showing signs of having been poisoned.

"I—for someone like me, this place is like pure energy. It's incredible. And miraculous! I didn't know so many people could actually be in such good spirits."

"Uh-huh." Germaine shakes her head. "You better watch yourself. You're acting *different*," she warns.

Different? Shouldn't everyone be equally affected by whatever is causing such high levels of energy? I look around at the effervescent vitality, trying to get a sense of whether its flow is uniform.

While I'm distracted, Germaine leads me to a long table filled with all sorts of appetizers. She picks up a little plate and starts serving herself.

"Aren't you going to get anything?"

I shake my head. "Not hungry."

Germaine groans. "*Your kind* of energy is not *this kind* of energy," she grumbles, pointing first at the sky and then at the food. "You need to eat. Free food, dummy." She pats my arm and hands me an empty plate. "Don't make me fill that plate up for you."

I sigh and roll my eyes, looking skyward. That's when I notice that a small, languid whirlpool of energy has gathered above me.

Y'jeni. Like this, I'm completely conspicuous. But I can't think of anything that will help; my body naturally generates a small amount of Death energy. Death energy from little microorganisms and cells accumulate in my body, rather than exiting through the skin.

But why would that matter? I wonder in exasperation. My passive energy generation has never been a problem before. It's only when I've actively cycled external energy that people have noticed anything. *Though technically, that's not quite true,* I muse, recalling the nurse in the school loop. She seemed to have noticed that something was off during my visit.

I decide to funnel accumulating Death energy through my feet and into the ground.

I despondently grab a few bite-size pastries and follow Germaine to a table serving as a bar. Fifteen or so bartenders decant wines of all shades into glasses before passing them off. Despite the volume of guests, fifteen bartenders seem sufficient to prevent the formation of a line. Germaine and I step right up to the first open bartender, with Germaine ordering for the two of us.

"I'll take a water for him, and your best red wine for myself."

"I'm fine, Germaine," I say in protest.

"Then order for yourself."

"A glass of white wine, please." Soon enough I'm holding a thin flute of water and a glass of wine, forcing Germaine to tug me around by my jacket's sleeve. After walking around for a few minutes, she finally leads us over to an unoccupied swinging chair. It's easily large enough to fit the two of us.

As a waitress passes by, we place our finished glasses and empty plates onto her serving platter. Having disposed of our trash, we lean back in contentment, listening to the strumming of music and indistinct chatter as the sun starts its descent.

"It's been a lonely few years without you, Germ."

Germaine snorts. "I'll bet." She pumps her legs forward, setting the swinging chair into motion.

"I wish you could remember this. When I leave, I'll be the only one who'll remember."

Germaine remains silent for a moment. "When I paint, sometimes I spend weeks working on a piece that nobody understands but me. I often have to redo those pieces entirely, either throwing them out or painting over them. Anything my agent doesn't approve of gets cut.

"There was one piece that I've never forgotten. I drew it on a small canvas, as a practice, but as I continued to work on it, I decided that I would try to finish it. The more I painted, the more I felt as though enraptured, enlightened.

"When I completed it, my agent then—I've since replaced her—sneered and threw it onto a candle flame." Germaine fiddles with a napkin as she speaks.

"I've wanted to recreate that painting many times, but I've never done so. Why? Because it was perfect the way it was. I can't even think about making it again. The painting was a beautiful and unique little flower in my heart." She turns to me. "Do you understand?"

"I'm not sure," I answer truthfully.

She sighs. "Just because I'm the only one who remembers that painting doesn't make it any less precious or beautiful. Doesn't make it so that it never happened."

We lay on the chair, rocking up and down for a few minutes in companionable silence.

"Oh, it's you two," a voice says. I look up and notice that Matteo has found us again, though this time he's accompanied by two others. "Funny running into you again."

"Who are they?" one of his companions asks.

"Dunais," Matteo says, giving us a knowing look. "C'mon, let's find the bocce courts."

"I can't believe he called Aunt Julia a slut," Germaine says after he's gone. "Ridiculous."

"Do we have any idea if Aunt Julia's here?" I ask.

Aunt Julia is a seasoned Life and Beginning practitioner. She boasts one of the highest Beginning affinities of those present—something over 70% last I heard. Her Life affinity shouldn't be too far behind. Therefore, if there was anyone who might notice anything off about me at this party, it would be her. Thankfully, though, the swirling vortex of energy above me has mostly gone away.

"Maybe we can find her," Germaine says. "Seems like the entire family is here, so it wouldn't surprise me to see her in the crowd."

"We can ask one of the security guards to check if she has entered," I propose. After sitting down for a little while, my limbs are thrumming with unspent energy.

"Now that's a plan." Germaine gets up and beelines for the closest guard—a young man who's standing stiffly in front of a side entrance.

"Hello," she begins, voice saccharine as she stands before him, "I was wondering if you could see if a guest has arrived yet."

"Certainly, miss. What's the guest's name?"

"Julia Verina Dunai."

The guard looks down at his glosspad. "She's here, miss. Not sure if I can help you find her, given the volume of guests, but she's somewhere."

Germaine turns back toward me and heads off into the crowd with excitement. However, this time, she fails to grab my hand, forcing me to try and push through the crush of guests after her. After a minute of pushing, I lose her in the crowd.

I look to the saffron sky, taking in a deep breath of vitality. Even though the whirlpool above me is gone, a cloud of loose vitality clings to me like a stubborn odor.

"Y'jeni, the energy here is ridiculous," I whisper under my breath. I'm not completely ignorant to the fact that the abundance of vital energy is influencing me more than others and impairing my judgment. Rather, I'm not sure what should be done about it—I'm already grounding my Death energy. What else can I do?

"And who's this strapping, unfamiliar young man?"

I turn around. *Me?* "Pardon?"

A coterie of white-haired gentlemen chuckle. "Your name, son."

I grin. "Julian Ignatius Dunai." I study their reactions, finding nothing noteworthy.

"So it's Demetrius's son," one of the men says, practically shouting to be heard over the background noise."

A few of them nod in remembrance. "He does look like Demetrius," one of them says, squinting. "Sure has the same kind of swagger."

Swagger? I've never heard myself described as having swagger.

"Tell me a story about my father, then, if you knew him," I say, giving the older gentlemen a small challenge.

One of them chuckles. "A story about Demetrius?" He elbows the man next to him. "Melvik, tell the kid a story about Demetrius!"

Melvik takes a swig from a flask. "Y'jeni, I need to be drunk before I can think that far back. Oh, Demetrius was a troublemaker."

The gentlemen all clink their wine glasses together.

"But he was a fun brat to be around," Melvik continues, chortling. "Recall, gentlemen, that Demetrius was a damn-well competent Beginning practitioner. Recall, also, that he liked to pretend that he had no affinity whatsoever and challenge people to all sorts of gambling games."

I snort at the shamelessness of it all. Someone with a Beginning affinity would have no trouble analyzing and exploiting any kind of game or human behavior. Their power revolves around analyzing the world around them like a preternatural glosscomp and performing auguries, or predictions. In my native state of Solar, people with over 20% Beginning affinity are outright banned from gambling houses. I'm vaguely aware that my father had this kind of shameless hobby, though, unsurprisingly, I haven't heard many stories about it from Mother.

"So one night he challenged someone to a game of poker. Utterly destroyed them, took their money. Shameless, right?"

"Aye!"

"So the person he conned turned out to be a powerful fire elementalist, and the man challenged him to a duel. And guess what Demetrius did, when faced with a duel against an angry fire elementalist?" Melvik asks, looking around. "He said *yes!*"

"Oh, I remember this story," one of the men says.

"Right. So Demetrius went onto the dueling ground and had his pick of the weapons, given that he was the one challenged. So he went over and asked for swords. Live swords, mind you, with sharp blades. Keep in mind that Demetrius had no talent for the blade."

I have to admit, I'm curious where this story is going.

"So the fire elementalist entered the dueling plot, sword in hand, and faced Demetrius. As soon as the starting flag hit the ground, the fire elementalist wasted no time in conjuring up a ball of flame and sending it toward him. Demetrius moved forward and tripped over his own two feet, falling in a most spectac-ular manner. The fireball missed, of course.

"Demetrius scrambled to stand, fumbling with his sword. The elementalist, meanwhile, sneered and threw another ball of fire just as he began to move forward again. Demetrius made it three paces before he tripped yet *again*." Melvik chuckles. "He tripped at least eight times before he got within a sword's length of the elementalist and drew first blood."

"It's an apt metaphor for how he went about life," another of the older gentlemen says wistfully. "But then one day, the joke was on him." The man looks at me. "I hope that things turn out better for you than they did for your father."

"I hope so, too." I turn to the storyteller. "Thanks for sharing the memory, Melvik. I don't have many of them that involve my father."

"Ian!" a voice calls out, almost lost amongst the background noise.

I turn around and see Germaine tugging our aunt through the crowd. Aunt Julia is attired in an azure dress composed of many pieces of thin, layered cloth. As she draws closer, her green eyes stare warmly into my own.

We embrace. "Aunt Julia," I exclaim as we separate. "It's been too long."

"At least two years," she says, nodding. "I heard from your mother that you graduated top of your class. I am so very proud of you!"

"Thanks, Auntie."

"It's almost time for the main dinner. Let me introduce you to the better half of this side of the family."

Aunt Julia thrusts us upon a tide of relatives, most of whom are complete strangers. Germaine seems to remember more of them than I do. Every time, whoever we meet greets us jubilantly, oftentimes insisting on embracing and clinking glasses. To be honest, I wouldn't even recognize the bride; I've maybe seen the Adricaius family once before—and that was many years ago.

Aunt Julia is much more popular than I imagined. It seems like every time she turns around, more people are waiting to speak with her. Some of the guests have a kind of intensity in their gazes as though they hope to get more out of the conversation than just exchanging warm regards. I have the feeling that she's likely using the two of us as a diversion to avoid hearing requests for favors.

"Aunt Julia, why is it that everyone at this party seems so happy?" I ask. Maybe she can explain the abundance of vital energy.

"Marcus asked me for a favor, to set up a vital growth array. It's an extravagance, but Y'jeni, I can feel my skin growing more rejuvenated with every passing moment," she says, chortling. "Doesn't it just feel wonderful?"

"It feels fantastic," I reply.

"Nephew, you're fairly sensitive to the array's effects," she observes, giving me a scrutinizing look.

I shrug innocently. "I wouldn't know."

Germaine interrupts the conversation, exclaiming, "Oh, look, the dinner tables are ready." She's right if the surging flux of human bodies is anything to go by. She gestures her head to the right. "Shall we all sit together?"

Aunt Julia takes one of our hands in each of her own as she strides toward the amassing crowd. "Of course." Her warm hand squeezes down tightly, and I notice her sending a trickle of vitality into my fingers as through probing for a reaction.

I'd better prepare an explanation for later.

A FORCED HAND

Dinner proceeds uneventfully, with Aunt Julia directing the conversation. I listen quietly for most of it, only speaking when necessary. People seem vaguely interested in me before they realize I'm the talentless son of Demetrius, at which time they tend to leave me alone. By the time dessert is served, the conversation has directed itself on Germaine's art.

At the end of dinner, Aunt Julia invites us to accompany her in refreshing the vital growth array. Germaine gives me a look, widening her eyes and pressing her lips together.

Yes, I know she's on to me. It's not my fault!

Aunt Julia leads us to what appears to be a service building. Upon entering, she immediately takes a staircase down and turns right at the fork. Filling the span of the entire underground hallway is the vital growth array, its power so potent as to be visible with the naked eye.

I freeze in place and hang back. I would normally have Death energy to center me in the presence of so much vitality; without it, I can already feel myself getting dizzy.

"Wow," Germaine coos, crouching down and letting the pooling vitality stretch around her fingers like bubbles of green taffy. "This is what's making everyone feel so good?"

Aunt Julia nods. "This hallway stretches around the perimeter of the main property."

"How does it work if it's just around the perimeter?"

Our aunt smiles. "The array only needs to be drawn in an unbroken circuit. The area within it—in this case, either the building's cellar or even solid ground—will also produce vitality."

"What do you think, Ian?" Aunt Julia says. I can practically see the gears turning in her head. "Don't be afraid and come on forward."

I can barely process her words.

"Uh, Aunt Julia, he's strongly affected by the vitality, isn't he? Are you sure that's a good idea?" Germaine asks.

Aunt Julia gives Germaine a stony look. "Don't interfere." She looks back toward me. "Come."

I shake my head limply. "I'm feeling ill. I should go back up."

"Fine. You stay there; Germaine, step back. I'll just be a moment refreshing the array." She holds out her hands at hip height. A stream of vitality erupts from her palms, and her eyes shine a viridescent green. The vitality streaks around the hallway like lightning over metal, blisteringly fast. I watch, dazed, as the energy circles faster and faster.

I gag and begin to sag against the wall, leaning on my right arm. I close my eyes, but the scene doesn't go away: I can easily see the energy beyond my eyelids. I turn my face away and try to turn my whole body around.

Germaine rushes over and holds my free arm in concern.

"Aunt Julia, can't you see he's really ill?" she cries out. "You *idiot,*" she whispers. "It's not worth it."

But isn't it? If I can't even go to a single party without needing to use decemancy, it's like I've become dependent on a drug. I should be able to get through this, even if it requires me to feel sick. If I give in just because the loop isn't real, I'm not doing myself any favors.

I steel myself and walk toward the stairs. But just as I'm about to go up, something catches my eye. I see a seedling of Death energy hidden behind the stairs, behind two layers of walls, its energy signature mostly obscured. What is that?

I stagger up the stairs and wait for Aunt Julia to finish. Before she comes over, I whisper to Germaine, "There's something hidden in the wall. Ask Aunt Julia if she feels anything weird coming from behind the stairs."

Sensing something in my voice, Germaine's eyes widen, and she nods resolutely.

With a flash, the array grows dark; the procedure has finished. Our aunt saunters over, walking toward the stairs.

"Aunt Julia, I think I might have dropped something under the stairs," Germaine says. "Do you, uh, see anything under there?"

I take in a deep breath. *Germaine is a terrible liar.* If I could just send out a little tendril of Death energy to inspect the seedling...

"No," Aunt Julia says, crossing her arms.

Germaine groans and throws up her hands. "I give up." She points at me. "You know what he is, right?"

Aunt Julia rubs the bridge of her nose. "Dear, I'm a Beginning practitioner." She says this like it's an explanation in and of itself. "My nephew has the most acute Life sensitivity I've ever seen. Every other second he fidgets like he's in withdrawal. There's a web of vitality suspended around him. He's subdued and doesn't speak like he's afraid he'll say or do something. Or because he's concentrating on doing something else."

I frown, annoyed that she's so coldly dissecting my behavior. She's right that I've been concentrating on something else—namely funneling Death energy into the ground. It's a deceptively tricky exercise; much finesse is required to manipulate so little energy.

"There are a few reasons why people might have life sensitivity. First, they're born that way. Second, they're suffering from some kind of curse or degenerative disease. Third, they're a practitioner of opposite alignment. That is, they're a decemancer.

"As far as I know, my nephew is none of these things. So how is it that he suffers so?"

"You could have just asked me from the beginning," I grumble. "Instead of acting like a sleuth."

She ignores me and continues, "The last explanation is that he's been compromised by a soul seed."

I blink once, confused.

Germaine asks, "A what?"

"A soul seed. Someone who has been implanted with a soul seed will slowly be taken over by a malevolent spirit. The seed is attached to someone's soul and is discreet, barely detectable by even the most powerful Life and Death practitioners. After a few years, the person will be fully possessed by the spirit, their soul completely devoured." She says this all in a quiet, steady voice.

I've never heard of a soul seed. I suspect from the technique's use of spirits that it comes from necromancy. Despite the fact that modern decemancy derives from necromancy, necromancy is fundamentally more ritualistic and mired in the occult, dealing with embodied souls and disembodied spirits. Contrastingly, decemancy's domain is Death energy. Even decemantic soul gems are just deposits of Death energy, so named because they subtly carry the imprint of whatever creatures they derive from.

It seems like, at least for a time, Aunt Julia suspected me to be affected by a soul seed. I feel a bit guilty for making her worry.

"Aunt Julia..." I murmur, my eyes flashing violet. "I didn't mean to make you worry."

I finally give myself some leeway to seize the vitality around me and convert it to familiar, grounding Death energy. It's easy to do so by drawing the energy into my body. While I can intentionally damage my own cells to quickly generate Death energy, the deluge of vitality allows me to do so without fear of injury.

She steps back, pale. "So...you really are a practitioner."

I nod. "It's a long story, but I didn't plan on bringing it up here, tonight. Unfortunately, this vital growth array of yours has forced my hand."

She shudders. "What happened to you to awaken your affinity?"

I avoid her stare. "We can talk about it later. But first..." I send out a thick vine of energy and make contact with the deposit of Death energy behind the stairs.

"Ian?" Germaine says, shaking my shoulder. "Hello?"

My countenance turns dark. "There's a dead child behind the stairs." But more than that...there's something more nefarious: a blood array. I wouldn't have noticed it from behind the walls, but I can detect it after probing the child's surroundings.

"A what?"

I clench my teeth. "A dead child! Can't you sense it?" I point downward and saturate the area around the child with my own energy. "See it now?"

Our aunt grimaces and runs forward. "I see it, though it's faint." Her eyes momentarily flash green. "They've only been dead for a few hours at most."

"What do we do?" Germaine asks, sitting down on the stair steps. "I didn't think there were any young children allowed into this party. Doesn't that mean that this isn't related to the family?"

"It's not just a dead child, Germaine," I spit in disgust, "it's a sacrifice. There's a small array of blood around it." I scoff cynically. "Someone's decided to use your vital array as part of a blood offering, Aunt Julia. Isn't that wonderful?"

Her face turns red with fury. "Nephew. Are you sure about this blood array? I can't detect anything."

I smile icily. Why would I lie about something like this? "Positive."

"Why are you only mentioning this now, after I've called you out?" she asks, clearly suspicious.

"If I knew about this, I would have told you immediately. But I didn't see the energy signature until now. It's well-hidden."

Aunt Julia appears pensive. "There are at least three decemancers at this party. They should have noticed something."

"Not with all the vitality flowing around," I argue defensively. "I bet that all of them are distracted. Besides, like I said, the sacrifice is well-hidden, obscured by both earth, walls, and vital energy."

"I should fetch Arno—"

"Don't worry. I can take care of this."

Aunt Julia looks at me with a tired expression. "I'm happy for you, Ian, that you've awakened an affinity. But with such a sensitive matter, I would feel more comfortable consulting Arno Dunai."

Haven't heard of him. "Is he a decemancer?" Germaine asks.

"He is."

"What affinity?" Germaine continues, giving me a sidelong glance.

Julia pauses. "I'm not sure. But certainly over 50%."

"With all due respect, I think you should trust Ian with this. You don't know—"

Aunt Julia snaps. "Of course, I don't know, because he didn't tell me!" She points a finger at me. "I can tell that you aren't a complete novice, so you must have awakened your affinity at least a year ago. Yet you never told me, never asked for guidance or support. I—" She stops suddenly, then takes a deep breath, regaining her composure. "What is your affinity?"

I sigh deeply, then look at Germaine. "So much for trying, right?" I give her a weak smile, then look Aunt Julia straight in the eye. "You think you know, don't you?"

"It's impossible. You were able to sense the sacrificial child from behind the walls, even with the obfuscation of vital energy. To do that, you'd need an affinity upwards of forty percent. There's no way you could hide a moderate affinity for so long."

"You're right, it is impossible. That's why I tried not to say anything or draw attention to myself." Aunt Julia just stares at me. After a second of silence, I give her more information to consider. "Have you heard of a time dilation array?"

"Yes," Aunt Julia replies, eyes narrowing. "Were you approached to make use of one?"

Approached? "I don't remember the circumstances that lead to entering the dilation array; possibly?"

She has a calculating look in her eyes. "...How long were you in it?"

I laugh; it's a cheerless, self-mocking sound. "What if I told you that I was still within one?"

"I wouldn't believe you," Aunt Julia says dismissively. She pauses, then rubs the space between her eyes, as though nursing a headache. "Of course, I believe you. Y'jeni, why would you lie? But all the same..." She takes a deep breath. "Let me try to help you understand my perspective. As you should have assumed, I'm using my Beginning affinity to direct my intuition. Practically, that means that I can retrace my steps over the course of the evening, see your behavior in a new light, and try to piece all my observations together to form a coherent theory. The results of this augury?"

I frown at the question. "...That I've been afflicted by a soul seed?"

She shakes her head. "No, that was before what I just learned. Based on every interaction we have ever had, and even this conversation now, my auguries are inconclusive. That's nearly impossible. But if I discard all prior knowledge—treating you like a stranger—and conduct an augury based on what I've observed tonight and only tonight…" She glances at Germaine, then back to me. "There's only one conclusion that makes sense. What is your affinity?"

"Over ninety-nine percent, Aunty."

I can sense Aunt Julia's chest constrict, the breath catching in her throat. Her heart begins to race.

"Believe it or not, it's the truth." I walk a few steps closer. "Do you understand, now, why I didn't want to tell you here, in the middle of the party?"

"You should believe him about the time loop, Aunt Julia," Germaine adds. "After you deal with this sacrifice situation, let him explain."

After hearing Germaine's appeal, Aunt Julia sighs and rubs the bridge of her nose. "How do you intend to deal with the sacrifice?"

I turn back around, gazing through the wall to see the dark, doll-like figure. Death energy wisps off it, its outline appearing somewhat smudged like a charcoal sketch.

"I think it should be enough to dispel the energy. The sacrifice has provided a fresh, potent power source for the inscribed ritual. Removing the source of energy should be sufficient to neuter the ritual's effects."

"Why not just destroy the ritual?" Germaine asks.

I walk to the stairs and sit down, facing the two of them.

"I could also do that. But even if the blood inscription is ruined, it's possible that there's a countermeasure in place, such that breaking the ritual sigils causes an unexpected—and unpleasant—effect."

Aunt Julia nods. "Often, these kinds of blood arrays compress and store energy until they hit a critical point, then they'll release their spell."

"Sounds like it might be a bit explosive," Germaine adds.

I take a deep breath and stretch out my shoulders. "Aunt Julia, shall I proceed?"

"Go ahead; it seems like you already know a great deal about blood arrays."

I snort. "I don't know that much." Hercates' Grimoire actually had a chapter that discussed the ideal way to "package" Death energy for different purposes, including ritual consumption. He was quick to mention the explosive downside of using raw energy in the event that a ritual failed or was interrupted.

I stand and angle myself toward the wall, then begin to siphon away the energy from the sacrifice, taking care to do so slowly and steadily, lest I risk the blood array flaring up. If I didn't feel confident, I would've taken precautions, such as sending away Aunt Julia and Germaine.

But I *am* confident. Like a river flowing into the sea, the energy passes into me without issue, melding with my own. After siphoning the Death energy from the sacrifice, I control its bones to swipe at and ruin the blood array's sigils.

"Done."

"That was quick, Nephew. Your control is unquestionable."

"Thanks," I reply, not exactly sure how to respond. I sense something deeper in Aunt Julia's words. Her tone almost sounds...bittersweet?

"You two go back up and see if you can find anything suspicious; I'm going to stay here for a spell and see if I can discern anything."

"We'll keep an eye out," Germaine assures her.

Germaine and I head out of the basement, leaving Aunt Julia to conduct her Beginning auguries. We spend the rest of the evening wading through the sea of people, trying to find a clue. Though I'm not sure when the array is supposed to activate, by the time we decide to leave, I'm confident its failure should have been noted. Unfortunately, nobody acted particularly agitated, the festivities and good cheer remaining uninterrupted the entire evening.

The two of us leave the party by one of the side gates, returning to the path we took on the way in. We sit on a bench overlooking a small pond lined by willow trees, moonlight reflecting off the still water.

"That could have gone better," Germain says. "Yeesh."

"That was a complete trainwreck," I say, agreeing wholeheartedly. "I'm not sure how any of us thought we'd be able to detect suspicious behavior." Aunt Julia is *much* better suited for that kind of task.

"Maybe Aunt Julia was able to find something."

Our aunt came back up to the party after dinner, though she went off on her own, informing us that it was easier to judge people's behavior when there weren't extra variables hanging around.

"If she did find something, she'd inform us," I point out, holding up my glossY. "But so far, nothing."

Germaine picks a willow branch off the ground with her liberated feet, passing it to her hands. The branch is long and supple, and she casts it into the pond like a fishing line.

I decide to bring up something else that had been nagging at me.

"I can't believe Aunt Julia thought I was afflicted by a soul seed. As if that were more likely than me simply awakening a latent affinity despite coming from a lineage of powerful practitioners."

"Don't take it personally," Germaine says, squeezing my arm. "Her augury probably said it was the most likely possibility, given everything that she knows about you."

"I guess."

"You even said it yourself: it's impossible for you to hide such a high affinity for long. You struggle to hide it for a month, isn't that right?" she says, recalling my explanation of the Academia Hector layer.

"Sometimes it feels hopeless, Germaine."

"Hopeless? Ian, you're incredibly powerful. When you get out of this loop, you'll get to do amazing things."

"Do you really believe that?"

"Why wouldn't I?"

"My affinity is *too high*. Don't you understand?"

She smiles gently and leans her head on my shoulder. "What is there to understand? You're Julian, my little brother. A less timid, more powerful version of my little brother, but that's not a bad thing."

"What am I supposed to do when I get out of here, though?"

"Whatever you want."

"I don't *know* what I want." I lean my head against her shoulder. "The problem is that as soon as anyone catches wind of my power, I'll never be let alone again. I wouldn't be surprised if I end up assassinated."

Germaine is quiet for a while. "Didn't Euryphel tell you to find him when you get out of the loop? He's the Crowned Prime. He can protect you, right?"

"He seems to think so."

"So what's the problem?" she asks.

* * *

After half an hour of sitting and thinking, I take Germaine back, flying us over the water and onto Menocht Bay's main beach. We return to the hotel room without saying much, Germaine correctly sensing that I'm not in the mood to talk.

We wake in the morning to a knock on our hotel door.

"Who is it?" Germaine asks sleepily, pulling the sheets over her face.

"It's Julia," a voice calls out, muffled by the door. "If you're both sleeping, you should get up. Brunch is in an hour and a half."

I pull out my glossY and look at the time. Sure enough, it's just before 10:30 am.

"Can I come in?" the voice asks again. I roll out of bed, walk over to the door, and open it. An impeccably dressed Aunt Julia stands before me.

"Germaine, you take a shower first," I say, knowing that she needs more time to get ready. I walk over to her sleeping figure. "Come on, get up."

She opens her eyes and groans. "Fine, fine, I'm getting up." She stands and pads over to the bathroom, her legs heavy. The door closes behind her with a click, leaving me and Aunt Julia. Aunt Julia walks out onto the balcony, gesturing for me to follow. Closing the sliding door behind us, I sit across from her and wait.

"I do believe that you're stuck in a dilation loop," she says, not mincing her words.

"What made you change your mind?"

"If I complete my augury assuming that you've spent a few years in a dilation loop, everything becomes improbable, rather than impossible."

I chuckle. "How improbable is improbable?"

Julia gives me a small smile. "Improbable." She folds her hands over her crossed legs.

"I assume that nothing unexpected happened on your end, either."

"Yes; I couldn't find anything out of place. It suggests that it really was someone outside the guests who devised the sacrificial array. And even though nothing happened last night, that doesn't mean we're in the clear. Someone with the audacity to attack a gathering of powerful practitioners won't give up after being thwarted once."

"Makes sense."

"Julian..." Aunt Julia murmurs, her voice growing tender. "What happened to you?"

Conscious that we have only a limited amount of time before I need to get ready, I mostly just state a basic outline of events, omitting any in-depth descriptions. She listens without interrupting, her face stoic. I can tell that she's probably running auguries as I speak, trying to understand how my experiences have shaped me...and whether anything I say raises any discrepancies. Whether I'm lying.

Though I explain everything coarsely, none of it is false. I finish my story in twenty minutes.

"Well?" I ask, giving her a look. "What do you think?"

"I'm glad I'm not a Remorse practitioner," she says thoughtfully. "I think what you've been through is best considered from a distance."

"I'd have to agree," I reply, grimacing. "This loop is like a nightmare that never ends."

"I think I have an idea of why this is happening to you," she says suddenly, her eyes intense, "though I can't be certain."

I incline my head. "Really?"

"Yes, really. The National University of Selejo has been working on a project that's garnered a lot of ire in the past few years. It's caused quite a stir in bloodline practitioner circles," she explains. "It's a project that, at its heart, seeks to overturn the belief that being a noteworthy practitioner is largely determined by blood."

"What does it have to do with me?" I ask, genuinely confused. What use is someone who comes from a powerful bloodline to such a study?

"The researchers on that project are trying to find a method to awaken latent affinities. The idea is that far more people have the potential to be practitioners than we believe." She raises an eyebrow. "You can see why a family like ours would be against such a project, right?"

I nod slowly. "Is there any evidence that the project's hypothesis has any merit?"

Aunt Julia sighs and looks away wistfully, though there was a hint of some other emotion in her gaze. Was it...guilt?

"The project has been going on for a few years now, receiving a sizable amount of funds from the Selejan military. As far as I know, they've only recently secured the funds to start conducting clinical trials on people.

"One thing I do know is that the researchers have some evidence suggesting that some people never naturally awaken to strong affinities because the barrier to do so is too high. In other words, the more powerful the dormant affinity, the more likely it is to be latent."

I nod along. Technically, all infants, whether destined to be practitioners or otherwise, have low affinities. It's only after a few years that children differentiate and strong affinities start to manifest. What Aunt Julia's saying is that it might be easier for lower natural affinities to manifest naturally. Meanwhile, for someone like me...the affinity might lay dormant, too powerful to awaken without an extreme stimulus.

"You think that I might be in a dilation loop as part of this clinical trial?"

"It's more than a little probable, going off what information I have. Especially given your family, your exceptional status as a non-practitioner, your close proximity to the National University, and...well"—she coughs—"if they had a suspicion that you would awaken as a decemancer, it becomes even more probable."

"Why?" I ask.

"Latent decemancers are known for awakening in life-or-death situations when they're subjected to extreme duress. A dilation loop is thus the perfect stressor: It's a nightmare where you can face death in the face repeatedly. If there was any kind of affinity most likely to awaken in a dilation loop, it would be Death."

I ponder her words. "I see." I thrum my fingers against the arm of my chair. "And you think that this experiment is the most probable cause of my current situation?"

"Augury is imperfect," she cautions me. "I wouldn't put too much stock in what I've said. Anything is possible."

The warning is valid, but I think she's being modest. "It's a plausible theory. More plausible than anything I've come up with before." Perhaps this means that I *won't* wake up to find myself chained into servitude by a life-death oath.

Germaine knocks on the glass door to the balcony while holding a towel over her hair.

"We can talk more about this later," Aunt Julia says lightly. "Get ready for now. It's important you come to this brunch in case anything else threatening shows up. And given the fact that this is likely just a layer in the dilation loop, we should expect trouble.

"Also...I'm sorry. For yesterday. For doubting you—and for everything that you've experienced. It must have been difficult."

I stop for a moment, considering her words. "Thank you."

SOUL SWARM

Germaine takes my place with Aunt Julia as I head inside to get ready for the brunch. As I finish combing my hair and adjusting my tie in the mirror, the glass door slides open.

"We'll be late if we don't head down now," Germaine announces. "Let's go."

We walk over to the Glass Palace—a venue only a few blocks from Hotel Denochs. Whenever I've been in Menocht before, it was always autumn. Now, in spring, I'm seeing a new side of the city. The Flower District is visible from the hotel, a relatively circular, flat hollow cradled by tall buildings. Its upper level has transformed into a garden just coming into bloom, foliage intermixing with stalls and shopfronts.

As I gaze on the vibrant surface, my thoughts stray to the dingy level hidden beneath the main thoroughfare. I shudder involuntarily, though Germaine doesn't seem to notice. A part of me wants to go over, just to make sure there's nothing sinister brewing below.

There's nothing there, I tell myself. *There's no ginger in this Menocht.* I would've noticed if there were infected people by now: Detecting the infection's gray taint to vitality is a well-honed reflex.

When we arrive at the eponymous glassy facade, the restaurant's front doors are open to the cool breeze gusting off the bay. While we queue to enter, Aunt Julia introduces us to yet more unfamiliar members of the family, though she seems distracted. I notice her eyes scanning over the people beyond the doors, probably looking for anything out of the ordinary.

Nothing unexpected happens during the brunch. We arrive, eat our fill, and leave. There were a few points when I thought Aunt Julia was going to out me as a practitioner, but each time, I noticed her giving me an appraising look before pivoting the conversation.

After double-checking the exterior of the building for any shady figures, I lead the three of us out of the heart of the city and into a residential neighborhood. We enter a small tea house, order a hot pot of tea, and theorize about what group might have enmity with our family.

Aunt Julia outlines several possible organizations and individuals with the means and motive. I can tell from the length of her list that she is grasping at straws, speculating. No group seems particularly more likely than any others.

"I should talk to Marcus," she mutters pensively. "I want you at the rehearsal dinner and Zebede's party."

"Too much trouble." It's not worth it for Aunt Julia to owe Adricaius a favor. "I can just lurk around. I have a lot of experience lurking," I say, chuckling.

"This isn't a joke," Aunt Julia states firmly. "I want you with me."

"I'm not joking. I think I can do more good without than within. It's much easier for me to focus on foiling a plot when I don't have to worry about socializing with the family. Besides, how would you justify yourself to Adricaius without telling him about my awakening?"

"I could just tell him," Aunt Julia mutters.

Germaine nods. "You could probably tell the whole clan without risking a restart. It doesn't seem like telling either of us has been a problem."

I give her a pointed look. "You can't know that for sure."

"Aren't you curious, Julian?"

I freeze. "About what, exactly?"

Aunt Julia sips her tea. "About how the family will react. You're going to emerge from the loop eventually; the clan will find out about you."

"They'll find out when they find out," I murmur. I'd rather not think about it: The Dunai-Adricaius-Fiorencia conglomerate won't hesitate to take advantage of whatever influence I gain post-loop.

"It would be good practice," Germaine says.

Aunt Julia meets my gaze for a solid second before sighing. "Fine. You can stay outside if you think it'll really be easier."

"Much easier. If you really want, you can tell the family later, once we're surer of the purpose of this loop layer."

"What about me?" Germaine asks, fiddling with a teaspoon. "Anything I can do to help?"

If this were outside of the loop, I'd sooner lock her in the hotel room than let her help investigate a shadowy group of practitioners—Germaine isn't a practitioner, nor is she a trained officer of the law. If anything happened, it would be my fault for tangling her in a dangerous mess.

But now, when she's giving me such an eager gaze?

"Why don't you stake out from farther away. I can get you a telescope, and we can use quantum channeling to communicate if you see anything I miss."

Aunt Julia looks like she wants to say something but holds back, biting her lip.

* * *

I secure a telescope created by a Light practitioner during the day, stealing it from the personal observatory of a wealthy drug lord. When we arrive at the Bridoc Yacht Club, I create a command and control base on a distant overlook. As Germaine and I set up the telescope, she gives me a funny look.

"How did you get this so quickly?" she wonders.

I snort. "Stole it."

She raises her eyebrows, expression shadowed by the dim light of the sunset coming through the clouds. "It's bizarre to think of you stealing from anyone. You really have changed... It's hard to put into words, but I feel like I've missed a critical part of your life, the time when you were at your worst, when you really could have used someone."

"There's nothing to be done about it. It's not like I *couldn't* contact you when I was in the first layer at Menocht Bay. But it wouldn't help—you'd never remember. Not worth calling you and explaining everything, only to have everything reset the next day."

She chews her lip, obviously unsatisfied with my answer, but lets the subject go. She pulls out her glossY and projects the event's attendance list. "So, to confirm, I'm watching and keeping tally of who shows up."

I nod. "And whether anyone uninvited makes an appearance."

"Doesn't sound too bad. What do I do if someone comes and attacks my position?" she asks.

"I'll send a construct to protect you. In fact..." I reach for the sword at my hip, only to remember that glosSword is no longer with me. No matter. I wave my hand forward and bones emerge from the surrounding trees and knolls, pooling into a spider-like construct above my hand. I add a large soul gem to its central body, then lower it down next to Germaine and appreciate her spirited response.

"Ian!" she hisses, recoiling. "Seriously, a zombie spider?"

"It's not a spider," I retort. "Spiders don't have bones. This construct is just a bunch of bone pieces connected together at the center; nothing remarkable."

"Yeah right," she quips. "Ninety-nine percent decemancer spider construct, and all you have to say is, 'nothing remarkable'? Can it shoot lasers from its eye or something?"

I chuckle at the thought. To her credit, the little construct's soul gem glows with dark-violet light—I could imagine it flaring up to create a light beam if I didn't know better. "He'll defend you while I'm closer to the yacht club. That's all you need to worry about. Remember, if you sense anything suspicious, you have a way of contacting me." The quantum channel we established today is more than sufficient to convey our thoughts.

After Germaine is all set up and comfortable, I take my leave, heading for the yacht club. I wait until no one is nearby, then dash under one of the deck balconies, pressing myself up so that I'm only visible if someone passes directly underneath. While I have almost no visibility of my surroundings with mundane sight, I can use my vital vision to track people coming and going.

Before long, two hours pass. The wait is nerve-wracking in the beginning, but as the night wears on, I struggle to stay vigilant.

Suddenly, I sense an ovular shape radiating Death energy pass by the yacht club's side. It comes from Germaine's direction, likely darting out from one of the bluffs bordering the coast.

"Ian," Germaine whispers over the quantum channel. *"Something's come. Do you sense it?"*

The unidentified object would probably look invisible against the building's dusk-lit grounds. In the telescope's special Light monocle, I'd expect Germaine to see something.

"Yes, I was just about to tell you. Did you see what it looked like?"

"It was shadowy. I can't say much more—it flew away so quickly. Do you know where it is? I can't see it anymore. Maybe it went inside."

"Don't worry; I've found it." The object flits around the other side of the yacht club, hidden from Germaine's scope. *"It's behind the building."*

"Are you going to engage?"

"I could, but it might be better to wait and observe what it tries to do. Keep an eye out for anything—I'll keep you updated."

We wait in silence for another hour, the Death shadow making no movements. It must be passively waiting for some kind of signal, but I have no idea what.

"I see something!" Germaine exclaims, re-opening the channel and nearly scaring me half to death.

"Really?"

"It's coming from behind the house, over the water. It's a dark cloud."

Sounds like trouble. *"I'm going to intercept it before it gets too close."* And that means it's time to disarm the stationary shadow: It'd be horrible if this was some distraction to draw my attention away so it could attack.

I dart out from under the yacht club, my movements like those of a marionette guided by powerful, invisible strings. My form-fitting clothing ripples ever so slightly; covered by a plain black face mask, I must look more like a faceless puppet than a man. The shadowy object seems to sense my approach and begins to fly away, but it has no chance: It resists my energy for a moment, but is soon flying behind me, its loose robes fluttering madly in the breeze. *Who would have guessed that the object is really an animated mannequin dressed in clothing?*

As I fly toward the dockside, I move my hand and the figure speeds up. Eventually it arrives next to me as though yanked forward by a sturdy rope.

Off in the distance, the dark, formless smog looms. After a minute of flying, I get close enough to discern the purpose of the smog. *Soul swarm.* It's a literal swarm of thralled mosquitos, hundreds of thousands of them given how completely they blot out the sky.

Not on my watch. I swipe my hands down and the mosquitos crunch together into a ball, their buzzing cut off as wing smashes into wing. I expand the ball out again, stretching it like putty before smashing the mosquito corpses together again. I let them fall into the ocean like shards of broken glass.

Now that the soul swarm is taken care of, I turn to the shadowy figure frozen beside me. *"Germaine,"* I begin, opening up the channel. *"What do we do with this thing?"*

"Isn't it a person?"

"No. It's a vessel. It was being controlled by someone, though now it's harmless."

"What was that black smog you just destroyed?"

"Oh, that? It was a soul swarm."

"What's that?"

"Nothing too complicated. Normally, people condense Death energy into soul gems, but as we saw with the blood array, raw energy can be used for other purposes. In this case, to empower and control swarms of insects."

"Like mosquitos? You know, there have been a lot of those out tonight."

"There are always mosquitos," I say dismissively. *"It's probably nothing."*

"How would I know if it's a normal mosquito or an evil mosquito?"

"Well...what would be the point of sending a mind-controlled mosquito to bite you?"

"I—"

Germaine's voice suddenly cuts off. I feel my stomach sink. *What happened?*

Taking one last look in the direction from which the soul swarm came, I fly back towards her hiding place, keeping well above the yacht club. The shadowy vessel next to me bounces along like a limp corpse, though it's dark enough against the twilit sky that it should be practically invisible.

By the time I get close to Germaine, I can see numerous dark pinpoints on her skin where Death energy is funneling into her body. The spider construct is busily yanking them free, but it isn't fast enough to deal with an entire swarm. When I get close enough, I pull all of the energy-siphoning anchors free, the sensation similar to uprooting weeds.

I touch down lightly on the ground, then walk over and support her kneeling, shivering form. I see rivulets of blood flowing from each of the decemantic mosquito bites.

"At least I'm wearing black," she whispers, her voice hoarse.

"What?"

She turns her head to look at me. "It won't stain my clothes," she explains, gesturing to the blood. She pushes herself out of my arms and stands up, her legs shaky. "I'm fine, Ian. Thanks for the save."

I tug the mask down so that it hangs like a bandana below my eyes, covering my nose and mouth.

"You have hat hair," Germaine observes lightly.

That's exactly the kind of thing she'd say to stop me from worrying about her. "You should be feeling weak," I admonish. "You lost a good deal of vitality just now."

"I feel fine," Germaine says, crossing her arms.

"Liar."

"I'm not lying!" she protests.

"Germaine, it's okay to admit you got hurt—I won't hold it against you. I promise to continue accepting your help and including you. Fair?"

She blinks, then nods slowly. "In all honesty, I really don't feel terrible. You came quickly."

I hope that's the truth. "Anyway, I think the rehearsal dinner is wrapping up. People inside are all gathering by the threshold to depart."

Germaine angles herself toward the yacht club, its wood-and-brick form a solid half-mile away. "Don't worry about me. Go and make sure no mosquitos attack them on the way out."

"It's been a minute, and you're already cracking jokes. Stay here; I'll be back soon." I push off the ground lightly, though surge forward as though tossed by a powerful giant, disappearing into the gloom.

"*Uh, Ian?*" she calls out over quantum channel.

"*What?*"

"*Did you forget something?*"

I turn back and see the captured humanoid vessel standing at attention next to the telescope. Shadows swirl across its surface like oily flames, giving the impression that the vessel is constantly changing shape. I see Germaine inch toward the telescope, only for the shadows to writhe with greater intensity, seeming to grasp in her direction.

"*I don't want to bring it back to the yacht club; leaving it with you should be harmless. Just ignore it.*"

"*It looks like it wants to eat me.*"

I snort. It's just a wooden mannequin with necromancy applied to it—I can't imagine it ever eating anyone. And now that I've forced it under my control, it's no longer beholden to its master's commands. "*You said something similar about the spider.*"

"*Fine.*"

* * *

I return to my previous hiding spot. My mask is damp with sweat, the heat of spring not fully tempered by proximity to the bay. I pull it off my face, running fingers through my hair.

Germaine...Y'jeni, I wasn't careful enough.

In hindsight, I should've taken precautions against a decemancer thralling insects. What I'd seen previously indicated expertise with arrays and souls—both characteristic of necromancy. But this latest attack suggested our adversary also had excellent skills as a conventional decemancer.

The practitioner had set up three layers of attack: first, the vessel, sent directly to the Bridoc Yacht Club; second, the soul swarm off in the distance, approaching only near the conclusion of the event; and third, the scouting mosquitos, searching the area for suspicious individuals and lying passive until triggered. I could imagine the strategy in my mind: detonate the vessel, send in the swarm to attack survivors, and use the mosquitos to kill witnesses or stymie those planning to intervene.

And it had been done carefully: the vessel, in particular, was practically a work of art, its surface covered in inscriptions and what looked like foreign calligraphy. Even the Death energy visible on its surface served to obscure, rather than signal its presence; if I hadn't been specifically looking for an intruder, attending the party instead as a guest, I might have missed it completely.

Whoever this practitioner is, they've taken precautions to avoid the combined observational skills of the entire family.

The guests at the yacht club slowly trickle out—many probably heading over to Zebede's for continued revelry. Unlike the rehearsal dinner, Germaine and I are welcome. I originally opted to continue the lurker plan, but Germaine convinced me to bring a change of clothes "just in case" I changed my mind.

I have to admit, after a few hours of sheltering in the fragrant mulch of the yacht club, attending Zebede's after party as a guest sounds significantly more appealing.

"Aunt Julia's leaving," Germaine reports.

"Be over in a moment." Aunt Julia's departure was my sign to reconvene at Germaine's location. Aunt Julia would meet us there shortly after detouring around the property.

I shake off as many wood chips and soil bits as I can before kicking off the ground and dragging myself into the air by the scaffolding of my own bones. Controlling my body in such a way allows me to decelerate before touching down; using a little more Death energy to bleed my acceleration is much more cost-effective than protecting myself against a forceful fall.

"Can you do something about the vessel?" Germaine says out loud, no longer using the quantum channel.

"What did you have in mind?"

She looks up from disassembling the scope. "Get rid of the shadows around it."

I shake my head. "I can't do that without ruining the array, but I'm hoping to study it a bit."

"Do you think you can use it to trace back to its creator?"

I shrug and remove the mask, using it as a fan to cool my face. "I've never had to deal with any necromancer ritualists in the past who did these kinds of inscriptions." The blood array used to summon and control the leviathan back in the Godora layer was similar, but I also have little understanding regarding that array.

It's at this point that Aunt Julia arrives, leaping from a root snaking up from below. Her eyes glow green as she steps toward us, the root she used to scale the bluff withdrawing behind her.

"Why is your sister covered in blood?" she asks.

"Aunt Julia—" Germaine begins, her voice anxious.

"It's my fault," I interrupt. "A decemancer skilled in thralling insects controlled a few mosquitoes to bite Germaine without me noticing. Then, while I was distracted by a soul swarm, Death energy entered her body through the mosquito bites."

"Mosquitos?" Aunt Julia echoes. "Be more careful next time. Tell Ian if you see anything out of the ordinary."

"Not that it really matters..." Germaine mutters bitterly.

I sigh at the remark, then pivot the conversation. "Tomorrow's the wedding. It's the last real chance for whoever we're up against to make their move."

"We'll need to be vigilant now that we're certain someone's actively targeting the family," Aunt Julia adds. "We also now know that they're after the immediate family, else they would have waited until Zebede's party or the wedding to attack."

Germaine's eyes dart between the two of us. "Aunt Julia, who do you think is the target?"

"It's probably Adricaius." Aunt Julia smirks. "He probably insulted someone he shouldn't have. Who knows, maybe someone feels slighted that they weren't invited to the wedding." Her smirk quickly turns into a grimace. "But even if it's because of Adricaius, they've made the mistake of targeting his entire family."

As Aunt Julia says this, Germaine's eyes meet mine, her expression strange. I wonder if she's thinking the same thing I am: the extended Dunai-Adricaius-Fiorencia clan would have suffered an attack that first night without my intervention.

For all Aunt Julia's talk of the power of our family, the one protecting them is essentially an outsider—the talentless scion they cast out. I feel a sense of strong indignation rise within me, followed by disgust.

Why am I even bothering to help them? Why did I assume that just because I was on my way to a family wedding, I was supposed to protect my relatives?

My eyes are still locked onto Germaine, studying her face. I have a powerful, inexplicable feeling that just saving her would be enough.

"What next?"

Germaine turns my way, eyes narrowing. "We head to Zebede's estate for another stakeout—unless you're willing to dress up."

Aunt Julia crosses her arms. "Julian, stop acting so stubborn."

I sigh. I just can't see the point of forcing myself to socialize with people who look down on myself and Germaine, not to mention Mother. If becoming a practitioner is all it would require to gain their favor, I'd rather cut myself off from them completely.

"I don't think there's going to be a second attempt at an attack tonight," Germaine continues. "There's really no need to hide in the bushes or dirt on the off chance something will happen."

I can see her perspective, but I can't agree with it. There were numerous times back in the first loop layer when I thought something couldn't be so complicated, so convoluted. At every step, I questioned how I was ever expected to find the correct approach, the right answer. Was I really supposed to assemble the strewn pieces of a torn-up map within the captain's chambers, just to determine the approximate location of the ship? And how was I ever supposed to guess that the next step of the puzzle was changing the course of the cruise ship for Menocht Bay? The list goes on and on.

It's easy to think that there won't be another attack, but that's just what our opponent would *want* us to think.

"You can go in and do some scouting on the inside with Aunt Julia. I'll stay outside to keep watch."

* * *

I eventually convince them to attend the party while I keep watch outside. The itinerary for the wedding claimed that Zebede Dunai's party would commence at eight in the evening, though that failed to account for the rehearsal dinner running late. By the time we arrive at Zebede's expansive estate, it's already half-past nine.

"It's just you and me, now," I murmur, giving the vessel a knock on the shoulder. The two of us are hiding out in a large tree at the edge of the estate, between the entrance gate and the rightmost boundary. Zebede's property is larger than the Bridoc Yacht Club by a wide margin, though it isn't overlooking the ocean. It's immediately surrounded by forests and pastoral fields, though half a mile down the road in either direction lies another similar property.

While lying in wait, I decide to inspect the vessel a bit more thoroughly.

Just how does the obfuscation work? I wonder, rotating the vessel's torso between my hands. Death energy is conspicuous; normally, I'd ascribe this kind of shadowy concealment to a Dark practitioner.

Why couldn't this be the work of a Dark practitioner? I ask myself, thinking of the most obvious question. I frown, dragging my fingers lightly across the vessel's featureless face and neck. I *know* that it's a product of decemancy, though it's difficult to articulate *why* if someone like Germaine were to ask.

A Life practitioner like Aunt Julia would likely agree with me. While Germaine can see the shadowy whorls on the vessel's surface with her bare eyes, the shadows appear to me like thin, overlapping strips of dirty, gray gauze. I presume that Aunt Julia sees something similar.

There's something about it...something peculiar that renders it particularly difficult to focus on.

As I run my hands along its smooth, wood-like surface, I suddenly hear a small click. The strands of Death-energy-gauze freeze in place before melting away into nothing, giving me the first unobstructed view of the vessel. The inscriptions I could see vaguely through the shadowy exterior now look like dark wounds, stretching across the vessel's entire body. It's almost as if someone decided to take a human cadaver and carve a ritual array across its surface, using brown blood and broken skin as ink.

Though the vessel looks and feels like sanded pine, pairing its human contours with violent inscriptions creates a disturbing image.

Good thing Germaine couldn't see what it really looked like when it was just the two of them, I muse. It looks far spookier now than it looked originally.

After the removal of the obfuscating shadows, I notice the presence of a small oval embedded in the hollow of the vessel's neck. I hover a finger over it, then tentatively begin to feed it energy, hoping to observe some kind of reaction.

What I didn't expect was to be drawn into a vision. I blink, and the world becomes black. For a moment, I'm left wondering if I've somehow already satisfied the conditions to move on to the next loop layer.

Before I can do anything, the world blinks into focus. I'm standing still within the halls of a grand estate, resting against the wall. I can see in my peripheral vision that I'm wearing a suit of historic armor. Across from me lies a matching suit of armor dressing a mannequin.

Where am I?

The scene shifts again. This time, I'm lying in what appears to be a dark closet; around me are other wooden mannequins and puppets, though my vision is restricted to what's directly in front of me.

The closet opens with a flash of light. I'm facing the wrong direction and am unable to see the face of the figure that grabs me from behind, snagging me by my shoulders and hoisting me onto the floor. I collapse in a heap, my line of sight unfortunately restricted to the floral pattern on the rug below.

The floral pattern shifts as I'm dragged down a long hallway. The person dragging me turns the corner, knocking me across a small wooden bump marking the transition between the hall and an enclosed room. Bumping shifts the position of my head, allowing me to get a better sense of where I've been dragged.

At the center of the room are two metal tables covered in straps. I see that a naked human body is fixed to one of the tables, though from my low vantage point, I can't tell whether they're dead or alive.

After listening to a few minutes of shuffling sounds, the person who brought me to the room returns, lifting me up under my armpits and dragging me over to the base of the other table. With a grunt and a drawn out-groan, they heave me onto the empty table and strap me down. Now I can see the human strapped to the other table more clearly.

They're most certainly alive.

I hope I'm wrong about what's going to happen next.

RITUAL

The person on the table struggles weakly at the bindings, her face partially covered by a gag. Her nose and eyes are red as though she'd been crying before my arrival.

The person who dragged me onto the table walks over to the gagged woman. All I can see is his back, garbed in a pair of khaki trousers and a black argyle sweater. I'm not sure what I expected him to be wearing—perhaps something similar to the black robe I always spawned onto the dinghy with.

I notice a small cart next to him filled with trays carrying assorted metal instruments. He unhesitatingly reaches out for a scalpel, holding it in his fist like a dagger. I've never used a scalpel before, but it's obvious that his grip is unconventional. He leans forward over the table, blocking the woman from my line of sight.

I hear a series of muffled squeals and wet slicing noises. I've witnessed, experienced, and perpetrated no small number of violent acts while in the loop, but I'm glad I don't have to watch the woman's butchering.

When the man steps away a few minutes later, I see that the woman's bare upper torso is covered in familiar-looking inscriptions. They weep profusely, trailing rivulets of blood across her legs and pooling on the ground, where I now realize a rubber tray has been placed. The cuts don't look like anything a scalpel would produce, their edges jagged and deep, as though the intent wasn't so much to carve as to torture.

The woman's eyes are manic, nearly rolling back in her skull. The man returns after half a minute, now wearing a black smock over his sweater and a pair of plastic spectacles. I catch the briefest glimpse of his face before he resumes his gruesome task, though it's not enough to recognize whether the man is a stranger...or someone I know.

Time suddenly jumps forward. The man is gone, leaving the woman's figure unobstructed. Inscriptions cover nearly every inch of her skin, giving the impression that she's been painstakingly flayed. There are some thinner lines traced across her body as well, these ones looking like they might actually be the work of a normal scalpel.

With a jolt, the head of the vessel rolls and lifts off the table. As the vessel, I feel myself walking over to the still-breathing—though unconscious—woman like an overgrown toddler, my legs shaking beneath me and causing my vision to lurch forward. I stand over her, then cock my head.

Without any warning, my sight lunges forward. I feel a jaw I didn't even know I had unhinge; sharp, jagged, and splintery teeth dig into tender flesh. It takes me a solid second to comprehend what's happening: the wooden vessel is *eating* the woman.

Y'jeni, I'd really like to skip viscerally devouring the now-reawakened, terrified woman. I have a general sense of how to cut off my connection to the vessel, to end the vision; however, I'm wary of doing so without seeing the vision through its entirety. It's possible the vessel's perspective will allow me to see the face of the necromancer.

She's not real, I remind myself as the vessel rips at her intestines.

A few minutes later, after only blood and bits of gore remain, I hear a sharp clapping sound come from behind. The vessel freezes in place, its head sagging. I can see part of the vessel's body, noting that the inscriptions from the woman have somehow reappeared on its surface.

"What a mess you've made..." the necromancer's voice calls out. As though following an unspoken command, the vessel's torso bends at the waist, its head squarely facing the floor. "Let's clean you up a bit."

The leftovers of the woman rise off the vessel as though freed from gravity, and I hear them dripping down across the room. The vessel straightens a little, and a piece of flowy, black cloth drapes over its face. After a brief period of tugging, the cloth is pulled down and away; I see that the vessel is now dressed in the black robe it wore at the Bridoc Yacht Club.

The man clears his throat; I can hear him stepping back and flipping through the pages of a tome.

"Yz'vor, maru gorem, shanadel'ora'we."

I can barely understand a few of the words; the man is reciting an archaic dialect of Swellish. It's something like, *'Something, mage moment death, binding something something find.'* What I understand only serves to confirm that the man is articulating ritual verses.

"Gor ren nais, gor ren sum. Skoda'nel no'we."

The next line I almost entirely understand: *'Man is born in a moment, and man dies in a moment. Something not missed.'*

The man walks in front of me, though the slack head of the vessel is angled such that I can only see the point of his clean-shaven chin.

"Devesta ti erterra ashar'le."

'Save to earth our ashes.' Perhaps, bury our ashes?

"Vara skai'sum'we!"

'Go forth and raise death!'

At the utterance of the last syllable, the vessel's head creaks forward.

Look up! I shout mentally. *Up!*

As though reluctantly heeding my words, its head hinges up, giving me the first clear view of the man's face.

I feel oddly relieved to discover that the man is completely foreign to me. He has pale skin, black hair, and black eyes flecked with green. He appears to be middle-aged, though he has aged well, still bearing the figure of someone far younger.

If I saw him on the street dressed in the very same pair of trousers and sweater, I'd have no reason to suspect he practiced necromancy. Just who is this man, and why did he create the vessel? Why is he targeting my family?

The man lets out a soft sigh and removes his blood-speckled glasses.

"Yes, go forth. Let's see what mischief you cause."

He begins to clean off the glasses, wiping them on a patterned handkerchief.

As the vessel turns toward the exit, the necromancer falls out of view. The vessel's motions have become more fluid since devouring the woman, though it still struggles with using its fingers to open the door. It eventually makes its way into the hall; after following the familiar floral carpet around and down the corridor, it stops to open another door.

The vessel walks outside, closing the door behind it and ducking into the shadows covering most of the street.

I nearly have a heart attack.

It's the upper, sun-kissed boulevard of the Flower District...forever the root of my problems.

* * *

The vision ends, the world seeming to distort into a swirl of color before my perspective returns to my body. I hold my head and take in a deep breath, wincing at the throb of a headache.

The vessel is standing next to me, its face devoid of features, its demeanor harmless; it's unsettling to know that not only can its eyeless facade see, but that its smooth wood hides a mouth.

I take a few moments to orient myself and think through what I should do next.

First, I try to understand just what the vision *was*. I frown and run my hand over the vessel, trying to get a feel for the energy radiating out from the oval embedded in the hollow of its neck. It feels tainted, distressed; it's almost what I'd imagine a soul gem to feel like if made from the energy of a creature tortured to death. I've killed practically everything imaginable to make soul gems at this point, and my gems never had the same wretched taint.

I pluck at the energy swirling slowly around the oval, pulling out little wisps of gray-black. Removed from the oval, they begin to smolder and fizz away into nothingness.

I've never tortured anything to death, I think coolly. But then I pause, wondering at the truth of that statement. What qualifies as torturing something to death? I've never flayed anything like the necromancer in the vision, but...there were times, in the first loop layer...

I scowl. Perhaps it's something aside from the method of death that's affected the taint of the energy. Maybe it's the fact that the woman was eaten alive as part of the ritual?

I tighten my grip around the oval, trying to angle my nails under the groove where it lies embedded. I wither the wood around it, giving myself enough purchase to yank the stone free. As I do so, the vessel lurches forward and hangs limp, its head nearly touching the ground.

The stone fits comfortably in my hand; it's about the size of a typical woman's brooch. I spend the next half-hour meditating with the stone in hand, moving Death energy between it and myself.

Suddenly, a thought comes unbidden into my mind: *"Help..."*

| 313 |

I freeze, my eyes opening. I concentrate energy over the stone, eyes narrowed in concentration.

"Kill...me..."

My nostrils flare. Whatever consciousness the stone possesses, it doesn't seem to be aware of its current state. It's as though it's stuck in the moment of its death, begging for—yet never granted—release.

I have the odd sensation that the stone is leaking something oily onto my hand. I drop it on instinct and it falls onto the grass. A moment later, it trembles before flying to the vessel and latching onto the neck where it had rested before.

This is some crazy shit, I think bitterly. All the more ritualistic pursuits are a bit odd, from elementalism to enchanting to necromancy. Glossy programmatics is itself a form of ritualistic inscription, though it is easily separated into three parts: design, compilation, and inscription. My degree just teaches the former, modern technology enabling compilation of human-readable commands into an indecipherable script.

I spend the rest of the evening both surveilling Zebede Dunai's estate and inspecting the carvings on the wooden vessel. I decide to leave the stone alone for now, instead directing my attention toward understanding the inscriptions causing the shadowy obfuscation effect. I ruminate on blocks of similar script, passing Death energy along the inscription conduits and trying to sense deviations. I figure that if two bits of scrawl look similar, with minor differences, I might be able to start making sense of what function they perform.

However, when Germaine and Julia emerge from the party a little before two in the morning, I haven't made much progress. Even though the obfuscation effect is disabled, I grow distracted after staring too long at the inscriptions, images of their hewing onto the woman's skin bubbling to the surface of my thoughts.

"What happened to the vessel?" Aunt Julia asks.

"It's no longer so shadowy," Germaine observes.

"I accidentally deactivated it. I ran my hand over it and pressed some button or switch."

"Did it only deactivate the exterior?" Aunt Julia wonders.

I nod. "I depleted the interior cavity of all Death energy earlier; it's just the exterior that appears to be cut off from the power."

Germaine comes up to the vessel, seemingly no longer hesitant now that the shadows are gone. She runs her fingers along a jagged, illegible scrawl of text over the vessel's shoulder.

"What do you think?"

She turns toward me. "I wonder how they got these kinds of grooves in the wood. It would be pretty difficult to carve this; you can see here how the wood grain is actually deformed in a few areas."

I open my mouth to speak, then pause; it might be better to explain back at the hotel. "It's complicated."

Aunt Julia narrows her eyes and comes forward, inspecting the vessel. "These inscriptions don't look like they were carved in wood."

"That's because they weren't." I take a deep breath. "They were transferred onto the wood from the skin of a person."

Aunt Julia recoils. "These inscriptions were carved on...a person?"

I nod.

"How do you know?"

"While investigating the vessel, I entered into a vision, taking on its perspective for a time. Within, I saw a necromancer conduct a ritual to empower it with a human sacrifice."

"Did you see the face of the necromancer?" Aunt Julia asks.

"I did, though I didn't recognize him. I also saw that the place where the necromancer performed the ritual is in the Flower District."

Germaine's face lights up. "Isn't that the place where that plague came from, in the first loop layer?"

"One and the same."

Germaine sighs, rubbing one of her eyes. "Looks like we'll be up early tomorrow. We should see if we can find the necromancer's place."

"We?" I murmur, looking between her and Aunt Julia.

"We," Aunt Julia repeats firmly. "Now let's backtrack a bit; what did you mean by the plague starting in the Flower District?"

Germaine and I share a knowing look. I didn't give Aunt Julia as detailed an explanation of the first loop layer.

"Let's go back to the hotel first."

"What are you going to do with *this*?" Germaine cradles the vessel's head in her hand. I can almost imagine its jaws swallowing her unsuspecting arm.

"Couldn't I just bring it to the balcony of our room directly?"

Germaine deflates. "...Sure."

Aunt Julia chuckles, bringing the first bit of mirth to the conversation. "What were you expecting, that the three of us would have to explain why we're bringing in a necromantic vessel through the hotel lobby?"

I can just see Germaine blush in the dark. "It'd be more fun that way! Think of all the gossip we'd start..."

DECONSTRUCTION

A fter we get back to the room, Germaine focused on transfer-ring the vessel's inscriptions to paper. I didn't have any faith in my own ability to do an accurate copy of the inscriptions, but Germaine took to the task with confident diligence.

Glancing over at what she's transcribed so far, I'm impressed: she's managed to unravel several patches of criss-crossing scrawl into distinct phrases. She's essentially recreating the text from which the necromancer might have learned the ritual, though the ordering of the phrases is likely jumbled.

After discussing the first loop layer, Aunt Julia and I sit around a glossY, our eyes glued to a dictionary translating what we sus-pect to be the archaic Swellish dialect used by the necromancer. I don't have perfect recall, but I can remember a few of the words I was missing and can accurately transcribe the bits that I un-derstood. We go sentence by sentence, clause by clause, trying to determine what might have been the necromancer's complete rit-ual.

Sounding out words and painstakingly comparing definitions isn't exactly *fun*, but we suffer and laugh together over our fail-ures. Germaine is in the background, but she frequently calls us over to ask for second opinions on the shape or curve of certain transcriptions.

It's relieving not to rely only on myself. It's true that back in the Godora command layer I collaborated with Euryphel, but unlike his assistance, that given by Germaine and Aunt Julia is unconditional: I don't need to read too much into it or second guess its intentions. I'm comfortable trusting that the two of them are fully invested in helping me escape for my own sake, versus fulfilling some political agenda.

After an hour of effort, Aunt Julia and I manage to decipher what we believe to be the original ritual used on the vessel:

Yz'vor, maru gorem,	Golem, last sight of the magi,
Shanadel'ora'we.	Now bound to the hunt.
Gor ren nais, gor ren sum.	Man is born in a moment, gone in a moment.
Skoda'nel no'we.	Borrowed but not missed.
Devesta ti erterra ashar'le.	Deliver our ashes to the earth.
Vara skai'sum'we!	Go forth and raise hell!

The first part of the ritual seems to us more specific to the task at hand—controlling a vessel or golem—while the latter stanzas seem more generic.

Germaine presses a pencil to her lips. "The third stanza references mortality, while the fourth...'borrowed but not missed,' makes me think of someone stealing a soul away before it returns to wherever souls normally go after death."

"That would make sense here, considering how the woman's soul appeared to be appropriated by the necromancer to empower the vessel," I affirm.

Aunt Julia sighs. "And the last two lines, deliver our ashes to the earth, go forth and raise hell..."

"Within the vessel was a highly compressed reservoir of Death energy. I know we haven't deciphered the phrases that Germaine has written down yet, but after dabbling around a bit earlier, I'm certain that most of the inscriptions serve a more destructive purpose than mere obfuscation. Likely, the vessel was prepared so that it could destroy the yacht club."

"Like an explosion?" Germaine asks.

I nod. "Like I mentioned with the blood array at the winery, using raw Death energy, rather than soul gems, is less stable and prone to exploding when disturbed. However, in this case, the hard exterior of the vessel and the wide, interconnected inscriptions suggest that the vessel was prepared against exploding when handled the wrong way." Or attacked, for that matter.

"Why not just use a soul gem, then?" Aunt Julia murmurs.

"That's the question of the moment, isn't it? I don't think we can determine much more definitively without trying to make sense of Germaine's transcription."

While Germaine continues to transcribe, Aunt Julia and I begin to translate what's currently there. Unfortunately, we're not met with much success. Looking up different types of alphabets and runes, we don't find any matches for the language that decorates the vessel.

"Aren't you both exhausted?" Germaine suddenly asks, yawning.

Aunt Julia and I share a sheepish look.

"We've actually...well, we've been giving ourselves jolts of energy. For Aunt Julia, it's easy: She can give herself a boost of vitality. For myself, the process is a bit more convoluted, but I can accomplish the same result."

Germaine gives each of us the stink eye. "Didn't it occur to you to do the same kind of vitality shot to me?"

"If you aren't used to it, it can be a bit jarring," Aunt Julia explained.

I nod, recalling the first few times I experimented with keeping myself alert. "Like severe caffeine jitters. The dosage is key as well, and giving you too much concentrated vitality might render you—"

Aunt Julia lets out a groan. "Julian, that's enough. Germaine, if you wish, I can give you some vitality."

"Yes, please. And, Ian, I'm not positive where you were going with that train of thought, but I don't need to hear it."

I chuckle. "Fine, fine."

A few seconds later, Germaine literally jumps in place, springing like a frog from her seat on the floor.

"That! Is! Something!" she huffs, eyes wide. I can see the formerly sluggish vitality in her vessels pulsing much faster as though going into overdrive. In a few minutes, it should equilibrate, but until then, she'll be feeling something of a small, jittery high.

"Now that everyone's properly wide awake, back to work," Aunt Julia says firmly.

* * *

An hour later, Germaine holds up a piece of paper with her transcription.

"We're looking at it all wrong!" she says, her voice tinged with awe.

Aunt Julia and I immediately look up, the glossY forgotten.

I gesture at the vessel. "Please explain."

"It's not a language—not one that would be written or spoken by us. What is this inscription, other than a channel? These...they're like rivers, cutting through a landscape. Based on the density of the rivers, and the flux of water coursing through them, the landscape is turned to swamp, to desert, to volcanoes!"

My eyes slowly meet Aunt Julia's, the two of us sharing a confounded expression.

"The vessel isn't a landscape, Germaine. Moreover, the inscriptions seem to follow certain patterns, with repeating words and phrases. They aren't haphazard lines, are they?"

"Aren't they?" Germaine replies, her eyes alight. "In the vision, you said that the man carved the woman without a reference, correct? You never mentioned him consulting anything. But when he was reciting the ritual at the end—which has far fewer lines than what I've transcribed, if you couldn't already tell—he needed to consult a tome."

She has a point.

"So you're saying that the similarities in the script that we're mistaking for words and phrases are coincidental?"

"Not coincidental at all. By carving in certain ways—with a certain depth, width, length—and placing more carvings in some areas than others, energy may be channeled differently over the vessel's surface. Depending on the kind of groupings of carvings, you might get different effects, like I said in the beginning with the landscape example."

I scooch across the floor, sitting beside the vessel. Germaine steps away, a victorious look in her eyes.

"Ian, what are you thinking?" our aunt asks.

I close my eyes and raise my hands above the vessel's spine. "I'm going to try my hand at understanding the inscriptions again."

I can see her cross her arms with my eyes closed, vitality coursing through her body like thick, white electricity.

"Very well. Remember though, that outside the loop, what we've been doing with the vessel would be enough to warrant our arrest. Inside the loop, it's justifiable, given our circumstances. But pouring Death energy into the inscriptions and trying to make sense of them...well, it won't look good to whoever eventually sees the footage of you in the loop."

"I'm not planning to become a necromancer, Aunt Julia," I say dismissively, opening my eyes. "I'm just trying to understand how the vessel works in case we come across another or have to deal with a necromantic array using similar principles of construction."

"Do you really think you're going to be able to glean anything useful in a few hours? I think it's a waste of time; we should instead start our investigation of the Flower District while most people are still asleep."

I run my fingers over the vessel. "Just give me fifteen minutes. If I can even learn a bit about how to neutralize these inscriptions most efficiently, it might be helpful. I'm concerned that when we enter the Flower District, the necromancer will be ready for us; all it would take is one well-placed array hidden under the pavement. If I can't see a trap with my eyes, or my decemantic vision, I'll be at risk of blindly walking into danger. The same goes for you as well, Aunt Julia."

"Well said. I suppose it's worth spending at least fifteen minutes on, but if you don't make much progress, we should go."

I nod, then close my eyes once more, running my fingers along a set of grooves. I trace them, all the while trying to envision them as metaphorical rivers. I sink into my thoughts, fingers trailing across the inscriptions while leaving threads of Death energy behind. If I can simulate the course of the energy on the vessel's surface, then hopefully I can find a way to disable it.

After a few minutes, the vessel is covered in what looks like a web of nodes. If the nodes were red, rather than grayish-black, the connections between them might almost look like tightly bunched muscle sinews. Instead, they look like translucent wires, their surfaces shimmering as though freshly oiled.

I lay my finger on one of the Death energy wires, then pull at it as though plucking the string of a harp. The force passes through the node, dispersing amongst the other connections.

I think that I'm starting to understand. To quickly neutralize the power of the vessel without first depleting its energy source, I could try interrupting the flow of energy along the carvings. Unlike depletion, interruption is instantaneous: I'll be able to disable any traps so long as I can react fast enough.

Aunt Julia seems to have a similar insight. "Julian, do you see the way the energy resonates? Is there a way to cancel it out?"

I furrow my brow, then pluck at the energy wire again, then once more. On the third time, I manage to prevent the force from transferring into the node and its connectors, using a bumper of Death energy to reflect the force out and away from the vessel.

"Amazing...and can you do it again, with more of the nodes?"

This time, instead of manually plucking a single wire, I pull several of them at once; moving my own Death energy with my mind takes trivial effort. After successfully shielding the nodes, I escalate once more, pulling all the wires at once. Again, I manage to redirect and disperse the force outward.

"Now remove the nodes, but keep whatever you're using to dissipate the force."

I see where she's leading me—while it's good to be able to deflect energy coursing through my web of nodes, the nodes are just a stand-in. It's time to transition to something more realistic.

"Alright. We should see if the original obfuscation spell is affected by my shielding."

"There's a small button on the back of the neck to turn it on," Germaine interjects.

Sounds about right. I open my eyes and visually inspect the neck for the button. Sure enough, I see a tiny, circular depression, barely noticeable amongst all the carvings. I press my finger against it, and the obfuscation springs back into place.

Despite the reflective energy bumpers, the obfuscation activates without issue. I feel like I'm close to a solution, but there's still something subtle that I'm missing.

Aunt Julia's previous question comes to mind: why would a necromancer choose to use raw Death energy over a soul gem to power this vessel?

Gritting my teeth, I begin to condense a soul gem out of ambient energy within the vessel. It's weak and non-uniform, but that doesn't matter. The key point is that I can test it as a power source.

When I activate the obfuscation spell again, energy flows unevenly as though pulled in conflicting directions. The spell still functions, though its shadows are less substantial.

"Julian, take this," Aunt Julia says, tossing me a bracelet. As it falls into my lap, I notice a soul gem socketed in it. It's not particularly powerful—it's half the size of a pea—but it's quite pure, likely sourced from one entity.

She resumes her previous stance, crossing her arms over her chest. "It bears the imprint of a lupine riftbeast."

I suspect it's probably worth several thousand auris; anything associated with riftbeasts is sold at a premium. I crush it without hesitation, plunging its dispersed mist into the vessel's center before reforming it anew.

Now, energy flows along the carvings erratically; the obfuscation spell is almost non-functional, with only a few shadows remaining on the vessel's surface. My suspicion is confirmed: Powering the vessel with soul gems disrupts the effects of its inscriptions, their energies somehow incompatible.

I wave my hand, reforming both gems outside the vessel. This time, instead of trying to reflect and dissipate the obfuscation spell using my own energy, I use Aunt Julia's soul gem as a power source.

I breathe a sigh of relief as the obfuscation breaks. The whorls of gray, cloth-like shadow freeze and then shatter roughly. I feel a tug of resistance on the soul gem, its surface buzzing as the reflective bumpers receive and disperse energy.

"I can't believe that worked," I murmur.

Aunt Julia shakes her head and steps forward, nudging the vessel's arm with her foot. "Neither can I. To disrupt the necromantic inscriptions, it's enough to spread out a thin web of energy powered by a soul gem."

Germaine gives both of us a lost look. "If it's so simple, what's the big deal?"

I open my mouth to speak, but Aunt Julia beats me to it.

"Nature seems simple, but within it hides infinite complexity. Such is elegance." She turns toward me, giving me a serious look. "It's been nearly an hour; it's time we try to track this necromancer down."

REMORSE

When we set out from the hotel, dawn is still several hours away; everything is awash in moonlight.

Instead of heading directly to the Flower District, we first head to the beach. I fish up shells and small bones, weaving them into pieces of chain-like bone armor for the three of us. I also spend half an hour creating three soul gems from fish, affixing each to a set of armor.

Normally, when outside of my control, the armor sets would fall apart, bereft of Death energy to link the shell and bone shards together. Because the soul gems serve as a stand-in for my own energy, the armor sets are persistent. Additionally, while I only have my experimentation with the vessel as a basis, I'm hopeful that powering the armor with soul gems will offer protection against necromancy.

I turn away while the women strip their black shirts and pants, don the armor, and slip back into their garments. It's easier for me as I construct the armor directly under my clothes.

Before we leave the beach, Aunt Julia proposes a contribution of her own. "I'm going to try and mask our vital signatures. The armor you made, while protective, is also conspicuous."

"But it's under our clothes," Germaine says.

"Doesn't matter," Aunt Julia replies. "To any Life or Death practitioner, it'll show up clear as day."

I nod. "Unless there's something like the obfuscation array on the vessel." Unfortunately, I still have no idea how to emulate such an effect.

Aunt Julia crosses her arms. "It's a bit tricky, but I should be able to mute the energy."

"How?"

"You'll have to keep close to me since it'll be an active effect."

"That's fine," I reply, still waiting for an explanation.

"It's easier just to show you." She holds out her arms and a stream of vitality flows forth. I feel it wash over me just as I see motes of light green energy float around the three of us, reminiscent of the vital growth array back at the winery. It's not nearly as strong, however; I glance at Germaine, who seems to be looking aimlessly around.

"Is there something happening?" she asks.

I consider making another soul gem to crush and send into Germaine's eyes but decide against it. First, seeing vitality takes some getting used to, but more importantly, it's useful to have someone without it on the team. We're dealing with an adversary who may plan to use our perception against us.

"Aunt Julia's sending out Life energy. But unlike back at the winery, or when she gave you a jolt of energy to keep you awake, she's concentrating it around the armor."

"I think I understand what's happening."

"Really?"

"Clothing normally shows up as a certain color to your vitality perception, correct?"

"Indeed," Aunt Julia affirms.

Germaine continues. "Adding in Life or Death energy would alter its coloration, leaving it conspicuous. However, by layering the two types of energy, it can become less noticeable..."

She's mostly right. "If you look closely, it's clear there's something odd under our clothes. But from afar, it'd be difficult to tell." I turn toward Aunt Julia. "This is excellent; let's go."

* * *

When we finally step foot in the Flower District, it's nearly half-past four in the morning, and the sun is just starting to cast its glow over the earth. It's expansive and open, with numerous large trees and thin walking paths that span from the central commercial boulevard to the edges. From above, the district looks like a green, bisected oval within the heart of the city.

Aunt Julia performs Beginning auguries, leading our small party about the district's residential blocks. The few residential areas in the Flower District lay at the periphery, so we walk along the district's circumference.

She prompts me intermittently about whether anything looks like it did in the vessel's vision. Unfortunately, nothing rings a bell—the vessel hadn't looked back when it shut the door and ventured out of the necromancer's home. What it did see of the surrounding buildings didn't stick out. And while I've spent a lot of time in the Flower District, most was underground.

While I let Aunt Julia focus on finding the most likely location of the necromancer, I remain vigilant against any ambushes. However, after searching around for nearly an hour, we don't encounter anything suspicious—hidden traps, necromancer mansions, or otherwise.

"Let's try going below," Germaine suggests.

"Why?" In the vessel's vision, the necromancer's abode was on the upper level, its neighboring buildings covered in sunlight and bordered by trimmed grass.

Germaine asks, "Do you think that the necromancer is expecting us?"

I open, then close my mouth, thinking.

"He likely figured we'd come for him at some point before the wedding," Aunt Julia assesses.

Germaine nods. "That being the case, he's possibly already taken precautions, like leaving his place of residence."

I see where Germaine's going with this, but her reasoning isn't exactly adding up.

"Why would he have reason to suspect we know where he lives in the first place?" From the vessel's perspective alone, anyone besides a Menocht native—or some unfortunate looper like myself—would be hard-pressed to recognize the residential outskirts of the Flower District.

Moreover, all the above assumes that the necromancer is aware that I experienced the vision in the first place.

Aunt Julia sighs. "There's nothing to go off on the surface, so I don't think it's a terrible idea to see the lower level. With the wedding ceremony starting in ten hours, we have time to spare."

"Fine," I relent. It's true that we have more time than we anticipated: We'd allocated most of our morning to tracking the necromancer.

"Let's do it." Germaine motions to the nearest lift, its entrance half-concealed by a line of shrubs. The entrances to the lower level are by no means hidden, though their dim interiors do look cold and uninviting.

As we head into the lift, a few dim lights illuminate our steps. We step onto the platform, and within a few seconds, it begins to move, sliding downward. Before we reach the lower level, I know something is off. I turn around, meeting Aunt Julia's eyes.

"Do you see the plants?" I ask.

"I see the plants," she confirms, lips curling into a frown. "The entire ground is carpeted in them."

"I don't see anything yet, but that's par for the course," Germaine mutters.

Finally, the lift comes to a stop. When we step out, we can all see the plants in the low light.

The ceiling above us has numerous thin slits and grates where light streams down onto the lower level, but they fail to dispel the place's dusty, dark aura, and few plants survive the oppressive environment. But now, the dusty corridors around the lift have transformed into a garden. Grasses and flowers appear wild and overgrown as though they'd been growing in the corridor for a while. Their appearance is unquestionably preternatural. I wondered if we'd see more people still awake on the lower level, but there isn't anyone nearby.

"Ian, do you know what this place normally looks like?" Germaine wonders.

"The last time I was here, the lower level had almost no plants at all."

"Makes sense...but why are these plants wilting? Pretty sure they were fine a moment ago." She points to a cluster of flowers to our right. Unlike before, where the entire area was an uninterrupted glow of vitality, there's now a growing field of gray and black.

Observing the mysteriously wilting flowers is all the stimulus I need to get us out of here.

I feel like I'm so close—I'm not leaving anything to chance.

"These ones are wilting now, too," Aunt Julia murmurs, her eyes flashing green. From the opposite direction, I see more flowers lose their vitality.

Nope, nope, nope, time to leave!

This is when everything's supposed to go downhill. At the end of the day, I'm in a stupid loop, with stupid rules and a stupid plot, and now we've probably stepped into a stupid trap.

As though activated by those very thoughts, the remaining plants wilt and wither, their green stalks turning brown and black. I drag my two companions over by their armor and brandish Aunt Julia's soul gem, using it to create a tight-knit cage of energy around us.

"Aunt Julia, do you have any idea where the trap array might be?"

"No idea!" she shouts. "We should go up *now*."

Keeping the women close to my side, I drag the three of us into the lift.

Of course, as soon as I enter the lift, the world goes ballistic. The field of death erupts into motion, withered plants twining together and elongating into thin, gnarled vines. They stab toward and latch onto the just-arrived platform. I can control them—meaning that my decemancy is (unsurprisingly) stronger than that of my opponent—but in the second it takes me to react, the platform has already been tilted off its side, some of its circuits lying exposed.

Though the lift platform is destroyed, so long as it isn't blocking the exit to the surface, I'm more than capable of taking the three of us up. Before I leave, I enervate all nearby plants of their Death energy. Then, I direct our three sets of armor upward.

When we touch down on the upper level, we realize the extent to which events have progressed beyond our control. The plants here also appear to have wilted and begun lashing out. In fact, enormous, desiccated vines partly sourced from trees have already started a fire and toppled a shopfront.

Residents have begun to come outside, screaming and running away from the frenzied plants.

It's a good thing the residential buildings are on the edges. People shouldn't have too far to run.

After a brief moment of disbelief, Aunt Julia and I spring into action. Since we've apparently given up all pretenses of subtlety, and the loop still hasn't triggered a restart, I give myself permission to do whatever needs to be done to shut this insanity down.

While I keep the three of us moving as one unit, Aunt Julia is able to send vitality into the dead plants, disrupting the flow of energy and rupturing them from within.

I begin to condense soul gems while we move, using Death energy harvested from the plants as a medium. The density and uniformity of the energy help the process along, and I'm able to condense the first gem in just under a minute.

As I take control of the plants, I begin twining them together, forming misshaped, sinewy constructs from hundreds of vines. After I implant the first completed soul gem within the new construct, I move to create the next.

Plant constructs are frailer and less powerful than bone constructs, but they are sufficient to cut through vines and defend escaping passersby from attacks. Less than two minutes into the battle, I've managed to make four such constructs. As I glance over at one of them defending a man from the aggressive swat of a tree-sized tendril, a team of six uniformed Menocht Bay practitioners arrives.

They don't dawdle or ask questions, instead throwing themselves against the plants, cutting them down, incinerating them, and freezing them. They also don't seem confused that a decemancer is ostensibly on their side, working to ameliorate the situation.

Aunt Julia's voice suddenly sounds out. "Where's Germaine?"
She's—

I stop moving our armor; Aunt Julia and I freeze in place a few feet off the ground.

I certainly expect that one of us would have noticed if she disappeared right from under our noses. I'd been controlling her *armor*; how could I *not* realize? I briefly consider whether Aunt Julia would have noticed, but I realize that she stopped actively muting the energy of our armor after the chaos broke out.

I cover my eyes with a hand, a bitter chuckle escaping my chest. Even though this is a loop, and I can always try again...I'd like to think I've grown powerful enough to do things right the first time.

Seems like I've still a long way to go.

In the real world, there are no do-overs. In the real world, there's one Germaine. And if this were the real world, I might have already lost her.

A voice calls out from the left.

A uniformed individual hails us from the ground, her voice difficult to hear over the sounds of battle. I lower us down. As our feet touch the ground, Aunt Julia gives me a reassuring look, motioning for me to stop attacking plants.

"They're wrapping up, Nephew," she whispers. "Our job is done here."

If we hadn't lost Germaine, her words might give me a sense of relief.

As though reading my thoughts, she adds, "Remember, she's not real. None of these people are real."

"I know!" I snap.

"Then act like it."

She then turns toward the uniformed individual, a smile plastered on her face. "Hello, Officer. How can we assist you?"

* * *

By the time we leave the Flower District, the practitioner squadron has put an end to the chaos. Despite our combined efforts, the district is an unrecognizable warzone. Of the scarce flora still alive, most are uprooted or partially destroyed. The formerly verdant lawn has entirely turned into a blackened mud pit, while the shops on the main boulevard have all sustained critical damage.

Thankfully, Aunt Julia and I seem to have been able to protect most people on the surface, though I do notice one or two corpses off in the distance. Below, though, on the lower level...I'd rather not think of what kind of damage the corrupted plants sowed, or how many lives they reaped. I briefly consider going down to investigate and amass Death energy, but I table the idea for the moment.

One of the six practitioners, an officer named Eugenia Frasia, takes us to the consulate for a debrief. As a wind elementalist, she's able to move agilely through the city. I assure her we can keep up, and so we quickly proceed to the consulate building.

"Since you both were at the scene before anyone else, you're valuable witnesses. I've been instructed to take you both to the captain." She leads us through the consulate gates, the doorman bowing his head in deference to our party. Eugenia stalks through the pathway leading to the front door with purpose. It seems like she's eager to leave and search for the culprit behind the Flower District attack.

"Come in," Conningway's familiar voice calls out, muted behind the closed door of her office.

Eugenia turns around and gestures for us to enter. "Again, thank you both for intervening when you did. You've both doubtlessly saved numerous lives." She gives us each a meaningful look before proceeding back toward the exit.

Aunt Julia and I meet eyes, then nod; I open the door and step through the threshold. Conningway is waiting in her chair, her eyes puffy as though she hasn't gotten much sleep.

"Good morning," she says, gesturing to the two empty seats in front of her. "Take a seat."

"Are these seats new?" The words pop out of my mouth before I can stop them. I've seen Conningway's office enough times to be surprised by new furniture.

She gives me a look. "They are, yes. Like them?"

I clear my throat. *Not particularly.* "They're quite shiny."

When we sit down, Aunt Julia kicks me lightly under the table.

"Captain Conningway," Julia begins, her hands clasped in front of her. She exudes the aura of an executive, her voice clear and refined. "I believe you have questions for us."

"Yes. First off, I want to know what brought you foreigners to the Flower District at such an early hour."

After interacting with Conningway in the past, I see no reason to be completely dishonest.

"We've been tracing a necromancer who we believe has been using his affinity to torture and kill people for their souls. We have reasons to believe he has been hiding in Menocht and are also fairly confident he's behind this morning's attack in the Flower District."

"A necromancer?" Conningway repeats, bristling. I figure that if she hates decemancers so much in the Menocht loop, she must hate necromancers all the more.

"Yes, a necromancer," Aunt Julia affirms. "As Julian here was explaining, we were investigating the whereabouts of the necromancer. We believed him to be hiding in the Flower District, and thus, we conducted our investigation there. Unfortunately, not only were we unable to find him, but he managed to activate a trap that encompassed the entire district, potentially facilitating his own escape, or destroying evidence of habitation and ritual practice."

I hadn't considered that the plant trap might have multiple uses as an attack, distraction, *and* evidence-eliminator.

"During the chaos of the ambush our companion disappeared without a trace," Julia continued. "We're still not sure what happened. We'd like to see footage of the Flower District during the attack—anything that might help us figure out what happened."

Conningway nods slowly. "Hmm...very well. You wouldn't normally be able to see the glosscam footage without first going through a few bureaucratic hoops, but Y'jeni, we're living in crazy times. Might as well go now."

Conningway heads out of her office and down a long hallway, leading us into an unfamiliar room filled with old glosscomp workstations and several individuals in uniform. They salute Conningway as she enters, and soon the captain has made her way over to a glosscomp station in the middle of the room. She drags her glossY over the comp, unlocking it and pulling up a list of applications.

Conningway is quickly able to find the latest video clip. After a few minutes of trying to track down the moment the plants go haywire, she plays the footage in real-time.

Her expression is unreadable as she watches Aunt Julia and I zip in and out of the camera's focus, destroying plant monstrosities as we go.

"There," Aunt Julia intones harshly. Conningway stops the footage two minutes into the battle.

"Please rewind five seconds, then play at a tenth of the normal speed," she murmurs, eyes narrowed in focus.

The three of us are hovering stationary in the air while Aunt Julia and I dish out damage. Germaine, meanwhile, appears to be observing the battle, her eyes darting all around. I wonder offhandedly if even then, amongst all the chaos, she's still searching for a lead on the necromancer.

We both see what comes next at the same time. The flash of a dark robe flits across the screen, careening straight into Germaine. Instead of headbutting her, however, the figure tackles her into an embrace before disappearing outside the glosscam's field of vision.

Conningway pauses the video a few frames too late and rewinds the footage again.

"It's another vessel," Aunt Julia says softly, shaking her head.

"It probably came from the underground...and from Germaine's direction. We were all facing away from her, so it wouldn't have been outrageous for *you* not to notice. But I was controlling her armor!"

"I think that it was probably after you, Julian, but grabbed Germaine instead. The three of us were all wearing your armor and surrounded by Death energy. And if Germaine was the first person in its path...it might have taken her instead."

I don't find anything objectionable about Aunt Julia's logic. However, she still hasn't answered my question.

I say each word slowly and deliberately. "How did I not notice her disappearance?"

"That's what I'm still trying to determine." Aunt Julia sighs, her brow furrowed. I can't see her use Beginning affinity, but the intensity in her eyes leaves no question that she's running auguries.

Conningway looks between the two of us. "I have some experience fighting necromancers. From what I understand, the strongest among them can create vessels from the souls of humans. And if they take the soul of a practitioner, they can sometimes create vessels with unique characteristics."

My mind immediately jumps to the obfuscation effect on the vessel. I *thought* it was the sort of thing a Dark practitioner would cast, but I had justified that its power was the result of the array's inscrutable inscriptions. But what if its power had come from elsewhere...perhaps, from the tortured, devoured woman herself?

"That's it. If I factor in the vessel with the powers of a Remorse practitioner, what we observe is feasible." Aunt Julia turns toward me. "I suspect that the array on this vessel isn't one of obfuscation but of confounding, interfering with someone's perception to prevent them from noticing something abnormal. Even under the effect, you would've normally noticed Germaine's absence after a few seconds, but since you were distracted by combat, it probably would have taken longer."

Conningway continues to let the video play. Seventeen seconds later, Aunt Julia notices Germaine's disappearance.

"Is there any other footage that might have captured the vessel's path through the city?" I ask.

Conningway rubs her forehead. "Technically yes, but unfortunately, there's no way for us to quickly process the camera footage when we're looking for just a few frames showing a thin vessel slipping through the shadows. We'll find out eventually, but it could take weeks."

When the captain takes us back to the office after watching the end of the clip, I sense a sort of tension that wasn't present before. She asks us a few more questions, but I can tell her words are carefully chosen as though she's nervous about how we'll react. She didn't show it while watching the video footage, but I suspect that she's afraid of me.

Or, knowing Conningway, more likely disgusted.

THE WEDDING

A fter we make an appointment to report to the consulate the next day, Aunt Julia and I return to the hotel to reconsider our strategy. It's quiet on the way back; while 7:30 am is early for a Saturday, I suspect people are staying in out of fear. The Flower District incident isn't a secret, especially for people in the neighboring districts. They would have heard the screams, seen the smoke.

Aunt Julia dusts ash from her sleeve. "If I knew you'd be disconsolate, I would've told you to leave her behind."

My head snaps up. "I'm not *disconsolate*. I'm disappointed."

"Even if you prepare for seemingly every contingency, Nephew, you might still fail if you don't understand the enemy."

I roll my eyes. "So there's always a chance of failure—is that what you mean to say? It's a high bar to understand anyone, let alone a hostile practitioner. Might as well just lock everyone I care about away, then, since I can't protect them. Is that your advice?"

Aunt Julia snorts. "Stop projecting. First, I was going to point out the merits of surrounding yourself with keen allies, people who will round out your flaws. There are numerous practitioners who focus not on combat but on intelligence-gathering. Second, I was going to remind you that family—and political connections—can help protect the people you care about. As a peak practitioner, it's critical you internalize this point."

I've already thought about her second point considerably, ever since meeting Euryphel. Just what would it mean to go to the SPU in the capacity of a decemancer?

"Sorry. I'm just—I don't know how to explain it. I haven't felt so antsy since I first entered the school layer." I chuckle bitterly. "I feel like I should be doing something."

"Going after her."

I give Aunt Julia a sidelong glance. "Yes."

She hums thoughtfully. "I don't fault you for wanting to find her, but a few hours after disappearing, it's most likely already too late." She reaches out and gives my arm a squeeze, her fingers recoiling slightly at the ridges of my bone armor. "Don't think I didn't notice how tense you were in the beginning, when we first left with the officer for the consulate."

I give her an icy smile. "Tense?"

"It's not weak to want to go after her. Nor is it callous to stay behind."

"I feel guilty: For letting her be taken, and for not following in pursuit."

At this point, we're near the hotel. Aunt Julia tugs my arm in a different direction, extending our journey by a block.

"Nephew...you're powerful but not invincible. The more time I spend with you, the more apparent this becomes—no offense intended."

"None taken."

"Have you ever fought against a Remorse practitioner before?"

I consider her words for a moment. Would Ajun'ra intruding on my dreams count?

"No."

She sighs. "I shouldn't have assumed anything, considering your unique circumstances. Most everyone at your level will have

trained themselves specifically to deal with Remorse practitioners. There are tricks to realizing when you're being influenced,
and there are items that can help to defend against attacks if you
find your aptitude for mental defense inadequate."

"If I'd have had this kind of experience, would I have noticed
Germaine being spirited away?"

Aunt Julia hesitates. "It all depends on the power of the practitioner, and your natural talent for mental defense, but considering that the enemy here is a vessel, rather than a live person,
almost certainly."

"Good to know for the future, I guess."

We finally find ourselves facing the hotel's facade.

"I'm going to change clothes," Aunt Julia explains. "I smell like
I've just returned from war, which isn't altogether inaccurate. I'll
meet you shortly to plan our next move."

* * *

I return to my room and collapse on the bed. Despite keeping
myself artificially energized, my limbs feel like lead; I have the
urge to sleep as though after doing so I'll wake to a world where
the morning was just a nightmare. I should probably strip and
take a shower, but I don't have the will to get up.

My gaze falls upon the deactivated obfuscation vessel. With a
surge of hatred, I focus the Death energy I've accumulated into a
churning ball of black, oily flame, flinging it towards the inscribed
wood.

When my energy makes contact, the vessel seems to respond
as though revived from death by a fairytale kiss. It jolts to a seated
position, its head hanging limp.

I realize that compared to how much energy the vessel had
when I captured it at the Bridoc Yacht Club, I have enough raw energy to fully fuel it four times over.

There's the question of morality involved: The vessel is the
product of an unusually cruel ritual. Moreover, the key com-

ponent of the vessel—its ability to channel an obfuscation effect—is only possible because of a direct and continuous use of the woman's petrified soul, still embedded in the crook of the vessel's neck. Repurposing the wooden construct for my own ends feels like I'm dirtying my hands by dipping them in someone else's permanent stain.

I grit my teeth.

She isn't real.

I repeat the words in my head like a mantra, to the point where I'm not sure if I'm saying them for the tortured woman, Germaine, or both.

With each recitation, the vessel floods with more energy, its conduits seemingly filled to the point of breaking. It twitches and writhes as though shocked.

I almost miss the door opening behind me.

"Should I have knocked?" Aunt Julia asks. I turn around, realizing that I probably look a bit crazed.

I cut off the stream of energy and cough lightly. "You cleaned up quickly."

Aunt Julia raises an eyebrow. "On the contrary, it's been almost an hour since I left. You need to wash up, then we can talk."

I cover my face with my hands, massaging my eyes. "Fine."

Taking a morning shower makes the new day more real.

When I look in the mirror and begin to comb back my hair, my thoughts once more wander to Germaine. I close my eyes.

Today...is a day of reckoning.

* * *

Aunt Julia looks up from her glossY when I reenter the main room. "Feeling better?"

I grunt noncommittally and sit on the edge of my bed.

"What were you doing earlier, when I walked in?" Aunt Julia asks, her voice soft, uncharacteristically cautious.

"Venting."

"What were you doing to the vessel?" she persists.

"...Venting."

"Julian."

I tug at the towel draped around my neck. "I was seeing if I could try and repurpose the vessel to use against the necromancer."

"Just wanted to confirm. You realize that you can never do something like this in the real world, right?"

"Of course."

"And how do you intend to control it?"

The vessel currently lies on the floor like a de-stringed marionette. Whatever energy I pumped into it earlier hasn't fully dissipated, but neither does it seem to have produced any effect.

"I have a few hours to figure it out. I think this method holds the most promise to locate and defeat the necromancer."

Aunt Julia's gaze is difficult to parse, her expression aloof and calculating. "Fine. I'll check back with you in a few hours. Once the wedding commences, you'll need to handle the necromancer in a one-on-one confrontation."

"Where are you going?" I ask, confused by her sudden departure.

She chuckles dryly. "I'm late for the planning breakfast. Members of the main wedding party do more than just show up to the main event, Nephew."

"So you're leaving? Just like that?"

She gives me a tired look. "What am I supposed to do at this point? We have no leads, other than the vessel if you can even count that."

"I suppose that makes sense."

Aunt Julia gives me a small smile. "I might not remember this, but I'm glad I got to spend more time with you these past few days."

I feel a sudden tightening sensation in my throat. "Me too."

* * *

"I didn't think you were going to open." Aunt Julia sighs in relief. She's standing in the doorway dressed in an elegant blue dress, her heels putting the two of us at around the same height.

"How long were you knocking?"

"Over twenty seconds. At least you had the foresight to lock the door—we wouldn't want a maid finding her way in."

I rub my nose. "Sorry; I was a bit absorbed."

"I figured you might be, which is why I came to check on you before heading to Gosophal Orchard. I'll be going with the immediate family; can you find your way there alone?"

I nod. "Shouldn't be a problem; I'll see you there."

"Best of luck, Nephew. I'll support you in any way I can."

"Thanks."

She shuts the door.

I close my eyes and stretch, yawning.

"Just us, now," I murmur. I flex my fingers and the vessel sits up, its movements limber and graceful. I sense a sort of tacit understanding from it. It's similar to the kind of recognition I sense in my bone constructs socketed with soul gems but subtly different. I have the impression that if the vessel wanted to rebel against me, it could.

"But you won't, will you?"

After spending the past five or six hours infusing the vessel with my energy, I stripped something away that felt conceptually like a pair of shackles to which I lacked a key. After yanking off this veneer, the soulstone has felt significantly more *present* but never once has it fought against me. The only explanation I can think of is that it understands—and supports—my intentions. Which is good, considering I have no idea (and no interest in learning) how to dominate and suppress a soul in the style of the necromancer.

I consider how to keep the vessel hidden en route and at the wedding. The obfuscation array primarily serves the role of masking the vessel's vitality signature, doing relatively little to hide the vessel to mundane sight. If anything, the obfuscation spell makes the vessel stick out in broad daylight, thick, oily wisps of energy coiling over its surface.

I dress the vessel in the same clothes it was originally wearing. The draping black robes should downplay the visual effects of the obfuscation array on the way over. From afar, it should look like I'm traveling with a human companion rather than a necromantic construct.

After cleaning myself up and donning a suit to look presentable for the wedding, I walk over to the glass door and head onto the balcony. The vessel follows behind, its movements inhumanly lithe. Seeing nobody around, I leap from the balcony, hoisting myself into the air and landing lightly on the ground. The vessel follows me, the two of us adroitly fast-walking through the city until we reach the beach.

The vessel and I disappear behind some rocks, then fly into the air. To maximize the obfuscation effect, I bear-hug the vessel from behind, keeping both arms wrapped around its neck and shoulders.

While I've never been to Gosophal Orchard before, I have been to a nearby landmark: a small sepulcher on the banks of the Zimbadi River. Pulling up a compass on my glossY, I navigate myself in its general direction. Eventually, I spot what looks to be a wedding party off in the far distance. In the vicinity are a few silos and a farmhouse, along with countless rows of fruit trees.

I continue forward, scoping off an ideal drop-off point on the road close to the entrance. Upon touching down, I condense my energy into soul gems, stringing them together as a bracelet. I'll be able to pull the energy out of the gems when needed, and they won't arouse suspicion the same way shrouding myself in raw energy would.

After divesting myself of raw Death energy, I direct the vessel to hide. It promptly lopes off into the rows of trees, hiding in foliage. I've instructed it to proceed carefully over the grounds; if it detects the necromancer, its instructions are to inform me and home in on his position.

In the meantime, I walk along the path for a moment before reaching a clearing. The wedding has been mostly set up by the time I arrive, garlands of lilies and peonies stretching over rustic country stone. Trimmed hedges, small tables, and bubbling fountains lay scattered over the grounds. I see well-dressed family members walking around and chatting, while staff offer up cooling towels and glasses of ice water.

I succeed in keeping a low profile as I hunt down Aunt Julia, eventually finding her directing staff to set up chairs in front of an ornate stone podium.

"Nephew," she calls out, noticing my approach from a distance. "Everything has been sorted out?"

"As well as can be hoped. Since I'm currently just waiting around, is there anything I can do to help?"

"You can help them fold booklets." She chuckles, pointing at four staff members creasing wedding programs.

"Sure." I won't refuse a simple, repetitive task when the alternative is stewing in my own thoughts.

Time flows like water; before I know it, it's time for everyone to be seated. I feel a knot of tension in my stomach. Shouldn't the necromancer have come by now? Perhaps the vessel isn't working properly or the necromancer has already discovered and disabled it without my knowledge.

As the number of people present exceeds five hundred individuals, it takes a few minutes for everyone to find their seats.

As the last few people trickle in, I sense the vessel accelerate as though locking in on a target.

Though I don't exactly understand how, the remorse vessel was able to track us down in the Flower District. Since the obfuscation vessel acknowledged receipt of my command to find the necromancer and possesses an intimate familiarity with its former master, it should have the man in its crosshairs.

This is it.

The tension in my stomach doesn't dissipate, but rather than coming from worry, its source is now anticipation. I wonder if the necromancer felt similarly excited when we fell into his trap in the Flower District.

I excuse myself quietly, drawing a few looks. As soon as I'm out of the immediate vicinity, I weave through the trees in the vessel's direction, waiting for it to come to a stop. After twenty seconds of travel, the vessel's movement halts, suggesting that it's successfully located the necromancer.

Steeling my resolve, I push off the ground with a burst of energy and rocket into the sky. I count down the seconds as I approach until at last, I crash to the earth feet-first, my arrival tearing up grass and cracking the ground. We're still within the orchard, though probably around half a mile from the wedding party. We're surrounded by fruit trees, their pink flowers hinting at fruit to come later in the year. It's hot, and the angle of the sun is such that the shadows of the trees are short, barely extending from the soil into the grass.

In short, the orchard doesn't possess the typical ambiance I'd expect of a necromantic ritual.

While the necromancer successfully ducks out of my way, a tome falling from his hand to the ground, his ritual array has no such luck. The array seems to be mostly complete; it looks similar to the array back at the winery, with foreign sigils and sloping geometric shapes, though I notice several new cracks running throughout. Two fresh corpses lay face down at the center of the array with burlap bags over their heads; I don't have time to pay them much attention.

I'm lucky he was still in the middle of inscribing his array when my obfuscation vessel located him, and I rushed over. He's probably unable to suddenly halt such a ritual, forcing him to remain stationary for a few extra seconds; otherwise, he might have already disappeared once he sensed my approach.

The two of us stand still, facing one another for the briefest of moments as though we're both frozen in time. His dark hair is disheveled, while a skintight black shirt and a pair of black trousers are blotted with dust. His right hand is covered in bright crimson; in it, he grips a curved, bloody dagger.

Without warning, we react. I try to crush and rip out the man's heart and spine, while he goes directly for my throat. I feel an acute pressure exert itself under my jaw, but I grin through the discomfort, narrowing my eyes as I try to increase the intensity of my own attack.

I've never met someone who could directly fight back against me before by resisting my intrusion. The necromancer seems equally perplexed at the futility of his own attack.

Nevertheless, by the time the first second of our battle is up, the necromancer leaps backward and clutches at his chest. He makes a gesture with his hand before coughing up blood. In the next second, three new vessels arrive and position themselves around the injured necromancer.

It's subtle, but now that I know what to look for, I can feel one of the vessels muddling my brain. I pick it out as the vessel on the left.

You're the one that stole her.

I whip forward between the vessels and land a kick on the necromancer, using the point of contact to send a deluge of energy into his leg. I can feel him resisting against me, but I'm ultimately successful. He gasps in pain, and his leg buckles beneath him, forcing him to place most of his weight on his other leg.

I can see the surprise on his face at my swift movements. I wonder if he realizes that I'm essentially controlling my own body like I would a decemantic construct.

Meanwhile, I send a stream of bone shards out of my inner jacket pocket, the pieces as sharp as knives. I consider animating the two corpses at the center of the array but decide against it.

No need.

The vessels come at me from behind, striking with clean, scythe-like movements. At this point, my obfuscation vessel darts out of the undergrowth, engaging one of the other vessels in combat and leaving two for me to deal with on my own.

I turn back to give the necromancer an icy stare. Though his lip is curled in contempt, I can see that his uninjured leg is trembling, and while he managed to neutralize my bone shards, his clothes are covered in weeping lacerations.

Just as his vessels are about to land a strike on my shoulder and lower back, respectively, they begin to rapidly shudder in place as though subjected to powerful vibrations.

The necromancer watches as I begin to slowly strip his vessels of energy. While draining them, we exchange a few more tentative blows, neither of us taking any damage. His attacks are growing more powerful, though also increasingly frantic.

After a few seconds pass, I throw the two drained vessels to the ground, planting my foot upon the head of the one that took Germaine. Fully draining them will not only prevent the vessels from attacking—or exploding, for that matter—but it also empowers me.

The necromancer kicks off the ground, intending to flee, but I keep pace and toss out more bone shards while throwing a punch at his ribs, pushing even more Death energy into his body. He inhales sharply and coughs awkwardly as though coughing itself is agonizing.

We both know how the battle will end. While the man may be a powerful necromancer, skilled in setting up arrays and creating puppets, he's an inferior decemancer, and he seems unfamiliar with close combat. That's not to say he isn't still powerful, relatively speaking—if Aunt Julia's ~70% affinity being considered high is anything to go by, he'd likely come out ahead in single combat against most of my practitioner relatives.

I chuckle darkly before planting another punch on the man's shoulder, sending him reeling forward through the air. I follow behind and send a kick into his back, the necromancer crying out and tumbling to the ground, bouncing unceremoniously from a tree on the way.

He tries to stand, but his body doesn't seem to listen. Hacking up another mouthful of blood, he forces himself back into the air, controlling a bone girdle now lying partially exposed beneath torn vestments. I briefly entertain questioning the man about Germaine, but I decide against it. It's probably better not to know.

Before he's able to return to the air, I once more try to grip his heart at a distance, as I did during the first moment of combat. The Death energy I've sent into his body responds, circulating wildly within the man's organs. He falls back to the ground and props himself up against a tree trunk.

He chuckles, blood spilling over his teeth and dripping down his chin. "Who knew...that your clan was hiding a peak decemancer..."

I step forward, staring down at him with disdain. Yes, who knew indeed?

"Takes a real bastard to advance so far while so young," the necromancer murmurs, his ragged breath slowing down his speech. "Still, to not even look for your sister..." He tries to laugh but only manages to wheeze.

"For taking her, I'm going to take pleasure in killing you."

His brow furrows as though I've misunderstood his point.

I'm not going to dally any more than I need to and risk the necromancer miraculously getting away. I make a squeezing gesture with my hand, and the man topples to the side with a groan, landing face-down on the grass.

Trepidation fills my heart as I stand there, my eyes wide open. What if when I close them, I'm still here?

What if this is the last layer?

Heart racing in my chest, I walk toward the fallen necromancer and stand over him, his death not yet quite sinking in. It wasn't anti-climactic, per se. If anything, it was refreshing to feel in control.

I stay there for a few seconds, resisting the urge to blink, my eyes beginning to tear up.

Just get on with it! I think self-deprecatingly.

I take a deep breath, clench my fist, and then close my eyes.

INTO THE BLACK

I keep my eyes closed for several seconds and crane my face downward, unwilling to open them to see the orchard—or worse, the dinghy.

For a first test...do I still possess Death energy? If I'm still in the orchard, it should be oozing around my body, visible through closed eyes. Moreover, I should be able to feel its presence.

The energy...is gone.

My ears strain to detect a difference in the ambient noise. After the battle, birdsong and typical animal noises had ceased; the present surroundings are similarly silent. The air smells woody, almost like pine.

My heart accelerates. This place can't be the dinghy: There's no harsh sunlight, no seagull cries, and no sound of the ocean.

I open my eyes, then collapse to the ground on my knees. I rub my face with my palms as though unwilling to trust my senses.

Y'jeni.

I open my eyes again.

"What is this place?" I turn my head, surveying the interior of what appears to be a lodge made of layered logs. There's a hearth with a crackling fire, as well as a simple bed, an old dresser, an antique mirror, and a round table.

"There's nothing here," I murmur, getting up and heading to the small, icy window by the table. Outside the warped glass of the window is an endless expanse of snow and mountains. The sun casts a blinding reflection over the snow, and evergreen trees stretch over the landscape.

My eyes search the outside for any signs of animals but detect nothing. Even the empty blue of the sky is devoid of life.

I turn away from the window and head for the lodge's single door, a stocky, rough cut of wood that looks like it would splinter to the touch. A thick fur coat lies draped on a hook next to it, along with a pair of leather boots. I slip into the coat and pull on the boots, finding that both fit me uncannily well.

I open the door with a twist of its knob and squint into the reflection of the sun off the snow. Before I can take a step outside, I'm assaulted by a bitter, biting cold. I close the door and turn back, looking for any other vestments, such as a pair of gloves or a hat. Seeing none, I step outside and begin to walk around, turtling my head into the jacket's collar.

While there are no animals or insects in the area, the trees are plentiful, and I'm able to quickly wither one and generate Death energy. I circulate the energy around myself as a small bit of insulation against the cold, then I throw myself into the air, soaring up high over the trees and into the cloudless horizon.

I've never been in such a climate before. While the Solar province can get quite cold in the winter, Shattradan, as a whole, is quite flat. On the opposite side of the spectrum, the region around Menocht and the Ho'ostar peninsula is mountainous; lofty Mount Ziggura is typically visible on a clear day. But the Ziggura range lies on the equator. While the peaks are white and strewn with evergreens, most of the range is either tropical or temperate.

I wonder if I'm in northern Corneria's endless peaks or the southeast's renowned Adder Spire.

After flying for a few minutes, I can't help but feel that I'm going in circles. Flying past the peaks begets only more of the same as though I'm passing over the same ground over and over again. I turn back around, and sure enough, I still see smoke in the distance. Somewhat confused, I decide to escape the cold and do some more thinking about the possible objective of the new layer.

When I reenter the cabin, my teeth are chattering and my fingers are numb. I kick off the boots and pad over to the fire, warming my hands and face over its blessed heat.

While the cold is nothing to scoff at, this layer seems oddly peaceful. Unless there's an angry tree monster lying in wait, there don't appear to be any creatures that could do harm.

After warming up, I throw the coat on the floor and walk over to the slightly cloudy mirror over the dresser. My hair is damp with perspiration, while my face is sallow as though I haven't recently had anything to eat.

I notice something shiny poking out from a small towel folded on the dresser. I pull the cloth away to reveal a long knife. While the blade is smooth and curved, looking very much like a typical knife blade, the hilt is a masterwork.

The metal of the hilt is filigreed and shaped with a superior level of detail. Minuscule gems of either blue, white, or yellow lie socketed in the hilt's tendriling metal, so numerous and small as to look like reflective scales. While most of the hilt appears to be made of steel, inlays of what might be gold and platinum lay like bi-color stripes along its surface.

Wrapped around the central span of the hilt is a thick ribbon of cyan silk. My hand seemingly moves of its own accord, gripping the hilt and holding it carefully aloft.

What would something so precious be doing here, in this remote lodge? Everything else here is simple and pragmatic, aside from the knife.

I bring it over to the window and hold it up to the light, its hilt dazzling. I snort as an idea crosses my mind. "Wouldn't it be funny if I'm supposed to use it to kill myself? There's nothing here, nothing to eat. Maybe the point of this layer is to end my own suffering."

I don't actually believe my words, though there is truth to them. I genuinely have no idea what I'm supposed to do about food. Perhaps the cabin has some rations stored away, but they won't last forever. It's possible I was wrong about going around in circles over the mountain, and that it's possible to fly away and reach civilization, but some part of me feels that this desolate mountain range might be all there is.

While I turn the dagger against the light, the floor tremors, almost wresting the dagger from my loose grip. A few seconds later, another tremor shakes the lodge, rocking the furniture.

Just as I think it might be over, the earth seems to unnaturally lurch behind me as though the entire house is being pushed backward. In the far distance, I can make out a muffled crushing sound as though a giant has stepped on wet snow.

I hastily don my coat and boots, then fasten the small towel on the dresser around my mouth as a scarf. I don't have a hilt to store the knife; keeping my hands exposed to the cold while holding it, rather than tucking them into my sleeves, isn't a valid option.

I go with the first solution that comes to me. I use the knife to tear off a strip of leather from the fur coat. I tie the leather around the hilt, then fasten it to the jacket, Death energy serving as stitching.

As I head for the door, the echoing rumble of falling ice and snow resounds, the sound waves accompanied by minute shuddering of the earth. When I exit the lodge, I can't see anything amiss from the ground, most of the distance obscured by tall trees. I kick off the ground and launch into the air, rapidly gaining altitude.

A snow tsunami is making its way across the landscape, snapping trees like twigs and covering everything in a blanket of white. Even at a distance, the avalanche is earsplittingly loud, the groaning, crashing sound of surging snow drowning out everything else. I draw closer to the avalanche's source, figuring that something must be responsible for setting the avalanche off.

As I fly, my heart nearly skips a beat. There's someone buried under the snow. I draw in energy from the countless freshly snapped trees, then shape one of them into a gnarled shovel. I dig into the snow; while the snow is powdery and easy to shovel, it's quite deep. As I draw closer to my quarry, the shovel's movements grow slower, more careful—I wouldn't want to accidentally kill the person with an errant swipe.

The first thing I see is a crown of long, dark hair. While continuing to dig, I begin to pull on the person's bones, trying to drag them up out of the snowy trench.

I eventually unearth a nearly frozen young woman and pull her up to my side. The air tosses her hair to the side, revealing a familiar face: Germaine.

I don't bother to consider how or why she's here. Instead, I immediately strip out of my coat and place it on her body. She's dressed only in a summer dress as though she's come straight from Menocht Bay; I'm not sure the coat will be able to help all that much, given that her legs are still fully exposed, but it's better than nothing.

Teeth chattering, I send the two of us back to the cabin, following the plume of smoke like our lives depend on it—which they probably do. I roughly barge through the door, sending Germaine across the room and next to the fire. Shivering uncontrollably, I grab a blanket from the bed, swaddle myself, then sit down next to her.

Her vitality is gray but seems steady; it isn't growing any darker. The two of us lay by the fire for the better part of an hour.

At some point, I nod off, the weariness of mind and body asserting its influence.

"Ian?" a voice calls out, thin and soft. I feel a slight shaking of my arm, then snap to consciousness.

"Germaine!" I exclaim.

She smiles. "You're awake."

"That's my line. I found you buried under an avalanche—it's a wonder you're still...well."

She gives me a confounded look. "An avalanche?"

"You don't remember?"

She shakes her head. "No... Where are we, exactly? This can't be Menocht. Are we in a different country?"

"It's definitely not Menocht," I chuckle bitterly. "We're in the middle of a mountain range."

Germaine's mouth pops open. "Let me guess, we're following the necromancer out here, right? Did he try to escape? Is this Mount Ziggura?"

So many questions...

"No to all three. Germaine. You remember a necromancer?"

"Of course; why wouldn't I?" She frowns. "I suppose I've lost a bit of my most recent memories if I don't remember coming here or getting stuck in an avalanche."

"I see."

While I try to keep my composure for Germaine, my thoughts are a mess. I've never had something like this happen before, where someone from a previous layer appears and has memories of past events. It's almost easier to believe that I'm still stuck in the previous layer and that some strange spell of the necromancer transported me—and somehow Germaine—across the world.

Almost being the key word: There's no way to send us to a far-off area without a transport array, and I have no explanation for why Germaine seems to have appeared here several hours after me. More fundamentally, if this were really the previous layer, I don't think she'd still be alive.

"What's the last thing you remember?"

"Um...perhaps...investigating?"

"Where?"

"The yacht club?" She sighs and rubs her hands up to the fire. "It's all kind of fuzzy."

I notice that Germaine has taken off the fur coat. I scootch over and turn it on its side, revealing the knife. I hold it up in front of me, watching the dancing light of the fire reflect in the metal.

"Did you have a chance to see this knife?" I call out. Hearing no response, I turn around, only to realize that Germaine has disappeared. She isn't dead, nor is she hiding in the cabin. She's just *gone* as though she'd never been here in the first place.

My thoughts turn to the danger of Remorse practitioners, recalling Aunt Julia's warning about needing to train myself against people who can meddle with my mind.

But this *can't* be that. Aside from Germaine, I'm all alone here. I hold up the knife uneasily. When first inspecting the knife, the avalanche occurred, suggesting Germaine's appearance. When I inspected it again, Germaine disappeared. It seems far too convenient to be a coincidence.

"Why must everything be a damned mystery?"

* * *

Suddenly, the cabin shakes again, though this time more forcefully. The window shatters, cold wind rushing inward and scattering shards of ice and glass.

"Mind if I come in?" a familiar voice calls out. A moment later, I see Euryphel's face in the window. Though he gives me an easy smile, his entire body is violently shivering.

At this point, I'm just about ready to give up on trying to understand this layer. I drop the knife on the coat, then run over to open the door, ushering the freezing prince inside. He staggers over to the fire, then breathes a sigh of relief.

"It's a good thing all fate in this loop points toward you, else I'd be hard-pressed to find you—or anyone else, for that matter."

"Do you know me?" I ask.

"I feel like I should, but my memory is disturbingly hazy. If I'm not mistaken, though, we're stuck in a dilation loop. Rather, you're stuck in the loop, while I'm around for the ride."

"It doesn't seem to bother you too much, being stuck in a loop."

Euryphel shrugs, his teeth still chattering despite the warmth of the fire. "It's not something I can change."

"Sounds...reasonable."

"You know, your fate is quite unusual."

Unusual? Euryphel never mentioned anything like this before.

The prince continues without prompting. "While my own fate points to you—as can be expected—your fate points *outward* like numerous vectors pointing so far away as to become invisible. If I had to hazard a guess, the world here in the loop is struggling to contain you. Perhaps it's simply running out of energy, though there are numerous more interesting possibilities."

"Like what?"

A gale rips through the cabin, tearing the door off its hinges. Visible beyond the door is the expanse of mountains, but they're growing indistinct. After a few seconds, everything beyond the cabin appears to be stark white, without definition, conveying a sense of nothingness.

The prince hums. "It might be better not to say. Whatever the cause, the loop is breaking down." He reaches over, grabbing for the knife, then stands up and walks over to the empty door frame. He slashes out and the emptiness opens up like a piece of torn paper, revealing abyssal black.

He gestures to the door. "It's time for you to leave."

It's impossible not to understand the implications of his words. We're not discussing leaving the layer but leaving the *loop*.

I hesitate, suddenly feeling unprepared: I still need to train myself against mental attacks; I never had the time to experiment with freeing myself from oaths. What if I leave the loop, only to find myself trapped in a life-death oath?

Euryphel suddenly chuckles, then hands me the knife.

"If you're afraid, you can try to turn back, but even if you can ignore the effects of the loop's collapse for a few days or weeks, your time here is approaching its conclusion."

"It sounds like you think I should leave, but you don't even know me."

The prince cocks his head. "Why not leave?"

I sigh. "I'm worried. If I step through that door...I don't know what's waiting for me on the other side."

"What's the worst that could happen?"

"What if I've agreed to an oath I can't remember? What if I have to live the rest of my life following the bidding of someone else? A weapon?"

The prince gives me a blank look. "I don't have a good understanding of your circumstances, but there are ways to deal with such things."

I move to ask another question, but he interrupts me.

"Stop worrying about what you can't change. Hasn't this place stolen enough time from you already?"

"Yes."

"Then you know what you should do."

I take a deep breath, steeling myself. I give him a nod, then step into the black.

AUTHOR'S NOTE

Thank you for reading *The Menocht Loop*, my first professionally published book! It's been a long journey from inception to publication. Writing words to paper and sharing them with the world is an exciting, nerve-wracking experience.

If you enjoyed the book, please consider leaving a review. *The Menocht Loop* is book 1 of a 5 book series. Coming February 2022 is book 2, *The False Ascendant*.

Subscribe to my newsletter to receive updates about new releases:
http://eepurl.com/hBDqW9

Join my discord to talk with me and other readers:
https://discord.gg/35atMsv

Check out my website:
https://www.timelesswind.com/

Lorne is an avid reader whose favorite series tend toward grimdark fantasy, such as *The Broken Empire Trilogy* by Mark Lawrence and *The Acts of Caine* by Matthew Woodring Stover. She enjoys time spent with loved ones and traveling the world.

She spends her days as an AI/machine learning software engineer.

www.ingramcontent.com/pod-product-compliance
Lightning Source LLC
Chambersburg PA
CBHW072113250626
47159CB00007B/2432